ISLAND OF GHOSTS

GILLIAN BRADSHAW

*I*sland
of
*G*hosts

A TOM DOHERTY ASSOCIATES BOOK

New York

This is a work of fiction. All the characters and events portrayed in this novel are either fictitious or are used fictitiously.

ISLAND OF GHOSTS

Copyright © 1998 by Gillian Bradshaw

Edited by Jenna A. Felice

A Forge Book
Published by Tom Doherty Associates, Inc.
175 Fifth Avenue
New York, NY 10010

Forge® is a registered trademark of Tom Doherty Associates, Inc.

Design by Sara Stemen

Map by Mark Stein Studios

Library of Congress Cataloging-in-Publication Data
Bradshaw, Gillian.
    Island of ghosts / Gillian Bradshaw. —1st ed.
        p.   cm.
    ISBN 0-312-86439-6 (acid-free paper)
    1. Great Britain—History—Roman period, 55 B.C.–476 A.D.—Fiction.   2. Rome—History, Military—30 B.C.–476 A.D.—Fiction.   Sarmatians—History—Fiction.   I. Title.
PS3552.R23517   1998
813'.54—dc21   98-13572
                                                CIP

First Edition: August 1998

Printed in the United States of America

0 9 8 7 6 5 4 3 2 1

To Robin

ὦφίλτατ᾽ ἀνδρῶν, ὁ μὲν χρόνος
παλαιός, ἡ δὲ τέρψις ἀρτίως πάρα.

Eur. *Hel.* 625–26

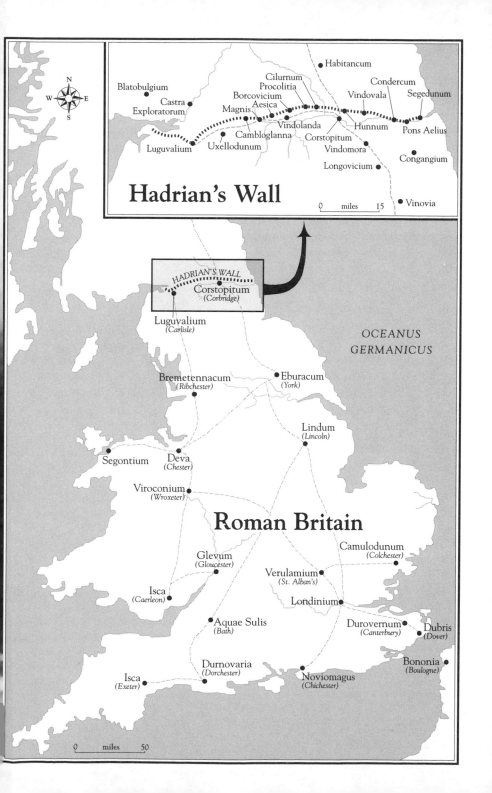

Hadrian's Wall

Blatobulgium
Castra
Exploratorum
Luguvalium
Uxellodunum
Cambloglanna
Magnis
Vindolanda
Borcovicium
Aesica
Procolitia
Cilurnum
Habitancum
Corstopitum
Vindomora
Longovicium
Hunnum
Vindovala
Condercum
Segedunum
Pons Aelius
Congangium
Vinovia

0   miles   15

N
W   E
S

HADRIAN'S WALL
Corstopitum
(Corbridge)
Luguvalium
(Carlisle)

OCEANUS
GERMANICUS

Bremetennacum
(Ribchester)
Eburacum
(York)
Lindum
(Lincoln)
Segontium
Deva
(Chester)
Viroconium
(Wroxeter)

Roman Britain

Camulodunum
(Colchester)
Glevum
(Gloucester)
Verulamium
(St. Alban's)
Isca
(Caerleon)
Londinium
Aquae Sulis
(Bath)
Durovernum
(Canterbury)
Dubris
(Dover)
Durnovaria
(Dorchester)
Bononia
(Boulogne)
Isca
(Exeter)
Noviomagus
(Chichester)

0   miles   50

I

W<small>E MUTINIED WHEN</small> we reached the ocean.

We'd been riding for fifty-one days, three companies of us with half a legion and two troops of Roman auxiliaries to guard us. We left Aquincum late in July, and rode through the heat of August: the dust and the flies were appalling. Most of the army bases where we stopped along the way didn't have proper supplies laid up for such a large body of men, as nobody had sent messages telling them to do so; of what they did have, the Roman troops took the best for themselves, leaving us sour barley soup and coarse black bread. We weren't used to the diet, and it made us ill. The hooves of our horses wore down on the paved Roman roads, and the beasts went lame. The Romans refused to give us leather to make horse-sandals, so we cut up the leather bindings of our wagon awnings. Then, early in September when we left the Rhine and turned west into Gaul, it began to rain, and the water ran through the loose awnings and soaked everything: bedding, food, clothes. Everything stank of wet wool, wet horses, rotting barley, and unwashed wet men, and we hated the feel of our own skins. Only our armor and weapons were safe: they had been wrapped in oilcloths at Aquincum and packed into twenty wagons of their own, which the Romans took charge of.

Then one afternoon, just before the middle of September, we were starting down from the hills when we saw it: the ocean. It had rained all that morning, but the rain had stopped about midday, and now the sky was clearing. The clouds parted and let down a watery light westward beyond us, and we looked up and saw a huge gray plain turn suddenly and impossibly blue. We had never seen the sea. We reined in our horses and stopped in the road, staring at it. The sun shimmered on the waves as far out as our eyes could see: no shadow of land darkened even the farthest limit of the horizon.

"It's the end of the world!" whispered Arshak.

Gatalas gave a long wail of grief and dismay and covered his face. The sound rose up above the clatter and rumble of the troops behind us and before us, and when it stopped, there was complete silence. Then there was a rustling whisper—"What is it?" "The sea, we've reached the sea"—running back down the line. A few dozen men and horses trotted forward, leaving the road and fanning out across the hill. Then there was silence again.

Marcus Flavius Facilis, the senior centurion in charge of us, came galloping up from some discussion with his subordinates. He was a stocky, bull-necked man, white-haired, with a face that went crimson when he was angry. It was beginning to go crimson now. "What's the matter with you bastards now?" he demanded, in Latin. He always spoke to us in his own language, though few of the officers and even fewer of the men understood it. During the long journey he had not bothered to learn Sarmatian even enough to give us orders.

Arshak, who did understand it, pointed at the sea. Gatalas didn't even look at him, but sat with his hands over his face, rocking back and forth in his saddle.

Facilis only glanced at the sea. His eyes slid lightly away from that shining vision of blue and silver, and fixed instead on the city down the hill from us, a comfortable huddle of red tile and gray thatch. He sat back in his saddle with a grunt of satisfaction. "Bononia!" he exclaimed, almost cheerfully. "Bononia at last! That's where we'll be staying tonight. And tomorrow I can say good-bye to the whole stinking lot of you. Come on, you bastards: hurry up and you'll sleep in dry beds tonight."

"And tomorrow?" asked Arshak, very quietly. "Where will we sleep tomorrow?"

"That depends how long it takes to embark you all," replied Facilis. "I imagine it will take a few days to ferry all of you across."

"They said there was an island," said Arshak, still very quietly. "They said that we would be sent to an island called Britain, and there we would have our weapons back, and be accepted as soldiers of the Romans, and receive honorable appointments and payment for our service. That is what the emperor himself swore to us at Aquincum."

"Yes," agreed Facilis, "and the sooner you get down this hill—"

"There is no island," said Arshak.

"May I perish!" said Facilis, going red again. "What the hell do you mean?"

Gatalas took his hands away from his face. "There is nothing there!" he screamed. "Nothing! Nothing but ocean!" He turned his head away from that terrible immensity.

"You pigheaded barbarians!" shouted Facilis. "You stinking idiots! Of course there's an island. It's across there"—he waved his hand at the sea—"about thirty miles off."

Arshak shook his head. "No," he said, "no. You lie to us, Roman. You lied to us all along. You, the emperor, all of you. You lie. There is no island."

Facilis' face was growing steadily redder. "You stupid bastard! By every god on earth or under it! Why would I march a troop of lunatic Sarmatians all the way from Aquincum to Bononia if there wasn't anywhere to send them when we got there? I wouldn't do it for the love of barbarian company, I can promise you that!"

"You would do it to cause our deaths," replied Arshak, still very quietly. He never raised his voice when he was angry, never swore, and never boasted. He was a member of the royal clan, second son of the king's own brother, and he had been taught that a nobleman answers insults only with his spear. It was lucky that the spear was stowed away in the weapons wagons, with Facilis' men guarding it. Otherwise Facilis would have been dead several times over, and Arshak as well, executed for murdering a Roman officer.

Facilis glared at him. He wiped his hands down the sides of his tunic. "The emperor wants you alive," he declared. "He wants you in his army. He swore to give you honorable posts, and you swore to serve him faithfully. Do you mean to break your oaths now, just because you've seen the sea?"

"The emperor wanted to kill our whole nation," Arshak returned. "He lied to us."

"If we go there," said Gatalas, jabbing a hand fearfully toward the sea, "we will die in the water."

"No!" Facilis insisted. He did not bother to deny that the emperor had wanted to exterminate our whole nation—everyone knew that was true—but he returned instead to his first point. "There is an island there."

We all stared at him.

"There's a huge island there, you stupid bastards! There's a whole Roman province, with cities and roads and three legions and the gods know how many troops of auxiliaries! The ocean's bigger than the gods-hated Danube, you idiots: you can't expect to see clear across it!"

Arshak glanced up the hill behind us. Behind a handful of our officers, Facilis' legionaries waited, leaning on their javelins and watching us. Two full cohorts of them, sixteen hundred men, drawn up six abreast: their ranks stretched up the road out of sight. The rest of our men were behind them, and the wagons with the weapons were still farther away, with the baggage. Of the two troops of Roman auxiliary cavalry, one was strung out down the road before us, waiting, and the other was guarding the baggage.

Arshak looked back at Facilis and smiled. Then, saying nothing, he touched his horse and started down the hill again, and the rest of us followed him in silence. Facilis sat still on his own horse, swearing as we rode past.

"We will not go on their ships," said Gatalas, in Sarmatian, when we were well ahead of him.

"Of course not," replied Arshak. "It's a trick. We'd be helpless on a ship, with our horses packed in a hold like sheep, and our weapons left onshore. They wouldn't even need to use swords on us. A few good swimmers could take us out, sink us and the vessel, and escape themselves without the least danger."

"Death in battle is better than drowning," Gatalas declared, rubbing the hilt of his dagger. "But I'd prefer it if I had something more than this and a rope to fight with. Do you think we could get our weapons back?"

"Probably," said Arshak, almost eagerly. "My men have managed to keep thirty bows, forty quivers of arrows, and sixty swords hidden in our wagons. How many do your troops have?"

"Fifty bows and twenty-seven swords," Gatalas replied promptly. "But only thirty quivers of arrows."

"Ariantes?"

"Fifty-nine bows, sixty quivers of arrows, and a dozen swords," I said, reluctantly. "But they're all well hidden, and it will take a little time to get them out. Facilis is suspicious. He'll find some way to obstruct us. Either we won't be allowed near our wagons, or we won't be allowed near our men, or both."

"Facilis won't be in charge in Bononia," Arshak answered confidently. "The camp will have its own commander. Bononia's a big place; the commander will be an important man, a legate or a procurator. You must have noticed how even tribunes don't like taking orders from centurions, however senior. It won't take much to ensure that we're sent off to the wagons with our men." Arshak smiled again, then added vehemently, "Facilis is mine."

I sighed. I was not sure what I felt when I looked at the sea, but it was not anger or fear. Perhaps it was hope. I'd had enough of the worlds I knew, Sarmatian and Roman both, and here we'd ridden to the world's end and were climbing down to touch something huge and mysterious beyond it. Why should I stop, here in this Roman city? Why not go on? I remembered the time long before when I had journeyed east, hoping to reach the Jade Gate of the Silk Country. I had been called back, halfway there. I regretted that still. Why stop again now, just short of the ocean?

Of course, I was tired. Some things had happened in the Roman war that had left me stunned, and when the war ended, I felt like one of the dead. I had a leg wound, too, which had meant that I'd ridden the first seven hundred miles of the journey with my leg in a splint, dazed with pain, and I'd floated through them in a kind of dream. Sometimes I woke up with a start and stared at myself in astonishment, but mostly I rode, ate, made camp, and gave orders to my men, all as though I were trailing behind myself and watching.

"What if they're telling the truth?" I asked. "What if there is an island?"

"Why should you believe them?" returned Arshak, swiftly and angrily. "Why should we trust them?"

"I don't trust them," I answered wearily. "But we swore oaths to the emperor, and we aren't yet certain that he was lying. If we fight them now, we will all die. You want to kill Facilis—but if you have to pay for the pleasure with the blood of all your men, is it worth it? Even if we managed to win our weapons, even if we gave them such a battering that they locked themselves in their forts and us out, still we couldn't get home, not through a thousand miles of land held by our enemies. And the emperor would look at what we'd done, and note that even when Sarmatian troops surrender in a peace settlement, they can still rebel and shed Roman blood. He'd have no use for Sarmatian troops ever again. What could our people give then, to buy peace?"

Arshak scowled. "He wanted to kill us all anyway. He has betrayed us and he will betray those at home, whatever we do."

"Better to die on land than in the water," agreed Gatalas. "At least on land the soul can fly free to the sun."

"But what if there is an island? If there is an island, it would be we who first betrayed them."

"An island in the ocean, beyond the limit of the world!" scoffed Arshak. "And what's more, an invisible one! If Facilis told you that there was an island in the sky and that you must climb up a mountain and jump off to reach it— would you believe him, and jump?"

"I wouldn't choose a path that would end with all my men dead without at least tossing a stone off the mountain and looking where it landed! And I am not sure that the Romans would invent a Roman province across the ocean, simply to trick us. Britain may well lie thirty miles from here."

"I will not cross the ocean!" cried Gatalas. "I will die cleanly in this world, and so will my men!" He stretched his hand toward the sun. "On fire I swear it!"

We rode on for a moment with the oath ringing in our ears. There didn't seem to be any point in continuing the argument.

But I couldn't leave it. When we reached this camp, we would have to begin planning our mutiny—and the more I considered it, the less likely it seemed that the Romans had invented Britain to deceive us. I had five hundred men who depended upon me to do what was best for them. "If I went," I said at last, reluctantly, "on my own, without you, without any of my own people—if I went to see if this island was there, and came back and reported to you that it was—what would you do then?"

Gatalas looked at me fearfully. "What if it's not an earthly island?" he asked, in a low voice. "If it's there, beyond the ocean, it might be . . . a place where the dead walk. What would you be like if you came back then?"

"You'd still know, then, from looking at me, that you should not cross. You'd be free to fight the Romans with a clear conscience."

"I'm not sure we'd notice any difference if you came back as a ghost, Ariantes," Arshak said, trying to lighten the air a little. I met his eyes, and he dropped his smile: the joke was too true to be funny.

"Someone should check what the truth is before we take up arms," I said.

"And if they refuse to let you go and come back again?" Arshak demanded.

"Then, again, we'll know that they're lying and we need have no doubts about fighting them."

"Very well, very well," Arshak said quietly. "Very well. You're right: we must toss our stone off the mountain and see where it falls. A pity: my hands ache for a spear every time I see Facilis, and I will regret it as long as I live if he goes home to Aquincum unharmed." After a moment he added, "And you're willing to go? Because I'm not. It would mean swallowing what I said to Facilis."

"I am willing to go," I said. "I'll tell Facilis as much this evening. Can I tell him that if we know he's acting in good faith, we will go on their ships?"

Gatalas flinched, but, after a moment, nodded. "I will not be the first to break an oath."

"Nor will I," said Arshak again, unhappily. "But we'll see what we can arrange for the Romans if it happens that they're lying."

Arshak was quite right about at least one thing, however: the procurator of naval base where we stopped that night did not want to take his orders from Flavius Facilis. He'd had letters about us, and when we arrived he came out to the gate to look at us. It was easy for us to guess who the figure standing on the battlement was: he was wearing the long crimson cloak and gilded armor, and when we got closer we could see he had the narrow purple stripe on his tunic, marking him as a member of the Roman equestrian order. Arshak galloped up to the gate, stopped his horse, saluted respectfully, greeted him as "Lord," and asked him where we could put our wagons. By the time Facilis had cantered up and suggested that we be confined to barracks instead, the procurator had already granted us leave to arrange the wagons in the shipyard, and wouldn't back down: an equestrian appointed by the emperor doesn't change his arrangements because a centurion who struggled up through the ranks thinks he ought to. Facilis turned crimson and swore under his breath, but had to accept it. He followed us to the shipyard, where he told us that if we "tried anything," he would see to it that our bodies were burned. He knew enough about us to be aware that this was a terrible threat—but luckily the men couldn't understand it.

I waited in the shipyard for my men, then waited, with them, for the wagons, then saw the wagons arranged and the men and horses settled. My bodyguard—the thirty men and two officers of my personal squadron—

offered to come with me to see Facilis and the procurator, and also offered, though fearfully, to join me if I was allowed on a ship: I refused both offers. They had a great sense of the respect due me as their prince-commander, and Facilis would only offend it and them—and there was no point in dragging their proud loyalty in terror across the ocean when at best it was an unnecessary voyage. It was dark when I set off for the center of the camp.

The camp headquarters were shut and locked; the guards told me that the procurator was next door, in his house, and that Facilis was with him. I went to the house and asked to speak with them. The servants told me to wait, and when I'd tethered my horse, they ushered me into the courtyard so as to keep my smell of horses and camp dirt out of the house. The courtyard was colonnaded and paved with flagstones; a few bushes of rosemary straggled from terracotta pots. There was lamplight in the glass windows and a smell of cooking. I sat down in the shelter of the colonnade and waited, resting my head on my knees and rubbing my stiff leg.

"If it were up to me, sir," came Facilis' voice from behind me, "I'd have killed them all before they ever left Aquincum."

That made me raise my head. A shuttered window on the courtyard had been pushed open, and the procurator was standing in a cloud of lamplight, looking out at the night. Facilis must have stood behind him. I remained where I was, in the shadow of the colonnade, and listened.

"But the emperor wants them alive," Facilis went on, "so it's my job to make sure they get to Britain that way. Sir, he appointed me himself. I'm Pannonian by birth, and I know the Sarmatians. He knew he could trust me to make sure of them."

"You haven't said anything to me that indicates there's the slightest reason for concern," the procurator replied irritably. "I know that the emperor put you in charge of them, Marcus Flavius, but he put *me* in charge of the British fleet. I can use my own judgment about how to get these barbarians across the Channel, and it seems to me that if I go clapping chains on their leaders, the men will be sure to mutiny." (In the back of my mind I made a note that, although Facilis called him *dominus*, "sir," he addressed Facilis by his first two names, informally: he spoke with the confidence of noble birth and high rank, and the centurion was forced to honor that.)

"You don't know anything about them!" Facilis said. "You seem to think they're like the Gauls or the Germans, nice safe *conquered* barbarians, who'll more or less do as they're told if you treat them kindly! Sarmatians are different. They've taken it into their heads that we've tricked them and mean to murder them, and they'll try to hit us hard while we're not looking. I'd stake my sword on it they've managed to hide some weapons in those wagons, for all our precautions, and they're sitting about their fires now plotting how to kill us."

He was perfectly correct on that.

"Really!" exclaimed the procurator in disgust, turning away from the window. "I seem to recall hearing that our invincible emperor *did* conquer them, by the favor of the immortal gods."

"His 'Thundering Victory,' " Facilis answered, in a tone of equal disgust. "Yes. I was there. But maybe you haven't heard the details of what came *before* that victory. They'd been raiding us for years—they thought it was a brave and manly thing to slip across the Danube with a troop of cavalry and steal the flocks and property of Romans, killing anyone who got in their way. They weren't afraid of us in the least. The cities cried out to the emperor as the raids got worse and worse, and the emperor decided to settle the Sarmatians for good. For a year we fought. We caught a raiding party on the Danube in the winter, and fought a battle actually on the ice of the river—but that only meant that the next raiding parties were bigger. We negotiated and got nowhere, and at last we set off to conquer the Sarmatians, with all the Danube legions, detachments from all the western legions and some of the eastern ones, more auxiliaries than I could count, and the emperor himself as commander. Twice the number of their army, at least; three, four times their number. We marched out into the plains—and found no one. You can't besiege their cities, because they don't have any; you can't burn their crops to force them to give battle, because they don't have any of those, either. They keep herds and live in wagons.

"We had reports, though, that their king was in the northeast of the country, and his army with him, so we marched on. And when we'd gone a long way, they attacked our supply train and chopped our rear guard to pieces, cutting us off. We sent out foraging parties, looking for food and water, and sometimes the foraging parties came back, and sometimes they didn't. I've been out myself, and come across a dip in the hills and found a party of thirty lads lying there, shot full of arrows, with everything stripped off them but their tunics, and their skulls looking like peeled grapes—and all the hills around empty, just grass and dust. Didn't you see the scalps hanging from their horses' bridles when they came in? Arshak has thirty-seven, ten on the bridle and the rest stitched onto his coat, all from Roman soldiers he's killed with his own hands—and he'd love to add mine to his collection. Jupiter! he would!"

"Those tassels on the bridles?" said the procurator. "Those are scalps? I thought . . ."

"Those are scalps. It's a custom of theirs. But that was just playing with us. One night when we were making camp, their army turned up. Good! we thought. Our turn at last! I tell you, sir, the heavy cavalry rode right over us. Twice. They used the lance on the way there, and the long swords on the way back, and all the while the light cavalry rained arrows on us. Twenty men I lost from my century that day, and the rest ran into our camp as soon as it was built, and hid. Next day we tried to retreat—and we couldn't. We managed to reach a patch of hills, the one damned patch of hills in that whole dry plain, and there we sat like a weasel up a tree, perishing of thirst, and didn't dare come down. And we would have died there, all of us, if the gods hadn't favored the emperor and sent the most torrential thunderstorm. The horses slipped in the mud, and we rushed out and caught them. By Mars, it was sweet, to catch them on the ground for once! They had enough fighting pretty quickly then, and galloped off, and a party of our auxiliary cavalry went after them and found one of their base camps, where they had some of their herds and some of the women and children: we drove off the herds and killed the bitches and their brats, and that was our Thundering Victory!

"It hurt them, all right, hurt them enough that they started begging us for peace. But they're not conquered yet. You can't conquer a people who don't build cities: it's like trying to carry water in your hands. The emperor thought of exterminating the whole horde of them. But it would have taken time to catch them all, and by then he had no time, and a rebellion in the East screaming for his attention. So when they offered to give us eight thousand troops if we went away, the emperor accepted, with the provision that all the troops had to be heavy cavalry. He wanted the troops—we'd all seen how good they were—and he knew that if we had them, they wouldn't.

Only the important men, what they call *azatani*, can afford armor: the commoners fight as mounted archers. To get eight thousand heavy cavalry, they had to send us practically every nobleman between the ages of sixteen and thirty—the very men who'd started the whole war with their raids across the Danube, and who'd poured out rivers of our blood. They won't start any wars now until the next generation grows up. But there's no province of Sarmatia yet, and while there's a Sarmatian alive, there never will be. There'll be more wars, in ten, fifteen years' time, and this lot know that just as well as I do."

"Yet they've been disarmed, and come quietly all the way from Aquincum."

"I've already said: they're not as thoroughly disarmed as I'd like, and I've heard of them killing armed opponents with just a rope and a dagger. And they won't come quietly now. Sir, I *know* they're planning to mutiny. You've got to step on them hard. There'll be another four thousand of them coming through Bononia next year, and if you let this lot cause trouble, you'll have trouble with them all."

That made me blink. We hadn't been told where our fellows were being sent. So, another four thousand of us were also on their way to Britain? I wondered if they included my sister's husband. I wondered how my sister was managing, overseeing the cattle alone. The picture of her, riding out to check on the herds, with little Saios bouncing on the saddle in front of her, suddenly seemed more real than the courtyard of the procurator's house and the voices in the room behind me.

"They're vicious brutes," Facilis was urging. "They don't respect anything but force. You need to show them you're stronger than they are. You need to break their spirit."

"And you think I should arrest . . . who?" asked the procurator, resignedly.

"All the squadron captains," Facilis said promptly. "All forty-eight of 'em. And the three company commanders, the prince-commanders of the dragons—them especially. They're all from the great families, what they call the scepter-holders. The rest of the men are their dependants."

The procurator winced and turned away from the window. "If that's true, Marcus Flavius, it seems to me that their men are almost certainly going to mutiny if we arrest them. I would expect my own clients to defend me, in such circumstances. There'll be bloodshed."

"But if we arrange it right, it will be Sarmatian blood, not Roman," returned Facilis.

"Marcus Flavius, I'd rather no blood was shed, Sarmatian or Roman! It would reflect very badly on me if I couldn't get these people across the Channel without killing half of them. The thing I'd expect to do would be . . . well, talk to the most reasonable of the company commanders, win his support. Set him against the other two, if need be—divide and rule, eh? Calm them down, give them a few days to realize that we're not tricking them or planning to murder them, and then ship them across quietly."

"A reasonable Sarmatian commander?" said Facilis. "Sir, that's a contradiction in terms. I wouldn't trust any of the bastards. Look at them! There's Arshak, the king's nephew: he'd rather kill Romans than feast on figs and sweet wine, and he hates me. Then there's Gatalas. He was green with fear at the sight of the sea this afternoon, but by reputation he's a lunatic of a fighter and completely unpredictable—you won't win him over. And then there's Ariantes, the quiet one: I trust him least of all. He's clever, and he's led more and worse raids into Roman lands than either of the others. Give them a few days and they'll hatch some plan to slaughter the lot of us. Arrest them, search the wagons for weapons, and give a good flogging to anyone caught hiding arms and anyone who resists."

I'd heard enough. If the procurator followed this advice, I'd end up with half my men dead trying to free me. Perhaps that was what Facilis wanted. I stood up. "Flavius Facilis!" I called, going to the window as though I'd only just arrived in the courtyard. "Lord Procurator! May I speak with you?"

The procurator jumped back from the window like a man who's put his hand in a hole and found a snake there. "Who are you?" he demanded. He had not particularly noticed me when I came into the camp. Arshak had done all the talking.

Facilis answered that question for me. "Ariantes!" he exclaimed, pushing past the procurator, gripping the window frame and glaring at me. "How long have you been listening?"

I didn't answer. "May I speak with you both?" I repeated.

"Certainly, certainly," said the procurator, though looking at me rather doubtfully, as though I were a wild animal—which, after Facilis' account of us, was hardly surprising. "Uhh . . . will you come in . . . um, *Lord* Ariantes?"

I knew, when I heard that *Lord*, that he would listen to me. Perhaps he didn't like being pressured by Facilis and wanted to try his own plan; perhaps he was genuinely afraid of bloodshed; perhaps it was simply that we were both noblemen. For whatever worthy or unworthy reason, I would be heard. Facilis realized it as well, and began to go crimson. "Thank you, Lord Procurator," I said, bowing my head. I walked round the courtyard to the door and found my way in.

The room was a dining room. It had a mosaic floor, painted walls, and the couches had feet of ivory. The light from the lamps on the gilded stand glowed on the polished table, where a glass wine bowl stood half-empty with two silver cups beside it. I held my hands at my sides, afraid to touch anything: my clothes were stiff with dirt. I'd been in such a room before only when a raiding party I'd led had sacked some rich man's villa in Pannonia. The cups there had sometimes been gold, though.

Facilis had swollen like a bullfrog and was glaring at me. "How long were you out there listening?" he demanded again.

It would be no use talking to him. He must have been aware where the path he'd been urging would have led. I wondered if there was any one in particular of the "lads" who died in the war whose death he held against us—he was old enough to have had sons. I turned to the procurator instead. "Lord," I said, "I have come to tell you that my people are afraid to cross the ocean."

"You've come here to *announce* the mutiny?" snarled Facilis, rigid with indignation. "Sir—"

The procurator raised his hand for silence, then nodded to me to continue.

"When we surrendered at Aquincum," I told him, "we swore oaths to obey the emperor. We do not wish to break them. But we cannot see any island out there, and we do not entirely trust the good faith of the Romans: we know that the emperor wished to exterminate us. We have never seen the sea before, nor have we been farther in a boat than across the Danube, and our religion holds that those who die by water must expect a wretched fate in the afterlife. Some of us are saying now that we have been betrayed, and we would do better to die on land. Some of us are desperate."

"Lord Ariantes!" exclaimed the procurator, in amazement and distress. "Let me assure you, we haven't the least intention of harming your troops! I am the man responsible for seeing them ferried safely over to Britain, and I would be disgraced if there were serious trouble: it's the last thing on earth I want! And Marcus Flavius Facilis here was charged with seeing you safely to your journey's end: he, too, would be disgraced if any harm came to you."

"Lord Procurator," I said, "I am sorry, but you cannot give any assurances that my people would trust. But I do not want serious trouble, either. If you would be disgraced, we would die, and die for nothing if you are acting in good faith and this island of Britain is indeed across the ocean, just out of sight. Now, I have suggested to the others that I cross the ocean myself first, if that is agreeable to you, and then return to report on the island, if it is there. They would believe me where they would not believe you, and if I can prove to them that they have not been betrayed, they agree to embark when you wish."

"Arshak and Gatalas agreed to this?" Facilis demanded incredulously.

"They agreed," I said. "Why would they want to die in Bononia?"

The procurator beamed. "Is that all it needs?" he asked. "Of course, Lord Ariantes, of course I accept your suggestion! I can send you across on a fast galley first thing tomorrow morning." He looked at Facilis triumphantly. "I should have had this man arrested, eh? All Sarmatians are unreasonable, eh?"

Facilis looked bewildered. "What are you playing at, Ariantes?" he demanded.

"I am not playing at anything, Flavius Facilis."

"Come on! I know you hate all Romans. What kind of game is this?"

"I am a servant of Rome," I told him. "I accepted that servitude to buy my people's freedom, and I could hardly go on living if I hated all Romans. Why should I wear out my heart? With any luck, you can go back to Pannonia in a few days, and I can go to my posting in Britain. I will not lie awake, regretting that you live. I intend to forget about you completely."

All the journey, he'd gone red when he was angry. He had shouted and sworn and hurled insults. He'd spoken of Arshak's hatred with relish. I hadn't expected him even to pay attention to my declaration of indifference. But he went pale—or rather, yellow-gray, leaving the red in uneven blotches of broken veins across his cheeks—and he stared at me without saying a word.

The pupils of his eyes contracted until he looked almost blind. I'd seen that look before, on the faces of men who've gone mad, in battle or grief. The crimson rages had been nothing: this was serious. I backed away.

"You killed my son," said Facilis, in a choked voice. I stopped with my hand on the door. "You killed my only son and you intend to forget about me completely?"

He had his sword out. I didn't dare move.

"Centurion!" cried the procurator. "Centurion! Put that weapon away!"

Until that moment I had never understood how powerful Roman discipline could be. Facilis stood rigid for a moment longer, fixed on me with that insane passion of rage—and then he began to shake. His head snapped away, and he fumbled the sword back into its sheath. "You stinking Sarmatian bastard," he whispered. "It might have been you that did it. It might have been any of you." He rubbed his face with one of his thick hands, and I saw that he was starting to cry. Coarse, cruel, miserable old man. I wanted, stupidly, to console him. But he was right: if his son had died in battle, it might have been me who did it. It might have been several thousand others, but it might have been me. So how could I console him?

"I am sorry, Facilis," I said after a moment. "I also have dead to mourn."

"You!" he exclaimed in disgust. "Sorry! Don't make me sick! You bastards started that war."

That was true, too, as far as it went. I turned to the procurator and said—quickly, so as to get out—"My lord, I will go tell my fellows that you are arranging for me to cross the ocean in the morning. Good health, my lord."

And so the next morning I set out for Britain.

II

*T*HE SUN WAS shining again, and the water sparkled in the light when I
came down to the quay; on the sea's plain, the waves curled whitely in the
breeze. I smelled the sea for the first time then, salt and alien, and for all my
bold offers, I was afraid. The procurator had arranged for me to travel in his
dispatch vessel, a small bireme that carried letters and messages between the
base in Bononia and one on the British coast opposite, a place called Dubris.
It was a quick, light galley with one large sail and fifty oars arranged in two
banks: it was shallow-decked, thin-skinned, and seemed to be held together
only by a few bits of rope. When I stepped down into it I felt it shiver under
my weight. The flimsy thing seemed to me quite certain to sink. But my fellows and all my men were watching me, so I waved to them, called "I'll see you
tomorrow!" and tried to look confident as I searched for a place to sit. My leg
wound had left me limping and clumsy, and I bumped into the rowing
benches. The captain hurriedly ushered me to the back, out of the way, and
arranged me beside the steersman. One of the sailors began to beat time on a
small drum, the ship was loosed from the dock, the oars dipped into the water,
and we slid out across the blue-green waters of the harbor. I clutched the
ship's side until my fingers ached, desperately praying that it wouldn't sink.

It didn't, of course. It was accustomed to make the voyage every few
days, and the crossing was a matter of such routine that the sailors found my
fears ludicrous. (I was seasick, and they found that funny, too.) They sealed
up the lower oar-ports when we were well out to sea to keep out the waves,
pulled up a corner of the sail to hold a straight line against the wind, and galloped cheerfully over the salt water in less than five hours. It was still early afternoon when I saw Britain for the first time: a row of cliffs, white above a
blue sea, and beyond them, green hills; then the city of Dubris, with its lighthouse overlooking the deep harbor, and its streets climbing up the steep hill
behind. The bireme brailed up its sail, let out the lower bank of oars again,

and splashed up to the quay amid the shrieking of seagulls and the shouting of men.

I sat in the stern watching even after the vessel had been made fast. The oarsmen gathered their packs and strode off to their barracks in the naval base, their oars slung over their shoulders; the captain and drummer collected the sacks of dispatches and came aft to talk to me.

"Lord Valerius Natalis has offered you the use of his own residence in Dubris tonight, Lord Ariantes," the captain told me. (It took me a moment to remember that Valerius Natalis was the procurator's name.) "If you like, I can show you where it is and introduce you to his slaves. Or, if you prefer, we can meet here this evening, after I've delivered these." He hefted the sack of letters.

"I will meet you here later," I said. He was pleased to be rid of the burden of a clumsy oaf like me, and went off without another look.

I sat by myself for some time after he'd gone. The water lapped against the dock, and the ship rocked gently, like a wagon in a wind. It was extraordinarily quiet—no sound of men or horses, no clattering of harness or weapons. I could not remember when I had last been alone.

After a while, I picked myself up and stepped hesitantly onto the gangplank. I could see the shadow of it falling through the shallow water, making it dark, and a school of small fish nibbling at the stones of the quay. I limped very slowly down the plank, stepped onto the quay—and stopped. I had set foot on Britain, the island that was to be prison or home—and the action seemed almost too simple for such a consequential thing. Was this really the invisible island beyond the world's end, the island of ghosts we all feared so?

After a moment, I walked on down the docks, out of the naval base surrounding the harbor, and into the town. It felt very odd to go on foot—my people are accustomed to ride everywhere—but somehow the simplicity of it was right.

Narrow houses overlooked the paved street, some of timber and stucco, a few of stone. A tavern sign shaped like a ship swung above the door of one; it had glass windows on its lower floor, wicker interlace shutters above. A man sold fish from wooden tubs outside his shop. Two women talked by a public fountain, one of them holding a baby. A girl carried a bucket of water, her tongue between her teeth as she tried not to spill it. I walked slowly, trying to take it all in. The cool clear afternoon light was the first light on a new world.

The street opened into a marketplace where the region's farmers had set up stalls. I limped slowly through the bustle and the cries, looking. Some of the people there, the wealthier ones, wore Roman dress of tunic and cloak, but most were clothed in what I presumed was the native fashion. The men wore trousers and sleeved tunics that came to the middle of their thighs, and the women wore longer tunics and shawls. Most of their clothing was made of plain gray-brown wool, but they had a fondness for checked cloaks, which they pinned on both shoulders. They were, I thought, on average a bit shorter than my own people, and a bit darker—not so many blond and red heads, though plenty of blue eyes. Their faces were different, too—rounder, wider about the eyes, without the high cheeks and long thin bones. The more Romanized men were short-haired and clean-shaven, the native men long-haired and bearded, like me. They looked at me as curiously as I looked at them, and I could feel them staring after me, trying to work out where I came from. I was not wearing Roman dress, of course. I had trousers like their own men, but a shirt and sleeved coat instead of the tunic and cloak. I was wearing the coat with the sleeves loose, since the day was warm, but I'd pinned it on my right shoulder, the opposite way from them, and I had a leather hat with a peak, while they were all bareheaded. I was obviously a foreigner and a barbarian—but I was also obviously wealthy. My clothes might have been dirty, but they had been dyed expensively red, decorated with gold beadwork and fastened with gold, and my dagger had a jeweled hilt. I was a contradiction. It was not surprising that they stared.

I paused to look at some sheep that were penned between three wicker hurdles. They were an unfamiliar breed, more lightly built than the ones I was used to: most were grayish brown, but a few, a longer-tailed, squarer sort, were white. I stopped for longer by a horse dealer. His horses were small shaggy animals with large heads and thin necks: I didn't think much of them. But I noticed that they all wore iron shoes. My own people never trouble to shoe their horses—it's unnecessary in a land without roads—and most of the auxiliary cavalry I'd met didn't either. I'd seen horseshoes before, but never had a chance to inspect them. I went over to one of the horses, patted it, and knelt to check its hooves. Its owner came over and asked me a question in an unknown language.

"I am sorry, I do not understand you," I said. "Do you speak Latin?"

"Indeed, man . . ." he said, then, correcting himself, "My lord, indeed I speak Latin. Are you interested in the beast? He's a fine worker, pulls well at the plow or the cart, only four years old; you may have him for just thirty denarii."

"How far can he go in a day?" I asked—the first question any Sarmatian asks when buying a horse.

The horse dealer stared at me. "Indeed, my lord, I don't know."

It shocked me almost to tears, and I had to look away and pretend to study the hoof again. I felt utterly foreign and alone. "How far can he go in a day?"—the question came from another world, a world where people lived in wagons and traveled from grazing ground to grazing ground, a world to which I could never return. Here the question was "Can he pull well at the plow?" and I wouldn't even understand the qualities that answered it.

I put the horse's foot down, stood, patted it on the shoulder. "Thank you," I told the horse dealer, and limped off.

I stopped at a public fountain on the other side of the marketplace and had a drink of water. A fat woman selling apples offered me a cup to drink from. As I returned it, with thanks, I looked at the apples, which she had in a large wooden barrel. They were small and red. "How much are they?" I asked.

"I'd sell a basketful for a couple of eggs, my lord," the woman replied, beaming, "but you may have one for nothing, seeing that you're a foreign gentleman." She handed me one. "Have you come from across the sea, my lord?"

Plainly she had a lively curiosity. I took a bite of the apple: it was sweet. "I have," I told her, when I'd swallowed it, "and I have some fellows there. I would like to buy your apples to give to them, freewoman. Will you sell me the barrel full?"

"What? The whole barrel?"

"If it is agreeable to you."

"Indeed, my lord! The whole barrel? Then you'd want the barrel, as well as the apples? That would be . . . let me see . . . You may have the apples for four asses, and another five for the barrel."

I had some coins in a purse, and I dug nine coppers out. The woman looked at them and shook her head. "My lord!" she said. "These are sestertii!"

"Well, how many of them make up one as?" I asked.

She stared at me in amazement, then giggled. "My lord!" she cried. "There are two and a half asses to one sestertius! Where are you from, my lord?"

I set my teeth. I'd acquired the money on raids, and kept it in case I ever needed to do any trading with Romans: my own people don't use it. Now I would have to learn what things cost. At least the apple seller hadn't tried to cheat me. I gave her five of the sestertii.

"Only four, my lord, only four, and I owe you one as change!" she said, laughing and trying to give one back.

I shook my head. "The fifth is in thanks for your honesty. Will that buy the apples?"

"Indeed!" she said, beaming. "Will you bring a cart to collect them, my lord? Or should my man drop them off with you when he comes this evening?"

I hesitated. Should I send the apples to the procurator's house or to the ship?

There was a sudden commotion from just up the street, and I looked up to see a white stallion trotting into the marketplace. I stopped worrying about the apples. This horse was altogether different from the sorry animals I'd looked at before. It was several hands higher, straight-backed and deep-chested, and moved with a light step. It was a fine horse. I had finer ones myself, even in Bononia, but I might have bargained to buy the animal in the days when I lived in my country and owned herds; I liked its hindquarters and the line of its neck. It had some harness on but no bridle, and it was clear from the shouting of the people around it that it had slipped its tether and was running loose. A young man in a fine cloak ran into the marketplace after it and stopped. "Oh, Deae Matres!" he groaned, seeing the stallion trotting away across the paving stones. "Fifteen denarii to the man who can catch that horse!" I watched to see how they would do it.

I never would have credited it: a whole marketplace of people, and no one knew how to catch a horse. They lunged at it, their cloaks flapping—and of course, it shied. They ran after it, and it snorted and laid back its ears. They yelled advice at each other, tried to grab its nose, tried to shoo it into a corner like a sheep, and it began to kick. The few, like the horse dealer, who had some notion of how to go about calming the animal were swamped in a crowd of eager helpers who threw the poor beast into a panic, and in a few minutes the stallion was reduced from alert interest into blind frenzy, rearing and lashing out at everything around it.

"Do you have a rope?" I asked my apple seller, who'd been watching the excitement with horrified delight.

She had a rope, and she handed it to me eagerly. I limped toward the stallion, making a lasso as I went. It was now bucking madly, striking sparks from the cobblestones, and the young man was wringing his hands.

I stopped about fifteen paces from the stallion and began swinging the lasso. The onlookers were now frankly running away from the horse instead of toward it, and it didn't take me long to get a clear shot. I tossed the rope about the stallion's neck; when it lunged away, I let it pull me a few steps, then drew the rope tight and began talking to it quietly. The horse stopped and stood still with its ears back, trembling. I walked forward very slowly, still speaking to it soothingly, until I was near enough to touch it. The ears flicked nervously forward as I ran my hand down the sweat-damp neck.

Then a large red-faced man gave a yell and lunged at the horse from the other side. "I've got him!" he shouted. And of course, the horse tried to bolt—toward me. I was knocked onto the pavement, and the horse stepped on me—and, worse luck, stepped exactly on my wounded leg. The pain was sudden and excruciating, and I screamed. A lifetime's instinct made me lie still and let go of the rope—one doesn't hold a frightened horse on top of oneself—and the horse clattered on over me. The red-faced man grabbed the rope, and then a dozen hands were clutching the horse and leading it away.

"I've got him!" shouted the red-faced man again. "I caught him!"

"You never did!" retorted my apple seller, bustling over. "The foreign gentleman caught him, we all saw that, and when you shoved your greedy hands in, you nearly lost him again. My lord, are you all right?"

I was lying on the ground clutching my leg. The apple seller bent over me and tried to pull me up, but the movement twisted my leg again and made me gasp with pain. The young man in the fine cloak dropped to his knees beside me. I noticed, for the first time, the narrow purple stripe on his tunic. "Deae Matres!" he exclaimed again. "I hope you're not hurt. You practically saved my life, catching that animal. Did it kick you?"

I set my teeth and managed to sit up. "You can catch your own horse next time," I said.

"It's not my horse; it's my commanding officer's wife's horse. If it had got hurt while I was in charge of it"—he whistled—"I might as well have resigned from the army at once. Priscus would never forgive me. By Maponus! Your leg's bleeding."

I looked: there was blood on my hands. The wound must have torn open. I let out my breath in a hiss.

The apple seller began to shout at the red-faced man in British. The red-faced man shouted back. I wanted to get away; I tried to climb to my feet, but when my weight came onto my injured leg, there was a spurt of such red-hot pain that I had to sit down again.

"Lie back, lie back," said the young man, "Let me see your leg . . ." He began pulling the trouser leg up.

"No," I said. "The horse caught an old wound. Leave it."

He paid no attention whatsoever. "I know a bit of field surgery," he told me. "My name's Comittus, by the way, Lucius Javolenus Comittus, a tribune of the Sixth Legion . . . Hercules!" he'd shoved the trouser leg up above my knee, and seen the scars. There were three, one above the other, and since I'd only got them that summer, they were still red. To my relief, it was the top cut, the one just above my knee, that had broken open, and that only a little down half its length. The pain had been so hot I hadn't been able to tell where it was. But the top cut had been the least serious of the three. It was the lowest slash that broke my shinbone.

"Lucius Javolenus?" came a woman's voice. Comittus looked round quickly, and I looked too.

I guessed that this was his commanding officer's wife, the owner of the horse. She was certainly a lady of some importance. Her fair hair was piled on her head in the kind of elaborate curls that require a trained slave to arrange them, and the cloak held modestly closed before her was of the most expensive kind, dyed a rich blue throughout, and bordered with patterned flowers. And despite the modesty, it was plain she was both young and beautiful. The rounded eyes were vividly, liquidly blue, an intensity of color I had never seen among the Romans before, though it's not uncommon among my own people—Arshak's eyes were much the same shade. The oddly familiar eyes stared into mine with impersonal curiosity. I did not look back at her gladly. Bad enough to look a fool; worse to look a fool in front of a beautiful woman.

"Aurelia Bodica," cried Comittus, "this man caught your horse, but it kicked him on an old wound when he caught it. Do you think we could find Diophantes? I think he needs a doctor."

The blue gaze sharpened. Aurelia Bodica ignored Comittus and stared at the scars. "It looks as though someone tried to chop off your leg with an axe," she said, in a dispassionate, assessing voice.

"With a Dacian long sword," I corrected her.

And suddenly the memory of it came over me with a terrible clarity: my horse falling in the mud, and the swordsman screaming and running at me as I rolled free, holding his sword two-handed above his head. His face was white, and there was a smear of blood down the side of it; his teeth as he screamed were like dogs' teeth. I tried to scramble away, and the sword came down; I screamed, tried to roll over and get to my feet, and the sword came down; I rolled onto my back again, trying to get my own sword up, and the sword came down. Then somehow I managed to strike his sword with my own from a sitting position, and knocked it out of his hands. Then someone else hit me in the back, I was thrown forward onto my face, and the next thing I remember clearly is lying in the mud, soaked with blood, too cold for pain, and watching the moonlight silver the bronze eye-guard of the dead warhorse before me.

I pushed Comittus' hands away from my leg. "I do not need a doctor," I told him. "It is sore, but not serious."

The apple seller plonked herself down and offered me a handkerchief of threadbare linen. "You can use this for a bandage, my lord, and I'll get you a nice piece of raw beef to put on it. That's the best thing for a bruise."

"Thank you for the bandage," I said, taking it and tying it around my leg, "I do not need the beef." I pulled my trouser leg down and got my good leg under me, then rose cautiously to my feet. Everyone in the marketplace had crowded round to look at me. The white stallion had been tied to a post at one side. I felt an idiot.

"Do you want the fifteen denarii for catching the horse?" asked Comittus.

"I do not catch horses for money," I said, straightening my coat and looking about for my hat.

"I didn't think you did, somehow," said Comittus cheerfully, "but I thought I'd offer. Can I buy you a drink, then? Would you care to come to dinner? You practically saved my life."

I spotted my hat under the red-faced man's foot, and limped painfully over. "My hat," I told him, looking at it pointedly. He moved over at once, picked it up, and tried to dust it off. I took it from him and rubbed it clean on his cloak. He spluttered angrily, but couldn't quite bring himself to protest: he knew he'd acted stupidly. Besides, I was a few inches taller than he and might have been dangerous. I pulled the hat onto my head.

"We're staying at the naval base," Comittus told me. "I escorted Aurelia Bodica to the temple of Minerva, just out of town, and we'd stopped for her to do some shopping when the horse got loose. I don't have much space in my quarters at the base, but there's a very good tavern just outside it . . ."

"I thank you, no," I said. I turned to the apple seller. "Have the apples delivered to the naval base, to the house of Valerius Natalis. Say that Ariantes bought them, and they're to be shipped to Bononia tomorrow."

"You're Sarmatian, aren't you?" said Aurelia Bodica suddenly.

I turned back to her and met her eyes for a moment. "Yes," I said. For a moment I was tempted to introduce myself—"Ariantes son of Arifarnes, scepter-holder and *azatan* of the Iazyges of the Sarmatians, prince-commander of the sixth dragon." But what was the point? The titles would mean nothing to her, and I was not a scepter-holder or prince now: I was the commander of a troop of Roman auxiliary cavalry.

"Are you really?" exclaimed Comittus excitedly. "Then we're comrades! We've come down from Eburacum to meet you!"

"What?" I demanded, staring at him.

"My commander, Julius Priscus, is legionary legate of the Sixth Victrix in Eburacum, and commander in chief of all the forces in the North. We were told to come down to Dubris to meet three troops of Sarmatian cavalry which were expected from Bononia. I'm going to be in command of one of them."

"You?" I asked, in confused disbelief. "How, 'in command'?"

"Well . . . as prefect of the *ala*, you know. The troops will have their own officers—I suppose you're one of them—but I'll be in charge, as they won't . . . that is, I'd heard you wouldn't be very used to Roman ways."

I stared at him, appalled. My imagination suddenly shaped another picture of him, etched with a ferocity I hadn't felt for months, and precise with details only too familiar: Comittus lying on the cobblestones with my spear in him, and my dagger's edge running across his forehead, around the sides of his head, and lifting the curly brown scalp away from the reddened skull. How could any Roman, let alone this one, be in charge of my men—my dependants, my followers, my own people? And if the Romans expected to appoint some of their own people as prefects, what did they plan to do with Arshak, Gatalas, and myself? Second-in-command, joint command, what?

Even a joint command would end in disaster. Here I was, determined to safeguard my followers by keeping the peace with our Roman masters—and I ached to scalp the first Roman colleague I met. What would my officers do? Or my fellow commanders? I thought of Arshak and his coat of Roman scalps. This Comittus was as cheerful and bouncy as a puppy. Members of the equestrian order often begin their careers by serving as military tribunes on the staff of a legion. They don't need any previous military experience, and I doubted Comittus had supplied any. He would manage Arshak about as well as the red-faced man had managed the white horse, and the result could easily be death and grief all round. Someone in Britain had miscalculated badly. Perhaps, like the procurator Valerius Natalis, they thought we were conquered barbarians.

I found that my hand was on the hilt on my dagger, and I made myself rub it slowly, trying to banish the images of blood. "I think perhaps we had better have dinner together," I said quietly. "Perhaps I might speak with your commanding officer, as well. What you have said . . ." I shook my head. "Javolenus Comittus, if you had said that to Arshak, that 'I will be in command,' I think he would have taken your life."

Comittus looked bewildered. The woman, Aurelia Bodica, smiled. "Is this . . . Arsacus . . . your commanding officer?" she asked.

"He is my fellow officer, Lady," I said, "but senior to me in honor, being of royal blood."

"Is he here in Dubris too? We hadn't heard that any of your troops had even arrived in Bononia yet."

"We arrived in Bononia yesterday afternoon, Lady. The others are still there. I came over on my own this morning. The others will follow when I have told them all is well."

"I see." She smiled again, very prettily this time. "I'd thought perhaps we could all have dinner together this evening, Sarmatian and Roman officers together, and you could explain to us how we should manage your troops. Instead, I'm afraid it will have to be you and four Roman legionary officers . . . What did you say your name was?"

"Ariantes."

"*Lord* Ariantes? I'm afraid I can't even invite you to dine out, because my husband and I are also staying at Natalis' house. But I hope you will share a meal with us, and I will invite the tribunes as well—I'm inviting you now, Lucius Javolenus! You can tell us all about your people's customs and how we can avoid offending them."

I thanked her and agreed. Comittus thanked her too. She smiled again and said she would have to rush back to arrange the dinner party, wished me good health, and set off back up the road. Comittus collected the horse and followed her.

My leg was still too painful to allow me to walk any distance. I limped back to the fountain and sat down on the rim. The curious crowd at last tired of gaping at me and began to take down the market stalls and pack up for the day; even the apple seller excused herself. I supposed that it was not really surprising that Bodica had guessed I was Sarmatian, given that she knew we were expected and I had mentioned Bononia. Yet I had felt something strange in that stare, and in the smile when I referred to Arshak killing the tribune. It unsettled me. I wondered how much authority she held. It was odd that Comittus had called her by her own names: she should have been Aurelia Julii, after her husband. Was it really so clear to everyone that she wasn't Julius' Aurelia, but her own? And the name itself was an odd one for a woman of rank. When they acquire Roman citizenship and Roman names, many people retain their own name as their last and take the family name of the Roman they received the citizenship from, often the emperor. The obvious "Aurelius" was the man I'd met at Aquincum, or perhaps his predecessor.

But that would make the citizenship of Bodica's family very recent, and she didn't carry herself like an upstart. And even without that puzzle to trouble me, I was staggered at the task of trying to explain the Sarmatians to four Roman officers at a dinner party. If I couldn't convince them to change their plans, though, there'd be a mutiny in Britain even if there wasn't one in Bononia. I might even lead it myself. I could not—*could* not—yield command of my own men to some ignorant and inexperienced young Roman.

The white horse trotted down the street again, this time pulling a flimsy little chariot of painted wood and leather. Bodica was sitting on the bench seat while a groom drove, and Comittus rode behind on a flashy but shallow-hocked black stallion. Bodica noticed me and waved as she went by, and Comittus turned his horse aside.

"Is your leg really all right?" he asked, stopping in front of me. "If it isn't, you can ride Thunder back to the base. Here, I'll walk." He slid off the black and offered me the bridle.

I looked at him for a moment. I do not like borrowing anything, but I doubted that I could walk the distance without straining the wound, and I'd had enough trouble with it already. (Riding's no strain. I have ridden while asleep.) "Thank you," I said, and took the bridle.

"I'll give you a leg up . . ." he began—but I was on top of the horse by then. I checked how it was trained, remembering to use my knees in the Roman fashion, instead of my heels as I would with my own horses. Comittus looked as though he had expected to instruct me on the horse, but thought better of it. "Well," he said, and swallowed. "If you want to ride him to Natalis' house, just give him to one of the orderlies when you get there and tell them I'm in the north barrack block; they'll return him."

I looked at him for another moment. It had been a kind gesture to offer me his horse. He'd been trying to make friends. "I do not know where Natalis' house is," I confessed. "I have not yet been there. If it is agreeable to you, Javolenus Comittus, perhaps you could walk with me and show me the way."

He brightened and agreed at once.

"What did you mean when you said this Arsacus would kill me for saying I was in command?" he asked as soon as we set off.

"Was it unclear?"

"No, but . . . what's wrong with saying it?"

"Arshak's troops are Arshak's men. He is . . ." I groped for a Roman parallel. "He is their patron, they are his clients. Their families also were clients of his father, and his father before him. You are a Roman—until this summer, an enemy. How would your clients feel if things were reversed? If they were marched out into the plains among the Sarmatians, and then told that you, their patron, were no longer their patron, but that they must look instead to a Sarmatian prince who knew nothing of their ways and could not even speak their language? Would they not refuse? And Arshak is the nephew of a king, and will not want a Roman tribune to interfere with him. He is not a patient man."

"Oh. I hadn't thought of it that way." After a moment, he asked earnestly, "So what should we do?"

"Could you not call yourself an adviser? Or a mediator? Or a . . . liaison officer, who speaks for the legate, but leaves the command to us?"

"I could! That's all I will be, really." He began to brighten again. "That's all right, then! Though I hope I'm not appointed to . . . liaise with . . . this Arshak. If there are three troops of you, and he commands one while you command another, who commands the third?"

"Gatalas. I do not know that you would find him easier to liaise with than Arshak, Javolenus Comittus."

"Call me Lucius. So if I'm lucky, I liaise with you."

"If you choose to view it that way."

"I do," he announced, grinning.

He was undoubtedly right to prefer me to Arshak or Gatalas. "How far is it to Eburacum?" I asked.

He was perfectly happy to tell me about Eburacum and his journey from there, and did all the talking the rest of the way.

Natalis' house at the naval base in Dubris was even larger and finer than his house in Bononia. I slid off the horse, thanked my companion, and wished him good health—though I called him Lucius Javolenus, not Lucius. I couldn't bring myself to use his first name alone, not while my mind still teased me with the image of his scalp hanging from my bridle. When he'd ridden off, I went in and introduced myself to the slaves.

The dispatches I'd voyaged with had contained a letter about me to the steward of the house, and I'd been expected even before Bodica had appeared to arrange a dinner party for me: the slaves were polite, despite my smell of dirt and horses. I gave directions about the apples and remembered to ask for someone to go to the ship to explain to the captain why I wasn't waiting there. The steward escorted me up the stairs to a bedroom overlooking the courtyard, murmuring that Lord Julius Priscus and his wife were expecting me in an hour, after I'd had time to wash, and would I like a bath?

I wanted to clean myself, particularly if I was to dine with these important Romans, but the Roman custom of immersing oneself in hot water was still alarming to me. I asked about a steam bath, and was told that only the public baths, outside the base, were equipped for that. I settled for some oil, and cleaned myself as well as I could with that and a strigil. There was nothing I could do about my clothes; after the long journey, I didn't have any clean ones, even in Bononia. I combed my hair and avoided the mirror on the bedroom table.

There was still a long time before the dinner. I turned my attention to the room. It seemed very large to me—I had never actually slept in a house before. The walls had been covered with painted plaster, but at least the floor wasn't stone, and had a carpet: it didn't feel as much like a tomb as a room on the ground floor would have. I took the mattress off the bed and put it next to the window, draped a curtain to fill in some of the cavernous space, and hoped that it would feel enough like a wagon that I'd get some rest. Then I sat down on the mattress and put my head on my knees. I imagined what my men would do if they were told that they were to be commanded by a Roman. I imagined what the Romans would do to them afterward. I prayed to Marha, the Holy One, the god whom we worship above all other divinities, to open the ears of the Roman legate to my words and make him change his plans. The steward knocked at the door at the appointed time, and I limped apprehensively downstairs.

Aurelia Bodica reclined on the middle couch with her husband, the legate Priscus, snaring the lamplight in the web of her hair. Priscus was considerably older than her, a thickset man in his late forties, very dark. (I later found out that his full name was Tiberius Claudius Decianus Murena Aufidius Julius Priscus. Important Romans collect names as Sarmatians collect scalps.) No one got up to greet me. Priscus and the two tribunes I had not met before looked at me as the procurator Natalis had, as though I were a dangerous animal; the wife of one of the tribunes, who sat with her husband, flinched when I came in and seemed afraid to look at me at all. Comittus gave me a smile of extreme embarrassment and looked nervously away.

"So you're Ariantes," the legate said in a harsh voice, looking me up and down.

"Greetings, Lord Julius Priscus," I returned, now feeling quite dizzy with anxiety. "Greetings to you all."

He grunted, and nodded for the steward to begin serving the wine. The others were all reclining on their couches, the legate and his wife in the top place, the married tribune and his wife on the right, and the two others on the left. I did not know where to sit, so I remained standing. I sipped my wine when it was handed to me, wondering what they had heard to make them so disapproving. Then I noticed a letter lying on the table in front of the legate, and guessed that Facilis had sent it, and that it had been read aloud just before I came in.

"Is it true," growled Priscus, "that you've been telling Lucius Comittus that he should call himself a liaison officer to your troops, instead of a prefect?"

"Yes," I agreed. I repeated my explanation of why. Comittus gave me another nervous smile, then plucked up his courage and moved over on his couch, allowing me to sit down. I was glad to sit. My leg was aching.

"And you're threatening us with trouble if we don't go along with this?" demanded Priscus when I'd finished. "You told Lucius that your friend Arsacus would kill him if he called himself commander?"

"No, my lord," I replied. "I am not threatening, but warning you of trouble. I should not have spoken as I did about Arshak; I cannot say for certain what he would or would not do—but I know our men would rebel. They are angry and afraid anyway. To them the ocean is the end of the world: I am here because they doubted there was anything beyond it, and were afraid of a Roman plot to drown them. A foreign commander could hardly escape offending them. I do not want problems any more than you do. It is my own people who would suffer most."

"We've been hearing about your own people," said Priscus.

"My lord," I said, "if Flavius Facilis has written to you, I would ask you to remember that his son was killed in the war this last summer, and he is tormented with grief. His judgment of us is not altogether reasonable."

The shot went home. I could see them all realizing that Facilis had not written as a senior centurion handing over a charge, but as a man driven by passions like the rest of us, and that I'd known he hated us. They all relaxed a little.

"So it's not true," said Priscus, "that this fellow Arshak has a coat stitched with Roman scalps?"

I was silent a moment. "It is true," I admitted.

"And that he, and your other colleague Gatalas, made themselves bow cases from the skin of Romans they killed in battle?"

"That is true, as well."

"And that you yourself," Priscus demanded, glaring at me, "once killed a Roman centurion who tried to stop you when you were attacking Roman settlements in the province of Lower Pannonia—killed him with a rope and a dagger, cut off his head, and made his skull into a drinking cup, which you have to this day?"

"I do not have it to this day," I replied. "The man's family came to me at Aquincum and I gave it to them for burial."

"But the rest of the story is true?"

"Yes."

"I do not see how you can think yourself fit to be a Roman officer. Jupiter! You're not fit to live!"

"My lord," I said tightly, "I have not observed that the Romans at war behave with decency and moderation. Perhaps you do not collect scalps, but you murder indiscriminately to injure your enemies, killing even young children. And I have heard Roman soldiers complaining at Sarmatian women, calling them vicious bitches because they took up arms to defend their babies, and had to be killed before they could be raped." I had to stop for a moment. A shadow of the helpless rage I'd felt when I'd heard the complaint choked me. I managed to continue more calmly, "My lord, you yourself must have decorated men for their bravery in doing things in war which, if they had been done under other circumstances, you would have punished with death. What is the point of scratching old wounds? From my people's point of view, we are dead, I and all my fellows. They have held funerals for us. Those who had wives now have widows, who are free to remarry as they please, and our property is divided among our heirs. What I or anyone else may have done in the past concerns no one now."

"On the contrary, Ariantes, it concerns me very much. How can I hand fifteen hundred Sarmatians their weapons, give command of them to men who drink from Roman skulls, and turn them loose in a Roman province?"

"My lord, we have sworn oaths to the emperor. We cannot go home. I understand that Britain contains three legions and more auxiliaries than I could count, more than enough to destroy us. We must become Roman auxiliaries, or die. Do you mean to help us become auxiliaries, or to kill us?" I hesitated, then went on, deliberately, "The emperor was pleased to get us. Even when he thought of killing us all, he wanted cavalry like ours. I saw him at Aquincum when we rode in and surrendered. He was like a boy with a new horse. He would not be pleased with you, my lord, if you provoked trouble with us."

Priscus glared at me wordlessly, his jaw set and his nostrils white with anger.

"Why did you use a rope and a dagger?" asked Aurelia Bodica, as though it were the obvious question. When I looked at her she gave me that same sweet, unsettling smile. "When you killed that centurion, I mean."

"I wished to match his own daring," I answered, after a silence. She looked at me quizzically; the others stared with incomprehension and disgust, and I went on, reluctantly, "I had a hundred armored horsemen and three hundred mounted archers, and we had crossed the Danube to raid. We were driving off the flocks and the cattle from a settlement when a centurion came up with just one century and ten legionary dispatch riders, ninety men in all. I do not know whether he had thought we were fewer, or whether he had expected reinforcements to join him. My armored troops alone could have dealt with twice his numbers easily. But he shouted at us to return the beasts to their owners and leave Roman land at once, and I was astonished at his courage. I thought I would have no glory from the contest unless I could match such bravery. So I offered to fight him man to man, and made my men swear that if he killed me, they would not harm him, but leave, as he'd ordered. Then I got off my horse, put my weapons and armor aside, and came to fight him with a lasso and a dagger. He had his armor, javelin, and sword;

he told me I was mad, and I told him he had no right to say so, and we both laughed. I spared his men when I'd killed him. I would not have taken his head as a trophy if I had not admired him."

I remembered riding back with the centurion's head hanging from my saddle, absolutely drunk with glory, and my men laughing and shouting and singing. What an exploit! Worthy of songs, worthy of a hero! I had never been so proud of anything in my life. When I came home, to my own wagon, my men shouted out the story to my wife, Tirgatao, waving the skull—now scalped and cut in half and scraped clean to prepare it for use as a cup. Tirgatao took it and stared at it in amazement, then put it down and slapped me so hard I nearly fell over. Then she grabbed my shoulders and shook me. "Do you want to make me a widow?" she asked. "Don't you want to live to see your son?"—she was seven months pregnant at the time. "I want my son to be proud of his father," I told her, putting my arms around her. "Proud!" she shouted, putting hers around me and kissing me. "You lunatic! Oh, my dragon, my eagle, my golden hero! Don't you ever do that again!" She was crying with pride and anger, and under both of them was love. And now I was one of the dead, and the story I had gloried in was told by the Romans to disgrace me.

Though they thought the details less disgraceful than they'd expected. They'd obviously taken Facilis' reference to rope and a dagger as some kind of Sarmatian torture, and now they were looking at me with puzzlement, rather than disgust.

"You don't want your people to cause us trouble," said Bodica. It wasn't a question. The blue eyes studied me as they had before, dispassionately, assessingly.

"I do not want my men to get into trouble," I agreed. "I want them to live. Enough have died this summer already."

"Why were you buying them . . . apples?" Again the smile, sweet and unsettling. "It was apples you were buying in the market, wasn't it, Lord Ariantes?"

That she asked that question then, after making sure I didn't want trouble, made me think that she'd already guessed why I wanted the apples. I looked at Priscus: he was puzzled and irritated. He had not guessed. "When I go back," I said slowly, wondering why she was trying to help me, "if I tell them that there is no trick, and that there really is an island of Britain here, they will believe me, but they will still be afraid. If I give them something from the island—if I give them apples, which they can see, and smell, and taste, and eat, and feed to their horses—then they will be confident. It will be much easier for them then."

Bodica looked at her husband. "Tiberius," she said softly, "he'd manage them much better than Lucius or Gaius or Marcus would."

"I suppose so," Priscus grunted, releasing whatever he'd intended to do with me, like a dog backing reluctantly away from a bone. "Very well, we won't tinker with the command of the Sarmatian troops. We won't make them proper auxiliary *alae* yet: they can be *numeri*, under their own native officers. You and your two friends, Ariantes, can command, and you three tribunes can call yourselves liaison officers and make sure the barbarians follow orders. We can work out the arrangements now." He clapped his hands for the slaves to bring in the first course. "If there's trouble, though," he said, glaring at me over the boiled eggs in garlic, "and if you're responsible, I'll have you flogged to death. Now I'll tell you exactly what's required of you."

When the wretched party ended and they stopped lecturing and interrogating and allowed me to crawl off to the bedroom, I stood for a minute looking out the window. My head was aching with anxieties and I was dizzy with the newness of it all. I remembered, with a stab of terror, how Natalis had wanted to deal with us. Find a reasonable Sarmatian commander, use him to divide and rule. Other Sarmatians had been reasonable and had ended up betraying their own kind. Was that what Aurelia Bodica wanted? And I realized what it was that I found so unsettling in her: that assessing stare, like a craftsman looking for a tool, and the craftsman's smile at finding one. I was afraid—afraid of the island, of the Roman army, of the honor and passions of my own people, of the legate, his wife, and myself. But I felt, strangely, more awake than I had for a long time. I could see only the courtyard below, barred with lamplight, and hear only the sounds of the slaves cleaning the dining room and the other guests going to bed. But I could smell the sea. Gatalas' fears had been all wrong: I was not going to come back a ghost. By passing the salt water, I was forced back into the world, painfully born into another life.

The next afternoon found me back in Bononia.

III

*T*HE APPLES HELPED. I tossed them out as soon as the bireme docked in Bononia, the men passed them from hand to hand, examining them and tasting them, and when I rode back into the center of our camp and made a speech about Britain, they were ready to be convinced. Nonetheless, it was no easy job to tear ourselves loose from the land and set sail on the unfathomable water. I asked the procurator Natalis to allow us a day for preparation and prayer before embarking.

"Of course, Lord Ariantes," he said, smiling benevolently. "Roman soldiers often want to purify themselves before a voyage, too. I've even seen Italians afraid to cross the ocean, and we often have trouble with the Pannonians and the easterners. Your people aren't the only ones who think the world ends at the Channel. Do you need any cattle for the sacrifice?"

"We use horses," I told him, and he offered to provide some.

Facilis apparently argued with him after I left, telling him that a delay would only give us more opportunity to mutiny, but, fortunately, Natalis didn't listen to him. He was eager to help us. In Dubris I'd learned that he usually resided on the British side of the Channel, and had only based himself in Bononia to supervise us. He saw to it that we had proper food, access to water for washing and enough fuel, and medicines for sick men and sore-footed horses—all the things we'd missed on the journey. I began to realize how much we had endured before because Facilis was the only one responsible for us. Of course, perhaps a part of it was that I was willing to go and ask for what we needed, instead of drifting blindly in the nightmare—or enduring proudly and dreaming of revenge, like Arshak and Gatalas.

So we were able to commit ourselves to the gods before embarking. We washed our clothing, groomed our horses, and set up some steam tents to clean ourselves properly. Then we assembled at noon to sacrifice to Marha and read the omens for the voyage. The sacrifice, of three horses, went well, and the omens were, on the whole, encouraging. Each of our companies had its own diviner, who knew how to read the patterns made by the willow rods, marked black with charcoal and white with chalk, that we use to discover the will of the gods and to foretell the future. Gatalas' diviner foretold life and good fortune for the dragon across the sea, but warned of danger from lies and from fire; he promised the company glory in war—which they received with a loud yell of pleasure—but warned the commander to beware of deceit, and foretold that he would die in battle. Arshak's diviner was less skillful. His company was indeed promised good fortune, but also disaster. The message for Arshak himself was equally confused: danger in lies, danger in darkness, life and death appearing equally balanced. Arshak received this prophecy with a smile. "I will die when it is fated," he said, "but I trust I will not die unavenged."

For my troop, the omens promised victory, which pleased them very much. But I myself had a divination as confused as Arshak's, and rather grimmer: danger from lies, battle, death by drowning, death by fire, and victory.

"What does that mean?" Arshak asked Kasagos, my diviner. "You've killed Ariantes twice there, and had him win a victory afterward. You Roxalani can't read the rods properly." (I had five squadrons of men from the Roxalanic tribe in my company, and the men in the other companies sometimes jeered at them. The rest of our army were all men from the tribe of the Iazyges, as I am myself. The Roxalani are just as much Sarmatians as the Iazyges, but are a less ancient tribe, and have a slightly different history.)

I thought Arshak had no business scoffing at Kasagos for making a confused prophecy, since his own diviner had produced an equally puzzling one. "Perhaps I will be wounded winning the victory, and die by either water or fire afterward," I suggested. A horrible thought occurred to me: that I would be wounded by a defeated enemy, drown, and when my body was washed ashore, some Romans would treat it with their own funeral customs and burn it. But I kept the thought to myself. Death by water is a wretched fate, and to burn the body, so my people believe, is to destroy the soul. The bare suggestion of such a fate would upset my men.

Kasagos frowned at the rods. "The sign for victory comes *after* the two deaths. I think, my prince, that the deaths must be read as warnings. If you avoid death by water and fire, you will win a victory."

"In other words, don't go swimming, and be careful when you light a fire," said Arshak, grinning. "Good advice at any time, but you hardly need the divining rods to tell you that."

Still, the omens had promised good fortune to every company, and when we followed the ceremony with a feast (courtesy of the procurator of the British fleet), the men were inclined to look on the bright side, especially after the wine started flowing. There was no resistance next day when the time came to board the ships.

But even without resistance, it was hard work. Fifteen hundred men and nearly four times that number of horses had to be loaded onto transports. The transports were larger, sturdier, and slower ships than the fast bireme, but only three of them were suitable for carrying more than a handful of horses at a time. The horses had all been on boats before, to cross the Danube—but many still had to be blindfolded to get them aboard, and their owners had to go with them to soothe them on the voyage and prevent them from harming themselves when the ships rolled. Since most of the men had three horses and we also had extra horses for the wagons, it meant that some men had to make two trips to cope with all the animals. Then, of course, there were questions of precedence. Put two Sarmatian nobles in front of a gate and they'll spend all day arguing over who goes through first—and we had fifteen hundred Sarmatian nobles in front of three horse transports. It helped that our companies had had their order of march established long ago. Arshak's company was called the second dragon, because his dragon standard followed second behind that of the king; Gatalas led the fourth dragon, and I commanded the sixth: Arshak's company thus went first, Gatalas' second, and mine last. But each commander needed to stand on the dock the whole time his dragon was embarking, to give each squadron, and each man in the squadron, his proper place.

Then there was a problem with the wagons: the Roman sailors saw no reason to transport these at all. Why couldn't we live in tents and barracks, like their own soldiers? they asked. I had to insist and threaten, coax and cajole them about it for some time, and when they at last gave in, it was as much from exasperation with the wagons clogging the shipyard where they were as from any desire to help us shift them.

Then there were more problems, with supplies.

My fellow princes remained proudly aloof from the Romans and left all the insisting and cajoling to me. I became, as I'd feared, the reasonable one, the one the Romans could work with. The procurator Natalis turned to me to say which troops went when, and asked my advice about how to secure the wagons or restrain nervous horses. I disliked the position, but could not shrug it off, and the more I cooperated, the more they turned to me.

Halfway through the first day of the transportation, Natalis came down to the ships while they were being loaded, carrying a set of wax tablets.

"There you are, Ariantes," he said, and offered me the tablets. "I'm trying to get a week's supplies for your people together for you in Dubris, and I've drawn up a list of what we think you might need. Can you just look it over and correct it if there's anything you don't need?"

I stared at the tablets, not touching them. "I cannot read," I told him.

"Oh," he said, pulling the tablets back. "No, of course you can't. I don't have time to go over them with you. I'll find you a scribe." And he went back to his headquarters.

About an hour later, a man of about forty, small, dark, and weary, trotted up with the tablets. "You are Lord Ariantes?" he asked me, and when I nodded, he went on, "I am Eukairios, a slave in the office of the procurator. Lord Valerius Natalis sends me to you. He said you needed a scribe."

I have never forgotten the shock of that afternoon. Eukairios was very good at his work. We went over the list of supplies, and it was all wrong: it contained vast amounts of wheat, which we weren't used to, and no cheese or dried meat, which we were. There was no wood to mend the wagons, should one break; there was the wrong kind of horse fodder; there was no felt to patch the awnings and not enough leather to bind them—it was a useless list altogether. And Eukairios knew exactly what to do to put it all right. All the afternoon it went on, me saying, "What we need is . . ." and Eukairios answering, "That would take us over budget, Lord Ariantes, but what we could do . . ." and me saying, "Can you really do that?"

Letters. "Ariantes, commander of the sixth numerus of Sarmatian cavalry, to Minucius Habitus, procurator of the imperial *saltus*, greetings. My lord, we require a hundred barrels of salt beef from the imperial estates to be shipped to Dubris under authority of the procurator Lord Valerius Natalis . . ." "Ariantes . . . to Junius Coroticus, shipping agent, greetings. The procurator Valerius Natalis requests that you provide a ship to the port of

Durobrivae of the Iceni to transport a hundred barrels of salt beef . . ."

"Ariantes . . . to Marcius Modestus, head of the fleet workshops in Dubris, greetings. The procurator authorizes you to allot us a hundredweight of oak staves and two hundredweight of beechwood planking . . ."

"And now, Lord Ariantes," Eukairios would say, "you put your mark *there*, and I write 'Unlettered' *here*, and we seal it *thus*, and we can send it off first thing tomorrow." Take a thin leaf of shaved beechwood, mark it with ink, fold it and seal it with wax, put it on a dispatch vessel—and men a hundred miles away who'd never heard of Sarmatians would roll barrels of salt beef onto a ship that had appeared to move them, take them to a warehouse in Dubris that was expecting them, and have them stacked waiting for us when we appeared. Letters are wonderful things.

After that, Eukairios was assigned to me every day until I left Bononia myself, on the last transport. To say I found him useful is as misleading as it is true. I had carefully planned and prepared troop movements in the past— I'd organized raids and gathered the men of my dragon to fight the war. But always I'd relied on those I knew, drawn on my own resources and those of my dependants, and done without records. The freedom of the pen, which can run backward in time to take account and forward to draw up a budget, which can speak directly to unknown persons far away, was intoxicating. It terrified me that I liked it so much, that, within two days, I was waiting impatiently for Eukairios to arrive in the morning, depending on him to come so I could do my own work. It infuriated me that I should depend on a Roman slave, and I looked forward to leaving him and Bononia behind. But I dreaded being left voiceless, while around me the letters flew and Romans spoke to Romans about my people, and we stood like mute and bewildered children in an alien world.

In the end I set sail from Bononia with Eukairios—and with Valerius Natalis, and with Flavius Facilis. Eukairios came because we were finishing some accounts; Natalis, because he was returning to his preferred base at Dubris—but Facilis was an unpleasant surprise. We had seen very little of him once the crossing began, and I'd thought that he'd given up his charge of us and was preparing to return with his legionaries to Aquincum. I found that instead he'd been writing to the legate Priscus, offering his services as an expert on Sarmatians. I could not ask him why. I suspected, even then, that it was not because he had any straightforward plan for revenge, but because he felt his business with us was unfinished. He meant to finish it and make sure we would not forget him, as I had wished to do. I suppose, too, he had nothing waiting for him in Aquincum except regrets and painful memories: why shouldn't he start a new life in Britain? At any rate, Priscus had accepted him and had offered to appoint him camp prefect of some fortress in the North where he could keep an eye on us. I was not happy at Facilis coming— he would have provoked my men into mutiny twice, if he'd had his way—and I was still more unhappy that Priscus thought we needed him. But because I could do nothing about it, I avoided the man. I had eight horses on the transport, and I went into the hold with them instead of onto the deck with the Romans—but, of course, I took Eukairios and the accounts with me.

When we were three hours out from Bononia, however, Natalis sent a slave to invite me to have a drink with him. The horses were all accustomed to the ship by then, so I agreed to leave them—I'd relied heavily on the procurator's authority in Bononia and I couldn't afford to offend him. I told Eukairios to come up on deck as well, and to bring the accounts, since we'd finished them. (I was not seasick on that voyage. The transport bucked and rolled far less than the bireme had, and the sea was calmer that day.)

Natalis was in the covered cabin by the sternpost of the transport, sitting in a carved chair and looking out at the ship's wake. He gave me his most benevolent smile, had another chair brought up for me, and offered me a cup of wine. "I thought we might have a drink together to celebrate a job well done," he said. "I've been grateful for your help, Ariantes."

"We have been grateful for yours, Valerius Natalis," I returned. I sipped my wine uncomfortably.

"Yes—but I was obliged by my position to help you, and you might very easily have decided to . . . cause difficulties. I believe we might have had serious trouble in Bononia, if it hadn't been for you."

"It was my own people who would have suffered most," I said, just a bit too sharply.

"Oh, indeed, indeed," Natalis agreed quickly. "But one doesn't expect barbarians to be so reasonable—or to show such flair for administration. As a token of my gratitude, I'd like to give you a present."

"Lord Valerius Natalis, I did not act as I have through hope of reward from any Roman."

"I am quite sure of that, Lord Ariantes. It would be an insult to you to suppose otherwise, wouldn't it? Nonetheless, it's a Roman custom for senior officers, such as myself, to make gifts to those who have helped them. I am sure you could use a reliable scribe in your future career, so let me make you a present of Eukairios."

Eukairios, who'd been standing quietly by the entrance to the cabin all this while, dropped his accounts ledger with a clatter and stared at Natalis in horror. "Lord procurator!" he gasped.

"I could not accept," I said. "My people do not keep slaves." I spoke quickly because I was angry with myself. I already knew that if Natalis pressed me, I'd accept. Now that I'd been offered him, I knew I wanted the scribe badly.

"Oh, you must have some slaves!" protested Natalis. "How can a gentleman manage without them? What do you do with the captives you take in all your wars, eh?"

"We do not take captives, Lord Procurator. We do not keep foreigners in our wagons, and our own people are all free, the sons and daughters of warriors. What would I do with a slave? Eukairios cannot ride a horse." (I'd discovered this in Bononia when I asked him to take a message, and it had shocked and astonished me.) "Where would I put him?"

"I'm sure you could arrange something," Natalis said easily.

At this, Eukairios interrupted. "Lord Procurator," he stammered, "please, my lord, please don't send me away from Bononia."

"Be quiet, man! Well, Ariantes? It would be a shame to waste your talents because of a lack of pen and ink."

"But, Lord Procurator . . ." begged Eukairios.

"I said, be quiet!" Natalis snapped.

Eukairios staggered over to Natalis and dropped to his knees, reaching out a hand to his master. "Please, my lord, I beg you, my lord, please don't—"

Natalis shoved the hand away. "Why are you making a scene like this? You don't have any family in Bononia."

"No," pleaded Eukairios, "but I have friends, old and dear friends and—"

"I know all about your friends," Natalis said, now tight with anger, "and I don't want them connected with anyone in my office. You'd disgrace us all, Eukairios, if there was trouble here like there was in Lugdunum. Do you think I want to see a scribe from my own office—the office of the procurator of the British fleet!—killed in the arena to amuse the mob? You can go off to Britain with the Sarmatians. Even if you find some more of your 'friends' there, no one will pay any attention to them."

Eukairios went white. He knelt with his hands on the floor before him, like a beast. "I'm sorry, Lord Valerius Natalis," he whispered. "I'm sorry. I . . . I . . . you know . . ." He rubbed at his eyes. "Oh my God, my God!"

"Get out," Natalis ordered him. "You're embarrassing Lord Ariantes."

Eukairios staggered out.

Natalis turned back to me with a forced smile. "The truth of the matter is, I'd be glad if you'd take him off my hands," he said, apparently realizing he had to explain the scene. "He's a good, reliable scribe, but he's a Christian. I've overlooked that in the past, but there have been some demands in Gaul to stamp them out, and I don't want any scandal to attach to the office. He'd be all right in Britain. No one cares about the Christians there."

"What is a Christian?" I asked, torn between pity for Eukairios and suspicion of Natalis at this admission that he wanted to get rid of the man.

"A follower of an illegal cult. Christ was a Jewish sophist crucified for sedition under the emperor Tiberius, and some of the Jews were stupid enough to decide that he was a god—and not just any god, but the Jewish god, who can't even be spoken of by name. The rest of the Jews naturally turned on them with all their usual ferocity toward blasphemers, so they went Greek, and now there are adherents of this lunacy in every city in the empire where Greeks are found. It appeals to slaves and riffraff, of course, not the better classes."

He rolled his aristocratic eyes in contempt, and went on pompously, "The Christians practice disgusting rituals in private houses at night, hoping, poor wretches, that this will give them immortality, and they refuse to worship any divinity except their crucified sophist, and even refuse to make offerings to the genius of the emperor and the spirit of Rome—so, of course, the cult's illegal. It was banned almost immediately after it appeared, but that hasn't stopped it spreading. Personally, I don't see any point in punishing the Christians, and I've turned a blind eye to the business as much as possible. I don't believe most of the stories about them—they aren't wicked, just silly pathetic fools. And, as I said, nobody's ever bothered with the cult in Britain—and even if somebody did, no one would worry that you, a barbarian nobleman, had the least sympathy for that kind of nonsense. But if anyone took official notice of Eukairios and his ridiculous religion, he could be killed for it. Complete waste of a good scribe, in my opinion. Now you know the worst of Eukairios. The best—that he's hardworking, experienced, and able—you knew already. I can add to that that he doesn't drink, doesn't get into trouble with women, and keeps out of quarrels. This cult is the one great daring secret of his drab little life."

"There has been trouble with this cult in Gaul?" I asked, after a moment.

"They executed a pack of the cultists in Lugdunum," Natalis admitted, "and some administrators in the South have called for a purge. I'd intended to shift Eukairios to Dubris anyway. But I'd rather give him to you. I do believe you'd find him useful."

I was silent for another moment. I, too, believed I'd find the scribe useful. It was against all the customs of my own people to keep any slave, and I didn't like the sound of this cult at all—but I *needed* the man to write letters for me. I wouldn't know how to buy or hire another scribe. I had no idea how much a good scribe would cost, and I suspected that I'd need all the money I'd brought with me to secure a good position for my men. "Thank you, Lord Valerius Natalis," I said at last. "I accept him." I got to my feet. "But let me give you a gift as well, in gratitude for your efforts on our behalf." I unfastened the gold pin from my coat. It was dragon-shaped, set with rubies, and about as long as my middle finger. "This I have worn as prince-commander of a dragon of Sarmatian cavalry," I said. "Very few Romans have ever held one of these, my lord Natalis. Perhaps the emperor alone. I trust you will keep it and remember my people kindly." I set it in his hands.

Natalis went pink with pleasure. "You have quite outdone me in your generosity, Lord Ariantes! Thank you, thank you very much indeed!" He took his own brooch off and pinned his cloak with mine instead. He fondled it a minute, running his fingers along the curves of the gold. "I will certainly remember you with friendship."

I'd thought that morning of giving him one of my horses; I saw that I'd been correct to offer instead this, which a Sarmatian would have valued less. I was relieved. I had another pin—in fact, I had a wagonful of valuables I had brought along especially for bribing Romans—and it would have been hard to part with any of the horses. "As I shall remember you," I told Natalis. "But you must excuse me now, my lord. I ought to stay with my horses to make sure they come to no harm. I could not easily replace them."

Eukairios was sitting beside the horses with his cloak over his head. When I came up he pulled it off his head again and rubbed his face. The hold was only dimly lit by the light that came in down the gangways, but I could still see well enough that he'd been crying. "Wh-what happened?" he asked me. It was a sign of how distressed he was that he omitted my title.

"I accepted you," I told him. After a moment I added, to defend myself against his misery, "He would have sent you away from Bononia anyway."

"To Dubris?" When I nodded, he rubbed his face again. "I didn't realize he knew," he said wretchedly. "I always thought no one in the office knew." The one great daring secret of his drab little life, as Natalis had called it, had proved to be no secret at all, and he was trembling with the shock of it. "He told you I was a Christian?"

"Yes."

"Ah. And had you ever heard anything about us?"

"No. But I understand that it is illegal."

"It's all lies, what they say," Eukairios declared bitterly. "Wicked lies. People have died for them, tortured until there wasn't any sound flesh to use the irons on, but it's all, all lies. We don't"—he looked up and met my eyes directly—"we don't hold incestuous orgies and feast on human flesh. We are forbidden to shed blood; we are told to love our enemies and pray for those who persecute us. If I had any choice in the matter, my faith wouldn't allow me to work for the regular army, let alone for a man who decorates his horses' bridles with men's scalps and drinks from a Roman skull. God help me."

"I do not have that cup anymore," I said. I was touched by his defiance, the more so as he'd never referred to the scalps or the skull story before. In Bononia he had been attentive and deferential, and warmed to friendliness with his own efficiency. "I will not require you to shed blood, Eukairios, or to do anything else your faith forbids. I only want you to write letters."

He rubbed his face again, then, giving up on suppressing the tears, buried it in his hands. "God help me," he said again, thickly. "I thought I'd stay in Bononia for the rest of my life."

"Were you born there?" I asked, both to calm him and because I felt I should know more about him. "Your name is not Latin."

He understood what I wanted. "My name's Greek. I'm not," he said, still thickly but with his usual precision. "Many gentlemen think it adds a touch of elegance to a household to give Greek names to the slaves. My mother was a cook in a gentleman's house in the countryside, thirty miles from Bononia, and our master had me educated and sold me as soon as I was old enough and trained enough to be valuable, when I was fourteen. The office bought me. That is the only other time I've changed hands. I never expected to be sold again—or given away." His voice was growing thicker again. "I have my other clothes in Bononia, and a couple of books, everything I own. I haven't said good-bye to anyone. I thought I was going back tomorrow."

"Then go back, collect your things, say your good-byes, and return," I said. "I will ask Valerius Natalis to send you on his dispatch vessel. You know yourself that we must load the supplies for the journey to Eburacum and plan the itinerary; we will not leave Dubris for another two days. That should give you time."

"You're not worried I'd run off as soon as I got home?"

It hadn't even occurred to me. "I am not used to slaves," I admitted. "I have never owned one before. Would you run off?"

"It would be against my religion," he said, taking his face out of his hands and glaring. "If you're not used to slaves and won't keep foreigners in your wagons, what are you going to do with me?"

I sighed. "I suppose I will have to let you stay in my wagon, at least during the journey, although it is against our customs." I winced inwardly at what Arshak and Gatalas, and my own men, would think of it. The fear still twisted in the back of my mind, the terror that I would be turned by the Romans and used against my own people. I had to have the use of letters, though, to defend them. "You will have to ride in it, too, at least at first—though I hope it is not against your religion to learn to ride a horse. When we reach Eburacum, we will see what else can be done."

There was a long minute of silence. Eukairios sat staring at his hands. The ship rolled, and one of my horses—the courser, who was always a high-strung animal—neighed nervously and kicked. I slid into the stall beside him and coaxed him into calmness again with my hands and voice. When I slipped out, Eukairios had stopped staring at his hands and was looking at me doubtfully. What sort of treatment could he expect from a master such as myself—a barbarian prince who'd killed Romans freely in the past, and now not only owned him, but owned a secret that could cost him his life?

I pitied him. "I am sorry, Eukairios," I said, again answering the misery. "You do not want me for a master, and I do not want to be the owner of a slave. But you know yourself that I need someone to write letters for me; for the sake of my men, I need it. Serve me faithfully and I will deal with you justly and without treachery, and reward you, as soon as I may, with your freedom. This I swear on fire."

I meant to keep my oath. But I knew it would be a long time before I rewarded him with his freedom, and a part of me hoped that he'd forget his religious scruples and run off as soon as he set foot in Bononia.

It was night when the transport reached Dubris, and the ship wallowed into port with the guidance of a lighthouse on the promontory above. When it had docked it had to be unloaded, a task that promised to take some time. Natalis stopped to wish me good health before going off to his house to rest, and I asked him to send Eukairios back to collect his things.

"You're not afraid he'd run off?" Natalis asked, as Eukairios himself had done.

"He says it would be against his religion to do so," I answered. "I am content to let him go."

"Very well, very well. I'll take him with me tonight, shall I, and send him off first thing tomorrow morning?"

"Thank you, my lord." A wagon we were pulling out of the hold lurched, and one wheel slipped off the gangway. Its owners crowded round, trying to push it one way; Natalis' sailors tried to drag it another; behind it, the tired horses waiting to get out began to whinny and kick. "Good health!" I called, leaving Natalis and hurrying to take charge.

"Good health!" the procurator called after me, and, as an afterthought, "You know your people are all camped at the parade ground?"

"Eukairios read me that letter," I said, shooing my men away from the stuck wagon. "We can find it."

The parade ground was not hard to find, but it was after midnight by the time we reached it. The wagons of the men who'd crossed before us were already in their concentric circles, but the fires were banked down and everyone was asleep. It was beginning to rain, a fine drizzle that made the ground soft. We were too tired to prepare a meal, and simply moved our own wagons into the outermost circle, saw to the horses, and went to bed.

I was tired, but I lay awake for a little while, listening to the rain splashing in the felt of the awning, and the sound of the horses tethered outside. I remembered lying listening to the rain with my Tirgatao, warm in her arms, holding her and not needing to say anything. The grief was like a black chasm, more unfathomable than the sea; I could no more understand or limit it than I could the deep waters. What would she have said if I'd suggested keeping a Roman slave in our wagon?

I got up, went out of the wagon and checked my horses unnecessarily, then went back in and slept like the dead.

I woke next morning late, muzzy-headed and stiff-legged, to find Arshak and Gatalas waiting outside ready to raise another mutiny. It was still raining.

"They won't give us our weapons!" Arshak declared angrily as soon as I stumbled out of my wagon. "They swore we would have them in Britain, but now they say we must ride to a place called Eburacum. They don't mean to return them to us at all!"

"Let me eat first," I said.

Leimanos, the captain of my bodyguard, at once brought me a chunk of bread, then, with a grin and a flourish, presented me with a cup of milk. The milk was the result of letter-writing in Bononia: we hadn't had any on the journey, and I'd tried to arrange for the loan of some cows during the few days we were in Dubris. But I doubted that the neighboring countryside had spared us more than a few beasts, and most of the men must have had to make do with the sour beer we'd been given on the journey. I guessed that when Leimanos had set this cup aside for me, the others had squabbled over the rest. Another thing to sort out. I sat down on the step of my wagon and began eating.

"Did you know?" asked Gatalas, angrily.

"Of course I didn't," I replied sharply. "I'll join you in protesting—after I've eaten."

"Protesting?" Arshak snapped. "What's the point of 'protesting'? We must do something to *show* them that they cannot tell us lies and escape. Gatalas and I have decided that we will not leave this city without our weapons. When you've finished eating, you can go and tell them that."

"*I* can go and tell them?" I snapped back, beginning to lose my temper. "Why only me? If you and Gatalas decided it, you and Gatalas can tell them so."

There was an abrupt silence. I looked from one to another of my fellow commanders. Why only me? Because I was the Romanized one and compromised already. If I went alone, they could keep their own hands clean of ignoble bargaining, take the advantage, and leave the shame to me. "You perhaps think that my nature is better suited to dealing with Romans than yours?" I asked quietly. I half wanted to fight one of them just to prove myself a Sarmatian.

Arshak and Gatalas looked uncomfortable. "You've been able to deal with them successfully so far," Arshak said.

"I am still a prince of the Iazyges," I told him. "No less than you, Gatalas, or you, Arshak, for all your royal blood."

"I don't deny it," said Arshak, embarrassed now. "But you went to Britain before the rest of us, and you met this legate, Priscus, and you were managing well with the procurator in Bononia. I thought, since you knew the men . . ."

"Haven't you met this legate yourself now?"

"Briefly," Gatalas answered for him. "We both met him briefly when we arrived."

That "briefly" was probably to the good. I hadn't told anyone what the

Romans had planned to do with us, either what I'd overheard in Bononia or what I'd argued against in Dubris. It would have fed suspicions and inflamed resentment, and it was just as well there'd been no chance for the others to learn what I had. But I was not in the mood to be pleased about it. "Then why couldn't you go to him yourselves and tell him what you'd decided?" I demanded bitterly. "Why sit about like a couple of eagles with ruffled feathers, too grand to complain, waiting for me? And then, the moment I arrive, sending *me* to deal with them as though I were your message boy!"

"I am sorry, Ariantes," Arshak said—rare words for any Sarmatian prince to use, and rarer still in his mouth. "We were mistaken, Gatalas and I. We will all go and see this legate together."

At this I was ashamed of myself. The bread choked me, and I tossed it aside. "My brothers," I said, speaking now with the urgency of what I felt, "don't you and the Romans conspire to make a Roman of me. I have tried to deal with them on their own terms, it's true, but it's only because they won't listen to me otherwise, and we must make our voice heard. But you know what they say: *divide et impera*." (And I said the words in the language to which they belonged.) "I know perfectly well that they think I'm the man they can use, the reasonable one, and they'll make a tool of me if they can. Don't help them by pushing all the reasoning, and all the bargaining, onto me."

Arshak stepped over to me and offered me his hand. "We will stand by you," he promised solemnly. Gatalas nodded and followed him.

I stood and took both hands in my own. The fear that had twisted in the back of my mind was out in the open now, and it was an immense relief to throw it off, and stand joined with my brother princes. "Thank you," I told them. "We'll all go and see the legate, then. But, Arshak, I think you should change your coat first."

He frowned. He took great pride in his coat, and was wearing it that day tossed loose over his shoulders and pinned. The scalps had been stitched on in a kind of pattern, with the lighter-colored ones making a stripe down the back and each arm, and the body in shades of black: the red wool of the coat's fabric showed only at the cuffs. (I'd watched him carefully working out where he'd put Facilis' scalp, if the gods were kind, and which others he'd move to make space for it.)

"We want to ask the legate to give us our weapons back," I said, when he was silent. "It's not a good move to start by reminding him how many Romans we've killed with them."

Arshak sighed. "Very well! I'll wear the other one. But I'd thought we would *demand* our weapons back, not *ask* for them."

I hesitated. "Do you want my advice?"

"You know more about the legate than we do."

"Then we should ask first, and ask softly, before we demand. My impression of the legate is that he's a proud man and a hard one, and doesn't like to be corrected: if we demand, he may say no, simply to prove to us that he won't be dictated to. Then if we refused to leave the city weaponless, even if he had to back down now, for lack of troops to put down a mutiny, he'd punish us later. He doesn't like or trust us, and he's accepted Facilis into his legion to advise him about us."

"What!" exclaimed Gatalas. "Facilis isn't going back to Aquincum?"

I told him about Facilis' offer to the legate and its acceptance.

"No wonder we haven't been given our weapons back," Arshak said thoughtfully. "Facilis has got at the legate. Well, I'm pleased he isn't going safely home." He smiled.

I hated that smile. I wanted to ask Arshak to leave the centurion alone, say that the risk of trouble from killing the man far outweighed the pleasure of vengeance. But I knew Arshak would be offended if I did, so I said nothing.

"How do you think we can get round this legate, then?" Gatalas asked, while Arshak fingered the place on his coat that he'd chosen before.

"We go to him quietly, all three of us, and tell him that the men are upset because they expected to be given their weapons as soon as they had crossed the ocean. He may not even know that; he wasn't at Aquincum. We tell him that it will damage their confidence in him if they don't get the weapons, and that they'll be suspicious of any promises that he might make in future."

"What confidence?" asked Gatalas.

"The confidence we might have if he deals with us fairly. My brother, he'll know that the men must believe that he means what he says, or there's no reason for them to obey him. He knows he must give us our weapons sometime. We can pledge our honor that our people won't do violence to any Roman on the way to Eburacum. If we phrase it tactfully, I think he'll give in. Arshak, you know how it's done—you did it yourself in Bononia."

"Not exactly this," said Arshak. "But yes, near enough. Very well, we do it gently. In fact"—taking charge—"we don't even go to him as though our first thought was to complain. We appear before him to greet him as our new commander, and to give him a gift. Romans love getting presents. What do we give him?"

"A horse?" suggested Gatalas.

"They don't value them as much as we do," I said. "A jewel?" My hand went involuntarily to the unpinned top of my coat.

Arshak looked at me sideways. "What did you do with your coat pin?"

"Gave it to Valerius Natalis, as you've guessed," I replied—evenly, though I couldn't yet bring myself to admit that Valerius Natalis had given me a slave. "He was very pleased with it."

Gatalas winced. "Did you have to give him a dragon?"

"If it bought us one friend in the Roman camp, it was well given," said Arshak. "If Natalis has a jewel, though, we don't want to give the same to Priscus. I have a length of silk which I bought from a caravan from the East and took along for just this kind of thing. Would he like that, or would he think it was woman's gear and be offended?"

"He has a beautiful young wife," I answered. "She's influential too, or I'm much deceived. Give it to him, and mention her: that should be safe."

"We'll bring only ten men each from our bodyguards," Arshak went on, now in charge completely. "Enough to show that we're persons of importance, but not enough to be interpreted as a threat of force. Very well. I'll go fetch the silk and change my coat, and we can all collect our horses and our men. We'll meet back here in a few minutes."

He strode off, and Gatalas started for his wagon, less quickly, and scowling: he disliked asking for what he thought he should demand. I ran my hands through my tangled hair and turned to the captain of my guard.

"Leimanos, was there trouble over the milk?" I asked. "How much of it is there?"

His eyebrows bobbed up, and he snorted with appreciation. He was a kinsman of mine, a lean brown man with eyes as blue as Arshak's, loyal and hardworking: we'd ridden together since the battle where I'd killed my first man. "Enough for about twenty men in our dragon. The other companies got the same amount. I poured some for you, my prince, and told the men to be quiet until you'd drunk it and could say who got the rest."

"Good man. It's to go to the men who are ill. If there's anything left over when they've had their cups, make cheese." I picked my own cup, which I hadn't touched, off the step of the wagon. "Take this to whoever's most ill."

Leimanos frowned. "The rest can go to the men who are ill. You drink that, my lord. You didn't eat last night and you didn't eat the bread this morning: you should at least drink that. And the other commanders drank milk. It's true what you told them: you're no less a prince than either of them, and it's a disgrace to the dragon if you're treated with less honor."

I drank down the milk. A company's sense of its commander's dignity ought to be treated with respect.

Leimanos smiled with satisfaction. "Do you want me to take the first ten of the bodyguard and come with you to see the legate?" he asked.

"No, stay and see to the milk," I answered. "Tell Banadaspos and the second ten to get their horses. I'm going to dig out another coat pin and comb my hair."

"Yes, my prince." Instead of going off obediently, however, he hesitated.

"Anything else?" I asked.

"Only that I'm glad you put that brace of eagles in their place," he said vehemently. "They had no business thinking themselves better than you. They've been happy enough with the leather and the medicines and the food and the milk that you talked out of the Romans, to say nothing of their crossing the ocean safely instead of dying on Roman swords in Bononia—but their men have been whispering that you're Romanizing, and they've let the whispers run."

"Ah. There'll be more whispers to come, Leimanos," I said, steeling myself. "There's worse Romanizing that you don't know yet. I accepted the gift of a slave, a scribe, from the procurator Natalis. I needed someone to write letters."

"My lord," said Leimanos, "if you say you need a scribe, then you need one. No one who knows you, who's followed you through the war, will talk of Romanizing. You are our prince"—and Leimanos came and touched my hand to his forehead—"and we say the gods favored us. I can speak for the whole dragon when I say that if you can deal with the Romans successfully, we're glad of it. How would we live, otherwise?"

"Thank you," I said, liberated for the second time that morning. "I will see if I can't get us back our weapons."

IV

*T*HE MEETING WITH the legate went well. Priscus was still staying at Natalis' house, and we were admitted and ushered into the dining room as soon as we arrived. The legate had been working there with the three tribunes, but he rose and greeted us politely. Arshak, who could be very gracious and charming when he wanted to, made a little speech of greeting in return, saying we hoped and expected that our service under a nobleman as distinguished as Julius Priscus would bring us glory, and giving him the silk "as a token of our respect for you, my lord, in the hope that it will adorn your house and please your noble lady." Aurelia Bodica was not in evidence, but it certainly pleased the legate. His heavy frown vanished and he looked almost genial.

Arshak went on to mention the demand for the weapons with an air of embarrassment, as though he were faced with a problem he didn't know how to resolve and was only turning to the legate for guidance. Gatalas chimed in with expressions of sympathy for the men's fears, concern at the damage to their confidence in their new commander in chief, and guarantees that, if they were armed, they would not cause any problems. The legate began to frown again. Whatever arguments he'd heard against giving us our weapons back outside his own fortress had clearly been persuasive. But Arshak was persuasive too, and Priscus wavered visibly. Hurrying to catch the moment, I put in the other argument I'd thought of—that I'd planned to use the unloaded weapons wagons to carry a hundred barrels of salt beef, a hundredweight of oak staves, and two hundredweight of beech planking, none of which could easily be loaded onto horses, and that if we didn't have the weapons wagons for them, we'd have to buy carts, which would put us over budget. That did it: Priscus agreed. "After all," he said, "you were sent here as soldiers, not prisoners—and you can hardly sail yourselves back across the Channel. You swear to me that you'll keep your men in order?"

"On fire we swear it!" we exclaimed together, and stretched our right hands over the glowing coals of the brazier in the corner, set there to take the chill off the wet September air.

It was agreed that the weapons would be distributed from the tribunal on the parade ground that afternoon, and we set off to give the good news to our men. Just as we were about to leave, Facilis came in.

Arshak smiled at him. "I am pleased that you will still be with us, Flavius Facilis," he said.

"You still hope you can get a white neckpiece for your other coat, do you?" Facilis growled back. That was, in fact, exactly the place Arshak had been fingering.

Arshak only smiled again, though his eyes glittered. "Remember that you followed us. We did not follow you. You chose our company. But now I must prepare my men to receive their weapons again." He said it pointedly, to bait the centurion.

"What?" demanded Facilis, rising to the bait, looking at Priscus in alarm. "I thought, sir, that you'd agreed—"

"I hadn't realized that the Sarmatians were counting on getting the weapons back as soon as they were this side of the Channel," replied the legate impatiently. "If they were promised it, or even believed that they were promised it, it would damage the confidence they ought to have in their officers to make them wait. Besides, we need the weapons wagons for supplies."

Facilis looked furiously at me. "We need the wagons for supplies?" he asked. "So this was your idea, Ariantes. I should have guessed."

"Flavius Facilis," I said, "you know we all wanted to have the weapons back now. We had to have them sometime. Since you must give, why not give gracefully?"

"I don't give anything gracefully to you," he answered, and, under his breath, added, "You slippery bastard. The others would have asked for what they wanted straight-out, and been straight-out refused."

I shook my head and excused myself, and my brother commanders joined me. Just as we were mounting our horses, Lucius Javolenus Comittus ran out after us. "Hey! Wait a moment!" he shouted. When we paused, he trotted up grinning and out of breath.

"I've been talking to the two other, uh, liaison officers," he told us, "and we'd be very pleased if you could join us for dinner this evening. There's a very good tavern by the harbor . . ."

"It would please us better that you join us, instead," said Arshak, smiling pleasantly. It was beneath his dignity to sit in Roman taverns by harbors, and Comittus had just plummeted in his opinion for suggesting it. "We can have a feast at the wagons, and you can meet the captains of our squadrons . . . the *decurions*, you'd call them, yes? I will have my men buy an ox to roast, and we will put up awnings against the rain."

"Yes," said Comittus, in pleased surprise. "Excellent! I'll bring some good wine. What time do you want us?"

"Young idiot," Arshak commented, when we were riding back to our wagons. "What do you suppose a 'liaison officer' does?"

"It's obvious," said Gatalas. "He brings good wine to dinner parties and sits in taverns."

"Well, I suppose that's a light yoke to bear," Arshak observed. "He can sit in taverns, and I can forget about him. And we'll get our weapons back!"

"You spoke to the legate like a prince, Arshak," I said warmly. "So sweet-tongued and respectful that he began to doubt Facilis' judgment."

"I can fill my mouth with honey when I like," agreed Arshak, grinning. "But it was that business you came up with that really tipped the balance. Where on earth did you learn that phrase—what was it? Above the bugget?"

"*Over budget*," I corrected. "A budget is a list of how much money you expect to spend on something. The scribe I was lent in Bononia used the term a lot."

"Scribes' talk, money talk," said Arshak, disdainfully. "And that legate listens to it! But I'm glad you learned it."

It would be better to announce my status as a slave-owner myself, rather than have someone else report it to my fellows behind my back. "It is useful," I agreed. "Natalis gave me the scribe as a gift. If we need to write letters to the Romans, or read any letters they write, to us or about us, we will be able to."

The other two stared at me in shocked silence for a moment.

"Where is this slave now, then?" asked Gatalas at last.

"I sent him back to Bononia to say his good-byes. He should be here tomorrow afternoon."

"Ariantes . . ." Arshak began—then shook his head. "I can see it will be useful. To all of us. I would not keep a foreign slave in *my* wagon—but I can see it will be very useful, so how can I speak against it? You've proved the use of it already. This afternoon"—he stood up in the stirrups, stretching his arm—"this afternoon I will hold my spear again! And *that* is worth a few soft words to a legate!"

The weapons were distributed from the tribunal under a steady drizzle. Priscus sat on a seat set up for him on the stone platform with a slave holding an awning over him, watching with his tribunes while we collected our things from the twenty wagons. The silk tails of our dragon standards hung down limply, dripping, and the horses tossed their heads unhappily as their hooves stuck in the churned-up mud. But for the men, it was a white day, a day of pure sun. The wagons had been loaded company by company, squadron by squadron, and they were unloaded in the same way. The orderly line of horsemen filed past, each collecting a sword, lance, bow case, and the oilskin-wrapped bundle that contained the armor for himself and his charger. Arshak's men, first as ever, cantered off to the other end of the field to put the armor on as soon as they got it. Gatalas and his men armed closer to the tribunal; I was aware of them saddling and buckling as I waited with my men for our turn. The rasp of armor against armor, a sound that had once been as natural to me as breathing, sounded all over the field. I could see the Romans on the tribunal beginning to stare as the dragons of Sarmatian cavalry twisted into the glittering metal of their skin and came to life.

It was my own dragon's turn. First of my company, as befits a prince, I collected my own oilskin bundle, bow case, spear, sword: all the heavy illusion of invulnerability. I hefted the bundle of armor unhappily. I felt a strange grief to see it again.

"Why put it on?" I asked Leimanos, who'd joined me, smiling over his own package of armor. "With this rain, it will just have to be taken off and dried and oiled thoroughly again tonight."

Leimanos looked shocked. "We must put it on, my lord!" he said. "The other dragons have. Besides, it's been in the wagons for a couple of months, and it will need drying and oiling anyway, as well as wearing, to keep it supple."

I couldn't shame my men by choosing to stay ingloriously disarmed beside the other commanders, and thus requiring them to do the same. I dismounted and began arming, and my hands remembered the old sequence of actions even though my mind was numb. Farna, my charger, a mare of the Parthian breed, stood patiently as I unsaddled her, only occasionally stamping her foot in protest at the rain. I tossed the armored blanket over her back and saddled her up again, clipping the blanket to the saddle and buckling it firmly across her chest and around her neck. Then came the chamfron, the horse's head-guard with its delicate filigree bowls to protect her eyes, gold-chased bronze on scaled and painted leather. Next my own armor. I took off my coat and hung it on my saddle. First the leather trousers, heavily stitched with overlapping scales of gilded iron on the lower outside leg, but scaled more lightly farther up, and next to the horse. The three slashes on the left leg showed only on the inside, where the new piece of leather had been fitted in; the outside looked as polished, golden, and impenetrable as ever. Next the leather cuirass, scaled to give a double thickness overall. I pulled the wrist-guards over the backs of my hands, then picked up my coat, slung it over my shoulders, and pinned it: no reason to get the armor wetter than I needed to. I pulled on the helmet with the crest of crimson horsehair, hung the bow case on the left side of my saddle, slung my sword over my right shoulder, and mounted, slipping my spear into its holder by my right foot. Leimanos had armed more eagerly than I had and was finished already, but most of my men were still busy.

Over the rasp of armor came a roll of kettle drums, and then a roar of hoofbeats. Arshak came galloping up from the far end of the ground at the head of all his company. His armor was gilded, like mine, and, like me, he was wearing a coat over it—but his was the coat of scalps, and he had his lance lowered and his long sword drawn in his hand. The red crest of his helmet tossed; the tail of the standard behind billowed and twisted in the wind, and over the hooves and the drums we could hear the hissing boom of wind in the golden mouth of the dragon. I'd forgotten the terror of it, and the magnificence. The drumbeat altered; the squadrons divided, one going left and the next right, then right and left, spreading out across the field, encircling it in a ring of iron. Arshak and his bodyguard came straight on toward the stone platform where the legate was sitting, and the legate stood up and looked as though he wanted to turn and run.

I started Farna towards them at a gallop, cursing inwardly. I was quite certain that Arshak was only showing off—but the legate didn't know that.

Luckily, Priscus didn't jump off the tribunal in a panic, and Arshak reined in immediately before him, making his white Parthian rear up and tear the air. As soon as the horse's forelegs touched the ground again, Arshak kicked his feet out of the stirrups and jumped up to stand balanced on the saddle, his eyes almost level with those of the legate. He swept off his scaled cap, bowing his sleek fair head to Priscus, and laid his sword at the legate's feet. "Arshak son of Sauromates," he said, "scepter-holder, *azatan*, prince-commander of the second dragon of the Iazyges of the Sarmatians, at your service, my lord Julius Priscus."

Priscus let out his breath a bit unsteadily. He bent and picked up the sword. "Thank you," he said.

Arshak grinned. I'd forgotten how he was, how he could be—his revelry in his own splendor, his power and strength. He'd undone all his good work of the morning, swaggering before the legate in his coat of scalps, but my own heart leapt at the sight of his arrogant grace. "Show me an enemy, my lord," he declared, "and I will bring you his head before the sun is down."

"There are no enemies of Rome here in Dubris," Priscus answered. Slowly he reversed the sword's hilt and offered it back to Arshak. "Keep this dry, and use it only when you're told to."

Arshak grinned again. He slid the sword back into its sheath, pulled his helmet on, dropped easily back into the saddle, saluted, and galloped off. Priscus let out his breath again and sat down.

I turned Farna quietly and started back to my own troop. A stone wall ran from the base of the tribunal along the edge of the field, and as I passed the far end of it, I noticed the carriage on the road behind, and the white stallion yoked between the shafts. I recognized the horse, and because of that, recognized the legate's wife, peering through the carriage window with her cloak over her head to keep out the rain. From the way she held her head, her eyes were still fixed on Arshak.

"What are you doing over here, Ariantes?" came Facilis' voice. "It is Ariantes inside that armor, isn't it?"

I turned back to see the centurion standing at the end of the wall, where the stone gave some shelter from the rain. I did not like to explain that I'd come over in case the legate needed reassuring about Arshak, and I tried to think of a convincing excuse. Facilis, however, went on before I could come up with one. "You thought you might tell the lord legate that Arshak's not as dangerous as he looks, did you? Too late. Anyone can see that he is."

"Arshak will keep his oath," I replied. "He will fight as well for Rome as he did against her."

"And if all there is for him to do in the North is patrols and guard duty, with no fighting?" asked Facilis. "What will he do then? He has to fight someone. He might need to mend his coat."

There was no point in talking to the man. I started Farna on without saying anything.

"Will you stand up in the saddle as well, and offer your sword to the legate?" Facilis jeered as I went past. "Or is your leg too stiff to let you? Tell me, did you ever succeed in killing the brave man that chopped it?"

I stopped Farna and looked at him. For a moment I felt like contesting Arshak's right to the centurion's scalp. But a commander shouldn't think with his dagger. "Why do you want there to be trouble with us?" I asked.

"Because if we have the trouble out now and break you, you won't make trouble later, when we're off our guard," he said vehemently. "There are Roman lives at stake. I'm quite clear about that."

"Clearer about it than we are," I told him. "There does not have to be trouble. Peace will take work, yes. It will take great care, delicacy, close attention. But it is possible. We are willing to serve the emperor if we are not forced to betray the customs of our own people. You do not help. If one of my men had heard you say that, he might have killed you where you stand. Then he would die himself, for defending my honor. Is it just, Facilis? We are both servants of Rome now, or trying to be."

"And why should you want peace?" Facilis asked bitterly.

"Because I am sick of war," I said—and the strange grief I had felt when I held my armor again snapped suddenly clear.

He looked at me in open disbelief. "You? A Sarmatian?"

"I. A Sarmatian. And you, a Roman, you still love it?" I set my heels to Farna and sent her flying down the field without waiting for response.

I cursed him silently as I led my dragon in front of the legate and offered him my sword—without standing in the saddle. As so often, the centurion had been right as far as he went—and then completely wrong. Mine is not a peace-loving nation, and if I had told my own men that I was sick of war, they would have stared in dismay and begged me not to talk like a coward. And yet, anyone can tire of death and killing. I saw now that I was so tired of it that I dismayed myself.

At the dinner with the tribunes that evening, the talk was all of arms and armor and horses. It was friendly, though.

We'd made awnings of brushwood about the main campfire, covering them with straw, which was abundant in the surrounding countryside since the harvest was just in. With more straw on the ground to keep it dry underfoot, and rugs and cushions brought from the wagons, we were able to make ourselves and our guests comfortable. I'd arranged for fresh meat for all the men while I was in Bononia, and Arshak had purchased an ox in the marketplace for the officers, together with good Roman bread, apples, carrots and leeks, fresh cheese, and a kind of sweet made from nuts roasted with honey. One of the tribunes brought a scented oil, with which the Romans like to anoint themselves at banquets, and Comittus brought some wine, as he'd promised. I fetched the set of gold drinking cups from my wagon and we drank some wine and ate some cheese while we waited for the ox to finish roasting, the Sarmatians sitting cross-legged, and the Romans reclining against bales of straw. None of the tribunes commented on the fact that the drinking cups were of Roman design. Perhaps they thought I'd bought them.

We introduced our squadron captains to the tribunes, and received in return the important information that the eldest of the three men, the married one, Marcus Vibullus Severus, was assigned to Arshak; the second, Gaius Valerius Victor, to Gatalas; and Lucius Javolenus Comittus to me. Comittus smiled at me when he announced this. I was pleased as well. Severus seemed a more serious and responsible man than his younger colleague, and might do better with Arshak. Though Comittus had won back some esteem from my brother princes during the dinner—largely by admiring our weapons and our horses.

"I never realized what 'armored cavalry' meant until today!" he exclaimed enthusiastically. "By Andate! You hardly look human in all that gear. I'm not surprised that no one's ever beaten you on a field where you could use the horses."

Arshak smiled and rubbed the hilt of his sword. "We are the best cavalry in the world," he said complacently. He and Gatalas were still wearing their armor. I'd taken mine off, and told one of my bodyguard to see to it when he'd finished oiling his own.

"How strong is that armor?" asked Severus. "Is it as good as plate?"

In answer, Gatalas held out his arm in front of Severus; the tribune tapped it, then fingered the scales, and the other two picked themselves up to examine it as well. "Two layers deep?" they asked. "What about the men who have horn for the scales, instead of iron? How does that compare?" "How long does it last?" "How long does it take to make?" "Will it turn a sword?" Gatalas and Arshak smiled, preening themselves, and boasted of their armor's strength.

I watched them irritably. "A direct blow from a good sword will cut through it," I said, and at once regretted it. They all looked at my leg. I was sitting with the bad knee up in front of me because it still hurt to cross it.

"The man that hit your leg was Dacian, yes?" said Gatalas. We were speaking Latin, and he was less fluent than Arshak or myself. "He used one of the long swords with two hands."

Arshak's eyes glittered. He lifted his own two hands above his head, and brought an imaginary sword down on my leg, whack, whack, whack. I'd been warned by his eyes, and managed not to flinch. The gesture was not one of serious malice—but he wouldn't have done it if he hadn't been annoyed at my admission that the armor was not impenetrable. "It was almost an axe," Arshak said, abandoning his imaginary sword again. "And even so, Ariantes, without your armor, you would have lost your leg. A man in this armor is almost impossible to wound."

I remembered lying in the mud with the Dacian hacking at me. Arshak still believed in his invulnerability. That is the problem with armored cavalry; that had been the problem for all our people. If we'd believed we could lose a war with the Romans, we never would have started one. "A long spear, used as a pike or a lance, can go through it, too," I said, stubbornly. "And a catapult bolt. And an arrow from a Hunnish bow."

"But it's very good armor," Severus said, tactfully closing the subject. "I suppose, though, that you need a big horse to carry it all."

So we talked horses for a bit—the Romans were immensely impressed by the Parthian horses in particular—and then got onto hunting, and thus to shooting, and bows, and lances, and war. I said very little; my leg ached and I was tired. We ate the roast ox, and the carrots and leeks that had been used for stuffing the meat, and drank some more wine. The rain hissed in the fire.

"The thing that amazes me," said Comittus, as we started on the nuts and apples, "is how much the way your troops are organized resembles the way ours are."

"Like a legion?" asked Arshak, expressionlessly. He was sneering at Comittus, though the other man didn't realize it. A Sarmatian dragon has almost nothing in common with a Roman legion.

"No, no, like an *ala* of auxiliary cavalry," replied Comittus, again showing himself less foolish than he first appeared. "Your 'dragons' have five hundred men; our quingenary *alae* have five hundred men. You divide the men into squadrons of thirty; we divide them into *turmae* of thirty. You have squadron captains, we have decurions. It's exactly the same. Did you copy us or did we copy you?"

"I'll bet we both copied the Parthians," said Severus. "They use heavy cavalry arranged in 'dragons,' too. I read about it in a book. And the Sarmatians used to live in the East, near Parthia."

"In the days of Queen Tirgatao," said Arshak, "we fought both the Parthians and the Romans, or so the songs say."

I looked away. I did not like to hear my wife's name spoken, even when the person meant was the queen she'd been named after.

"What happened?" asked Comittus, with interest.

"She led her people to victory, and died winning it."

"Do even your women fight wars?" asked Severus.

"Not now," Arshak answered. "But in the days of our grandfathers' grandmothers, yes. There are many songs of the warrior queens. In those days a woman could not marry unless she had killed an enemy of her tribe." He shrugged. "It was easier for her to do it then, I think. People used less armor. Most women can ride and shoot with the bow, and I think that in those days that was all that was needed."

"Queens have led armies in Britain, too," said Comittus. "Cartimandua of the Brigantes, Boudica of the Iceni . . ."

"Bodica?" I said, beginning to pay attention again. "Like the legate's wife?"

"Yes," said Comittus, beaming at me. "And in fact, Aurelia Bodica is related to Queen Boudica, on her mother's side, through the royal family of the Coritani. The sister of King Prasutagus of the Iceni married—"

The third tribune, Gaius Valerius Victor, sniggered. He was older than Comittus, but he'd been hitting the wine harder, and was now slightly drunk. "Hear our *Brittunculus* on the royalty of the tribes! Sitting around a campfire's gone to your head, Comittus: you're raving in the poetry of your ancestors."

Comittus went red. *Brittunculus*: little Briton, a diminutive that oozed contempt. "You've got no right to use that word to me, Gaius," he said. "You're British yourself; your family's lived in Verulamium for generations."

"Yes, but *my* great-great-grandfather was a veteran of the army of the deified Claudius, not a Coritanic tribesman who used to paint himself blue!"

"My ancestors were kings!" replied Comittus, starting up.

"That's enough!" rapped Severus, glaring at both of them, and both fell silent and remembered us. We were all looking at them with blank, remote expressions and expecting the two to duel. No Sarmatian would have spoken so insultingly to another man's face unless he meant to fight him—and no Sarmatian accepted an insult to his ancestors peaceably. The fire hissed and spluttered as the silence dragged. Comittus reclined again, blinking angrily, and we realized that nothing was going to happen.

"You are a descendant of kings?" asked Arshak, to break the stillness. "And this lady also, the wife of my lord the legate?"

"Well—Aurelia Bodica is," Comittus said, still unhappy. "Her father is a descendant of the kings of the Regni, and her mother, of the Coritani. My family are related to her mother's. You probably noticed I have a British name."

We had not noticed, of course, and I wasn't even sure which of his names was the British one, except that it couldn't be Lucius.

"These . . . Coritani, Regni, Iceni . . . they are tribes?" asked Arshak.

"Native British tribes," supplied Severus. "Britain used to be divided into a number of different tribal kingdoms. A few tribal organizations are still used for administrative purposes, but otherwise none of them count for much."

"We also have tribes," said Arshak, "but I think ours are greater. We Iazyges hold all the land between the Danube and Tisza beneath our spears, and we count for much even with your emperor. We are all Iazyges here—except Ariantes' Roxalani. And it is because you share family with this lady, Lucius Javolenus, that you come to be a tribune?"

"Well—yes."

Victor was scowling again, and Severus looked uneasy. There was something about this topic that bothered them—presumably the same thing that had caused the squabble a moment before, and not the fact that Comittus had won his place through patronage, as the Romans take that for granted. I tested it, cautiously. "The lady Aurelia Bodica seemed to me very wise and perceptive," I said.

I'd hit it. There was something about the legate's lady that the other two tribunes disliked: they looked at me nervously. Comittus, however, beamed at me again. "She is, she is!" he exclaimed. "There's not a woman in Britain to match her. Julius Priscus fell for her head over heels the moment he met her, and he'd tell you himself what an immense help she's been to him, lucky man. You know, of course, that the legionary legate for Eburacum controls the civil administration of northern Britain as well as all its military affairs—" (we hadn't) "well, Aurelia Bodica can sort out a lawsuit so quickly it makes you blink."

"Yes," said Severus, hurriedly—then, turning to Arshak, he said, "You are also descended from kings, aren't you, Lord Arsacus?"

"My father is second in line to the crown," replied Arshak proudly, which effectively silenced everyone else's boasts about noble birth.

I LAY AWAKE for a while that night, trying to interpret what I'd heard. I had not thought about the natives of the province as a force distinct from the Romans who governed it. Victor, though, had sneered at Comittus as a Briton: there was some tension there. Aurelia Bodica was descended from two houses of native kings, and her position of influence made some of her husband's junior officers uneasy. Who were we going to fight in the North? Facilis had expressed doubts that we would fight anyone: "What if it's all patrols and guard duty?" he'd asked. That still meant that there was some force the Romans needed to guard against.

I had known nothing about Britain, and I was still trying to grasp how large the island was. All through the journey I'd believed that we were being sent there to prevent us from troubling the Romans, not because the Romans wanted us to deal with trouble from someone else. Priscus, though, had come to collect us with the assumption that we were something much closer to auxiliary troops, that he could appoint his own men to officer us and use us against Rome's enemies. Facilis' letter revealing how dangerous we could be had horrified him. From what I'd overheard in Bononia I knew that there were more Sarmatian troops to come. That did not suggest a province entirely at peace.

What were we going to do? The tribunes had said nothing whatever about that, almost certainly out of deliberate policy. Julius Priscus had carefully avoided showing us how many men he actually had in Dubris. At the tribunal he'd appeared with just the three tribunes and twenty of his dispatch riders: I guessed that Facilis had come on his own. Probably that meant the legate did not have many men with him. A handful of men from his legion, then, and fifteen hundred of us to move: he would certainly try to keep us ignorant, bewildered, and unsure of our directions, dependent upon himself and his officers not just for guidance but for the means of life. We had been given our weapons back—a thing I suspected the legate now regretted—but we were not Roman soldiers yet by any means. We were barbarians, and would be kept ignorant of everything we had no immediate need to know.

I could imagine the Romans busily writing letters at the naval base. Planning where we would go, how we would journey there, what we would eat on the way; alerting other troops to our movements in case there was trouble. I had no desire whatever to take advantage of the lack of guards, but I wanted some control over what was to be done with my friends, my followers, and myself.

THE FOLLOWING DAY, when I'd checked that the wagons and horses were ready for the journey to Eburacum and that we were well provisioned,

I took my horse, shooed off my bodyguard, and set out into the town look-ing for Lucius Javolenus Comittus.

I found him at his quarters in the naval base—a couple of small rooms at the end of one of the barracks blocks. He appeared himself at my knock, looking tousled, bad-tempered, and, when he saw me, surprised.

"Oh!" he said. "Lord Ariantes. Uh . . . I was just planning the itinerary for our troop."

"That is what I have come about," I replied. "May I speak with you, Lu-cius Javolenus?"

"Uh . . . yes, yes, of course! Come in out of the rain."

I unsaddled and tethered my horse, and limped in. The room was stone and narrow; I disliked the cold, enclosed feel of it intensely. Comittus had moved a desk underneath the window, to get the light, and it was littered with parchment, tablets, and sheets of wood.

"Thank you for the dinner last night," said Comittus.

"It was our pleasure. I have come, Lucius Javolenus, because I thought perhaps I could be of help. When my lord the procurator Natalis was trying to gather supplies for us, he allowed me to check his lists, and I found that he had much misjudged what was needed. He ordered wheat, and my men have complained at eating grain all the way from Aquincum. They are not used to it; it makes their teeth hurt, they say."

"Oh!" Comittus exclaimed in alarm, and picked up one of the sets of tablets. "I've ordered it, too. Don't you eat wheat at all?"

"Some, a little, to thicken a stew or make flat cakes. But in our own country we eat mostly meat—fresh and dried beef, mutton, and horse-meat—and milk and cheese from mares, sheep, and cattle. Now, I understand you do not eat horses or drink mare's milk, but dried and salted beef is eas-ily obtained, as is cheese. Would it be possible to replace a part of the order for wheat with orders for some of these things?"

We were soon going over what supplies would be collected where. Comittus made some effort to cloud the itinerary, and referred to "supply depot one, supply depot two," and so on, but I gathered we would reach the provincial capital, Londinium, on the third day of the journey, pick up more supplies four days later somewhere to the north, and two days later again would be at a place called Lindum, which was Comittus' home: Eburacum was three days' ride north of that. "And there we will stop?" I asked.

"Well, not us," he replied, "That is, we'll stop briefly, but . . . I wasn't supposed to tell you this."

"Why is it secret? Are we not meant to know that the three dragons will be split up?"

"Deae Matres! How did you know that?"

I was honestly surprised. "We have been sure from the beginning that we would be posted to different camps as soon as we arrived at our destination. All along you have feared to have too many of us together. When we left Aquincum there was some question whether our group was not too large to be safely contained on the journey."

Comittus laughed. "So much for secrets!"

"That was not much of one," I said. "Come, you are supposed to 'advise' me, or so you said. Can I not even know where I am to be posted?"

He laughed again. "Very well! You'd certainly know anyway in a few days' time. You and I and our company will go on to Cilurnum, on the Wall; Gatalas' dragon goes to Condercum, which is also on the Wall; and Arsacus' stays in Eburacum."

"What is this 'Wall,' then?"

Comittus pulled the sheet of parchment out from under the tablets and spread it on top of them. "Look," he said, pointing, and I looked and saw a meaningless huddle of lines, with the tiny black scratches of writing scattered about them. "Here's Eburacum," he went on—and the lines resolved themselves into a map. I leaned over it, frowning and trying to make sense of it. My people use maps, but ours are only lines scrawled to show camps, landmarks, the sun's position, and days' riding; Roman maps are different.

"All this territory," Comittus went on, spreading his hand upward from the blotch that was Eburacum, "belongs to the Brigantes. They're a big tribe, a bit wild, sheepherders mostly, with some farmers. They've caused problems in the past—uprisings. The last was twenty-five years ago, but they're still not entirely happy with being ruled by Rome—that's the way the government in Londinium puts it. If you ask me, they're just annoyed at having to take orders from a lot of southern tribesmen in togas. Anyhow, this"—he enclosed a similar area, above the territory of the Brigantes—"belongs to the Pictish tribes, the Selgovae, the Votadini, and the Novantae. Now, *they* are nothing *but* trouble. We pushed the frontier up to here"—he drew a line with his finger above the area he'd just shown me—"and put a line of forts through Pictish territory, but we had nothing but grief from it. They raided, they stole sheep, they sprung ambushes on the men that tried to get them back—and what's worse, they feuded with the Brigantes behind our backs. So about twelve years ago we dropped the frontier back south to the old wall, the one built by the deified Hadrian, and recommissioned that. That's the wall we'll be keeping. It runs from here to here"—he spanned it with his fingers, a line between the Brigantes and the Picts—"with a castle for a few dozen men every mile, a major fort every six miles or so, and a great stone wall, bank, and ditch across every inch. We also have some advance forts beyond the wall, to keep the Picts in order, but they still raid the Brigantes. They think it's a brave and daring thing to creep up to the Wall in the dead of night, murder the sentries, and slip into the South to steal the property of Romans."

"They could not bring cattle across a wall in the dead of night," I said.

"They can get sheep over, though," said Comittus, "and anything else movable. And slaves."

I'd forgotten about slaves, of course; I'd never taken any on my own raids across Roman boarders.

"They're allowed through at the forts," Comittus went on. "They can go to markets in the South, provided they leave their weapons behind and pay a toll. But the raiders have often slipped back through with returning market-goers, hiding their weapons and passing off stolen property as their own. And sometimes the raiders are killed, and that makes trouble, too, because their relatives to the north think we owe them the blood price for the dead. Every now and then there's a big raid, organized from a mixture of greed and vengefulness, and then troops have to be rushed from all over the Wall to deal with it. That's why we were so pleased to get heavy cavalry. A few of you could deal with a fairly big raid, and you can move fast. Whenever anything happens, the troops at Eburacum are always too far away."

"Then you should not keep Arshak at Eburacum."

"Well . . ." Comittus said, and coughed with embarrassment.

I looked away from the map. "You mean by that, that Arshak should not have changed his coat yesterday afternoon."

"Well . . . yes," Comittus said, and suddenly gave me a confidential grin.

I looked at the map again, and drew my finger along the line of the Wall. The situation did not seem as bloody as I'd feared in the darkness of the night before. And Arshak might fret angrily in a legionary fortress, but even he would hardly start a mutiny there for lack of bloodshed. "What is this place Cilurnum like?" I asked.

There was a stamp of feet outside and we both looked up to see Flavius Facilis glaring at us red-faced through the window. Absurdly, we both gave a guilty start, like two small boys caught by their father using his bow case to carry frogs.

"Julius Priscus wanted to see you, Tribune," grated Facilis. "We're all comparing notes on the itinerary."

Comittus hurriedly picked up his tablets and went to the door. I followed him.

"He didn't ask to see you, Ariantes," Facilis told me, "and I don't think the tribune did, either."

"He was giving me advice on what supplies to order," said Comittus defensively.

"He was digging for information," corrected Facilis. "Why else would he be slipping in here quietly and leaving his bodyguard behind?"

"Why should I not know things that concern my company?" I asked. "We are soldiers, not prisoners, as the legate himself said. And I thought, Flavius Facilis, that some advice on supplies was needed. I have nineteen men too ill to ride and a whole dragon complaining of sore teeth, to say nothing of nearly thirteen hundred horses with sore feet, because we were not supplied with what we needed on the way from Aquincum."

I expected an angry response to this. Instead, Facilis looked at me for a long minute, and then declared, "The legate said almost exactly the same thing to me yesterday. There are times, Ariantes, when you're just like a Roman. What do your men think of it?"

I picked my saddle up from the porch and went to my horse. "I have asked you not to insult me," I said, putting the saddle on the animal's back. The shaft had struck flesh, and I was angry.

He gave a snort. "Very well. You want to give your advice to the legate, then?"

"Would I be heard?" I asked bitterly.

"Yes. If you confine yourself to supplies."

I stopped buckling the saddle.

"Yes, you bastard, he'll hear you!" Facilis shouted. "He wants you in Eburacum in good shape and ready to fight. He's keeping me to balance your crew, but he'll listen to you sooner. Come now, and he'll probably send you off to arrange your damned supplies—with me to write the letters for you, since he knows I'll keep my mouth more tightly closed than the tribune."

"And you would be willing to write the letters for me?" I asked.

He was silent for a moment, still red in the face, still swollen. But his look was one of exasperation with himself, rather than of rage. "Yes," he said at last. "Yes, I'll have to work with you, won't I? You're going to be here, and you're going to be sending letters anyway, as soon as you've collected that scribe Natalis gave you. And I'm going to be camp prefect in Cilurnum. I can hardly go on hating you. Why should I wear out my heart?"

I began unsaddling my horse again. "We're not obliged to like each other," I remarked.

He snorted. "And a good thing, too."

V

THE SCRIBE EUKAIRIOS did not show up that day, and that night I began to believe that he had indeed run off in Bononia. The following morning, however, while we were busy striking camp and harnessing the horses, one of my men appeared at my wagon escorting him. I'd just finished arming myself for the journey and had climbed onto Farna, who was the best horse I had for carrying armor. The slave stopped in his tracks and stood looking up at me with a mixture of misery and resolution. He looked even smaller and drabber among so many glittering Sarmatian horsemen, and he was clutching a bundle of clothing tied to a stick.

"I'm sorry I'm late, my lord," he said. "The dispatch vessel didn't arrive back in Dubris until last night, so I stayed at the lord procurator's house until this morning."

"I am glad you arrived in time," I replied. "We will set out shortly; you should get into the wagon."

The men slept six to a wagon, but because I was commander, I had a wagon to myself. These were light wagons for campaigning, horse-drawn, not the heavy ox-wagons we would have lived in at home. But mine was still a large one, and both the body and the felt awning were stained red; the four horses that drew it were already harnessed. They were matched red bays, not large animals, but strong, enduring, and with some spirit, and they were tossing their heads and moving restlessly under the yoke. "I . . . don't know how to drive . . ." Eukairios began, looking at them and losing some of his resolution.

"No one expects you to. The men of my bodyguard take turns. Just climb in and sit down."

He climbed in; after a moment, he climbed through into the front and sat on the edge of the driver's bench, over to one side.

Comittus galloped up on his shallow-hocked black. He had a gilded helmet and breastplate, and was wearing the purple tribune's sash: he, too, had armed for the journey. "We're ready to go!" he called, his eyes dancing with excitement. I turned and gave the troop drummer the signal to give the call to assemble: I had a few things to tell the whole dragon before we set out.

A few minutes later the wagons had been whirled out of the way and the dragon was gathered before me. The rain had finally stopped, and there was a bright September sun. I looked out over a plain of steel and horn, gleaming in the light. The horses shifted and danced, the banners of the squadrons tossed in the light breeze, and behind me on my left I could hear the air singing in the mouth of the standard.

"My brother *azatani*," I shouted, trying to pitch my voice so they could all hear, "we are bound on the final stage of our journey, and I ask two things of you. First, I have sworn upon fire that we will do no harm to any Roman along the way: I entrust you with the keeping of my oath. I don't say just that I want you to respect the lives and property of those you meet; I say that even if a thief should visit *us*, you must be blameless. Take him alive and give him to the legate to punish. Second, remember, now that you are armed again, that we are not in our own country and not free to follow our own customs. If you fight duels among yourselves, not one but both the duelists will die, the first at the hand of his opponent, and the second executed by the Romans as a murderer. I cannot defend you from that; even if you fight a man of another company for the sake of my own honor, I cannot defend you. So if you must fight, do so with blunted weapons, and not to the death.

"In twelve days we will be in Eburacum, and four days after that, in Cilurnum, where we will be based. I hear that it is a pleasant place beside a river, with abundant grazing for horses and good hunting nearby. We will need to travel no more than thirty Roman miles in any day, and I trust that we will be well provided for along the way. There are no more oceans to cross, and we will travel now as warriors, armed and honorable, and not as wretched prisoners. May God favor us!"

They cheered, waved their spears, and shouted, "Marha!" I gave another signal to the drummer, and he rattled out the call to march, which was taken up by the banner-bearers of the squadrons. Arshak and Gatalas were still speaking to their men, so we circled the parade ground while we waited for them to start. I never like to keep the men standing about waiting.

"What did you say to them?" asked Comittus, who'd turned his horse beside mine.

I told him, roughly.

"Would they really start fighting duels if you hadn't warned them?" he asked in amazement.

I looked at him sideways, wondering what it must be like to lead a body of men who did *not* fight duels over every half-imagined slur. "Of course," I said. "Though not so much with men from this dragon. We all know one another. But there are one or two points of conflict with the troops that follow Arshak and Gatalas."

"What? I ought to know if I'm to . . . liaise properly."

True enough. "The others sneer at the Roxalani in my company, and the Roxalani sometimes take offense. I am lucky in Kasagos, who is senior to the other Roxalanic captains. He is a sensible man and a priest and diviner, and he knows how to calm his fellow tribesmen and soothe their opponents—but still they fight, at times. Then we are second to Gatalas in the order of march. The men do not mind coming behind Arshak, because he is of royal blood, but Gatalas, they say, is no better than myself. So they and Gatalas' men boast to one another that their horses are faster, their armor stronger, their own skill greater, and their commanders braver and more glorious—and sometimes they fight over it." After a moment I added, "They did it to some extent even on the way from Aquincum. But then they were unarmed, and they were too wretched with bad food and weariness to have much heart for boasting. It will be worse now."

I could have added that now Gatalas' men were certain to say to mine, "Your commander is a Romanizer," and my men would probably reply angrily, "Who got you that beef you're eating?" and there would be blows over that, too. But what would be the point of trying to explain the danger and dishonor of Romanizing to a Roman?

The Romans were waiting for us by the tribunal. Priscus had even fewer troops than I'd expected: fifty dispatch riders and one century. He sent Arshak's dragon in front, with a guide, and followed it with his own troops and their baggage. Gatalas' dragon came next, and then the wagons, and finally my own company brought up the rear. Normally I would have expected that to be a dusty position—but everything was far too wet. The worst problem was horses losing horse-sandals in the churned-up mud verge of the road. As soon as I'd arranged the squadrons, I was obliged to leave them to dig the horse-sandals out on their own while I joined the legate. Senior Roman officers usually ride together when their forces are on the march, though Sarmatians stay with their men. Facilis had imposed the Roman order of march on us during the journey from Aquincum, largely to keep an eye on the officers and separate us from our followers, and I wasn't surprised to find that Priscus retained this precaution.

Priscus was riding a solid and rather sleepy-looking gray at the head of the century—the legionaries, of course, marched on foot. Arshak and Gatalas and their liaison officers were already on his right when Comittus and I cantered up, and Facilis rode slightly behind them, keeping out of their way. Aurelia Bodica was on her husband's left, sitting in her flimsy painted chariot again, with both the white stallion and another white horse to pull it. (I'd noticed her covered carriage with the baggage train, drawn by a less exalted horse.) She was even lovelier than I remembered, and she smiled at us very brightly.

"Greetings, cousin! Greetings, Lord Ariantes!" she called. "Isn't it lucky the rain's stopped?"

"Just in time for the journey," agreed Comittus, falling in beside her.

She gave me a look of sweet concern. "Though I gather that you had very wet weather to travel in over the last month, Lord Ariantes. My husband"—she glanced toward him—"has been telling me that your troops have had such a difficult journey so far that you all have a number of men lying in the wagons with the baggage, too ill to ride. I hope we can recover them."

I felt ashamed of my distrust of her. "I trust they will recover, Lady Aurelia Bodica," I replied, "given better food and supplies." I was glad she'd given me the chance to call the legate's attention to the question of supplies again.

Priscus snorted.

"Well, I'll be glad to help if I can," declared Bodica earnestly. She glanced over at Arshak and Gatalas as well, and raised her voice so that they, too, could hear her offer, "As my husband can tell you, Princes, my family and my friends own a great deal of land and cattle in northern Britain, and I'd be glad to use whatever wealth or influence I have to help your people settle in happily."

The legate smiled, and leaned out of the saddle to pat her hand. "You needn't worry, my dear," he told her. "I'm sure we can settle them without digging into our private fortunes. But thank you."

Bodica gave him a lingering smile back. I bowed my head and thanked her for her kindness in making the offer; Arshak and Gatalas did the same. I gathered from their manner that they'd been introduced to her before I joined them, and that they found her impressive.

"Oh, and Lord Ariantes," Bodica went on, "I believe I never actually thanked you for catching my horse the other day. Please excuse me! I was so surprised to find one of your people actually in Britain, it went right out of my head. But really, I'm very grateful. I do love this horse, and who knows what might have happened to him if you hadn't caught him?"

"I am glad to have been of service to you, Lady," I replied.

Arshak turned his mount, cantered behind the chariot, and pulled in beside me. "What is this?" he asked me, speaking Latin in courtesy to the company. "You had the good fortune to be of service to the lady?"

Bodica laughed. "Didn't he even tell you, Lord Arshak?" (I noticed, with some surprise, that she said his name correctly, with the *sh* sound most Romans can't pronounce.) "Was that modesty, Lord Ariantes, or didn't you find the adventure worth repeating to your friends?"

I was taken aback: I hadn't considered being knocked down by a horse an adventure.

"Ariantes is not given to boasting," replied Arshak, giving me an affectionate look. "I think otherwise any service to a lady such as . . . your wife, my lord Julius Priscus" (the pause before he tactfully brought the legate into the conversation was only just noticeable) "is a tale he would gladly have told us."

Bodica gave him a look that said, "That is very pretty flattery, sir!" Priscus, however, was frowning anxiously. "How did the horse get loose?" he asked. "You hadn't mentioned that, my dear. You just said you'd met one of our Sarmatians in the marketplace. Blizzard didn't . . . that is, the beast didn't cause any trouble for you, did it?"

Bodica explained. Priscus gave Comittus a scowl, which the tribune received with a nervous, appeasing smile. "You were in charge of the escort, weren't you, Tribune?" demanded the legate. "What were you thinking of, to let the beast slip its tether like that? Blizzard is a very valuable animal, shipped all the way from Iberia! You should have seen to it that he was tied securely."

"I don't know how it happened, sir," replied Comittus. "I thought he *was* tied up securely."

Priscus snorted again. "Don't think. Check! That horse is not just a valuable animal, it's a powerful one: it might injure Bodica if it got loose at the wrong time." He glanced anxiously at his wife. "Really, my dear, I wish you'd use the gelding instead."

"Oh, but I adore big strong fiery stallions, Tiberius, you know that!" Her quick, laughing under-the-lashes glance reinforced the double meaning.

Priscus gave a pleased grunt. "All the same," he added, "there's such a thing as too much fire in a horse. You remember that last animal you had nearly killed a groom, and I don't like to think—"

"Tiberius!" she exclaimed, warningly, though she smiled on it, and he stopped. Her taste for fiery horses was evidently a sore point between them. No wonder Comittus had been anxious when the beast got loose.

"A stallion such as the lady Aurelia's is no more dangerous than any other horse, if it is well trained and well handled," I put in, trying to be helpful. What I said was true, though in fact, like most cavalrymen, I've always preferred a good quiet mare for any purpose, such as battle, that might frighten or alarm a horse.

Bodica gave me another dazzling smile, but the disquieting look was back in her eyes. Priscus gave me a hard glare. After a moment, Bodica began to ask questions about our mounts and our other horses.

It was an easy day's riding, as I'd promised my men. We stopped in the middle of the afternoon, only twenty Roman miles from Dubris at a place called Durovernum: it had been decided that an easy journey north would give us time to recover from the hard one we'd had to Bononia. The men were in a good mood, happy at having their weapons back, happy at having reasonable food, happy at riding through the green rolling hills with their dragon leaping before them, the first Sarmatians to have crossed the ocean. They sang as they rode and told stories. I was less cheerful, worrying about the future. They might be happy now, but when they got to Cilurnum they would realize that they were here forever. Then they would miss their wives and families, hate the fellows who shared their wagons, and long for the open plains and the herds and wagons they had left behind. There would inevitably be trouble with drink and women, if there were any nearby, and quarrels over precedence and honor. And up to now they hadn't spoken enough Latin to quarrel with Romans—but I guessed that they would learn it. When we stopped at Durovernum, I was eager to leave the legate and his party, with whom I'd been obliged to ride, and get back to my own men.

The legate, however, insisted that all the senior officers first come with him to the house at Durovernum where he would be staying—and then the local nobleman who owned the house obliged us to come in and have a drink with him. Arshak and Gatalas seemed pleased, but I did not want to stand about sipping wine and making small talk, leaving my horse untended in her armor and my men unsupervised in their camp, and as soon as I could, I made excuses and left. The local nobleman was some relation of the legate's wife, and Lady Aurelia Bodica offered to show me where her kinsman's servants had put my horse.

She picked her way carefully across the stable yard to where Farna was tethered, holding the skirts of her long cloak and gown high out of the mud. She had long straight legs and delicate ankles, and she stepped very proudly, so that it was a pleasure to watch her.

"What a beautiful animal," she commented when we reached Farna.

I nodded, warming to the woman. Farna was worth all the other horses I'd brought put together, and they were all exceptional. She was seven years old, a golden chestnut with black points; she had a finr head, broad neck, deep, powerful chest and hindquarters, a round barrel, and straight legs. In conformation and in temperament, in strength and in endurance, in patience and in courage, she was altogether without fault. She was of the breed called Parthian or Nisaean, the largest and noblest of all breeds of horse, and she carried her blanket of gilded armor easily. I'd slipped the bit out of her mouth and loosened the saddle girths when I'd dismounted, to make her comfortable, and I slapped her side and began adjusting them again.

"What is he called?" asked Aurelia Bodica, coming over to pat Farna's neck in the gap above the armor. The horse was so heavily armored she couldn't tell its sex.

"She is called Farna," I said.

Bodica smiled and patted Farna again. "What does that mean?"

" 'Glory.' "

"Glory," repeated Aurelia Bodica softly. "Glory! Is that what you hoped for when you named her?"

The question, like many of her questions, was perceptive. "It is what I hoped for," I admitted. "Then."

"Not anymore?" She was watching me closely, her head a little on one side. I suddenly suspected that she'd shown me to my horse simply to have the opportunity of testing me in private, to see if I were indeed the sort of tool she and her husband were searching for. The warmth I'd started to feel cooled abruptly.

"No," I said carefully. "I am not so ambitious now."

She reached over and touched the back of my hand, her eyes still fixed on me intently. "Why not? Glory, surely, is the noblest ambition of free men."

"I won glory in Pannonia," I said, telling her the bitter truth. "I and my followers and others like me. And our people have paid for it with war, defeat, and . . . this."

"You think I'm asking this for my husband, don't you?" she said, with that unsettling secretive smile I'd disliked before. "He thinks so, too. But I am a noblewoman, and I can speak on my own account. My ancestors were kings. My family was offered the citizenship of Rome many times, but refused it— until my father inherited, a few years ago. I'm no more a Roman than you are. My people used to love glory too, and I can't believe that it always comes at so high a price. War can bring victory as well as defeat, after all." Her fingers curled around my own. "Though I am grateful to your defeat for bringing you here. My husband values you above the other two commanders. So do I."

I turned away from the horse and looked at her in surprise. Her face, turned upward toward mine, was flowerlike, disturbingly beautiful, and her hand now clasped my own firmly. "Lady," I said, far less sure of myself than I had been a moment before, "Arshak is my superior in honor."

"But not in experience," she replied. "Nor, I think, in ability. You've achieved a great deal more for your men than he has. You might achieve more still."

"I hope that I will," I said, uncertainly. I wished I knew whether the way she held my hand was mere courtesy or something more. Roman customs in such matters are very different from those of my own people. "I wish them to have honor among the Romans and be content."

"And that is all? No glory? No . . . revenge?"

I shook my head.

"Because it brought you war, defeat, and this," she said, smiling again. "Is 'this' so terrible, Lord Ariantes?" She touched the side of my face lightly, leaning forward.

I knew that if I matched that movement, she would come directly into my arms and let me kiss that unsettling smile away. A part of me burned to do just that, but I stood as if I had been turned to stone. I didn't trust the place and the moment, in the stable yard of an unfamiliar house—and I didn't trust her.

"By 'this' I meant servitude to Rome," I told her harshly.

"So. Then it is terrible. What if someone offered you freedom? Do you *want* to become my husband's man and Rome's loyal servant?"

I couldn't answer. Even if this were a test her husband had suggested to her, I couldn't bring myself to say, "Yes," and "No" was a road that led only to death.

Bodica laid her palm against my cheek. "You hate Rome," she observed. "Ariantes, you don't need to worry about saying so, not to me. My own people have suffered too."

A door creaked open behind us, and Bodica instantly shifted her hand from me to Farna. "Such a beautiful mare," she cooed. She glanced round and smiled warmly. "Tiberius, I'm over here! Don't you think this is a beautiful horse?"

Her husband came out of the house and crossed the stable yard toward us. Arshak and Gatalas were behind him, together with the local nobleman, our host. "I thought Ariantes would be gone by now," Priscus told his wife. "Have you been discussing horses with him all this time?"

She laughed. "Haven't you noticed that all the Sarmatians can talk horses for hours? Seriously, Tiberius, don't you think a foal by my stallion Blizzard out of this mare would be the best horse in the world?"

When I returned to my wagon, I tended my horses and sat by the evening fire in silence, going over the scene in the stable yard again and again and trying to understand it. I couldn't. I couldn't even tell whether the way

Bodica had touched me was a sign of serious interest or meaningless flirtation, let alone guess what she'd meant by her talk of freedom and glory. I felt as though I were riding in a mist across a battlefield mined with pitfalls and scattered with caltrops that would lame my horse. Everywhere I turned there might be danger, but I could neither stand still nor go back.

The only thing I felt with any certainty was that I wanted nothing more to do with Lady Aurelia Bodica. I was bitterly ashamed of what I'd felt when she touched my cheek. I had not touched any woman since I last said good-bye to Tirgatao, and I was disgusted to find myself stirred by Bodica, however lovely she was and however noble. I had enough to worry about, too, without dangers from feuds between Roman factions or the threat of punishment for adultery with my commander's wife.

The only other man in the dragon who seemed gloomy was Eukairios. He sat silent by the fire while the rest talked and laughed in a language that he, of course, did not understand. After a while, he asked me where he could sleep, and I took him back into the wagon and cleared a space for him.

I WOKE IN the middle of the night to the sound of sobbing. It pulled me from deep sleep, and for a moment I could not remember when or where I was. "Artanisca?" I said, sitting up. "Artanisca, love, I'm here. Don't cry."

The sobbing stopped abruptly, and as it did I realized that it had not been a child's sobbing, but the hard, painful gasping of a man. I remembered Eukairios.

"I'm sorry, my lord," came the slave's voice out of the darkness, still rough with grief. "I didn't mean to wake you."

I dropped onto my back again and stared up blindly into the blackness. "No," I said. "I am sorry that you grieve so for Bononia."

"I didn't mean to complain," he told me. "You have been very kind. It was a great consolation to me to be able to say good-bye, and to have my friends' prayers supporting me as I set out. I do thank you. But it's . . . foreign to me. It will get better in time. I'll learn the language."

He was speaking to encourage himself. "Yes," I said. I closed my eyes, willing myself to be still.

"What does 'artanisca' mean? It is what you said just now, isn't it?"

I was silent for a long minute. "It is a name," I answered, at last. "My little son. He is dead."

"Oh!" After a moment, "I am sorry, my lord."

"Yes." I pressed my hands against my face, trying to stop my own tears at the thought that Artanisca would never wake me in the night again, never; Tirgatao would never get up to pluck him from his cradle and place him between us, round and warm, and slide her slim arm around my back, leaning her head against my own. Never, never, never.

"What do your people say of the dead?" I asked, saying something, anything, rather than gaze into that black chasm. "Do followers of your cult burn them, like the Romans, or do they lay them in the earth?"

"Either, my lord," Eukairios said, after a surprised pause. "Bury if we can, burn if we can't. We believe that if we have died in faith, it doesn't matter how our bodies are treated."

"But you believe in immortality." I remembered Natalis on the ship, mentioning the cult's disgusting rituals done in private houses at night, to give immortality.

"We believe that one day this earth will shed its skin like a snake, and be renewed; that it suffers now like a woman in labor, but when its pain is ended there will be joy. Then all things will be made new, and the dead rise from ashes or the grave, and all that was broken will be made whole."

"You believe that the bodies of the dead can return from ashes?"

"If they were made once in their mother's womb, they can be made again from the earth, or smoke, or ash. What matters is what they were when they lived, not what was done to them afterward."

"My people believe that when fire destroys the body," I said, "the soul is destroyed too. Fire is holy, and death pollutes it."

"If you think fire is holy, shouldn't it purify death?"

"That is not what we believe of it."

We were silent for a little while. I imagined Tirgatao burning, and the pain was so great I couldn't breathe. I spoke. I had to, even though I was weakening myself before, of all people, a miserable slave. "My wife's body was burned," I said, "and my little son's as well. They were in the wagons. The Romans came—the second Pannonian cavalry. Tirgatao took Artanisca and jumped out of the wagon, hoping to run with him to safety, but she was heavy with our second child, and slow; they saw her. She had her bow, and shot at them; they told me she killed one man. The rest fell on her with swords and killed her. Then they killed Artanisca. They were angry because we had made them suffer in the war, and because she had killed one of them. They looted the wagons and set them on fire. They cut her body open, and tore the child from her womb, and hurled it on the fire. I pray to all the gods it was dead! They took a horse's head, and put that in her womb, and flung her on the fire, like that, and Artanisca after her. Another woman who had hidden in a well saw it all. I was wounded on the field, five miles away; I was lying in the mud all the while, not conscious. When my men came to find me next morning, they did not tell me what had happened. I asked and asked for Tirgatao, and they said she was not there. I thought she had been sent to safety."

I heard the floorboards creak as he moved. "Christ have mercy!" he whispered.

"I do not believe a crucified Roman would help it."

"But you believe fire is holy, and your god, Marha, is holy and good?"

"That is what my people believe."

"Then . . . then surely, fire for your wife and child would be release, not destruction?"

"Perhaps," I said. "The Romans burn their dead to release the soul. Perhaps they are right. I hope they are right, and you also." After a moment I added, thickly, "It is the thought of Artanisca that hurts me most, when she was already dead, screaming beside her body. He was two years old. I think of him crying, and of her burning. I was helpless to prevent it, and helpless to revenge it, and I am helpless still. Do not repeat anything of what I have just said. To anyone."

"God forbid!" he said vehemently. "I'd as soon tear a man's skin off and wear it round the camp."

"My people do that sometimes." I felt very tired now, and ashamed. But the chasm had moved away a little, and I could breathe again. "I am sorry, Eukairios, that I have made you suffer too. I have seen enough suffering this year to wish to see no more of it. But if you should mention what I have said, I would have to kill you. A commander must be strong."

"You don't need threats, my lord, to make me be silent."

Not because I must be strong, but because he knew I was weak. It was a strange feeling, being pitied by a slave. It should have made me angry, but didn't. It was comforting, to have another human being in my wagon, not be alone; comforting to be able to grieve without fear. "Good night, then," I said, beginning to drowse off.

"Good night, my lord."

I DID NOT want to meet his eyes next morning. But he walked up to me while I was saddling Farna, and asked, in the dry quiet voice he'd used in Bononia, whether I wanted any letters or accounts done. I asked him a question about how the Romans handled accounts, and he began explaining it. Comittus appeared while he was still explaining, and joined in the explanations. The talk was interrupted by our setting out, then resumed and continued for a while on the road. I was aware, as Comittus and I rode back to the place beside the legate, that Eukairios had turned his attention to the man who was driving my wagon and was trying to learn a few words of Sarmatian.

"He's a good scribe," observed Comittus. "Natalis did well by you."

"Yes," I answered. Natalis had done very well by me—or perhaps very badly. I could not treat the man as a slave now. Property does not wake up crying in the night, or pity the tears you shed in return. I might grow to hate the man because he knew my weakness—or we might end up friends. How we would manage remained to be seen.

"I suppose I ought to learn some Sarmatian, too," Comittus said, thoughtfully.

I looked at him appreciatively. "I think the men will learn Latin. But a few words from you in their own tongue would please them."

"I'll try and learn some, then," he declared, eagerly. "Though I must say I'm glad you speak Latin as well as you do. Your Latin is much better than the others'—a little formal, maybe, but it's educated Latin. Where did you learn it?"

"My father had a . . . I do not know the word for it. A client or tenant; a man whom he permitted to farm some land where he had grazing rights, in return for some of the produce. There were a number of these people near the Tisza River, at the winter pastures. This one was educated. At any rate, my father used to remit a part of the tribute from this man in exchange for Latin lessons for myself and my sisters. He wished us to speak educated Latin. Nobles of our nation try to learn some Latin, but we have little opportunity to practice it, in our country, and only use it for trading, or raids. I had a better teacher than most." I didn't add the other truth about my Latin, that it was good because I'd enjoyed the lessons and gone to talk to the old man even when I hadn't needed to. I'd always been ashamed of that. "He used to read us poetry," I said instead.

Comittus laughed. " 'Arms and the man I sing, who first from the walls of Troy'?"

"Yes, he did read us that."

"Did you like it?"

I shook my head. "We have our own songs of heroes, which are bloodier, and more to our own taste. But I liked some of the other things he read us. Did you grow up speaking Latin?"

He flushed slightly. "Yes, of course! That thing Gaius said, that 'Brittunculus' gibe—that was just a joke. I'm as much a Roman as he is. My family's had the citizenship since my grandfather's day."

"I meant no offense. I was wondering if I should learn some British."

He relaxed again. "Ah. The fact is, British *is* my first language—though I learned Latin before I could read." He added it so hastily that I suspected he had learned Latin in order to read.

"Is Javolenus a British name?" I asked.

He looked astonished. "No, of course not. No, he was a procurator when my grandfather got the citizenship—the first Javolenus, I mean. Why did you think it was?"

"You said you had a British name, and Comittus sounded Latin to me," I answered. *"Comitia, comites, comitatus . . ."*

"That's only got one *t* sound in it. Completely different word." He gave me one of his sudden confidential grins. "At home they call me Comittus all the time; I'm only Lucius in the army. If you like, since you're not a Roman either, you can call me Comittus as well."

I nodded, and wondered if he realized how much he had just given away with that little word "either."

On the third day after leaving Dubris we arrived outside Londinium. Priscus wanted a day to conduct some business with the governor in the capital, but he did not want to take us into the city. He commandeered a house for himself and his lady, in a field with a clean stream in it about a mile south of the city, and next morning left us camped in the field while he rode in. He took a dozen of his dispatch riders but left the rest, and the century, under the command of Flavius Facilis and with instructions to keep an eye on us.

Eukairios asked permission to go into the city as well. "I could buy some tablets and some ink and writing leaves," he said. "And I'd like to look up some friends—with your permission, Lord Ariantes."

"You have friends in Londinium?" I asked. "Are there Christians there as well?"

He jumped, then gave an apologetic smile. "I forgot that you know. I wouldn't say the name, my lord, not so loudly! I was told a few names, and . . . and a password. I hoped . . ."

"See them if you wish. And buy the things. Buy yourself some better clothing, too. How much money do you need?"

He glanced down at his tunic with a surprised expression, as though the threadbare gray-brown patched thing were perfectly respectable. "How much better do you want it to be?" he asked.

I shrugged. "You know what a nobleman's slave should look like better than I. Buy what is fitting to my position."

He took a silver denarius for his writing supplies and twenty-five for new clothes.

"Is there anything else you wish to buy?" I asked him.

He stared at me a moment, then gave a sudden dry chuckle, stopped quickly in embarrassment. "You really don't know anything about slaves, do you, my lord?" he said. "I took a few sestertii more than I'm likely to need—and *I'm* honest."

I handed him three more sestertii. "Honesty is rewarded," I said. "Do you need to borrow a horse?"

He took the coins with pleasure and pushed them quickly into his purse. "Thank you very much, my lord! But you've forgotten that I can't ride."

It was still hard for me to remember that *anyone* could not ride. "Well then, walk—and enjoy Londinium. Stay in the city tonight, if you wish, but be back tomorrow morning."

When he was gone I went to the center of the camp, and I was there, discussing business with Arshak and Gatalas, when Aurelia Bodica came driving up in her little chariot. She had no attendants with her, not even her driver; she guided the white stallion herself, turning it neatly around the wagon shafts and past the tethered knots of horses, and drawing it to a smart halt in front of us. Her blue cloak had fallen back from her shoulders, her cheeks were flushed with the wind, and her eyes were dancing. "Princes of the Sarmatians!" she called, smiling at all of us. "I have come to ask you a favor."

Arshak instantly leapt forward and offered her his hand to help her down from the chariot; Gatalas, just a second behind him, had to content himself with catching the stallion's reins. "Lady Aurelia," Arshak said, smiling at her, "you need ask no favors, since we are yours to command."

"Oh, thank you, Lord Arshak! I've decided that I'd like to go into the city, and I need an escort. My husband has already gone, of course, and taken all the tribunes, so I've come to ask you if you could provide one."

"It would give me honor," replied Arshak at once. "I and my bodyguard will escort you."

"Lady Aurelia, your husband wished us to remain in the camp," I intervened. "Have you told the camp prefect what you want?"

She smiled at me, her eyes sparkling. "I have not. I know perfectly well what Facilis would say—'You can't trust Sarmatians; I'll give you a dozen legionaries.' But I'd much rather have an escort of Sarmatians. Legionaries are dull. If I went in with them, everyone would think I was a centurion's wife. But if I go in with Lord Arshak and his bodyguard, the whole city will be out on the streets staring, particularly if you put all your armor on. Please do put all your armor on! Why shouldn't we show off to the capital a bit? Don't worry about my husband being angry, Lord Ariantes. He won't punish you for leaving camp if you go with me."

Gatalas laughed. I cursed inwardly. From the way Bodica had phrased it, it sounded as though I were afraid of her husband. Perhaps she thought I was.

"Your husband's anger does not concern *me*, anyway," Arshak told her. "I am pleased to escort such a noble and beautiful lady, and I wish to see the city myself. Ariantes and Gatalas will remain here to look after the men, yes?"

"No," said Gatalas, "I will come too. I will leave Parspanakos" (the captain of his bodyguard) "in charge of the dragon, and I will take ten men."

I hesitated. I did not want to go into Londinium: I'd never liked cities, I didn't want to leave my followers unsupervised, and I'd resolved to avoid Aurelia Bodica. On the other hand, she thought I was afraid. Besides, if I didn't go and the other princes did, their troops would have yet another thing to hurl in the faces of my men—particularly after Aurelia Bodica's comment. "I will come as well, then," I said. "I do not wish to fail in the respect due to a legate's lady."

"Of course," she said, tossing her head. "So I shall ride into Londinium with three princes of the Sarmatians to escort me, one of them the nephew of a king! There are not many women can boast of that!"

So we all accompanied the legate's lady to Londinium, each of us with ten men from our bodyguard. Aurelia Bodica wanted to visit a temple and she wanted to go shopping. She had the length of silk Arshak had given her husband, and she wanted some of it unraveled and rewoven with linen thread, so that it would go further: Londinium, apparently, was the best place in Britain to have this done. She chatted pleasantly as we approached the city, about this, about the shops and the temples—but as we came up to the bridge that crosses the Tamesis River into the city, the talk became more serious.

"Londinium," she said, stopping her chariot just before the long wooden span and gesturing at the city beyond—the quays with the ships drawn up to them, the warehouses, the house roofs huddled behind. Across the river and to our left was a larger building with an elaborate facade. "That's the governor's palace," Bodica said, pointing to it. "Tiberius will be there now." She shook the reins and started the chariot forward again. "But you can't see the bridge from the palace. All the windows look inward. Very Roman, I think, to study your own imported magnificence rather than the circumstances of the province around you. Look there!"

She pointed along our bank of the river, to our left. There was a cross fixed in the mud by the waterside, with a tattered mass of flesh and bone sagging from it. A few birds fluttered about it, pecking.

"They often leave the bodies of criminals there," Bodica told us. "As a warning. You can't see them from the governor's palace, either. When my ancestress, the queen of the Iceni, sacked Londinium, she hung up the bodies of . . . Roman nobles . . . along the same bank. Hundreds of bodies."

Arshak's face sharpened. "She sacked the Roman capital, this queen? She had many followers?"

"Oh, very many! In those days the whole island longed to throw off the Roman yoke and live free under its own kings and queens. We were a race of noble warriors then, like your own people." As we rode into Londinium she recounted the story of Queen Boudica of the Iceni: how an unjust Roman official had ordered her to be flogged and her daughters raped; how she'd raised the South against the Romans and sacked the two greatest cities; how finally she had been defeated in a fierce battle; how she'd taken poison rather than grace a Roman triumph. It was a tale of courage and desperate heroism, and I was moved by it despite myself.

"That was a long time ago," Bodica finished quietly. "More than a century now. The British horse has been broken to the yoke now, and pulls the cart quietly—except in the North, where it still frets a little. I expect that, in time, your own people will be yoked beside it."

We all stiffened at that. "Our people have never been conquered!" Arshak said fiercely.

"But you're here," she pointed out—sadly.

"We are the price our people paid for a truce. My uncle is still king of the Sarmatians. The emperor hates him, but the emperor had to make terms with him nonetheless. Our nation is noble, not one of slaves."

Bodica bowed her golden head. "At times," she whispered, "I wish my own people could say the same."

Her voice was soft and sad—but there was a look in her eyes that contradicted that softness. It was like that of a wrestler who's found his opponent's weakness. Arshak noticed nothing: he was plainly enjoying himself. As we rode off the bridge into the city, the citizens did indeed run out into the street to stare at us, and he preened himself in their gaze. Bodica began to ask him about his own battles against the Romans, and soon the talk was of struggles and scalping. Gatalas was less happy, but largely because he had fewer scalps to boast of. I was not happy at all. My old distrust was back, stronger than ever, and I wanted only to get away.

"You're very silent, Lord Ariantes," Bodica said at last. "You've said barely ten words together to me since Durovernum. Have I offended you?"

I bowed my head. "Not in the least, Lady. You have shown me much honor."

"Are you keeping quiet, then, because you don't like boasting? From all I've heard, you've done as much damage to your enemies as Lord Arshak, if not more."

"Our brave raids against the enemy," I said harshly, "provoked a terrible war in which our people suffered defeat. I see no point in boasting of it."

The eager, satisfied, warlike look vanished from the faces of my listeners. The lady frowned; Gatalas became sullen; Arshak looked angry.

"I am proud to have fought for our people!" Arshak declared. "We were defeated, but we have never been conquered!"

The Romans didn't want to conquer us, I thought. They had no way to govern a people without cities. If we hadn't raided them, they would have kept the peace; because we had, they'd considered not conquest, but extermination. It was our own greed, for goods and for glory, that brought ruin on us, and that the ruin had not been greater was due as much to a Roman rebellion in the East as to our own courage. But I couldn't say that to Arshak without offending him.

"What good does it do us to recall this now?" I said instead. "We have all sworn on fire to serve Rome, and if we remember how we fought her, it will only make it harder for us."

"Is servitude what you want?" asked Bodica.

I had my answer to that this time. "Our heirs in our own country are free. For ourselves, it does not matter: we are dead men, all of us."

"You don't look dead to me," commented Bodica, smiling again.

"We're only dead in our own country," replied Arshak, smiling back at her. "Here beyond the stream of Ocean, even Ariantes will have to come back to life in the end, little as he wishes to. Be gentle, Lady: he isn't used to living with defeat. None of us are."

"But why should you think that here beyond the ocean, freedom and glory have become luxuries you can't afford?" Her smile was still directed at me, but her eyes had slid over to meet Arshak's.

"I don't," said Arshak vehemently—and suddenly they were allies. A part of me cried out its agreement with them, and urged me to join them, to accept the hinted offer now, quickly, before it was too late. I think I would have if I'd had only myself to decide for, despite the oath I'd sworn at Aquincum. I had five hundred others, though, who would be bound by my agreement, and because of them I could not choose rashly. Besides, I had, still, the sense that we were being played upon. Bodica was no more a Sarmatian than Facilis was, and enmity to Rome did not make her our friend.

WHEN BODICA HAD visited her temple I excused myself, saying that there ought to be at least one senior officer in the camp—though I left five men with her to make it clear that I was not afraid of the legate. The other five and I started back.

We weren't used to cities. The narrow streets of close-set houses, crowding windowless over the road, confused us, and we wandered helplessly for a while, looking for some familiar landmark. I eventually stopped and asked a shopkeeper for directions to the bridge.

"You mean the bridge to Ladybank?" he asked.

"It is the one that crosses the Tamesis," I replied.

"To Ladybank," he agreed, nodding. "You go back down to the corner and turn right, then left, and it'll be there in front of you."

"I thank you."

The shopkeeper looked up at me curiously as I gathered the reins again. "We call the other side Ladybank," he told me. "On account of all the ladies hung up there when Queen Boudica sacked the city."

I paused.

He nodded, pleased at seeing a foreigner suddenly so intent on his local knowledge. "You're not from Britain, are you? You've heard of Queen Boudica?"

"A little."

"You'll have heard, then, that she sacked Londinium. Well, they say that when the old queen took the city, the men were already dead defending it, so she revenged herself on the women. She had the wives and daughters of the Roman citizens stripped, tortured, mutilated, and impaled along the bank there. So it's been called Ladybank ever since."

"I thank you," I repeated. I nodded to him, and started in the direction he'd indicated.

Why, I wondered, had Aurelia Bodica left the cruel executions out of her hero tale and implied that the bodies were those of dead Roman officials? Because she admired her ancestress and believed no evil of her? Or because she knew that cruelty to defeated prisoners would offend her audience and lose their sympathy for the British cause?

We found the bridge, and I left it behind me with a sense of relief. The commandeered house was near the road, with the legionary tents pitched in a neat square in its stable yard; our own camp was behind. When I rode up to the road gate I found Facilis standing there fuming.

"Where are the others?" he demanded, "Where's the lady Aurelia Julii? Why did you go into the city, may the gods destroy it?"

He must have deliberately decided to call her by her husband's name; I'd heard nobody else use it. I told him where everyone was, and he swore again. "The lady's husband offered her an escort this morning, a *Roman* escort. She said she had a headache and wanted to stay quietly in the house for the day! She's left her little slave girl confined to the house in tears, and her driver sulking in the stables. May I perish if I know what she's up to!"

I shrugged and gestured for my men to go on back to their wagons.

Facilis looked at them sourly as they jingled past. "She was parading you, I suppose, like a triumphant general," he said. "I hope you enjoyed it."

"I did not," I replied. I sat for a moment looking down at Facilis. I had no love for the man, but he was shrewd and perceptive, a party to Roman debates from which I was excluded—and he plainly didn't trust Aurelia Bodica any more than I did myself. "You think, then, that she is 'up to' something," I said quietly.

Facilis let out a long breath through his nose. "I don't say anything against a legate's lady, Ariantes. Remember that."

"Lucius Javolenus Comittus admires her greatly. The other two tribunes are . . . unhappy at the mention of her."

"Afraid, you mean." Facilis' voice had dropped to a whisper now, and I had to pull my helmet off to hear him. "They, and most of the lads, are afraid of her. And I don't quite know why."

"Javolenus Comittus is a native Briton," I said, slowly. "He is related to her. The others are of Italian descent."

"And she's a descendant of the native royalty." Facilis glanced round, then came over and caught my stirrup. "May I perish, Ariantes, I don't know Britain any better than you do. I'm a Pannonian and I've never been here before. There's something going on, all right, underneath what they actually say and do, but I don't understand it and I can't make it out. The fact that she's native royalty is part of it, but not all of it by any means. All the lads in the century here are British-born and most of them are from the northern tribes, the ones that have had risings a generation or two ago, but they're good lads, loyal to the emperor. And they're afraid of her."

I dismounted and stood facing him, holding Farna's bridle. "And my people?"

He gave a hiss between his teeth. "So you've seen it. Yes, she's after you, all right. You in particular, but Arshak and Gatalas as well. She's asked and asked about all of you. It could be innocent curiosity, but it isn't."

"In Britain, queens have led armies."

"Just like Sarmatians. I'd feel pretty damned unhappy if a Sarmatian princess were married to a legate on the Danube. But it's much more complicated here. On the Danube, we were on one side of the river and you were on the other, and we all knew who was who. Here everything's all muddled up."

"Southern tribesmen in togas," I agreed, "and northerners, so you say, in strip armor."

We looked at each other for a moment. "What do the other two think about the lady Aurelia Julii?" he asked.

"They think she is a noble and beautiful lady, of royal blood, and they are pleased to find a commander's wife suited to their own dignity. They are flattered at her attention."

"Arrogant bastards! Them and their damned ancestors!"

I shook my head. "You should not say that to me, Flavius Facilis. It will . . ."

He joined me on the end of the phrase. ". . . only make trouble! Very well, very well, you're an aristocratic bastard yourself, and I'll keep my plebeian mouth shut about your ancestors. At least you've got more sense than the rest of them."

"What does the legate think?" I asked. That was the real question.

"Lord Julius Priscus is forty-two and a widower. He married the lady last year. He thinks she is wonderfully beautiful and the cleverest woman he's ever met, and he thinks she's after your lot to help him manage you. I don't know. Perhaps she is. They were all shaken to hear the truth about Sarmatians, and they still don't really believe it." He stared at me for another moment, then said, "I'd have expected you to jump at what she's offering, whatever it is. You're no friend of Rome, and maybe here's your chance to play 'divide and rule' for yourself."

"I have sworn oaths, Flavius Facilis. And . . ."

And, and. And I didn't like the woman. I couldn't explain why, even to myself. I'd known her only a few days. But I did not like that assessing gaze and the probing questions, and liked them even less coupled with the sweet smiles and girlish enthusiasm, the delicate touch of her hand against my face. To my people, lying is worse than murder, and too much of what she did had the sweetly foul scent of deceit. It was unfair, perhaps, to regard her with so much suspicion. I had dug for information myself, of late, and taken advantage where I could, of Comittus, of Eukairios, of Natalis to some extent. But still, I wanted to keep myself and my people away from her.

"I would have thought that you would . . . like her better yourself, Flavius Facilis," I finished instead. "Perhaps she is, as you say, trying to manage us."

"Perhaps she is," he agreed. "But I don't believe that any more than you do. Maybe it's just because I'm a stranger here, and notice things the others take for granted. And, I admit, there's another reason, which is no reason at all to suspect a woman of . . . whatever. I don't like the way she treats that little girl she has to do her hair. I could hear it, at Natalis' house and here as well. 'Please, my lady, I didn't mean to, my lady, please, no, please . . .' and the sound of the damned woman using the stick."

"What had the girl done?" I asked, shocked.

"Nothing. Got a curl out of place when she did her mistress's hair, or brought washing water that was cold. Crack, crack, crack, and the girl sobbing. Can't be more than sixteen. I wouldn't treat a healthy young recruit that way, let alone a skinny little girl—and one that's pregnant too, by the look of her. It makes me sick. Where's your slave?"

"You need not ask that now, Facilis, in the same breath," I told him, in a low voice, beginning to be angry. "He is in Londinium, shopping and visiting friends."

He looked at me a moment longer. "No," he said, finally, "I shouldn't have said that in the same breath. You wouldn't hit a slave. Even that business in Budalia" (the rope and dagger incident) "shows that. You wouldn't cut down a man that had dropped his sword and was using his shield as a stretcher for a wounded friend, either."

"Who says that I have?" I demanded, now openly angry.

"No one. One of you bastards did—but I guess it wasn't you." He turned and stalked back toward the house, slashing at the weeds along the road with his vine-stalk baton.

I remounted Farna and cantered back to the wagons. Now I knew how his son had died. It was some relief to know that, after all, the killer had not been me.

Arshak and Gatalas returned from the city late in the afternoon. They were in a loud and exuberant mood, laughing with each other over the sights of Londinium and the charm of Aurelia Bodica. But Banadaspos, who was second in the bodyguard and who'd been in charge of the five men I'd left in the city, seemed annoyed about something. I asked him what had happened, and he shrugged and said they had simply escorted the lady around the shops. "She is a very lovely lady, the legate's lady," he said, "and from what I could understand, very clever as well. But she's not good with horses."

He himself was very good with horses, the best in the whole dragon. I'd taken him into my bodyguard because of his skill with them, although he was a commoner by birth, and made him second to Leimanos because of his intelligence, his loyalty, and because I liked him. "What do you mean?" I asked him.

He shrugged again. "That stallion she has for her chariot smelled a mare in the marketplace. It kept trying to get to her, neighing and kicking at the traces. Well, stallions will! But she lost her temper and took the whip to it, and dragged at the reins until its mouth was dripping with blood. She has a bit on that bridle like a steel trap. What is the point of treating an animal like that? Any of us could have brought it around for her if she'd let us. If she can't manage a stallion, she ought to get a driver who can, or use a gelding or a mare. I tell you, my prince, I can't bear to see a good horse mishandled, and in my opinion the other commanders shouldn't have allowed her to do it."

"I don't think she likes admitting there's something she can't do," I replied. "And she likes asking for help even less."

"You're undoubtedly right," Banadaspos agreed at once. "But these Britons are all hopeless with horses."

VI

*E*UKAIRIOS RETURNED FROM Londinium next morning, in a good blue tunic and a checked cloak fastened with a fine bronze pin; he looked much more respectable and seemed very much more cheerful. We struck camp and continued north toward Eburacum.

For all my forebodings, the journey passed peacefully. Shamed by Eukairios' earnest attempts to learn Sarmatian, the bodyguard asked him to help them with their Latin—they all spoke the language a little, but none spoke it well. Every evening they would sit about the fire cross-legged, mending and cleaning their weapons and their armor, while the scribe pretended that they were visiting a dairy, or an armorer's, or a horse trader's, and got them to say the appropriate phrases. Before we reached Eburacum they had all forgiven him for being a blot on my reputation, and Banadaspos had grown sufficiently friendly to begin to teach him riding. Eukairios had no gift for it at all, and rather puzzled Banadaspos by the number of times he fell off.

At Eburacum, where we once again camped outside the city, a couple of my men did quarrel with a couple of Gatalas', but they fought their duels quietly with blunted weapons, and a broken arm was the worst injury endured on either side. I managed to avoid any private meeting with the legate's lady, and was relieved to escape her. She would remain in the fortress with her husband while I continued to my posting on the Wall.

Arshak was, predictably, furious when he understood that he and his company were to remain in Eburacum, particularly when he gathered that the greatest chance of action was farther north. But his liaison officer managed to soothe him with murmurs about a possible posting elsewhere, in time, and Bodica smiled at him, and in the end, even he accepted it quietly.

The division of our companies happened almost too casually, seeing that we'd journeyed so far together and were such a long way from home. "After all," Gatalas and I said to Arshak, when we parted in Eburacum, "we'll be only a few days' ride to the north, and under the same commander in chief. We'll meet often."

"After all," Gatalas and I said to each other, when we reached the supply base of Corstopitum a few days later, "we'll be only a day's ride from each other's camps. We'll have to meet for hunting trips, or let our dragons compete at mounted games." And he and his dragon turned east to Condercum, while I and mine turned west toward Cilurnum, and I never saw him again.

It was just my own dragon and the two Roman officers, Comittus and Facilis, who trotted the last few miles along the old road from Corstopitum, late in the afternoon of a golden day of late September. We went up the valley of the Tinea River—pleasant, rolling country, with patches of woodland; the trees were beginning to turn, and the blackberries beside the road were ripe. Northward we would sometimes get a glimpse of the uplands of Caledonia, purple with heather and spotted with sheep; cattle and horses grazed contentedly on the richer grass of the valley. At the place where the Tinea forks, one branch running from west to east along the valley, and the other descending to it from the north, we turned northward from the old road toward the new military way, and almost at once came to the Wall. Three times the height of a man, built of a golden sandstone, it strode off east and west as far as we could see. It crossed the river on top of a bridge that was built of the same stone and ran directly into the walls of Cilurnum. I stopped, looking at the fort, and Comittus and Facilis, who were riding beside me on the road, stopped too. Behind us, the drummer gave the signal to halt.

"That's the bathhouse," said Comittus, pointing at a building just outside the fort by the river. He'd visited the place before. "It's a good one. The water's good at Cilurnum, too—there's an aqueduct that carries it right through the camp from end to end, and flushes the latrines. And there's a water mill under the bridge, which grinds all the grain for the fort . . ." He coughed. "If you want grain, that is."

I nodded. My heart had risen at the sight of Cilurnum. The fort itself was the standard affair: a rectangular wall, four gates, watchtowers. I knew that inside it there would be the usual two main streets, the usual headquarters building and commandant's house facing each other in the center, and the usual narrow barrack blocks laid out in neat grids. It was, I knew, more than half-empty. It had been manned by an auxiliary *ala*, the Second

Asturian Horse, but most of them had been posted elsewhere, and there were only some five squadrons remaining. A village of the kind found around every Roman fort sprawled messily to the south. But the fort's setting beside the shallow brown river was beautiful, and to its north there were meadows—lush, intensely green, dotted with large trees. "We can put the wagons there," I said, pointing to them.

Comittus and Facilis both looked at me, Comittus in surprise and Facilis in exasperation. "You won't need the wagons anymore," Comittus told me. "You know yourself that all the letters have been written and everything's arranged. The Second Asturian Horse have left plenty of space in the barracks for you and them both."

"You're going to have to start sleeping in houses sometime, Ariantes," said Facilis. "We can't have Roman auxiliaries parked in wagons behind their own fort. Particularly not on the wrong side of the Wall."

I set my teeth, looking at the stone walls. I thought of sleeping in them, night after night. I thought of watching the seasons change, fixed in the same place, unmoving, buried like the dead. I had known that the Romans would expect us to follow their ways now, that they would ride us, as the saying is, with the curb bit and the iron bridle. Facilis was going to be in charge of the ordering of the camp, and the remaining Asturians were subordinate to Comittus. There were thousands of Roman troops in the region, more than enough to put down any mutiny. But this change was too great and too sudden, and as I looked from the walls back to my companions, I felt all at once certain that it was not something I had to bear. Comittus and Facilis might use force against us for many reasons—but this wasn't one of them.

"Not tonight," I said. "Not yet." I snapped my fingers for the drummer to give the signal and started Farna forward again. The drums rattled, and the dragon began clattering and jingling after me.

"But . . . really . . . I mean . . ." said Comittus, spurring after us, "barracks are much more *comfortable* . . ."

They did not give up easily. We rode into the fort—we had to, to get to the fields, since the Wall cut us off from them. There the senior decurion of the remaining squadrons of the Second Asturian Horse came hurrying to meet us, followed by his men and most of the inhabitants of the village. (Despite their name, the Asturians were not from Asturica in Iberia; their *ala* had been raised there originally, but that had been a long time ago, and they themselves were mostly born in the village.) The decurion was a mournful-looking dark man of about my own age, named Gaius Flavinus Longus—I strongly suspected that "Longus" was a nickname, as he was one of the tallest and thinnest men I'd seen. Comittus and Facilis rushed the polite greetings and at once enlisted his help to explain to me why we couldn't sleep in our wagons. He had put a considerable amount of work into getting the barracks ready for us, and argued more hotly than either of the others. I nodded, ignored them all, and took the men out the other gate of the fort into the fields. The three Roman officers, with most of the Asturians and villagers, followed us, exclaiming in amazement at our obstinate savagery.

"You bastards don't even entrench!" Facilis shouted at me, while I held Farna in the place I'd chosen for the main fire and waved the wagons round. "Listen, Ariantes, you'll have the damned villagers in and out of here every hour of the day and night, and half of them are thieves! And what are you going to do about latrines?"

"Lend us a few shovels, and we'll dig a spur from the ones in the fort," I replied, not looking at him.

"You're entitled to the commandant's house, you know," Comittus coaxed. "At least, we could share it. It's a big house, and it has a hypocaust and a private bathhouse with a steam room, and the last man there put in a very fine floor on the dining room . . ."

"Comittus," I said, "when I was in my own country and a prince, I did not have a big house with a mosaic floor. I do not need or want one now. Perhaps in the winter, if it is very cold, barracks and hypocausts may seem worthwhile. Not tonight."

"May I perish!" exclaimed Longus, exasperated at seeing all his preparations for us laid waste. "What sort of people have they sent us?"

I looked at him. "They have sent you Sarmatians," I told him. "We are accustomed to live in wagons."

"They've sent us a pack of raving lunatics! Who else would prefer filthy carts to good stone barracks blocks? Oh, *now* I know what the problem is! You've mistaken Cilurnum for the madhouse you escaped from!"

The Asturians, and the villagers, laughed. My men heard it. They interpreted the comment to each other. I noticed Facilis' face losing its red, swollen look as he became alarmed. He had called us similar things, and worse—but he was a senior officer, and knew exactly how far he could go, and in what circumstances. He would never have used language like that in front of an audience that understood.

I looked at Longus thoughtfully. He'd climbed onto his horse to greet us, and he was armed and wearing a shirt of mail. But he was off guard. "You should not insult us, Flavinus Longus," I told him quietly. "Remember we must work together." I raised my hand to keep my men still.

"I can say what I li—" began Longus.

Farna leapt sideways at a touch of my heel, and I swept my lance out and across to knock the decurion off his mount backwards. I turned my horse almost on top of him, and drove the point of the lance into the earth about two inches from his shoulder. By the time he'd recoiled from it, I had my sword out and at his throat. "No killing!" I shouted in Sarmatian. It had been sudden enough that the Asturians were all still gaping, and my men had not yet tried anything on their own. But I could hear the sound of the bows being strung behind me.

"You should not insult us," I told Longus again. He looked up the sword blade into my eyes. His face had gone gray. "If you ask Marcus Flavius Facilis, he will tell you how we deal with those who insult us. You should not have said that, on first meeting us, in front of all your men and mine. It was foolish. But I am sure you would not have said it if you knew us better, and you regret it now." I took my sword away from his throat and put it back in its sheath, then pulled my lance up and backed Farna away.

Longus picked himself up, still looking gray. One of my men had caught his mount, and I nodded for it to be returned. It was probably just as well we'd had a small, manageable incident of this kind. The Asturians had obviously needed to have it pointed out to them that it was dangerous to speak to Sarmatians as they would to Romans. I was sorry to have humiliated Longus, but at least he was junior to me and would have to admit to himself, when he'd calmed down, that he should not have used that tone to the commander of another unit, however stupidly he thought I was behaving.

"We swore to the emperor that we would fight for him," I told the Romans. "We did not swear to sleep in tombs. We must already learn to patrol and guard, to stay in one place, to use money. We must learn another language and another way of life. This we can and will do. Flavius Facilis, we can build a palisade, if you want to keep people out of our camp; we can make adjustments. But you must forbear a little."

They gave in, though Facilis still muttered darkly about latrines, and we parked the wagons in the field, loosed the horses, and settled down into a new life.

THE FIRST MONTHS we spent in Cilurnum were all I could have hoped for: quiet and monotonous. All my forebodings about trouble in the North seemed utterly misplaced. We could test the shape of our new position with very little to disturb us. The legate had given orders that the men were not to leave the fort—which we interpreted to mean not just the fort itself, but the village and fields attached to it—without the permission of the camp prefect. This was a measure to control us and protect the civilians of the region, but I was glad of it: it gave us a chance to learn the customs of the land before we entered it.

The chief business of the fort was the collection of tolls. Cilurnum was the official crossing point for neighboring people with business on the other side of the Wall, and it also provided the main bridge over the north Tinea River. Every day a trickle of shepherds drove flocks through the gates, and on market days there would be a crowd of carts, all paying their copper to the men on duty to be allowed to cross.

The fort was also responsible for manning six milecastles—small fortlets that were built every mile along the Wall. The milecastles, in turn, manned the watchtowers, where the sentries could sit watching the sheep on the hills northward. We sent men out to the milecastles for ten days at a time, and rotated them squadron by squadron. The squadrons not on watch were assigned chores about the camp—though these generally did not take up much time, once the work of building a palisade for our camp and digging latrines had been finished. I suggested to Facilis and Comittus that we buy some flocks and herds of our own, which would not only keep us supplied with meat, milk, and woolens, but also give the men something more to do. I was told that Roman soldiers were not allowed to herd or farm the land. Instead, one had to invent work for them—drilling, extra patrols, competitions. It seemed ridiculous to me, but I had to go along with it, if only to keep my dragon from squabbling with the Asturians.

If my men weren't very busy, I was, and quarrels with the Asturians were the chief thing that occupied me. The Asturians, my troops reckoned, were perfect to quarrel with, much better than Gatalas' men. Their spears were shorter, they couldn't shoot, they didn't wear nearly as much armor, and they weren't as skillful on horseback as we were: they were opponents who could reliably be beaten. My men were soon swaggering at the very sight of the poor auxiliaries. It was amazing how little Latin they needed to start a fight. And there was trouble, as I'd anticipated, with drink and women—the fort village had a collection of taverns and two brothels. Still, it could have been worse. The Asturians were so clumsy that no one actually needed to kill them, and I was allowed to impose punishments on my followers myself, rather than yield them to the Asturians for floggings and forced marches. I explained to the men that this would change if the Romans thought they were out of control, but even so I had a constant struggle to keep the most imperfect peace. I had to disgrace some of my men by taking back gifts I had given them and bestowing them instead on the Romans they'd injured, and one man I had to dismiss from my bodyguard for provoking trouble.

Longus was better at it than I was. Despite his mournful appearance, he had a keen sense of humor, and he told jokes against himself with a straight face and toneless voice that had his friends roaring. When I was faced with a quarrel, I could only give orders or administer justice: if he got to a quarrel in time, it dissolved in laughter instead of blows. Far from holding a grudge against me for knocking him off his horse the first time we met, he turned the incident into one of his favorite stories: "Next thing I knew, I'd fallen from my mare's rump like a lump of manure, and Ariantes sticks the spear he did it with next to my neck, chunk! and looks along his sword at me with an expression on his face like he's considering what bit to chop off first. I thought my last hour had come. Oh gods and goddesses, I thought to myself, get me out of this one and I'll never say a word against carts again, so help me Epona, goddess of horseflesh. And then he says, very reasonable and soft-spoken, 'You should not have insulted us,' and you know? I couldn't agree with him more; I want to nod, like that, but there's this sword at my throat, and I'm worried a nod will have consequences, if you take my meaning . . ."

I learned very quickly to value Longus. In fact, I liked all the men I worked with at Cilurnum, except Facilis, and even he no longer quarreled with me. Comittus had been friendly from the first, and once he'd agreed to take the commandant's house and leave me in my wagon, we got on well. Bouncy and inexperienced he might have been, but he was able and intelligent underneath it, and understood what the British were thinking far better than the rest of us.

After the first month or so, I sent Eukairios to live in the slaves' quarters of the commandant's house, as it was clear from his wistful look every time we left it that he far preferred stone walls to a wagon now that the winter was drawing in. Leimanos was unhappy with this: though he now quite liked the scribe, he still didn't trust him. "I think he is loyal to you in his own way, my prince," he told me, "but he's a slave, with a slave's courage. If the Romans order him to, he'll tell them anything he knows." But I wanted Eukairios to be content in my service. Besides, there were no secrets in the work I gave him: all the letters I had him write were to Romans. He had made an inventory of the goods I'd brought with me in my wagon, and reported that I had enough to buy the goodwill of the administration with plenty left in reserve, so we set out to arrange pay and conditions for the men to my liking, and distributed gold by the handful. In this I relied on Eukairios absolutely. He had an astonishing memory. Our language was his fourth, and he mastered it in only a few months and learned everything there was to know about the northern army at the same time. He knew who were the best officials to write to about what, and how much one should give them to make them friendly. I was satisfied at Cilurnum that autumn, despite the dragon's quarrels with the *ala*. But that satisfaction was shattered by Gatalas.

It was a chill, damp day early in December when I heard the news, and we'd had one of the ridiculous competitions. We'd divided into teams, with some Sarmatians and some Asturians on each team in the hope that this would reconcile them to one another, and played a game that involved much cantering about in full armor and the mud, hurling blunted spears—casting javelins was about the only thing the Asturians could do better than us. Now the men had gone off to steam away the mud and cold in the public bath-house, and the senior officers were doing the same in the commandant's bathhouse. Comittus and Longus sprawled along the benches; Leimanos, Banadaspos, and one of my captains, the dragon's priest Kasagos, whom I'd brought with me, sat cross-legged with their eyes half-shut against the heat. (Leimanos and Banadaspos usually came on such occasions, and Kasagos' squadron had distinguished itself in the game.) Facilis sat off to one side, elbows on knees, squat and silent. He had become the one who was out of place now, an aging foot soldier among the young cavalry officers, and he usually bathed, left, and went home before the rest of us. The exercise had gone well, and we were all tired but pleased.

"We ought to finish up the day with a few drinks," said Longus. "Or even a few drinks and a bit of action. Fortunatus has a couple of new girls."

"Any good?" asked Comittus.

Longus rolled his eyes. "I like the Greek. Trufosa, she's called. Little and dainty and hot as pepper—or so they say. I haven't been honored yet. You ought to go, Ariantes. Fortunatus has said that if you come, you can have any girl you like, for free."

"So that my men will go to his brothel rather than the other one?"

"I doubt it. They're not short of Sarmatian custom as it is. Every time I've been in there recently, the place has been full of drunks weeping into their wine as they tell the girls about the beautiful horses they had to leave behind." He clasped an imaginary cup in both hands, looked more mournful than ever, and began lamenting a lost horse in extravagant terms and a wickedly accurate Sarmatian accent. Kasagos and Leimanos laughed. Longus rolled his eyes, sighed deeply, and declared, still in a Sarmatian voice, "I miss my vife sometime, too." Banadaspos, who hadn't found the lament funny, realized at this that it was a joke, and laughed too. "No," continued Longus, in his own voice now, "Fortunatus just wants to give his place a bit of class. Patronized by princes and senior officers! But a couple of the girls have said they'd be delighted to oblige you any time. Lupicilla still goes into floods of giggles at the thought of you knocking me off my horse. You really ought to come."

I looked at him tolerantly. "Thank you, thank Fortunatus, no."

If the goddess of love herself had appeared to me, naked and golden and smelling of myrrh, I would have fallen on my knees before her and begged her to give me Tirgatao. I wanted, I wanted desperately, but a man who's parched with thirst cannot eat bread.

The door to the steam room opened suddenly, and Eukairios came in. "My lord," he said to me, "may I speak to you a moment?"

I gestured for him to sit, but he remained standing. He glanced at the door, which he was holding open. I got up and went toward the changing room to get my clothes.

Facilis picked his head up. "What is it?" he asked suspiciously.

"A piece of news, Lord Facilis," Eukairios answered politely. "If I may just speak with my master . . ."

"Wait a minute, man. If it's so important it can't wait until your master's out of the steam room, it's important enough that the rest of us need to hear it too."

Eukairios looked at me nervously. "What has happened?" I asked him.

He shook his head and closed the door. "In the post this evening there was a letter for me from . . . from a correspondent of mine in Corstopitum. It said . . . I am sorry, my lord. Your friend Lord Gatalas is dead."

"Dead?" I asked, in horror. "How?"

"In a mutiny against the authorities," Eukairios admitted miserably. "Apparently, two days ago he quarreled with the camp prefect of Condercum and with his liaison officer. He turned them out of the fort, so they went at once to the neighboring forts, collected troops, and marched back to Condercum. He came out of the fort this morning with just his bodyguard, thirty-two men. They thought that he wanted to negotiate with them—but he'd come out to die. He'd ordered the rest of his dragon in Condercum to surrender, but rode out to battle himself. He and the thirty-two killed four times their number, including the camp prefect, before they were killed themselves. The rest of his men have surrendered and are under arrest in Condercum."

"Marha!" I whispered. I bowed my head, blinking at it: Gatalas dead.

"Why didn't anyone tell us?" cried Leimanos, jumping furiously to his feet.

"Don't be stupid!" snapped Facilis. "It was over in two days. And no one would tell you anyway. You'd have gone to help him. A hundred and twenty Roman soldiers dead. Gods and goddesses! I tried to tell them!"

I went out into the changing room and began to put my clothes on. "Leimanos," I said, "we need to summon all the men."

"What do you think you're going to do?" asked Facilis, pushing his way out after me.

"You think it better that they hear this in the taverns?" I asked, fastening my muddy trousers. I picked up my shirt and glared at the centurion. "You need have no fear, Flavius Facilis. I will not throw away the lives of my men chasing vengeance. As for Gatalas, he revenged himself." I pulled the shirt over my head.

"Revenged himself for what?" demanded Facilis. "For being sent to a cavalry fort in pleasant country, well fed, well housed, well paid? A hundred and twenty Romans dead! And most likely because of a few words!"

"It needed forbearance!" I returned. "He was willing to keep his oaths if he could trust his commanders." I sat down and pulled my boots on. Banadaspos was weeping as he did the same; Kasagos was muttering a prayer for the dead; Leimanos was dangerously silent. "Eukairios, as soon as I've spoken to the men, we need to write some letters."

Eukairios coughed. "The letter that told me this . . . it came with some dispatches. They arrived by special courier. That's why I had to see you at once."

For a moment I couldn't think what he meant. Then I understood: the dispatches had included orders to Comittus, Longus, and Facilis to arrest me, disarm my men, and confine us all to camp.

I turned to the Romans. "If the dispatches tell you to do anything," I whispered, "do not do it yet! Please. Give me a chance to calm things down. Longus, if my men hear of this in the taverns, they will set on yours and there will be bloodshed. I need to assemble the dragon and speak to them all tonight. Tomorrow morning we can sacrifice to Marha and read the divining rods, and also pray for our friends' souls. After that you can do what you like. The men will be steadier and will not do anything foolish."

The three others were silent for a long moment. Then Longus said, "We weren't going to read the dispatches tonight—were we, Comittus?"

"No," agreed Comittus, understanding at once, "no—we've had a tiring day, and it's getting late. We were planning to have a few drinks and get some rest."

"And we can't open them tomorrow morning, either," Longus continued. "If you're having some ceremony to worship the gods, obviously we ought to join in. The dispatches can wait until lunchtime."

I looked at Facilis.

"May the gods destroy those dispatches!" he said. "I'm certainly not reading them tonight. I'm going straight to bed."

"I thank you all," I said, warmly, then grabbed my coat and hurried out into the chill dampness of the night to assemble my men.

When the drums had dragged them from the bathhouse, taverns, and brothels of Cilurnum, they heard the news with groans of dismay and wails of grief. There were no shouts of anger, though, and the promise of a sacrifice in the morning, and the chance of reconciling everything with the will of the gods, reassured them. They went to bed reminding each other that the divining rods had promised Gatalas death in battle, but had offered them, and Gatalas' dragon, life and prosperity. I was aware, during the night, that the Asturians were mounting a guard on the fort walls overlooking our wagons— but it was unobtrusive enough that no one was offended.

We were woken before dawn by the sound of trumpets in the fort sounding the call to arms. I rushed out of my wagon, jumped on the nearest horse without bothering to saddle it, and galloped wildly up to the gate, cursing silently. I was sure that the Romans must have decided to read the dispatches after all, and I was afraid of the consequences. But as I reached the north gate, Comittus' messenger came rushing out of it. "Lord Ariantes!" he shouted, waving his arms so that my horse reared up and put its ears back. "Lord Ariantes, the tribune wants you to come at once! And give the *numerus* the signal to arm! The barbarians have crossed the Wall!"

IT WAS VERY strange, setting out with Roman troops to catch a party of barbarian raiders. I had imagined it before—the raising of the alarm, the rush to arms, the gallop across country in what was hoped to be the right direction, the snippets of news gained from frightened shepherds or farmers, and finally the moment when you crest a hill and see the enemy there beyond you. I had imagined it because I was curious to know what it must be like for them, my opponents. Living it for myself was so like what I had anticipated that it felt unreal, as though I were imagining it again.

The signal fires told us to go east; the shepherds and farmers we questioned told us that there were "thousands" of the raiders. We left the road and moved across the hills to the north, sending out scouts to locate the enemy. In fact, we might have dispensed with their services: the enemy made no effort to conceal themselves. We arrived at the town of Corstopitum, the principal town of the region, to find it overrun. It was the beginning of December, a dull gray day, but not too cold: we stopped at the edge of a slate-colored wood and looked down at a city surrounded, smoking here and there with fires.

Corstopitum had been built as an army fort to control the bridge over the Tinea River, where the main road north meets the main road west. The fort was decommissioned when the Wall was built just north of it, then recommissioned for use as a supply base: in the time between the two events, the thriving city had grown so much that the old fort had been swallowed up, and the new one had to be laid out as two irregular enclosures on either side of the main road north, instead of the neat rectangle used everywhere else. The bridge was now held by a large party of invading cavalry—we could see the gleam of their whitewashed shields—and the fort appeared to be under attack: the fires were concentrated about it, and the marketplace before it was full of armed men.

Longus, who had been riding beside me, groaned. "They're after our pay," he said.

It seemed that the quarterly pay for all the men stationed at all the forts along the eastern Wall was distributed from Corstopitum, and that this huge sum of money was almost certainly inside the besieged fortress. The garrison at Corstopitum was an auxiliary *ala* called the First Thracians, a part-mounted force of five hundred men. It could be assumed that the number of the raiders was at least twice as great, or they would not have attacked at all.

Comittus bit his lip and struggled to control his horse. He had been pale and feverish with excitement during the ride, and his mood had communicated itself to his flashy black stallion, which was snorting and fighting with the bit. "There hasn't been a raid this big for years and years," he said unhappily.

Facilis snorted. "A quarter's pay for four thousand men's a tempting target. I doubt they meant to fight us as well as the Thracians for it, though."

One of my scouts galloped up and drew rein. "They are all in the town, my prince," he announced. "They have a detachment on the bridge, to prevent the townspeople from escaping, but no one in the hills."

No danger of a flank attack. Comittus had said that the Picts were in general lightly armed, and that their leaders tended to be jealous of one another, so that their fighting was disorganized. I judged that whatever their number might be, the enemy could not overwhelm us. I consulted the Romans on the order of battle, and then gave the signal.

The drums rattled and the dragon divided in two, eight squadrons to the left of the Asturians, eight to the right. Then the beat slowed to the steady one-two rhythm of the walk, and we rode out from the shelter of the trees and started down the hill.

The Picts noticed us quickly and began to pour out of the town. They didn't want to be caught in the narrow streets, trapped between us and the Corstopitum garrison. I kept our pace slow: I didn't want to fight inside the town either. The enemy grouped themselves into irregular squadrons along the road facing us. They began to beat their spears against their shields and give hawklike screams. They were indeed lightly armed—spears, swords, and wooden shields that had been whitewashed or painted in bright colors. Only a few of them wore mail, and not one in a hundred had a helmet. They wore the same kind of gray-brown tunics and trousers and the same checked cloaks as I'd seen on the shepherds who crossed the Wall to go to market, but as we drew nearer I noticed that they'd covered their faces with the blue and green war paint that had given them the name "Picts." There were too many of them to count—eight, nine hundred?—and then the first wave moved forward, and more Picts came from the city, and more.

I raised my right hand, and the half-dragons swung out, spreading across the hill to cut off the Picts' retreat. The drumbeat quickened, sounding sharp and high above the growing thunder of the hooves. The trumpets of the Asturians rang out, and they halted in the middle of the road, their red and white standard waving.

From within Corstopitum, more trumpets answered, faint with distance. The First Thracian Cohort was hurrying to join its unexpected reinforcements.

The Picts began advancing directly up the road toward the Asturians, obviously preferring them to us. The Asturians remained motionless, spears leveled—waiting, as we had agreed. I raised my hand once more, and the drumbeat quickened again: we began to trot down toward the Picts at an angle. The long tail of our standard twisted in the wind behind me, crimson and gold. The beat quickened still more, and the horses broke into a canter, into a gallop. We shouted our own war cry: "Marha! Marha!" with one deep voice, and drew our bows from their cases, setting the arrows to the string.

The Picts knew nothing about mounted archers. When we veered away from them, they began to hoot and jeer in triumph, believing, I suppose, that their numbers and their paint had frightened us off. Then the arrows struck, and the jeers turned abruptly into screams of pain and consternation. We galloped past them on both sides, shooting; some of the Picts hurled javelins back, but at that range these were useless against armored enemies, while our arrows found easy targets in the raiders' unarmored legs and sides. Their advance foundered, collapsing in a sea of dead and injured men and horses. The trumpets of the Asturians rang out, and they rolled forward. I drew rein and waved the men around, putting away my bow and pulling out and lowering my spear. I felt an unfamiliar dread as its weight came down into my hand. There was no glory in this contest. It was simple slaughter.

The Picts were brave men. They struggled to regroup themselves, to settle their shields on their arms, to gather up the reins, lower the spear, all the while we swept down on them. The same instinct that informed me must have told them that they were facing death—but they faced it with unaltered courage. The Asturians struck them first, but lightly: they clashed, halted, horses rearing, men fighting. Then our charge caught them on both sides, and they went under like a nest of field voles sliced open by the plow. We galloped over them, killing with the lance and the long sword and trampling the corpses underfoot. When we drew rein and turned again on the other side of the field, the remaining Picts flung themselves off their horses and begged for mercy. The First Thracians, hurrying up from the city behind them, were too late to do anything except secure the prisoners and bury the dead.

The aftermath of the battle was unreal. I sat on my horse among the Roman officers and watched as the barbarians were disarmed, bound, and led off. There had been about eighteen hundred of them, of whom half were now dead. My men busily stripped the corpses of valuables and, of course, scalps. I told myself that I was doing nothing more than honoring the bargain my people made at Aquincum, but I was revolted at it and at myself. I had fought in a great many battles, from the first, when I was fourteen and rode with the archers, to the Thundering Defeat, but the battle against the Pictish raiders at Corstopitum was the most pitiful affair I ever took part in. We might have dispensed with the arrows altogether and taken them with the cavalry charge alone. I was accustomed, though, to using a force of mounted archers at least twice as large as my armored troops, and didn't like the idea of employing no archery at all. Besides, we hadn't been sure of the enemy's numbers, and the arrows could have covered a retreat.

The prefect of the First Thracian Cohort of Corstopitum was elated, and told us several times that it was the biggest raid he'd ever seen, and that he hadn't expected anyone to come help him in time. He thanked the gods that Comittus, Facilis, and Longus hadn't read the dispatches that ordered them to arrest me and disarm all my men. When I finally got the chance to put a word in, I told him that I wished to go to Condercum and speak to Gatalas' men. The thought of them, lordless, disarmed, and imprisoned, had been weighing heavy on my mind.

"I'm sure the legate will arrange it as soon as he arrives," the prefect replied. "We sent him the news by fast courier when the trouble started." (By "trouble" he meant the mutiny, not the raid: he was being tactful.) "I'm sure he'll come himself in a few days. I'll put it to him then, Lord Ariantes."

"I would like to see them earlier, if that is possible," ' said.

He gave me an unhappy look, and I saw that I wouldn't be allowed anywhere near Condercum until the legate had arrived with more *Roman* troops. "I'll write Condercum about it," the prefect promised, to pacify me.

The prefect invited us to spend the night in Corstopitum, and was taken aback when Comittus told him that my men wouldn't sleep in barracks. "The Sarmatians at Condercum do," he said in surprise. We declined to squeeze in beside his own men, and rode back to Cilurnum. Comittus rode in silence most of the way. When we turned north along the river, I saw that he was crying.

"Had you never seen a battle before?" I asked him quietly. He had been very white and silent since it ended.

He shook his head. "No. Oh gods! Was it that obvious?"

"Not so very much. Nearly all men are nervous beforehand. But if they have seen war before, they are less dismayed afterward."

He sniffed. "I'd never realized . . . and . . . *damn* it, Ariantes, you know what they're going to do with the prisoners we took?"

"The arenas?" I asked. That was what the Romans had always done with their Sarmatian prisoners.

He nodded. "Damn it! Poor wretches. I know they started it, but poor, miserable men." He looked up and met my eyes. "You probably don't have any idea what it looked like. Gods and goddesses, you were like . . . like those reaping machines they use in the South. No, like meat grinders. Nothing human, anyway. Sweeping down on those poor miserable savages, chopping them up, and trampling over them while they screamed. It was horrible!"

"Yes. Who were they?"

He rubbed his face. "Mostly Selgovae. I recognized the emblems of a couple of their chiefs. And some Votadini—they were the ones with the hawk emblem painted on their faces. And that's an odd thing: the southern Votadini don't usually cooperate with the Selgovae. They've fought a lot in the past, and they have so many blood debts back and forth that they can hardly make a truce even when they want to."

I was silent for a minute. "It was an odd thing in many ways. They must have known that there was . . . trouble in the Roman camp."

He gave me a look I couldn't interpret. "They did know," he said, after a pause and in a whisper. "I heard them talking about it as the Thracians were tying them up and taking them off. But . . ." And he lowered his voice still further, so that I had to lean half off my horse and strain my ears to hear it. "But I don't see how they could have gathered their forces in time, particularly with all those blood feuds to settle—unless they knew about it *before* it happened."

"Perhaps there was trouble earlier, which we did not hear about," I said, after a pause. "As Facilis said, we are the last people who would be informed of trouble in Condercum."

"By Maponus! That's true!" exclaimed Comittus, brightening. There had clearly been another possibility that had worried him before. I suspected it myself, but in a vague way, not happy with details. I was quite certain that Gatalas wouldn't have been able to coordinate his mutiny with an invasion even if he'd wanted to: we were all of us too alien to this world to play its factions. But then, Gatalas' mutiny didn't sound planned at all: it had the feel of a desperate gesture undertaken to revenge his honor. Why? What had happened? Plainly he had been forced to bow lower to Roman discipline than I had, if he'd been obliged to use barracks. But that would not have been enough to make him resort to mutiny. He'd swallowed Facilis' insults all the way from Aquincum and had only threatened to rebel at the ocean crossing because he thought it a death trap. He'd hoped for glory in war, for a battle like the one I'd just fought. And still, he must have had some residual faith in the Romans, or he would not have ordered his men to surrender when he rode out with his bodyguard to die.

Danger from lies, the rods had warned in Bononia. I suspected, though still vaguely, that someone had lied to Gatalas, someone with contacts among the Pictish tribes—and from Comittus' unhappiness I guessed that the same thought had crossed his mind as well. And without details, without proof, like a man listening to echoes in the darkness, I wondered if the legate would bring his lady with him when he came from Eburacum.

VII

*J*ULIUS PRISCUS ARRIVED in Corstopitum five days later, and summoned Comittus, Facilis, and myself at once. We left Leimanos and Longus in charge of the fort, and rode down with my bodyguard. I also brought Eukairios. The scribe had ridden to the town a couple of times on his own, with letters, and he no longer fell off a horse unless the horse actively wanted to get rid of him. He still disliked being on horseback, but he wanted to visit the town to meet his "correspondent" there. I hadn't inquired too deeply about this person, since it was easy to guess he was another Christian, and it was better not to know any of the illegal details. I guessed that Eukairios must have been given the name and a password in Londinium, or perhaps in Eburacum. Whoever the man was, I was grateful to him.

When we arrived, we found that the legate had brought half his legion with him, more than enough troops to deal with any trouble, and had summoned Gaius Valerius Victor and another senior Roman from Condercum. He had also brought Arshak, but not Arshak's men. And he had indeed brought his wife. Aurelia Bodica sat beside her husband while the rest of us stood in the main hall of Corstopitum headquarters, and discussed the question Priscus had come there to resolve—"What should we do about the Sarmatians?" I suppose it was a major concession, which we owed to the Pictish defeat, that Arshak and I were allowed to participate. But it didn't feel that way at the time. It felt to me as though I were on trial.

"A hundred and twenty-four Roman soldiers dead!" said the legate, much as Facilis had, except he had the exact figure. "And why? Because the bloodthirsty savage who commanded the Fourth Sarmatians had somehow taken it into his head that he was going to be demoted and replaced! Who told him that, eh?" And he glared at me.

"My lord legate," I said, stunned by the accusation, "if that was true, I had heard nothing of it; and if it was false, I am the last man to spread lies about it."

"You were in Dubris before the others," snapped Priscus. "You were the one who said there'd be a mutiny if we went through with our original plans to make your troops regular auxiliaries. And you are the one who has a scribe, and has been deluging my office with letters and bribing my staff." It was true, I had—mostly in an attempt to improve the pay of my men.

"Yes, sir. But I did not write to Gatalas. He did not have a scribe and could not read."

"He could have found someone to read him a letter easily enough! You were dissatisfied with your troop's pay; it seems to me very likely you were complaining to him. I told you before that if I was sure you were making trouble, I'd have you flogged to death. As it is, if your troop hadn't defeated those tribesmen . . ."

He let the threat hang. "Sir," I said, trying to keep my voice level, "if I have been concerned at my men's pay, it is because I wish at all costs to avoid trouble. At the present level of pay they will get into debt, and if they are in debt, they may act wildly. I said nothing to any Sarmatian about your plan to make us regular auxiliaries under Roman officers: I believed that you had abandoned it, and to spread any rumor of it would only stir resentment." I glanced quickly at Arshak. The revelation didn't seem to surprise him. He must have heard it when the trouble first caught fire. He looked well, better than I'd expected. I'd been afraid to find him worn with tension, restless as a caged hawk, but he was sleek and golden and arrogant as ever—though the coat he was wearing was his plain one.

"Ariantes is telling the truth," Facilis put in, suddenly and unexpectedly. "He's had no contact whatever with Condercum, and he's not the man to stir up trouble if he had. He knows perfectly well that his own people would be the losers in any contest with the legions, and he'll go to any lengths to protect them. Javolenus Comittus and I were both with him when he got the news of the mutiny: he was shocked by it, and his first thought was to calm his own people down. If Gatalas believed he was going to be replaced as commander, it's probably because he heard some rumor, or misinterpreted something somebody said. Had he had a lot of disputes with you, Tribune?"

Valerius Victor shrugged. "We'd had nothing but disputes. They didn't want to sleep in barracks; they wanted more fresh meat and milk than they could get; they quarreled incessantly with the original garrison of the fort, and had to be confined to barracks half the time. A couple of the old garrison were killed, and the men responsible had to be executed. No, the air was pretty poisonous. But I never said that I was going to replace Gatalas as commander. I could see for myself I'd be murdered if I suggested any such thing."

Priscus let out a breath through his nose. "We had some of the same disputes in Eburacum." He glared at Arshak, who smiled. "Not as bad, though. And you, Lucius—have you been breathing the same poisonous air in Cilurnum?"

"No," declared Comittus at once. "We've got on very well in Cilurnum. We've had some quarrels between the Sarmatians and the Asturians, but on the whole, the dragon's been settling in very well. Hasn't it, Marcus Flavius?"

"Yes," said Facilis shortly.

"In fact," declared Comittus, gathering himself up, "I have complete confidence in the men and officers of the Sixth Numerus of Sarmatian Horse, and I believe they are, and will remain, an invaluable asset to the defense of the province. As for Ariantes, I'll swear any oath you like that he had nothing whatever to do with the mutiny at Condercum. No one could command the dragon better than he does, and I would be completely lost without him."

"Agreed," growled Facilis. "I agree to every word of that. And if you speak to Flavinus Longus or the other Roman officers in Cilurnum, Lord Legate, they'll tell you exactly the same."

There was a moment of astonished silence.

"Well," said Priscus at last, "I'm glad to hear it. I was glad of the Sixth Sarmatians when I heard what happened at Corstopitum. They arrived quickly, hit hard, and caused no problems afterward: I would've hated to demote their commander. This fellow Gatalas is dead, and the rest of his men took no part in the killing, and surrendered quietly. Very well, we'll keep the present command structure, and call the mutiny the result of passion in one unstable man. I'll give the Fourth Sarmatians a new commander and bring them back to Eburacum with me, and we'll put the Second Sarmatians in their place. Ariantes, since your liaison officer and camp prefect are willing to vouch for you, you can take temporary command of the Fourth Numerus as well as the Sixth."

"My lord legate, no," I said hurriedly, "It would offend Gatalas' men enormously, sir."

"Why would it offend them?" snapped Priscus, glaring again.

I spread my hands helplessly in the air. I had grown less aware of the gulf between Roman and Sarmatian at Cilurnum, but I was dropped in the middle of it now. "My lord, the fourth dragon were all . . . *clients* . . . of Gatalas. They kept sheep and horses of his when we were in our own country, and he gave them grazing rights and judged their disputes. He led them on raids and in war. I and my men, we were friendly rivals at best, and at worst, enemies. Now they have watched their commander die, and by his orders have not raised a spear in his defense. They have been disarmed and confined to their barracks as traitors, while I and my dragon fought a battle and won a victory. They have been humiliated—and to hand them over to me would only humiliate them more, however gently I spoke to them. They need forbearance and the hope of glory if they are to become loyal servants of Rome. No, my lord. Let me go to Condercum and speak with them. I will find out which of the squadron captains is most willing to work with the Romans, and you can appoint him and Valerius Victor to a joint command."

Bodica spoke for the first time. "Surely, Lord Ariantes," she said softly, "if they're under a joint command, they'll believe that Gatalas was right to rebel, since the thing he was afraid of has come about?"

"Not if it is done properly," I replied. "Gatalas was a prince of the Iazyges, a scepter-holder. His men will not expect to receive the same honor as their prince."

There was another silence—then the legate's stony face cracked unexpectedly into a grin. "The minds of barbarians are a mystery," he said. "The place of a Sarmatian prince can't be taken by another Sarmatian prince, can't be taken by a Sarmatian who isn't a prince, but might just be managed by a Sarmatian noble and a Roman tribune together. Lord Ariantes, you're a capable man. Even your letters on pay were sensible, little as I liked them, and now your camp prefect, who has no love for any Sarmatian, has vouched for your trustworthiness. Didn't you realize I was offering you a promotion?"

I hadn't, and the sudden reversal left me blinking. "My lord legate," I said, uncertainly, "I thank you. But if you wish to make the best use of Gatalas' dragon, you will arrange the command as I have suggested."

He snorted and leaned back in his seat. "When a man gives advice against his own advantage, the advice is probably good. Very well. You have leave to go to Condercum, with Gaius Valerius, and arrange the command of the Fourth Sarmatians in whatever way you and he can agree on. Lord Arsacus, you can go along with Lord Ariantes. When you get to Condercum make arrangements for your people to replace the Fourth Numerus. But first, Ariantes, you can explain to me why your troop can't manage on an auxiliary's pay without getting into debt. The rest of you are dismissed."

WHEN I LEFT the legate's office an hour or so later, I found Arshak waiting for me in the courtyard outside. "Greetings, my brother!" he said, jumping up and coming over. "Congratulations to you on the victory. I hope next time I'll be able to share it with you."

I caught his hand and shook it. "It wasn't hard fought," I said, "but I'd welcome you beside me. I'm glad you'll be freed from Eburacum."

He grinned. "So am I. I swear on fire, I never thought a man could hate stone so much."

"You look well, though, despite it."

"That is the doing of the legate's lady. I think that if it hadn't been for her, I would have killed someone. She is a wonderful woman, Ariantes, a wise woman, a true queen."

I didn't like the sound of that at all, and he seemed to realize it, because he changed the subject. "Victor is waiting for us at the military stables, if you want to start for Condercum. What was all this about pay?"

I explained it on the way to the stables. Our troops were being offered the standard auxiliary pay, two hundred denarii a year, plus the cavalry allowance of two hundred denarii for the upkeep of one horse. However, most of us had more than one horse and we all had more armor than a Roman would. Even though we had men who could replace worn-out equipment for the dragon and didn't need to turn to professional blacksmiths, still the cost of the upkeep of the armor would be high. Eukairios and I had worked out how big the allowance would have to be to take account of the differences, and had been pressing for the pay to be increased accordingly. Priscus had just offered me part of the sum, and suggested that we reduce the number of horses. For various reasons, I was not satisfied with this, and I told Arshak about it—warmly, because my mind was still hot with it. He frowned and asked questions.

"I don't understand," he said, when we'd finished. "How do you know these things, what it costs to repair armor or provide fodder for a horse?"

His tone was flat, and I suddenly understood all too well that what he meant was, "You've Romanized, more even than I expected." And I saw in the same instant that it was horribly true.

"I have a good scribe who explains it," I replied, cursing myself. "I needed to learn, and did."

He stopped suddenly and caught my shoulder. We were just at the corner of the stable yard, standing in one of the cramped alleys of the military compound. "What are they doing to us?" he asked, looking at me earnestly.

"What do you mean?" I replied—coolly, trying to step back from myself and find where I stood.

"Gatalas is dead, you talk of pay negotiations and get Facilis to vouch for you, and I . . . Ariantes, we are scepter-holders of the Iazyges. Or we were."

"We were," I said quietly. "But now we are commanders of *numeri* for the Romans."

"For the Romans! Neither you nor I love the Romans. How can we fight for them?"

"We swore to the emperor himself at Aquincum that we would do so."

"We didn't know what we were swearing. We had no conception of what it meant. We thought we would stay Sarmatians but fight under another commander—but they're making Romans of us. We eat bread and sleep in tombs and give bribes to officials. Marha! Haven't you sickened of it yet?"

I was silent for a moment. "I and my men have kept our wagons," I said at last. "No. I am no sicker of it than I was when we arrived."

"Our wagons were broken up," Arshak said bitterly. "The men got barracks, and I got a house. It stands in a row with the houses of the tribunes, and it's made of stone. Everything is in rows, and made of stone,"—he glared furiously at the featureless walls around us—"and the Romans think we must be grateful for the comfort. I'd set fire to it, if it would only burn!" He let go of my shoulder. "But you seem to like it here!"

"What did I have left, across the Danube?" I asked, very slowly.

He looked at me with hot eyes. "Things here could be different."

"And I'm trying to make them so."

"You're tinkering. Talking in their words, becoming more like them every day, despite yourself. Pay! Wagons! The problem is the Romans. The native Britons are a lot like us; we would agree with them very well, if this were a British kingdom. They have kings and queens of noble blood, who reward valor and not greed. Why should we fight them?"

"Who has been telling you this?" I asked, and saw the answering flicker in his eyes.

"Do I need anyone to tell me? You can't *want* to fight for Rome—for the people who murdered your wife and child, insulted their bodies, and tossed them into the fire."

I slapped him across the face. "Don't mention them to me, Arshak!" I told him, in a low voice, while he stared in angry surprise. "Don't ever mention them to me!" I turned and strode furiously on into the stable.

After a minute, Arshak followed me. I half expected him to whisper a time and place to meet to settle the argument, but he said nothing—and, as soon as he met Valerius Victor, became instantly all charm again.

The tribune had a squadron of the Dalmatian cavalry from Condercum, and we rode out with that to escort us: I was politely given to understand that my own bodyguard would not be welcome. When we reached the fort that night, I felt that I wasn't welcome either. "The air was pretty poisonous," Victor had said, and indeed, it was thick with bitterness and hatred. The Roman garrison watched me and Arshak ride in the gate with a heavy sullen stare that set my teeth on edge, and they kept it up the whole time we were there.

Though it was late, I asked to speak with Gatalas' officers in the main hall of the headquarters building at once. The garrison grumbled but, at Valerius Victor's insistence, agreed, and set up torches, which cast a flickering light over us and made the statue of the emperor, standing larger than life in the chapel of the standards off the hall, seem to be alive and watching. When Gatalas' men filed in, under armed guard, they gave the statue and the Romans the same heavy sullen stare that the Romans had given us.

I asked Gatalas' men how they were; they released a torrent of helpless grief and resentment. Their wagons had been broken up, some of their friends had been executed for killing the Romans they'd quarreled with, some had been beaten like slaves, their prince was dead, and they had been ordered not to defend him. Worse, far worse: the Romans had burned his body. They'd watched helplessly, disarmed, imprisoned, and disgraced. Their chief consolation was how many Romans Gatalas had managed to kill before he died.

"He revenged himself," I agreed, trying to put a hopeful face on it, though I was appalled. "And he has what the gods promised him, death in battle. He was warned of danger from fire, but not of destruction: perhaps his soul will escape. At Cilurnum we sacrificed three horses on his behalf, and prayed to the gods for him. But you were promised good fortune and glory in war, and your prince ordered you to surrender so that you could have what you were promised. I've come to help you choose a new commander who can offer prayers for Gatalas' spirit and for your own future."

"We have no power over who'll command us," they replied. "That was why our lord mutinied. He'd heard that they meant to depose him and set that tribune in his place." And they glared at Victor, who was sitting by the tribunal, looking blank. He didn't speak Sarmatian.

"It wasn't true," I said. "They thought of doing that before they met us, but they changed their minds, and there were no plans to replace anyone."

They looked at me sullenly, as though they were sure I was lying. Then they looked at Arshak, who was sitting on the table swinging his foot. "Didn't you send us a message of warning, Lord?" one of the captains asked. He was a young man, but I'd had him in mind as a possible leader for the dragon: he'd struck me as the most intelligent, as well as one of the most loyal, of Gatalas' officers. His name was Siyavak, a slim man, with dark hair and eyes that made him stand out from the rest.

Arshak stopped swinging the foot. "I?" he asked. "I didn't send any message."

At this they looked bewildered. "Lord Gatalas showed us the message and said it came from Eburacum," said Siyavak.

"If there was a message from Eburacum, it wasn't sent by me," said Arshak, angry now. "Do you still have this letter?"

"It wasn't a letter," replied Siyavak, "but we have it. Our lord left it with us, and if the Romans will let me, I'll fetch it."

The Romans allowed him, and he came back carrying a bundle wrapped in black. He set it down on the floor in front of Arshak and unrolled the cloth: a set of divining rods tumbled onto the floor. Moving with sharp, angry jerks, Siyavak counted them out, and I saw that they were tied together in sequence by a red cord. They were all black; none of the chalked ones were included. "They promise death and destruction," whispered Siyavak. "He had them read before us. And on the final rod . . ." He sorted through and picked one up. "This."

There was a pattern of scratches on the blackened surface of the rod, little lines parallel to one another or at angles. It was nothing like Latin writing, but it looked as though it might have a meaning. "What is it?" I asked, taking the thing, still bound to the others by the blood-colored cord. The whole bundle was one of the most frightening things I had ever seen: it seemed to vibrate with a menace of supernatural disaster beyond anything the mind could conceive. There would have been some white in any normal reading.

"Gatalas said that the messenger who brought the bundle gave him the name of a man here who could interpret it," Siyavak told us, still in the low voice, "and he said he had shown it to the man, and the man read the marks as though they were writing. 'Beware,' it says, 'the Romans have lost patience. You will be arrested and replaced by Victor.' "

I looked at the tribune, who was now standing over the rods and staring in confusion, aware that something had been disclosed but having no idea what.

"Have you seen these before?" I asked the tribune, in Latin.

He shook his head. "They're some of the divining rods you use to know the will of the gods," he said. "Why do they matter?"

I explained, and showed him the stick with the markings. Something shut suddenly behind his face. "Jupiter Optimus Maximus!" he whispered.

"What is it?" I asked.

"The writing's . . . British," he replied. "I can't read it."

And he didn't want to look at it. But he had understood something about it that we had not.

"Someone from one of the Pictish tribes must have sent it," he went on, "trying to provoke the mutiny, to distract our troops so that they could raid our lands."

"Didn't Gatalas show these to the Romans?" I asked Siyavak.

He sat back on his heels, looking at Victor intently. "He did not show them this," he said, in Latin now, and to Victor, not me. "No. He went to you, though, he asked what you would do about the command of the dragon."

"I didn't understand," said Victor. "I thought he was trying to find something else to quarrel about."

"You said that you had once planned to be commander in his place."

"I only said that because I thought he knew! I told him the plan had been abandoned!"

"How could anyone believe you, with things as they were?" Siyavak turned back to Arshak. "We thought this was from you, Lord Arshak, that you'd heard something in Eburacum."

"No," said Arshak. He took the rod and slipped it out of its loop of cord, then turned it in his hands, looking frightened. "No, they can vouch for me at Eburacum. I've had no chance to send anything. And it wasn't true."

"Who was the messenger who brought it?" I asked. "Who interpreted the markings?"

"I don't know," replied Siyavak. "My lord Gatalas didn't say." He looked at me bleakly. "So he died for nothing then?"

"No," I answered. "He died for a lie."

"We will revenge him," said Siyavak, his eyes beginning to smoulder. "Marha! Whoever sent him this murdered him, as surely as if they'd sent him poison! We will revenge him!"

"You will have to work with the Romans to do that," I said.

He looked at Victor again; all of them looked at Victor. "Very well," Siyavak said, angrily. "We can do that."

WHEN I LEFT next morning they'd agreed to a joint command by Siyavak and Victor and were planning a funeral service for the dead. The air was still poisonous, but no longer sullen; the hatred was balanced by a sense of purpose. I had hopes that when they got away from Condercum they might yet find a way to be happy.

Victor remained at Condercum to supervise the fourth dragon. He offered us some Roman cavalry as escort, but Arshak declined the protection of men who detested us, and I agreed with him. Arshak and I set out back to

Corstopitum on our own. It had turned colder, and there were a few flakes of snow drifting from a slate-colored sky. I was tired—I hadn't slept much in the stone barracks block—and the world of camps and war seemed more confining and oppressive than ever. I didn't want to put my armor on that morning; the weight and the sound of it set my teeth on edge. I packed it behind my saddle. No need to get it wet, I told myself, and my coat and hat were warmer. Arshak, who'd armed for the journey despite the snow, eyed me contemptuously.

We rode off in silence along a road that was almost entirely empty. We had not spoken to each other since his reference to Tirgatao, and now he sat on his horse with his head bent, eyes fixed on the animal's mane in a hot manic glare. We'd ridden the better part of ten miles along the military way, and had passed the fort of Vindovala, when Arshak suddenly sat up straight and turned the glare on me.

"You struck me in the face at Corstopitum," he said.

"I did," I told him. I'd had time to calm myself again, and I knew how to answer him. "I ask your pardon for the blow. But you mentioned a thing that's like a hot iron in my heart, and you can't be surprised that I was angry."

A little of the glare faded. "Do we have to be enemies?" he asked, almost pleadingly.

"We're not—are we?" I returned.

"You've taken the side of the Romans."

"We both swore at Aquincum that that was our side."

"It isn't! It never was! It can't be!"

"Then whose side is our side? The side of the people who sent that message to murder Gatalas?"

He drew in his breath with a hiss and looked away. What were they doing to us? he'd asked. Gatalas dead, me Romanizing, and himself . . . He hadn't said. He'd known, though, that what was happening to himself was terrible. "I don't know what you mean," he said, in a frozen, unnatural voice.

I was afraid that if I said anything more, I would have to fight him, and that would be disaster however it ended. So I said nothing.

We rode on for another mile, and were nearing the turn down to the old road and Corstopitum when we heard a jingle of harness ahead of us and Bodica's chariot turned onto the military way in front of us.

She was alone. The blue cloak she wore was pulled over her head against the cold, and she held the reins under it: for a moment the white stallion trotted toward us driven by a shapeless, faceless shadow. Then it stopped, the horse shivering under the yoke, and waited while we rode on toward it.

Just before we reached it, Bodica loosened the hood and turned into a lovely woman again. "There you are!" she announced, smiling prettily. "I thought I would take the horse out for some exercise, and perhaps meet you on your way back from Condercum. I wanted to talk with you."

Arshak said nothing. He dismounted, strode up to the chariot, and handed her the divining rod with the marks on it.

Her smile vanished. She turned the rod in her fingers, then shook her head and handed it back to Arshak, saying something I couldn't quite hear. "Can we stop and talk?" she asked, more loudly, looking at me earnestly with those vivid blue eyes. "I've brought some hot wine against the cold."

"Lady Aurelia, greetings," I said. "I thank you, no."

She looked at Arshak. "We need to talk," she told him. "We all do. Didn't you speak to him?"

He nodded. "Ariantes, stop with us a minute."

I looked down at them both and gathered the reins. The sudden openness about the fact of their conspiracy frightened me. I wished I'd put on my armor after all. But there was an obvious question to ask, and I had to ask it.

"Lady Aurelia," I said, "was it you who sent Gatalas that rod?"

She simply stared at me, neither nodding nor shaking her head, neither smiling nor frowning. "I've come here to speak to you," she said. "I would have spoken before, but you avoided me." Then, deliberately, she turned away and took a flask wrapped in a blanket out from under the bench seat. "I hope that I'm speaking to a friend. Let me treat you as one. I offer you hospitality, and we will all hold what we say under the sacred bond of guest friendship. Then, no matter what comes afterward, we'll know each other's minds."

I walked my horse closer to the chariot but did not dismount. Now it had come to it, I did not want to know. If I knew, I would be at odds with Arshak, perhaps with all my people.

"You said we were not enemies," said Arshak.

I was bound to hear his explanation. I sighed and nodded. Bodica pulled two cups from under the seat and poured the wine; it steamed slightly in the chill air. She handed one up to me, took a sip from the other, and handed it to Arshak. I took a sip; it was tepid, rather than hot, and had been sweetened with honey.

"You can't love Rome," said Bodica.

I said nothing.

"You're a very able man," Bodica coaxed, "and a prince in your own right. Why shouldn't you serve the kingdom of the Brigantes instead of the masters of a city in Italy?"

"There is no kingdom of the Brigantes," I replied.

"But there could be! Rome used to govern hundreds of square miles beyond that wall there, but it was abandoned because it became too costly to keep. If Brigantia became too costly to keep, they'd abandon that too. Don't you see that we're much more like you than the Romans are, that your natural alliance is with us? We don't worship money, kill men in the arenas for pleasure, or murder women and children when we make war."

"Your ancestress, the queen of the Iceni, murdered women and children when she made war," I replied, "or so I have heard. You exaggerate your likeness to us. And you are not Brigantic. Your ancestors were kings and queens, but of southern tribes. You would have no rights in any kingdom of the Brigantes if one did exist, and I do not believe you plan to set up an independent Brigantic kingdom with someone else as queen."

"She is a queen, by birth and by wisdom," said Arshak, angrily. "Why shouldn't she be one in fact as well? The Brigantes would rejoice to have her."

"And the Pictish tribesmen who invaded?" I asked. "They would rejoice, too? Someone had promised them that the Romans would be busy with a mutiny, Gatalas' mutiny. But Gatalas is dead, and so are most of them."

Bodica's eyes had narrowed dangerously. "Gatalas was meant to succeed! He should never have ordered his men to surrender. I made a mistake, I didn't speak to him myself. So he didn't realize that we could succeed, and he tried to spare his followers what he thought was the inevitable finish. I won't make the same mistake again; I am speaking to you. We can succeed; if we dare enough, we will! Still! As for the raid, it was you who stopped it, and that, too, was because you didn't know."

"No," I said bitterly, "it was because we had peace in Cilurnum. You meant me to be under arrest there, suspected of being in league with Gatalas, but my Roman officers trusted me, and left me free. I do not like these plans of yours, Lady. They are too full of lies, and too ruthless with your allies. I would not trust myself and my men to your good faith any more than I would lead them on horseback into the ocean." I swallowed the rest of the wine in one gulp and handed her back the cup.

She looked at me without expression. "You won't join us, then? You won't even hear the rest of what I have to say?"

I shook my head. I was aware of Arshak turning back to his horse and mounting. "I have no proof of anything," I reminded them both. "And what you have said has been under the bond of guest friendship. If you like, I will swear on fire, as well, not to mention this conversation to anyone. You will then have to see to it that I get no proof: that is a fair contest. Good health, Lady."

"You are on the side of the Romans, then?" said Arshak, his voice harsh with both pain and anger. His hand was on the shaft of his spear.

"I am on the side of my own men, who trust me to do what is best for them."

"Traitor!" shouted Arshak, drawing his spear from its holder.

I touched Farna's sides and sent her dancing backward up the road, and as I went I pulled my bow out of its case. Arshak yelled and lowered the spear. I turned Farna, stringing the bow, setting an arrow to the string, and cantered her onto the verge, going back toward the chariot. Farna reared as I stopped her, the arrow fixed on Bodica. "Let me go back to Corstopitum," I called to Arshak.

"Fight *me!*" shouted Arshak, trying to get his horse in front of the chariot. "Not her! Me!" But I turned Farna about and kept the arrow fixed on Bodica.

"I do not want to fight you. If we duel, the survivor will be charged with murder, and his dragon will suffer trying to protect him: I will inflict that on none of our men. I have offered you a fair contest. Accept it now, and let me go."

"Go, then!" said Bodica. She stood very tall in the chariot, her blue cloak draped close about her shoulders, but the hood fallen from her head, flung back proudly against my threat; she raised her hand. "Go if you can!"

I touched Farna and started back to the road, holding the bow bent and the arrow on the string. But before I reached the paving, something seemed to fall like a fog over my eyes. I felt dizzy. Farna's hooves rang on the stones, and she stopped, sensing something wrong. My hands, holding the bow, seemed suddenly very far away. As though I were looking at them from a distance, I saw the bow slacken. My fingers fumbled at the string, and I dropped the arrow. Arshak lowered the spear and stared at me in consternation. Farna blew softly and shook her head, puzzled.

Bodica tied the reins of the chariot to the post, climbed down, and walked over to me. I couldn't move. She pulled the bow out of my hands as though I were a child. I tried to rouse myself; I fumbled at my shoulder for my sword-hilt, but couldn't find it. Bodica gave me a shove, and I fell. I lay on my back, looking at the side of my horse above me, steaming in the cold, and beyond that, the gray sky and the few light flakes of snow. Everything seemed remote, as though I were looking at it down a long tunnel.

"What have you done to him?" cried Arshak.

"Did you think we could let him go back?" she demanded in return. "His Romanizing has cost our people a thousand lives already, and he'd do worse, much worse, now he knows we're his enemies."

"I would have fought him," protested Arshak. "He's good, but I could beat him."

"Everyone knew you left Condercum with him. If he were found killed by the spear—and, dear heart, I believe he would be if you fought him—everyone would know that you did it, and what would happen to us then?"

"What did you do?" Arshak repeated. "He's a prince of the Iazyges: he deserved to die fighting." But he sounded halfhearted now.

I thought, with a mind that was numb and fumbling like my hands, how she'd handed me the wine. It had been drugged. Not the wine, she'd drunk some of that as well, and Arshak. The cup, my cup, the cup she offered in the sacred bond of hospitality. Had she been sure I'd refuse to join them, or had it just been a precaution? How could Arshak accept it? I tried to get up. I twitched over to one side, and fell back.

"He deserves to die," Bodica answered Arshak. "That he was a prince of the Iazyges makes his Romanizing worse. Go back to Corstopitum, but stop on the way and do some hunting. Take off your armor. Say you and he saw a quarry, a deer or a flock of partridges, on your way back from Condercum, and decided to see who could shoot the most game. Say you lost him in the chase, and thought he'd be back in Corstopitum. It will look like an accident."

"But . . ."

"He betrayed you, my white heart! Don't you see that? My husband approves of him, and wanted to promote him above you. He would have become an adviser on all Sarmatian affairs and your lord. He would have ended up handing you over to my husband, and I couldn't bear that, I'd die. Go, quickly. I can deal with him."

"If it has to be, let me help. It's too much for you to bear alone."

"No! The road's empty now, but who knows when someone will come along? We mustn't be seen together. Just help me to put him in the chariot: I'll do the rest."

Arshak picked me up by the shoulders, slung me over my horse, and led her over to the chariot. I was aware of it, through the mist, but I could not move. It was the most I could do to pick my head up a little, and then I couldn't hold it. I was put in the chariot like a corpse and shoved under the bench seat. I was aware, in the dim scent of damp leather and wood, of Bodica and Arshak whispering good-bye, and then the chariot jolted into motion.

It rolled over paved road for some distance, and I struggled in the mist and darkness, half-unconscious, half-awake. When I could think at all, I wished, stupidly, passionately, and irrelevantly, that I had succeeded that time in reaching the Jade Gate. It was cold. After a time, I realized that we'd left the paved road and were bouncing along a rougher surface. Again I struggled to get up, and couldn't. I twisted my head, and saw beside me the edge of Bodica's gown, her feet in the expensive shoes of embossed leather, and a mud track beyond. The chariot turned, and the mud was replaced by grass, green winter grass with a light sprinkling of snow. The chariot stopped.

The world faded a moment, and I felt horribly cold and sick. Bodica hauled me out of the chariot and rolled me over on the grass, then went and did something with my horse, which I saw had been tied behind the chariot. She bent over me and unfastened the baldric for my sword, took it off, refastened it, and hung it from my saddle. Then she took the bow case out and put it in my hand. She knelt and looked in my face. "You can see me, can't you?" she whispered. Her eyes were very bright and she was flushed and smiling.

"I've given you the bow because they'll think you were hunting. I've hung up the sword because you would have taken it off if you were wading out into the water to fetch something you'd shot."

Water. I tried to move my head; after what seemed a long time, it shifted, and I saw the river, only a few feet away.

"Yes, there," said Bodica, gleefully. "You're going to drown. I've never drowned a man before. Only animals." She giggled, sat down, and began taking her shoes off. "You believe that people who drown are damned, don't you?"

I could not move or speak. Bodica leaned over me again, her face close to mine; she ran her hand up my arm and pressed my shoulder. "You're strong, aren't you?" she whispered. "A big strong warrior and a commander of men. And you're going to drown like a helpless little puppy." She giggled again, rubbing my shoulder like a lover, and then leaned closer still and kissed me, openmouthed, hot and wet. It was peculiarly horrible. It was my death she kissed then, and her pleasure in it was somehow even worse than the thing itself.

She stood up, put her shoes and socks in the chariot, and pushed me with her bare foot; I rolled helplessly over toward the river. I closed my eyes. Tirgatao, I thought, just let me find Tirgatao when I'm dead. Marha, Jupiter, any legal or illegal god you like—let my people's beliefs be wrong, and let me find Tirgatao and Artanisca.

Bodica gave me another push, and I rolled over into the water. She pulled up her skirts and stepped into the shallows after me, pushed once more so that I lay on my face. The last thing I was aware of was the weight of her foot pressing me down.

VIII

I WOKE IN the dark, smelling fire. I could not feel my own limbs, but the cold was like knives in my chest and stomach. I coughed and someone lifted me; I remember their skin seemed red-hot against my side. I tasted the river in my mouth and felt it, heavy in my chest. I struggled to toss it off, coughing, gasping, and vomiting, and the water gurgled in my lungs and ran from my nose. The other held me up, put a basin under my mouth, spoke soothingly, and at last, when the spasms stopped, set me down and drew blankets over me. I lay still, drifting numbly; slept; woke again feeling warmer. The fire-scented darkness still surrounded me. My hands and feet felt as though they were burning, my head ached, and I still felt sick. I struggled to move, and a woman's voice said something, softly and gently, and a hand smoothed my hair away from my face. I relaxed.

"Tirgatao," I said, feeling as though I were fitting back into life, like a sword into its sheath or a latch onto a door. I opened my eyes, trying to find her.

But it was not her. The reddish light of a fire showed me a woman beside me, but a strange woman with a long, oval face, hair indeterminately dark in the faint light, a gentle mouth, long hands. I stared at her for a while in bewilderment. "Where is Tirgatao?" I asked at last.

I spoke in Sarmatian, but the woman replied in another language. I looked at her blankly, and she said something else. I felt that I ought to understand the second time she spoke, but I could not, and I wept because I could not. The woman stroked my hair again, and said "shhh, shhh," which at least I could understand. I lay still; after a while I went back to sleep.

When I woke again, it was lighter, and I felt less ill. There was still the smell of fire. I lay on my side, staring out at a wall. After a time, I put my hand against it, and felt that it was made of stone. Then I knew that I was dead and in my grave. I lay for a while, considering this without distress. It didn't surprise me, but I couldn't remember how I had died.

It suddenly occurred to me that if I were dead, I might find Tirgatao. I pulled myself up onto my hands and knees, looking around. The stone walls enclosed me, but there was a hearth on my left, with embers glowing redly under a gridiron. The packed earth floor was covered with dried bracken, and herbs and dried meat hung from the ceiling. I sat back onto my heels. I was on a kind of bed, with a blanket over me, and all my clothes were missing. I pulled the blanket around my shoulders and stood up. My knees were weak, and my bad leg almost gave under me; I staggered and put a hand against the wall to balance myself. There was a door in the far wall, and I started toward it.

A woman came suddenly through another door, on the other side of the hearth, and ran over to me, saying something in an unknown language. I remembered her as the one who'd been beside me in the dark. She caught my elbow, speaking to me and trying to lead me back to the bed.

"I must find Tirgatao," I told her.

"You shouldn't be up," she said, in her second language—only now my mind understood it as Latin. "Do you understand me? You shouldn't be up; you're much too ill."

"But Tirgatao . . ." I said, in Latin now. "I must find her. She was burned, not buried, but perhaps she is wandering the air, and will come in when I call her. Perhaps she is outside. Please, I must find her."

"There's no one outside," said the woman.

I pushed her off and staggered to the door. I scrabbled with the latch a moment, then pushed it open. Beyond it was a farmyard, with chickens scratching in the fresh snow, and beyond that, white hills and dark leafless trees under a gray sky. I leaned against the doorframe, staring at it. It was all wrong. It was not my country at all. They'd buried me in the wrong place. "Tirgatao!" I called desperately, hoping somehow she could still hear me, "Artanisca! Tirgatao!"

"Please come back in and let me close the door," said the woman. "You should not stand half-naked in the cold. You were chilled and very nearly dead when we found you."

I let her close the door and lead me back to the bed. My strength barely got me back to it, and I collapsed on the floor beside it and wept bitterly, then coughed up some more water. "They burned her body," I told the woman, when I could speak again. "That is why she is not here. And they have buried me in the wrong place, and now I cannot find her."

The mouth lifted in a gentle, ironic smile. "It isn't because you're in the wrong place: none of the living can find the dead. You are alive."

I stared at her incomprehendingly. She took my hand, turned it in hers, and ran her thumb up my wrist: the blue line of blood went white, then leapt forward again with the force of life. "You are alive," she repeated softly.

I looked at her doubtfully. "If I am alive, why am I in a tomb?"

"Why do you think you are?"

I put my hand to the wall again. "It is stone."

"Do they only use stone for tombs where you come from? This is a house. You are at River End Farm, five miles from Corstopitum in the region of Brigantia. My name is Pervica, Saenus' widow, and the house and farm are mine."

I touched the wall again, frowning. My mind was still not clear. I felt that I'd heard of Corstopitum before, but I couldn't remember anything about it.

Pervica knelt and put my arm over her shoulders. "You should get back into bed," she said, and helped me into it. "Now, do you still feel sick, or could you eat some barley broth?"

I let her fetch the broth, and drank it when she brought it. When I handed her the empty bowl, I suddenly realized that I was still wearing nothing but the blanket around my shoulders, and I hurried to cover myself. "How did I come here?" I asked.

"We took you from the river yesterday afternoon," she answered.

"I do not remember," I said, frowning again.

"You wouldn't remember," she said soothingly. "You were very nearly dead."

I shook my head. "I do not remember going to this river at all." It troubled me.

She noticed, and continued gently. "Probably you'll remember in a little while. Where are your family, or your friends? In Corstopitum?"

"I do not remember," I repeated. "Sometimes . . . I have been there, I think."

"What is your name?"

"Ariantes."

"You remember the important things, then. Don't worry, the rest will come. I'll send Cluim into Corstopitum this afternoon to ask if anyone there has missed you. Cluim looks after my sheep; he was the one who found you. He saw your red coat against the green of the riverbank when he went to gather the sheep yesterday, and he went and pulled you out. He thought at first you were dead, but you coughed, so he covered you with his cloak and ran shivering back to the house to fetch help. We put you in the cart and brought you in by the fire, and the warmth recovered you."

I nodded, helplessly, and tried to sit up again. "Where are my clothes?" I asked.

"There." She pointed to a rack by the foot of the bed: there they all hung neatly, the hilt of the dagger gleaming in the dim light. "They're still a little damp, so I wouldn't try to put them on yet. Try and rest."

"You took them off me?"

"You needed to get warm," she said reprovingly.

It was warm in the bed by the fire. "Yes," I said, drowsily. "I thank you."

When I next woke, it was dark again and my strength was returning. I sat up and looked at the embers on the hearth. After a minute, I rose and put some fresh wood on, and watched the flames burn up, bright and yellow. Image of Marha, the holy one, the pure lord. I stretched my hand out to him, and suddenly the sight of it made me shiver. There my fingers, so cunningly articulated, moved at my will to honor the god: I was alive. For a long time I had regretted that life. In my heart I believed I should have died on that day of thunder, and never seen defeat or heard of the end of those I loved most. And now, all at once and without thinking, I was glad to be alive, to see the fire burning and smell the thick sweet smoke; to feel my strength rising in me again. The world of the dead is one we cannot share. However long we stand, gazing at the tomb, in the end we must turn and ride home. We are wonderfully and mysteriously suspended in a web of bone and blood, able to think and move, love and believe. Alive. Thank the gods!

I couldn't go back to the bed. Though I now knew I was in a house and not a tomb, I still found the close stone walls deathly. I fumbled my clothes on by the light of the fire, pulled on my coat, slung the blanket over my shoulders, and went to the door.

A full moon was shining on the snow in the farmyard, and the stars were white and high in a clear cold sky, scattered so thick that the night was radiant with them. The hills glimmered in the moonlight, and everything was still, frozen in an impossible beauty. My breath steamed. I stepped out, closing the door behind me, and limped along the side of the house. By the time I'd reached the corner, I was shivering, and I turned for shelter to a wooden barn just beyond it. I slipped into this and stood still, smelling the scent of cows, and the closer, more familiar home-smell of horses. At once I was tired again. I found a pile of clean straw in a corner, lay down in that, rolled up in the blanket, and went back to sleep.

When the cocks crowed I woke feeling hungry and myself again. I stretched and stood up, then shook the straw off the blanket and hung it over the wall of a stall. Outside the barn, dawn was breaking pink and radiant over the snow-covered land. Six cows watched me peacefully from the other end of the barn, chewing their cuds as they waited for someone to come and milk them. Two horses were loose-tethered opposite them, and a third horse was in the box stall I'd hung the blanket on, tethered with its head to the entrance. This last was looking at me with its ears back.

"Good morning," I told it.

It rolled its eyes and shifted nervously.

I walked round to the door of the stall and looked at the animal more closely. It was a stallion, chestnut with white socks and a blaze on its forehead, and it was a fine horse, round-hooved, heavy-hocked, and big enough to carry armor—though, like most British horses, a little light in the forequarters. But it had whip scars across its withers, and more scars on its nose and at the corners of its mouth: it was nervous because it had been mistreated.

It never occurred to me that Pervica could have been responsible. I had come back to life at the touch of her hand, and I could not associate any cruelty with that gentle face and ironic smile. I at once assumed that this was some beast she'd taken pity on, as she'd taken pity on me, and I looked at the animal with fellow feeling. I spoke to him soothingly, but the stallion still rolled his eyes, keeping his ears back as though to say, "Keep your distance. I won't let you hit me." There was no real hatred there, though, just fear.

I looked about and found a rag that had been used to clean harness. I picked it up and went over to the other horses. One was a mare, and I rubbed the rag against her rump, then went back to the stallion and let him smell it. His ears came forward again as he sniffed—an old trick, but a good one. I stroked his neck, talking to him quietly, and ducked under the door, which was the high kind with two bars at waist level. The ears flicked back and forth, the stallion snorted, but couldn't make up his mind to attack, and I went on patting him and crooning to him until he began to think he liked it. I went out, fetched a handful of grain, came back and fed it to him, mur-muring all the time to keep him calm. I noticed as he ate that at some point his tongue had been torn so badly that it needed stitches. I judged that the scars on his nose had been caused by a psalion, the metal hackamore that closes when it is pulled, which the Romans sometimes use for recalcitrant car-riage horses.

The barn door opened and a man came in. He was dressed in the com-mon gray-brown woollens of the Britons, but with a sheepskin cloak instead of a check one. He stared at me and gabbled something in his own language.

"Shh," I said, since the stallion was putting his ears back again.

The man ran out. A few minutes later, he came back, with Pervica. She stopped in the doorway, so suddenly that her companion bumped into her. The rising sun lanced around her shape, framing it black against the white winter light—a tall woman, wide-hipped, deep-breasted, extraordinarily graceful. She had drawn me back into life the way my heart had drawn the blood back into my hand. Desire is, some think, a simple thing, like thirst or hunger. But all I could feel of desire had been clenched upon the dead until that moment, when it opened all at once to Pervica's grace. The happiness I felt was like another sunrise, immense and shining.

"Very many greetings, Lady Pervica," I said, giving the horse a final pat and ducking back under the door.

"Greetings," she returned, coming forward slowly, looking at me in amazement. "Cluim told me you were in here, with Wildfire eating out of your hand. I'd just found your bed empty, and I had no idea where you'd gone." Seen in daylight, her hair was brown, and her eyes a light blue-gray. She was dressed just as most of the British women I'd met, in a gray-brown dress and checked cloak. She was attractive rather than strikingly beautiful. I might not have noticed her in the marketplace at Dubris, but if I had noticed her,

I'd have looked at her again: she had a grace and dignity that set her apart. I guessed already that her face was the kind that can grow on a man, becoming more beautiful as he comes to know it well.

"I am sorry," I said. "I am not used to sleeping in houses." I looked back at her companion, then asked, "You are the Cluim who took me from the river and saved my life?"

Cluim shuffled his feet and said, *"Non loquor Latine."*

"He is," Perdica supplied, and interpreted my question for him.

He grinned and bobbed his head at me. He was a small, dark man in his twenties, very dirty.

"Tell him I am grateful," I said.

Pervica interpreted, and Cluim bobbed his head again, shyly.

I unfastened my dagger from my belt and held it out to him, hilt first. "This is no repayment for a life, but it has some value. Perhaps he would accept it, in token of my thanks?"

"He is unlikely to refuse it," Pervica said dryly, and indeed, Cluim's face had lit up at the sight of it. He took it and ran his fingers over the jewels in the hilt, exclaiming; drew it and ran his thumb along the blade and exclaimed again as it cut him, then grabbed my hand and shook it wildly, beaming at me.

"And I am grateful to you as well, Lady," I told Pervica. "It is clear to me that I would have died even after I was taken from the river, if it had not been for your care. Such a debt I cannot repay but with thanks, and the prayer that one day the gods grant me the power to return your goodness."

Her cheeks flushed a little. "You are very courteous. I could hardly do anything else but try to help you, and you have repaid my efforts already, by living. I certainly didn't expect to see you looking so well this morning. But will you at least come into the house for breakfast?"

"If you wish it, Lady."

"I do." She said something dry to Cluim, who grinned, fastened the dagger to his belt, and went off toward the cows. The lady started back toward the house, and I limped after her. "So, you work with horses, Ariantes," she said, after a few steps.

It was a reasonable assumption, given that her stallion was so easily alarmed. "Yes," I agreed. "And that is a fine horse. Where did you get him?"

"My husband bought him at Corstopitum market—a great bargain at four hundred and thirty denarii. He was full of plans to use it for stud, and to start the business of horse-rearing here at River End. Nothing came of it except that he was four hundred and thirty denarii out of pocket: nobody wants his mares serviced by such a vicious animal. I'm astonished that the horse let you near him. He barely tolerates me, and we haven't been able to do a thing with him since we got him."

"He is not vicious, but frightened." We reached the door of the house and stamped the snow off our shoes. "He has been ridden too long . . ."—I hesitated, searching for the right words, then continued—"with the curb bit and the iron bridle."

"The iron bridle?" she repeated blankly.

"The psalion, I think it is called. The curb bit and the iron bridle: it is a saying my people have, but here it is true."

"Do you use this iron thing?" she asked uneasily.

I liked that unease. I shook my head. "If a horse needs that much force to control it, it is not a good horse, and I would not keep it. That chestnut is a good horse. He was punished too much, when he was willing to please as well as when he was not, and it is that that has ruined him."

"How can you tell?"

"He was afraid when he saw me first, but not angry. He enjoyed attention."

"Is he ruined forever?"

"I could handle him for you," I told her. "I have a mare I might breed to him." I was surprised that I mentioned her, then reconsidered. The stallion was tall enough, and I was unlikely to find a better one here in Britain.

She smiled at me rather crookedly. "Have you? Do you trade horses, or just raise them?"

"At the moment, neither. I used to raise some, but now . . . Still, I would not mind breeding Farna to him. I have a stallion, but he is a courser, and a bit light; I need an animal with some height to it."

She opened the door and went in, and I followed, ducking my head under the low threshhold.

There were two other women in the kitchen, one a lean redhead of about forty, and the other a dark girl of about sixteen who by her looks was Cluim's sister: they were both standing by the bed and talking animatedly. Pervica clapped her hands to get their attention and spoke in British; she gestured at me. The other two laughed; the girl clutched her hands together and looked at me admiringly. The older woman went to the fire and took a pot off a hook, calling to the girl, who brought some bowls. She spooned a kind of oat gruel out of the pot, and the girl set two bowls on the table, then took two more through the door on the other side of the hearth. "The dining room's this way," said Pervica, following her.

The dining room seemed to belong to a different house. The walls were plaster, the floor red and white tile, and there was a glass window. A couch with feet carved in the shape of eagle claws stood by a low rosewood table, and on the wall there was a painting of the three Graces dancing together under an apple tree, all lurid pink flesh and swirling draperies. The girl set the gruel down on the table, bobbed her head to her mistress, and went back to eat her own breakfast in the kitchen.

"It's not as warm in here," said Pervica, "but it's not as smoky, either." She sat down on one end of the couch and picked up her spoon.

I sat on the other end and stirred the porridge. I did not share the Roman taste for grains and pulses, but I was hungry, and did not want to offend the lady. "This is a large farm?" I asked.

"Neither large nor small," she said matter-of-factly. "Two hundred sheep, a dozen cattle, three horses, twelve acres of arable land, and an apple orchard. I have three families to help me with it. Elen and her two children live here, and the others are in their own houses nearby."

"You said you were a widow."

"I did, didn't I?"

I stopped stirring the porridge and sampled it. It wasn't actually unpleasant, so I ate another spoonful. "How long have you had the horse?"

She laughed. She had a pleasant laugh, low and soft. "You are tactful not to ask directly when my husband died. Autumn before last—a few months after buying the horse. I suppose I should have done more with the animal. He'll tolerate me, and I could show Cluim how to manage him, too. But it takes time."

"Yes," I said. "They learn fear quickly, but trust takes longer." And I thought of my men, and Gatalas'.

"I don't have the time to teach the horse trust. I'd sell him if I could, but he has a bad reputation in the area now, and no one would buy him."

"I would."

She smiled. "Now, should I take advantage of that? Friend, you don't have to buy my horse because I saved your life."

"That is nothing to do with it."

"I forgot—you can handle him, and you want a big stallion to breed to your mare. Well, perhaps . . ." She smiled crookedly again. "Talk to me about it in a few days, when you've recovered from the shock of finding yourself alive again. I confess, I'd like to sell him to a kind owner. He gulps food and is good for nothing—but I haven't felt able to dispose of him to the few who'd take him, given how much he's suffered already."

"Why could you not use him for stud? You have land here."

She shook her head. "We have land—but nobody on it is skilled with horses. Cluim's the only one who can ride at all, and he can't ride well. I can drive a cart, but that's it. My husband should never have bought the horse— but he was full of enthusiasms and ambitious projects"—the crooked smile—"mostly misguided ones." She waved a hand at the room around us. "This was another project. A fine Roman dining room, and an extra wing to the house. And the painting, another great bargain—hideous, isn't it? We couldn't afford that either. But I shouldn't complain. He was a good man; I pray the earth is light on him. And I was another one of his misguided enthusiasms. I'm a soldier's daughter whose father had been posted to the Danube, and I lost him all the dowry I never had, so everyone said he was a fool to marry me. Now you know all about me."

I didn't know what to say to this. Soldiers of Rome below the rank of centurion, in the infantry, and decurion, in the cavalry, are not legally allowed to marry. Most of them do anyway, but the army does not recognize the marriages, and if a soldier is posted far away, his family will be left behind impoverished unless he can scrape together enough money for their passage. I finished the porridge. "My wife died last spring," I replied at last, a confidence in exchange for a confidence.

Her look of amusement vanished. "The one you were calling for."

I nodded. "You have children?"

"No." After a moment she smiled a nervous acknowledgment of the curiosity that I could not quite conceal, and went on. "My mother was another soldier's daughter, and lived in the fort village at Hunnum: she made a living by weaving and selling vegetables after my father left. She died when I was fifteen. My sister died in childbirth three years ago, and my brother is also with the army on the Danube. I am entirely on my own, and quite independent. You?"

"I have two sisters who live in my own country, whom I can never see again. I had a little son, who died with my wife."

"I'm sorry." She paused, then asked, "Where are you from?"

"The Romans call the land Sarmatia."

"Oh! Oh, Deae Matres! *You're* one of the notorious Sarmatians?"

"Notorious?" I asked, amused.

She smiled back, with an air of surprise, but her reply was serious. "In the marketplace in Corstopitum they say you drink blood out of skulls and wear cloaks of human skin. People who used to go to Condercum or Cilurnum to trade started coming to Corstopitum instead. They were just thinking of going back again when there was that mutiny, and the battle against the Picts. We were glad, very glad, that the Selgovae and Votadini didn't have the chance to steal our cattle and carry us off as slaves—but we were frightened, too, to hear how completely they'd been crushed. And when the Sarmatians at Condercum mutinied, just thirty killed over a hundred . . ." She stopped. I could see the awful possibility running through her mind, that I was a mutineer who had escaped and was fleeing justice. "You're not from Condercum, are you?" she asked anxiously.

"No," I replied, "Cilurnum."

But I remembered now, going to Condercum and starting back with Arshak. At the bottom of my mind the memory of what had happened on the road heaved, like a serpent hidden in the dust. I was silent, the white morning dimmed.

"So you're a soldier," Pervica said, after a silence, in a flat voice. "I didn't realize that. You weren't armed, except for the dagger. You said you worked with horses—but of course, you're a cavalryman." After another silence, she said, "When Cluim went in to Corstopitum yesterday, he told the town authorities, not the military ones. That explains why they'd never heard of you."

"Lend me a horse and I will ride in myself," I said, trying to shake off a sense of horror at the shadow of memory. "I remember now, I was at Corstopitum on fort business. I think my friends will still be there. Lend me the stallion Wildfire, if you like; I think I can persuade him to carry me to the gates."

She looked at me with the crooked smile, but her eyes were sad. "Lend you Wildfire? Oh, he was never broken to the saddle; he's a carriage horse. And you certainly shouldn't try to ride all the way to Corstopitum. You were almost dead, night before last. When we brought you into the house, you were gray and cold as ice, and I thought we were carrying a corpse. I'll take you in in the cart this afternoon."

"I thank you. My men will be concerned for me."

Her face changed again, the faint regret shifting to wariness. "Your men? You're an officer?"

I nodded.

She dropped her eyes. "Oh, I'm a fool!" she exclaimed. She didn't explain why, and I had no chance to ask her, because she went on immediately, "It seems so strange that you're a Sarmatian. All my life I've seen troops leaving Britain for the Danube. My father went when I was seven, and my elder brother was recruited for the war six years ago. And now your people are being sent here to defend us!"

"Where were your father and brother posted?" I asked.

"My father was with the Second Aelian Cohort, at a place called Cibalae, in Lower Pannonia. We had one letter from him after he left, with some money, and then nothing more. My brother was further west, at Vindobona, with the Second Brittones. Do you know of them?"

I knew the places. Vindobona was well to the west of my own country, and Pervica's brother probably had to fight Quadi, not Sarmatians. But Cibalae was closer to home. The fort there had been at the western edge of the territory I used to raid, and I had an unpleasant feeling that I'd once scalped one of the Second Aelian Cohort. I struggled to clear the memory, and came up with the image of an auxiliary kneeling to brace his spear as I rode at him, a round-faced man in a long mail shirt. Yes. The scalp was brown, with no white in it, and the man had been about thirty. That had been three years ago—he couldn't have been Pervica's father, who would have had to be in his late forties. That was a relief.

"You fought them?" asked Pervica, who was still watching me.

"The Second Aelians, yes," I admitted, "but not your father."

"It must be very strange for you, after fighting Romans, to come here as soldiers of Rome."

That summary of our twisted place in the world was so simple and straightforward I could almost have laughed. "It is," I agreed. "It is very strange."

There was a moment of silence, and then she said, "Well, I can send Cluim in to town today, and tell him to go to the military authorities this time. Or, if you like, I can drive you in, in the cart. I need to buy some things in Corstopitum anyway."

At that moment there was a shriek of terror, shrill and piercing, from outside the house. Pervica leapt to her feet and pelted out the door. I followed her more slowly, still stiff-legged and clumsy.

The scream had come from the front of the house, and I hurried out into a columned courtyard to find the red-haired servant screaming again, Pervica running across the snow, and my own bodyguard, glittering in their scales, milling about the farm gate. In another instant I realized that one of the armored figures was Leimanos, and that he was leaning down from the saddle and clutching Cluim by the arm, shouting at the shepherd and hitting him in the face; and that Comittus was beside him, trying to restrain him.

"Leimanos!" I shouted. "What are you doing?"

He spun round in the saddle. "My prince!" he yelled joyfully.

"Ariantes!" shouted Comittus.

And the whole squadron galloped over. Leimanos swept Cluim up over the saddle and took him along, then reined in sharply in front of me and dismounted, leaving the shepherd to slip off dazedly on his own. Pervica, halfway across the yard, turned and began walking slowly back. The horses steamed and glittered, and I noticed Farna, tied behind Leimanos' horse.

"My prince!" said Leimanos, and he dropped to both knees in the snow in front of me and kissed my hand. "Thank the gods you're alive!"

"I thank the gods indeed," I answered, and pulled him to his feet. The rest of the bodyguard crowded round, shouting, slapping me and each other on the back, thanking the gods. Comittus, grinning and bouncing, pushed through them and shook my hand.

"But what were you doing to this shepherd here?" I asked, when they'd calmed down enough to let me speak. Cluim had picked himself up, and Pervica was wiping his face with a handful of snow. His face was blotched from the blows, his nose was bleeding, and he looked terrified.

"We found him outside the gate, and stopped him to ask the way," said Leimanos, glaring at Cluim. "Then we saw that he had your dagger. We feared the worst, my lord."

I shook my head. "I gave him the dagger. He found me lying nearly drowned in the river, and pulled me out. It is to him, and to this lady here whom he serves, that I owe my life."

Leimanos gave an exclamation of dismay and went over to Cluim. The shepherd backed away hastily, but Leimanos knelt to him. "Forgive me," he said, in Latin, in which he now had some fluency. "I did not understand. I thought you had killed my prince."

Cluim still looked terrified. Comittus interpreted for him, and the shepherd nodded, but did not seem inclined to come any nearer. Leimanos took the dagger, which he'd thrust in his own belt, and offered it back. After a nervous glance around, Cluim snatched it hastily.

"My lord gave you that," said Leimanos, "in gratitude for his life. And for his life, which I value above my own, let me add this." He laid his own dagger at Cluim's feet.

"And this," said Banadaspos, taking the gold pin from his coat and putting it beside the dagger.

And the others in the bodyguard, all thirty of them, copied them, each adding something—a ring, a purse full of money, a gold torque taken from a Pictish chieftain—until poor Cluim was shaking his bruised head in bewilderment. He exclaimed loudly in British and pointed to Pervica.

"He says these should belong to his lady," Comittus translated, then at once abandoned translation and gratitude together. "Deae Matres! Ariantes, I've never been so pleased to see anyone in all my life. As soon as you disappeared we realized you were the last man in Britain we could afford to lose. We've been going out of our minds with anxiety, and the men back in Cilurnum are ready to riot. We didn't dare tell the fourth dragon you were missing, and Siyavak has been asking to see you: we had to tell him you'd gone back to the fort. If you'd died so soon after Gatalas, gods help us all! Priscus wanted to sack Gaius Valerius for letting you and Arshak leave Condercum without an escort, and he was cursing your soul to Hades for deciding to go hunting. Don't worry, he'll forgive you anything when he sees you alive. But I felt sorry for that poor miserable magistrate."

"What magistrate?" I asked.

"The one who told the prefect of the First Thracians yesterday evening that a shepherd had reported finding a man in the river the day before, and was he possibly anything to do with us! We'd been turning the road between here and Condercum upside down all day, looking for you. The magistrate couldn't remember anything about the report, and Priscus practically had him flogged. Fortunately, his clerk had made a record of it. We all set off at full gallop at first light to find you. The men wanted to set out last night, but we weren't sure of finding the place in the dark. Thank the gods you're well! The report said you were too weak to stand and very confused in mind."

I nodded impatiently; I had just remembered that Leimanos should have been at Cilurnum. "Who is in charge at the fort?" I asked.

"Longus and Facilis," replied Comittus promptly. "I hope there hasn't been trouble!"

I groaned. "Leimanos!" I exclaimed, switching back to Sarmatian, "Who did you leave in charge?"

"Kasagos, my lord."

"Kasagos! You know perfectly well that half the men won't obey him because he's Roxalanic! What were you thinking of?"

"I'm sorry," said Leimanos, wretchedly. "I couldn't endure waiting there, with you perhaps lying dead or injured in the forest, and neither could anyone else in the bodyguard. Our duty is to defend your life or die beside you. We'd rather die than live in the disgrace of having abandoned our lord."

"We'll all be disgraced if the dragon has been killing Asturians in the absence of anyone to control them! Give me my horse!"

I went over to Farna and began tightening the girth on her saddle.

"What are you doing?" asked Pervica, speaking for the first time since my men arrived. She turned anxiously to Comittus. "You don't mean for him to ride to Corstopitum today?"

"Why not?" asked Comittus in surprise.

"Because it's perfectly true that yesterday afternoon he was too weak to

stand and believed that he was lying dead in his tomb. And he had good reason to believe himself dead: when I first saw him, I thought the same. I didn't
pull him back from the grave to see him catapulted into it from a horse's
back."

I left Farna and came over to her. "Lady Pervica," I said, "you need not
fear that your efforts have been wasted. I can rest on horseback as comfortably as in a bed. And I must return to Cilurnum at once. My men need me."

"To Cilurnum!" she said, frowning at me. "That's even worse! It's
farther!" Then she caught her breath. "You're the prefect at Cilurnum,
aren't you?"

"Not exactly. I am commander of the Sarmatian *numerus* there. My
friend Lucius Javolenus Comittus here ought to be prefect, but is called a
liaison officer instead. The titles have been changed because of our . . .
notoriety."

She didn't smile. "And . . . they said you're a prince? All these men are
your subjects?"

"That was how it was when we were in our own country. Here it is different. I ask you to understand, though, why I must leave at once. My brother
prince at Condercum died at Roman hands only a few days ago, and my men
will have been very alarmed at the news that I was missing. I left Leimanos
here, who is commander of my bodyguard, in charge of the rest of my company at the fort. But he believed his first duty was to find me, and has left the
rest of the dragon under the command of those whose authority will not
master them. I must return at once to reassure them."

She caught her breath again, angry, astonished, and bewildered. "We
can't possibly accept all the gold your . . . your men have given us. It's far too
much, and I couldn't justify keeping it. I don't want money from you."

"My bodyguard paid Cluim, and you, the debt they owed to their own
honor," I told her. "They were ashamed because they had been unable to defend me themselves and because they had attacked the one who had done it
in their place. I could never correct them in something that concerns their
honor: you must keep what they gave you. But for my own part, I know only
too well that I have given you nothing but thanks." I took her hand. "And
those I give you again, with the promise that my life is at your service." I

kissed the hand, pressed it to my forehead, let go of it, and stepped back. She stared at me with wide eyes and flushed cheeks. "May I come back in a few days to talk about the horse?" I asked her.

"Y-yes," she said. "Yes, if you like—but you shouldn't ride today!"

I went back to my horse. I slid the stirrups down the leathers and mounted. "Tell Cluim I regret it that Leimanos struck him," I said, unfastening the lead rein from Farna's bridle. "I will see you in a few days. Lady, good health!"

"You obstinate, arrogant man!" she replied. "I pray the gods give *you* good health!"

I looked back at her and smiled. Tirgatao used to talk to me like that. I gave the signal for the bodyguard to mount, bowed to Pervica from the saddle, and trotted away from the farm, leaving her standing on the porch and staring after us, a slim gray figure against the whiteness of the snow.

Pervica had been right to doubt whether I was fit to ride any distance. I could rest comfortably on horseback, as I'd said, but I was shivering with the cold before we'd gone a mile. It didn't help that I'd lost my hat. Comittus noticed and suggested that we go to Corstopitum after all, and said that we were expected there, but I was concerned about the situation at Cilurnum and anxious to return at once. I sent a Latin-speaking bodyguard to Corstopitum instead, to announce that I was safe and would go there the following day as soon as I'd reassured my men. I borrowed the messenger's helmet to keep my ears warm.

Comittus asked me several times on that ride whether I was really all right, whether I was chilled, whether we shouldn't stop and rest a bit. I found it exasperating and answered only by asking him questions about other things. In this way I learned that the Sarmatians in Cilurnum were confined to our camp, very sensibly, and the Asturians to the fort; that my weapons and armor, except for my bow case, were in Corstopitum; that Eukairios was still in Corstopitum; that the legate was also still there; that the fourth dragon was also there; that Farna had been found on the road the evening I disappeared, with my spear in its holder, my sword hung from the saddle, and my armor in its pack behind. My bow case was missing. "Arshak told us that you'd both seen a wild boar," Comittus said, "and had decided to hunt it. He said he lost you and the boar both in the chase. Why didn't you bring the spear? Those bows of yours are powerful, but I wouldn't have thought they're the gear to use on boars. We'd been imagining you lying wounded, gored by the beast, or perhaps eaten by wolves. How did you end up in the river?"

"I do not remember," I replied.

But even without remembering, I knew that Arshak was lying. I did remember how we'd argued in Corstopitum, and how we'd set out from Condercum, with Arshak glowering at the road before us: we had not gone hunting. I struggled to remember the missing hours, but they were fogged, and I was left only with the sense of horror at something forgotten. I knew, though, that what had happened was somehow bound up with the legate's wife, and I hadn't forgotten that she was Comittus' kinswoman and that he admired her. I said nothing to him about my doubts. I said nothing to my men, either: if they knew that someone had tried to murder me, they would be out for revenge, and that would only cause trouble. So I let Arshak's story stand.

The precautions taken by the officers at Cilurnum proved to have been sufficient, and my fears unfounded: though things had been tense, my men had not yet begun killing Asturians. When I appeared, somewhat the worse for the ride, the Asturians came running out of their barracks and the Sarmatians galloped up from the camp, and there was a great deal of shouting. Even Facilis seemed pleased to see me.

I was by this time feeling very chilled and utterly exhausted, so after letting my men see that I had not been murdered by the Romans and giving a few orders to my officers, I went to my wagon to rest. When I got off my horse, my bad leg gave under me and I fell, then, to my disgust, found I couldn't get up again. Everyone crowded about exclaiming and explaining to one another that I'd been practically dead of drowning two days before, and arguing with each other over how I should be looked after. The Romans would have whisked me off to the fort hospital at once, but I refused to allow it, and managed to pull myself back onto my feet, though I had to lean against the side of a wagon to stay there. We had by this time built shelters of wattle and mud daub out from the front of the wagons, put awnings over them, and covered the ground beneath them with straw to give ourselves somewhere warm to sit in the evenings. My men built a roaring fire in front of my own shelter, covered its floor with extra straw and several thicknesses of rugs, and there I sat to get warm. The bodyguard fussed over me like a pack of old women at a childbed, bringing hot compresses for my feet, fetching blankets and pillows, offering cups of warm milk and bowls of beef stew. It was some time before I could persuade them to go away and let me rest. Then I drank the milk and ate the stew, and lay still, looking at the fire and thinking about Pervica. I forgot Arshak, Bodica, and the nagging uncertainty about the Brigantes and the Picts. I realized now why she'd called herself a fool. When she learned I was an officer, she realized that I would be free to marry her, which I couldn't have done as a common soldier—and she'd at once told herself that it was far too early to worry about such matters and she was a fool to think of it. But she had needed to tell herself that: she was not indifferent to me. I saw her again, standing flushed and angry on the porch of her house, telling me I was obstinate and arrogant, and I was happy.

IX

THE NEXT MORNING I saddled Farna, collected the second ten of my bodyguard, and rode into the fort to see if Comittus also needed to go to Corstopitum.

I found the tribune in his house, having a late breakfast with Flavinus Longus and Facilis. They all jumped up and hurried over smiling when I walked into the dining room.

"A hundred greetings!" exclaimed Comittus. "I'm glad to see you looking so well. Sit down and have something to eat."

"Thank you, I have eaten already," I replied. "Did you need to return to Corstopitum?"

"You're not planning to ride there now, are you?" asked Longus.

"I sent a messenger yesterday, saying I would come."

"You can send another one today, saying you won't," growled Facilis.

I shrugged. "Are you coming, Comittus? Or any of you?"

"*Vae me miserum!*" exclaimed Longus. "Man, when you arrived yesterday you were the color of a dead fish and your teeth were going like castanets. There's nothing so urgent in Corstopitum that it can't wait a day or two, is there?"

I shrugged again. I was very uneasy about the hours I had forgotten, and I was aware that while I rested in the fort, things might be happening in the town that could devastate and destroy. I was particularly concerned about Siyavak and the fourth dragon, brought to the town as something very close to prisoners and at the mercy of the same lies that had killed Gatalas. Perhaps I'd find nothing to do even if I went, but I didn't want to risk it. "I am perfectly well enough to ride," I said.

"That's what you said yesterday," said Comittus.

"And it was true then, and is truer now."

"You're a very obstinate man," said Longus.

At that echo I grinned, and then found them all staring at me.

"What is the matter?" I asked.

"You were smiling," said Longus.

"So?"

"So I've never seen you smile. Not more than a lopsided, if-you-think-it's-amusing sort of twist of the mouth. I'd decided it was beneath your dignity. What did I say that was so funny?"

Comittus suddenly started to grin. "That woman on the farm told him he was obstinate as well, and he smiled then."

"A woman on a farm?" asked Longus, with lively interest. "What woman on what farm? A young woman?"

"A lady," I corrected him, beginning to be annoyed. "The widowed landowner whose people took me from the river and who drew me back to life by her care."

"She was young though," Comittus said, mischievously. "And rather pretty. And you're right, Gaius, I've never seen him smile like that. Is she why you're in such a hurry to get back to Corstopitum?"

I cursed inwardly. Romans manage love differently from Sarmatians, and I was uncertain myself how I should go about following what was still nothing more than an interest, a stirring of desire that had been dead. But I did know that my own people allow women far more freedom than the Romans do. The reputation of a Roman lady is a delicate thing, and rough jokes in the fort could break it. "The lady is a respectable woman of rank," I said severely. "I owe her my life, and I will not have her spoken of with disrespect because she showed me kindness. If anyone fails to treat her with the honor she deserves, I will fight him in earnest."

They were silent a moment, digesting this. Then Facilis laughed. He had a harsh, barking laugh, an unpleasant sound, but his face was genial. "I'm sure the lady is modest and highly respectable," he said. "And I suppose your wife back home is like them all, officially widowed."

"My wife back home was killed by the Second Pannonian cavalry," I replied sharply, "and my little son with her. Their bodies were burned. Do not speak of them."

I don't know why I announced it to them like that. No one had spoken of them. All my followers, and most of Arshak's and Gatalas' as well, knew what had happened, but they had kept silent about it for fear of offending me. The Romans had not known.

"I'm sorry," said Facilis, after a silence.

"Yes," I said. "As you once pointed out, we started that war."

"I'm sorry," Facilis said again, and sighed.

"The second ten of my bodyguard are waiting outside," I said. "Is there anyone else that needs to come, or shall I go speak to Priscus and to Siyavak on my own?"

"I left some things in Corstopitum," said Comittus. "I'll come. But I need to get my warm cloak and saddle my horse."

"We will ride on slowly; catch us up," I said, and turned to go. Just at the door, I remembered another thing I had meant to say, and turned back. "Comittus, Facilis—thank you for vouching for me to the legate."

"What were we supposed to do?" asked Facilis in his usual harsh voice. "Lie?" But he was smiling again.

The ride to Corstopitum did not tire me too badly and we arrived to find the town peaceful. (Most of the troops, both Sarmatians and Priscus' legionaries, were camped outside the city, as there wasn't space for them inside.) I left my escort at the stables in the military compound and went to the commandant's house, where Comittus and I announced ourselves to the slaves. I asked where Eukairios was, but nobody seemed to know. A nervous pay-and-a-half clerk said that he had been billeted in the commandant's house, but that he wasn't there anymore. They were sending out runners to find him when Priscus himself appeared.

"Huh!" he said, scowling at me. "So there you are. What happened to you? They said they pulled you out of the river."

"Greetings, my lord legate," I replied. "They said the same to me. I do not remember it."

"Huh!" he said again. "Well, at least you're alive. Your advice has been wanted. The fellow you put in charge of the fourth dragon has been full of complaints about supplies, and everyone seems to agree that you'd find a way to satisfy him. Come into my office. I'll summon him and Gaius Valerius, and we'll go over it all. Lucius Javolenus, did you need to see me?"

"No, sir. I only came to Corstopitum to fetch some things, but of course, if you have anything for me to do . . ."

"Go tell Siavacus and Valerius that Ariantes is here and they're to come at once."

"Yes, my lord. Uh . . ."

Priscus didn't wait for the question, but stamped off into the building. I followed the legate into his office—or rather, the prefect of the Thracians' office, which Priscus had taken over—and perched uncomfortably on the three-legged stool he'd indicated when he seated himself in the chair. (I would have preferred the floor, but knew it would embarrass us both.)

I was glad the officers of the fourth dragon had to be summoned; I had another matter I wanted to discuss. "My lord legate," I began carefully, "I have been giving thought to the matter we discussed a few days ago."

"What?" he exclaimed. "You worry about your men's pay even when you're drowning?"

Very likely I did give him what Longus had described as an if-you-think-it's-amusing twist of the mouth. "I considered the problem of the horses as I was recovering."

He gave a snort. "What about the horses?"

"Do you remember, my lord, why I was reluctant to sell the additional ones we own?"

"You said that the poorest man you commanded had once owned a dozen horses, and had two, and the richest once owned over a thousand, and had six. You thought it would be humiliating and distressing to them to lose any more. Distressing or not, Commander, the province of Britain cannot pay for barbarian *numeri* to keep six horses just to satisfy their vanity."

"That was one reason, my lord. I had another one."

He sighed. "And I must admit, the second was a bit more compelling than the first. You don't approve of native breeds of horse, and you want to keep those you have for breeding."

"The British horses, my lord, with a few exceptions, are not large enough to carry the armor. And the exceptions are extremely expensive. The dragon could not afford to purchase enough of them."

"Very well—but you know the rules. We do not let Roman troops engage in farming while on active service—and that includes Sarmatians taking time out to breed horses."

"Sir, the horses we have are in their prime. In a few years they will be past that prime and aging quickly. Without sufficient horses of good quality, we cannot use our armor. If we are to function at all, we must begin breeding the animals at once. Now, my lord, the thing I was considering was this. I understand that the army can lease out property to private companies, that in fact this is done with land used to provide supplies. Could we not lease out some of the horses to a suitable private farm? The breeding stock would remain ours, but the farm would feed and care for the beasts, and in return receive a set price for the offspring."

Priscus looked at me for a minute, rubbing a hand thoughtfully against his chin. "Did you think of that yourself?" he asked.

"Yes."

"You're a pretty damned odd barbarian. Yes, that's an excellent idea. We could fix a price that would make it worth the farm's while, but still be well below the market value of your bloodstock. If we had any foals surplus, we could sell them at a handsome profit. It's an *excellent* idea. But wouldn't your men be distressed and humiliated at this as well?"

"No. We are accustomed to . . . let out . . . our cattle. I had horses with every man in the dragon: they cared for them, I picked out some of the offspring, and they kept the rest. The men will understand it at once. But, my lord, we would have to give some of them leave to visit any farms that were chosen, to teach the British owners how to handle the animals, and to assist in the autumn when the mares are covered and in spring when the foals are born. We have not been impressed at how well the Britons handle horses."

Priscus gave a harsh laugh. "Setting your men horse-rearing by the back door, eh? Well, if it's just a few men, and just spring and autumn . . . we'd be hard-pressed to find the stud farms to manage such pedigreed beasts otherwise."

"I have found one, possibly," I said, coming to the point that had given me the idea in the first place. "The place where I was brought when they took me out of the river. The previous owner had purchased a very fine stallion, intending to use it for stud, but he died before fulfilling his intention, and his widow does not have the skill to complete it. They have some good grazing land, though, and some people who could learn horse breeding. I believe the lady who now owns the farm would be interested in such a proposal.

I was to see her in a few days, about the stallion, which she wishes to sell. If it is acceptable to you, I could put this suggestion to her then."

Priscus laughed again. "You don't waste your time, do you? Lying there, fresh from drowning, and planning to invest in horseflesh. Jupiter! Eh, Bodica, my dear!" I turned on my stool, and there indeed was the legate's lady, stopped in the office door and staring at me wide-eyed with a look not so much of surprise as of outrage.

"Come in!" her husband told her jovially. "Here's Ariantes back, alive and fit and with a very clever way to pay for all his horses."

Bodica smiled at Priscus and came into the office. I stood and bowed my head to her in greeting; when I raised my eyes, I caught the look of murderous hatred she shot me while her face was turned from her husband's. I knew, as soon as I saw it, that we'd met on the road from Condercum. The meeting was still hidden in the fog that covered my memory, but I could sense it there now. It was a relief. It hadn't made any sense that I'd fought Arshak and ended up in the river without a mark on me.

"Lord Ariantes," she said, sitting down on her husband's desk. "I confess, I never expected to see you alive again."

"No," I replied. "I myself believed I was dead, two days ago. And I can still remember nothing between leaving Condercum and waking half-drowned. I live by the kindness of the gods." I did not want a contest with her yet, and wanted her to know that. I still had no proof, and I suspected that even memory would afford me no proof—not the kind of proof I would need to convince the legate that his adored young wife was guilty of treason. The bare word of a man who'd been threatened with demotion and even flogging for "causing trouble" would clearly not be enough.

Bodica gave me another glare of rage and loathing, then looked quickly away before her husband could notice. "What is this clever plan about horses?" she asked.

Priscus was explaining it when Siyavak and Valerius Victor came in. Bodica gave a bright smile to Victor, which he returned, but a lingering, assuring smile to Siyavak—and I noticed that that, too, was returned. I decided I was right to have come to Corstopitum.

Both officers, and Bodica, joined in commenting on the scheme and suggesting modifications to it. Then we turned to the business of Siyavak's supplies (too much grain, not enough meat and milk) and the legate's wife smiled again, and said she hadn't meant to distract anyone, she'd just heard that I was there and she wanted to be sure I was safe and well, and she'd go. She went, leaving us to draw up comparative budgets. I missed Eukairios.

I could not satisfy Siyavak: I was not satisfied with the supplies for my own men. However, we agreed on an arrangement that was as good as we could get, and as soon as we had, Siyavak excused himself. It seemed to me that for a man who'd been asking to see me, he was now in a hurry to get away from me. I also made my excuses to the legate, and left with him: I wanted to talk to him.

He tried to slip away, and said he needed to go to the stables to see how his troop's horses were. I refused to be slipped away from, and said I would join him. He was not pleased, but endured it. As soon as we were private, in the same alley where I'd argued with Arshak, I asked "Has the legate's lady spoken to you?"

He stopped in midstride and whirled to face me. "What do you mean?" he demanded suspiciously.

"She has spoken to Arshak," I said. "I wondered if she had spoken to you."

"They've both said some things to me," he replied. "Some things I agreed with." He turned back and started on.

"Wait," I called after him. "The rod that was sent to Gatalas . . ."

That stopped him and turned him around again. "Do you know who sent it?" he demanded, eagerly this time.

I shook my head. "But listen, Siyavak. Whoever sent it knew how to make divining rods and set them in a pattern. But they used British writing on the last rod to make their message clear: therefore, the sender is British, but familiar with our own people. Further, the sender was able to get the message into Condercum when there was tension in the camp without the Roman authorities being aware of it: therefore, the sender was not Pictish, despite being in league with the tribes, but was probably a person of some importance within the Roman army. The messenger who brought it said it came from Eburacum. The lady Aurelia Bodica was in Eburacum. She is a British princess and a legate's wife. And she has spoken a great deal with Arshak, and could easily have learned, from him or from his diviner, how to construct her message. She was asking about such matters even on the road from Dubris."

He let out his breath with a hiss. "She had no reason to do it! Why would she want my lord to die?"

"If she's spoken to you, you know better than I. Is a mutiny against the Romans a thing that would please her?"

Siyavak walked back toward me, now frowning deeply. "Why?" he asked again. "She's a legate's wife. Why would she want to help raiders from outside the Roman border?"

This was a thing that puzzled me, too. She was an ambitious woman— but surely a legate's wife not only has a position of power already, but has further scope for her ambition in advancing her husband's career? Instead, it had seemed to me from the first that she wanted to use us for a purpose of her own. Why?

"I don't know why," I admitted. "I have no proof that she's the one who did it, and without proof I've already said too much. But I think I can guess what she said to you. Perhaps she welcomed you, promised you her assistance in Eburacum, told you that the Britons are the natural allies of our people, far more than the Romans. And when you agreed and she saw that you hated the Romans, perhaps she hinted that we might not always be enemies of the Britons, but could join with them against a common enemy. She's told you, certainly, that I've gone over entirely to the Roman side, and you should not trust me."

I'd struck the mark: his frown vanished in a look of consternation. "And you haven't?"

It hurt unexpectedly that he had believed it so completely, and I answered him more directly and passionately than I might have done. "I'll tell you whose side I'm on," I said. "I'm on the side of the sixth dragon. I'm on the side of my own people. They followed me on raids against the Romans, they followed me to war. Now everything we gained in raiding is lost, like the war, and we've become dead men to our own people, but they must follow me still, across the ocean to an island of ghosts. All that we had is gone, but as long as they and I both live, they are bound to me and I to them. I will do my utmost for them. If that means Romanizing, I'll Romanize, as far as I need to. I have as much reason as any man living to hate the Romans, but I can't choose my alliances from hatred. The honor and safety of my people is in my hands, and I would rather keep them secure than be revenged on any enemy—particularly an enemy we have all sworn on fire to serve."

"But if we could make an alliance against the Romans?" Siyavak asked—whispering now. "A successful one?"

"With whom?" I asked. "With someone who told a lie that sent your lord to his death and which would have left me disgraced, and my men, most likely, killed mutinying? And I'll tell you more: the Picts we fought here not ten days ago hadn't just heard that there would be a mutiny on the Wall to distract the garrisons, they'd heard it well in advance. They'd had time to settle blood feuds and forge alliances between tribes. Whoever sent that message acted deliberately and with forethought, and *chose* to tell Gatalas nothing except the lie that killed him. I don't trust allies who take no risks themselves but are very free with other people's blood. I trust them even less if they are, as I suspect, headed by a woman who smiles sweetly at her husband when she lies to him and slips from his bed to plot with his enemies. She says she is our natural ally—why should we believe she's truer to us than she is to the legate? It seems to me far more likely that she's playing 'divide and rule.' When we and the Romans have killed each other, she'll collect the spoils for herself. Look at what she does, Siyavak, not at her smiles, and think if you trust her then."

Siyavak thought, and gazed at me in distress. "I've always hated the Romans," he said, "and everything that's happened since we came to Britain has only made me hate them more. When the lady Aurelia Bodica talked to me and hinted at revenge, it gave me hope. But you're right. You're right. Very likely it was her who killed Gatalas, and her alliance would only kill us all. But I'm not used to bridling myself with reason. I never was a scepter-holder."

"You're the commander of a dragon now," I replied. "You and Valerius Victor. You'll have to learn."

"Help me," he said wretchedly. "You're saying that to revenge my lord's death, I must fight the enemies of my enemies? Not just on the battlefield, but in secret? How can I do it?"

"By all the gods! You mustn't even *think* of revenge yet. We don't know for certain that she sent the message, and if you were found plotting to murder the wife of a legate, we'd all be punished. No, all I have said is that the alliance we've been offered is no alliance, but a death trap. Our only choice is what it always was: keep our oaths or die. And how can we lead our people to death? Your prince commanded you to surrender to the Romans so that you'd live: do you want to throw his last gift away?"

"No," said Siyavak, soberly. "No—but it is my duty to revenge him." He rubbed a hand wearily along his face. "And you're right. It's my duty to see that the others of my dragon stay alive and reach the good fortune the gods promised us. Both duties make me an enemy of Lady Aurelia. But I don't know how to go about discharging either."

I'd won, made him a servant of Rome, and I felt only grief and weariness. I leaned against the wall. "I don't know any more than you," I said, "but I must warn you: she's won Arshak over, completely as far as I can tell—though you probably know that yourself. And you can add one more thing to what we know of her: she's dangerous. Arshak and I met her on the way back from Condercum. I can't remember now what she said or what came of it, but I do know that I didn't agree with her—and I ended up in the river."

He stared. "I thought perhaps Arshak had fought you," he said, after a silence.

"You believed that Romanizing has made me so feeble I'd lose without either of us putting a mark on the other?"

"No," he answered, flushing a bit, "I'm sorry. I didn't think at all. Then how . . . ?"

"I can't remember. But I don't think the details will make a great difference. The god warned us in Bononia to beware of lies and deceits, and we must take that warning to heart. It seems to me that if you're not going to join her, you have two choices. The first, the course I will follow myself, is never to see her privately, never to accept any gift from her, and to distrust every message you receive that she might have tampered with—and you'll have to be suspicious of Arshak as well, since he's firmly behind her banner."

"And the second choice?"

"Let her believe that she's won you over, discover her plans, and expose them. That's the way you'd get your revenge without harming your men. But you'd have to lie to her. She might either discover it, and kill you—or she might win you over in fact."

When I saw his eyes light, I knew which choice he'd make. But I'd known that he'd choose the more dangerous path if it offered him revenge. It was the path I'd both hoped and feared he'd choose—hoped, because he could learn things that would let us destroy our enemies; feared, because I was letting him take a course of danger and dishonor that I'd been too proud to take myself.

"Do you think I'd go over to her if she's guilty of Gatalas' death?" he demanded impatiently.

"I think you hate the Romans, and she's very persuasive. She might be able to convince you of something you wanted to believe."

"I am not blind or stupid," he said bitterly. "I heard her before in a fog, without thinking, but when a thing's been pointed out to me, I can see it. I will watch facts now, not pretty smiles. No. I will get revenge. But . . ." He stopped, then nerved himself. "But you must help me. I feel as though I'm riding an unknown plain without landmarks, and I don't know which way to turn to reach my goal. You must advise me."

I'd never expected him to humble himself that far, and I blinked at it. He went on quickly, in a low voice, "I don't know how to govern myself, let alone command a dragon subject to the Romans. You're a scepter-holder and you've learned to use the Roman roads. You must advise me, Lord Ariantes."

I said nothing for a minute. It was not that I didn't want to advise him, but I didn't see how I could.

"I know!" he said, misunderstanding my silence. "I've insulted you, now to your face and before in my own thoughts. But I've thought from time to time as well that the sixth dragon was lucky in its commander, and I beg your pardon."

"I have nothing to pardon," I answered, touched by it. "You served your own prince honorably. But how can I advise you if you're in Eburacum, under Bodica's eyes? For you to consult me would put your life at risk. But if you want my advice, I'm here. We'll talk through what we can here and now, and I'll try to find another way for you to reach me in future."

We talked for some time, first in the alleyway, then at the back of the stables, and parted in the end warmly. I'd been quite right in my first judgment of the man, that he was both intelligent and loyal. I could only pray to the gods that he was intelligent enough to deceive Bodica, and loyal enough not to be turned by her.

When Siyavak had left the stables, I remained for a while, sitting on a bale of straw with my head on my knees, rubbing my sore leg. I was tired—

not perhaps as exhausted as I'd been the day before, but still, deeply and immeasurably tired. I'd made no arrangements to spend the night in Corstopitum, and my bodyguard were planning to meet me back in the stables around the middle of the afternoon. The thought of the ride back depressed me; the thought of arranging accommodation in the town for the ten I'd brought with me depressed me as well. I was trying to work up the strength to do one or the other when I heard a polite dry cough, and picked up my head to see Eukairios standing in front of me.

I smiled, so pleased to see him that I surprised myself. He smiled back: I hadn't seen him smile like that before, and it transformed his drab, weary face into something quite different.

"I met Banadaspos in the town," he said, "and he said he was to meet you here, so I came looking for you. I'm very glad to see you alive, my lord."

"The gods have been kind to me," I answered. "But where have you been? I asked for you at headquarters and at the commandant's house, but they did not know where you were."

"I've been staying with a friend in the town. But I packed my things when I heard you'd arrived, and I'm ready to leave whenever you want to."

"Readier than I am, then. Eukairios, I am tired."

He hesitated, then said cautiously, "You look very tired, if I may say so, my lord. Well, should I take my things back to my friend's? I'm sure you have a standing invitation to stay at the commandant's house."

"I have, my bodyguard has not. And the town is overcrowded, with all the troops here. They might be sent to the servants' quarters, or somewhere else that would offend them. No, better to ride back tonight. I need to find my armor. Then we can set out as soon as the others arrive back here."

Eukairios sat down carefully on the straw beside me. "Banadaspos was fetching your gear from the armory, my lord. He told me about it when I met him just now. Why don't you go somewhere and rest for a bit?"

I was relieved to hear it. "Why go somewhere?" I asked, leaning back into the straw.

He gave his short, nervous laugh, and I looked at him questioningly.

"Your notion of what dignity demands is so different from a Roman's," he explained. "A Roman noble might swallow a dozen insults which a Sarmatian would kill for, but he'd be outraged at the suggestion he could rest in a stable."

"That is what houses are for, is it?" I asked. "Dignity, dignity."

"And comfort."

"For some." I remembered Pervica, her house and her barn, and I smiled again. I began to tell Eukairios about River End Farm and about my plan for the horses. "Do you think she would be interested?" I asked.

"If the set price for the horses was good, I would think so," he replied. I could see him calculating it in his head: budget horse fodder; budget vet's fees; take gross income from the foals at probable set price; take net. "It would be a good steady income," he concluded, "and there'd be a good chance of extra, as well, since the army officials coming and going would probably buy the wool from the sheep too, and other farm produce as well. Yes, a sensible woman would be very pleased with it."

"Good."

We were silent for a few minutes, me lying back with my eyes half-shut, contented now, Eukairios still sitting primly with his feet tucked under him. Then the scribe said, hesitantly, "I was glad to hear that you succeeded in calming things at Condercum. May I . . . may I ask what caused the trouble there?"

I explained. When I came to the markings on the rod, he caught his breath. "I'd . . . heard a little bit about this. I'd been wanting to talk to you when you got back, only you didn't come back. My lord, I was very frightened, and I could only pray for your safety. What did these markings look like?"

I sat up: he sounded like he knew something. "Not like Roman writing," I said. "The lines were not joined up, and there were no curved lines. It was more sticklike."

"Like this?" he asked, and he bent over and made a series of markings in the dirt of the stable floor.

"Yes," I said, staring at them, "Exactly like that. You know that kind of writing?"

"A little." He rubbed the markings out with his foot. Like Victor, he didn't seem to like the look of them. He sighed, staring at the rubbed earth, then looked up suddenly and met my eyes. "Have you ever heard of the druids?"

"No."

His mouth twisted. "No, I suppose you wouldn't have. They're . . . another illegal religion."

"Like yours?"

"No. Oh no. Not 'like' at all. But . . . we know of each other. We've shared hiding places with them, and the names of officials who could be bribed; we've exchanged information about arrests, journeys, boats that could smuggle a passenger to safety. I think we both know that if the other group became legal, it would be an enemy, but we're both threatened with death for our faith, and that creates a bond, even unwillingly. The druids think we're atheists and we think they're addicted to sorcery, but we help each other." He paused, then went on, "They are the old priesthood of the gods of the Celts. Britain was the center of their cult. That writing is the kind they use."

I had a feeling like the moment in a hunt when you sight the quarry. I knew that a number of things I hadn't understood were about to be explained. "If they are the priests of an old religion, why are they illegal?" I asked quietly.

"Because they are enemies of Rome." Eukairios looked at me levelly and spoke in a steady voice, though his shoulders were hunched with tension and his hands locked together in his lap. "They were enemies of Rome before there was a province of Britain, before there was a province of Gaul. When Italians first fought Celts, the druids cursed them, and they've been cursing them ever since. Britain was always the center of their cult, the place they came to study their sacred mysteries, and when Britain first became a province, the druids took shelter in the West and preached rebellion. The Romans marched on them and slaughtered them, together with their wives and their children. That was about a century ago, and they and all their schools have been banned throughout the island ever since. It's not true elsewhere in the empire. In Gaul they're perfectly legal—but in Gaul they're not the same. The ban hasn't destroyed them. I've sometimes thought that their power is greater as a thing of whispers and shadows than it ever would be if they were legal, as they are in Gaul. They even send out emissaries to the Gaulish druids, whom they regard as heretical, telling them to mend their ways."

He fell silent for another long moment, then went on painfully, "I met one of them in Natalis' house in Dubris, a man called Cunedda. He'd been an emissary to Gaul, and once I gave him some information about a ship which probably saved his life—he was being hunted by the authorities at the time. We were very surprised to see one another, but when he learned that I had become your slave, he was pleased. He knew who you were, my lord. He asked me my name—I never told him that when we met before—and then he asked what it means. When I said that it means 'well timed,' he said, 'I accept the omen! I pray that this meeting is well timed indeed.' He wanted me to arrange a meeting with you."

"But you didn't."

"No, my lord. I . . . didn't know what you would do if I did, how you'd answer him. I didn't want to betray him to the authorities, but I didn't want to get mixed up in anything seditious, either. I made excuses and hoped he'd go away. But I met him again in Eburacum, and then again here, in Corstopitum. He was growing impatient, and said that you were avoiding those who might help you. My lord, he has an ally in the legate's house."

It was everything I'd thought. "Aurelia Bodica," I said.

The hunched shoulders slumped with relief. "You know, then."

"I had heard nothing. But it fits."

"I saw her with him, in the legate's house when I was billeted there, my lord. I left the house to avoid them. I was afraid, I . . . You see, I wouldn't do what they wanted, wouldn't arrange the private meeting, and it would be so easy for her to destroy me; all she would have to do would be to tell her husband that I'd stolen from her. I went into the town and stayed with my friend. I told him about her and about Cunedda, and he told me what he'd heard about the lady from his . . . contacts. It's the same here as it was in Gaul: the Christians and the druids exchange the names of people who are sympathetic or bribable, or hiding places which the authorities know nothing about—though, of course, the druids are very much more powerful here, in their homeland, and the Christians are very weak. The lady is known to be eager to protect the priesthood of the old gods, and is thought to be devoted to one of the most extreme sects. My friend said that there's been a lot of tension just in the past year, with the druids pushing the limits of official blindness, and he found it very easy to believe that an extreme sect has been growing in influence. I was very alarmed. I realized that I'd been a fool not to speak to you about it before, and I asked Banadaspos to let me know when you got back. Only you didn't come back.

"I was very frightened. I asked around at the stables and I found out that the lady Aurelia had had herself driven out of Corstopitum, to visit a shrine of the god Silvanus. I rode out to the shrine myself, and I learned that when she'd arrived there, she turned her slave and her driver out of the chariot and drove on alone. There were troops searching the road for you by then, so there was nothing I could do but ride back and pray. I thank God that you are still alive! That's not the end, though. Yesterday morning, when I was here in the stables looking after the horse you lent me, Cunedda came in looking for me. He gave me this message: 'Your master refused to listen to us. It's true that he still lives, but he will not live long. Before this season is ended he will die, and die not by any human hand but by the power of the sacred ones. You will see it and believe.' "

So. A threat. I had heard many of them in my time, and it didn't trouble me unduly. "A curse or an assassination?" I asked.

He hesitated, then shook his head. "A curse, my lord, at least at first. They are famous for working magic, sir, famous. They claim superhuman powers. They're certainly used to killing people secretly. Before the Romans came they practiced human sacrifice, mostly on willing victims. The official druids in Gaul now say that human sacrifice is hateful to the gods, and even some of the other British druids say that if the victim's unwilling, the sacrifice is useless. But there have been bodies found, strangled and dumped in the sacred wells, or hung from the sacred groves, and it's been clear that they weren't willing. People are afraid of the druids. If they don't talk about them much, that's the reason."

I was silent for a little while. "This sorcery," I said at last. "Is it powerful?"

"The druids claim it is, my lord. For my own part," he said defiantly, "I know that no power on earth or under it can stand against my God."

"Who is not mine. Still, I trust Marha, the holy one, is not his inferior. And from what you say, the druids have been cursing the Romans for centuries, and the power of Rome has only grown greater. But I will be on my guard. What did this priest mean by 'before this season is ended'? Before the end of the winter, or before this matter is settled?"

"I imagine it means before the end of the month, sir," he said unhappily. "*This* season would naturally mean the season we're in now, midwinter. The midwinter solstice is holy to the druids. It's only ten days from now."

"So, I do not have long to wait? That is good."

He obviously thought I wasn't taking it seriously enough. "Be careful what you eat, sir!" he exclaimed urgently. "The druids study drugs and poisons as well as magic."

The memory of the lost hours shifted again in my mind, chilling me, but again subsided. "Thank you," I said then, looking him in the eyes. "Thank you very much. You have given more loyalty than I have deserved of you."

"No, my lord. I have given what my duty demanded, but given it later than I should. If I had warned you earlier . . ."

"Could this Cunedda inform on you?"

He went still—then nodded miserably. "If he knew I'd informed on him, he would," he added. "If he didn't know, I'd probably be all right. My lord, what happened on the road from Condercum?"

I shook my head. "I do not remember. I remember setting out with Arshak, and nothing afterward until my wakening in Pervica's house—but I am certain I met the lady Aurelia on the road. She is, I think, the head of this conspiracy."

He blinked at that. He had obviously put her down as this Cunedda's disciple, a rich and arrogant young noblewoman playing for excitement's sake with an old and dangerous faith. "You don't think that Cunedda . . . ?" he began—but trailed off helplessly, as though realizing that Aurelia Bodica was nobody's disciple.

"She wishes to be a queen," I said, trying to set all my assembled pieces in order. "Her family is royal, and was long hostile to the Romans. She resents the marriage that was arranged for her and admires her ancestress, the queen of the Iceni for whom she was named. She has great influence with her husband, and has been able to appoint her kinsmen and friends to positions of power—Comittus at least owes his place to her, and there must be others. Comittus will tell you, too, when he sings her praises, that she has influence in the civil administration of the North, which is also in her husband's hands. She has had the power to create an instrument of war against the Romans, and I do not believe she would create that instrument and set it in the hands of another. She is a proud woman, and hates to be crossed in any way."

He was shocked silent. We weren't facing just one or two people near the legate and a handful of druids, but a substantial conspiracy, an unknown large number of people in the army and in places of power throughout the province.

"Have you heard any rumors about what her husband thinks of this?" I asked. It was the crucial question.

Eukairios nodded wearily. "He's heard the rumors, but doesn't believe them. He's not British, of course: he's an Italian from Mediolanum. Her family is royal, descended from the rulers of two kingdoms: they could have had the citizenship generations ago, but they refused to have anything to do with the Romans until very recently. They say that the legate was proud of himself for winning them over."

"And recent events have not made him suspicious?"

"My lord, there are hundreds of British tribesmen in the Sixth Legion and thousands in the auxiliaries. Dozens of them might have been able to send that message: anyone with druidical training would have been interested in your people's method of divination, and you don't keep it a secret. Why should the legate believe it was his wife?"

"She has been after us," I answered, sharply.

"And he's grateful to her, my lord, for helping him with such an irritable and indomitable people. He believes that without her help, he would have had far more trouble with Lord Arshak's people in Eburacum."

"She's won over Arshak and tried Siyavak."

"My lord, I thought as much. But the legions are not united either. There are factions even inside the Sixth at Eburacum, and I suppose that the legate thought she was winning them to *his* faction. My lord, Facilis would know more about this. He's a good man; I'm sure he would help."

Facilis was a shrewd man. He had guessed enough to let him suspect the lady, even without knowing about these druids, or hearing the hints she made to me and my brother princes. I was not surprised that he'd tackled Eukairios on the subject as well. But there were reasons why I could not accept any help from that quarter.

"So," I said, ignoring the suggestion, summing up. "Our enemies may be anywhere. We have no evidence that we could bring to a Roman court. Even if I remembered what the lady said on the road, I could only pledge my word against hers and Arshak's, and my word will not be enough. I am not trusted. Her own servants are unlikely to testify against her. This Cunedda is protected by her, and unlikely to be caught unless you inform on him, which you cannot do. As for you, she would say that you are my slave and will speak as I order you."

"I can't give evidence in court anyway," he said hurriedly, looking sick. "Anything I said would be weighed as testimony, which doesn't count as much as evidence . . . and . . . and I'm not sure I could repeat it, sir, under torture: please don't ask me to."

"Torture?" I asked in surprise.

He looked surprised in turn, that I hadn't realized this. "The testimony of slaves is always taken under torture, sir."

"Marha!" I exclaimed in disgust. "No. We cannot say anything to the authorities—not yet. We must wait in silence until we have the power to strike in force. Do not repeat what you have just told me to anyone—and particularly not to anyone in my bodyguard."

He smiled weakly. "I imagine that they wouldn't take it quietly if they knew the legate's wife had tried to kill you."

"They would decide among themselves who would kill the lady," I told him, flatly and truthfully, "and that man would swear afterward under any torture that I knew nothing about it. They are brave and honorable men, and have sworn to defend me. I would not willingly lose any of them. And they would not understand that the Romans would be outraged and punish all of us, nor that the authorities are accustomed to lies and would believe me guilty anyway, nor that the conspiracy might survive the lady's loss, and strike back. I believe that the lady Aurelia heads it, but I have no doubt that she is not alone."

We looked at each other for a moment, and saw that we both understood that we could trust neither the honesty of the authorities nor the discretion of my subordinates. But perhaps I'd found a solution to another problem.

I told Eukairios about Siyavak and his resolve to discover and expose Bodica's plans. "Do you have friends in Eburacum as well?" I asked.

He looked nervous. "There is a small *ekklesia* in Eburacum," he admitted.

"A what?"

"A . . . an assembly. Of believers. We use the Greek word."

"Could someone in this assembly write letters for Siyavak, and send them to me secretly? He is a young man and still impulsive, and I am afraid for him if he's left entirely on his own with this lady—and even if he should discover something, it might cost him his life if he tried to reveal it himself. But I have no way of contacting him which she would be unable to interfere with—and for that matter, I do not completely trust Comittus not to spy for her in Cilurnum. He is her kinsman, and admires her greatly. I need some method of communication which she knows nothing about and cannot tamper with. Your friends could provide that. And I would welcome it very much if they, and your friend here, could continue to tell us what they learn from these 'contacts.' "

He was silent, looking at his hands, his shoulders hunched again.

"Do your fellow cultists perhaps have more sympathy for these druids than for the Roman authorities who persecute you?" I asked.

"No," he replied at once, but unhappily. "No, we pray for those in authority, and we know perfectly well that in Britain the druids would be far more ruthless with us than the Romans are. It's true what Valerius Natalis said: no one has bothered the assemblies in Britain very much. No, it's just . . . it's just you're suggesting we make an alliance with . . . with . . ."—*a tribe of bloodthirsty barbarians,* he meant to say, but didn't—"an earthly power, and we . . ." He stopped himself, reconsidering. "But we are a part of the province of Britain, even though most of us aren't Roman citizens or British tribesmen. If there were an . . . uprising"—he brought himself to say the word—"in Brigantia, and invasions by the Picts, we would suffer along with everyone else. We'd suffer more, if the druids had a kingdom of their own. I don't know, my lord. I can't answer for the Christians in Eburacum. I must pray, and write to them. Then they can answer for themselves."

"That is fair," I said. "Write to them. I will try to arrange for us to ride down to Eburacum when this season is ended." I remembered the other thing he had told me, and added, relishing the old challenge, "If I am still alive."

X

*I*N FACT, I didn't need to think up an excuse to take me to Eburacum. The legate left for the fortress next morning, taking his men and the fourth dragon with him, but before he set out he sent me a letter asking me to visit him early in January to discuss plans about the horses "and some other matters that have come up."

I was pleased at the invitation, though slightly apprehensive about the "other matters." I resolved to visit River End Farm as soon as possible, to give Pervica plenty of time to decide her response to the stud farm idea.

By this time, it was the middle of December, approaching the solstice, which we Sarmatians celebrate as Sada, the feast of the winter fire. The Romans celebrate a festival at about the same time, the Saturnalia in honor of the god Saturn, and we'd agreed at Cilurnum to celebrate the holy days together. I was busy making arrangements for this feast—all the officers were—but as soon as I'd recovered fully from the aftereffects of drowning, I decided to take a day out to ride over to see Pervica.

"I'll come along," said Longus, when I announced this to my fellows.

I looked at him suspiciously. "That is not necessary."

"But you might want someone to advise you about the farm! I have a farm in the area myself; I know how many horses they can support. And you might want someone to translate for you—Lucius isn't the only one who speaks British, you know." When I still looked at him silently, he raised his eyebrows and said, "You're bringing half your bodyguard anyway: you're hardly expecting a cozy chat with the lady."

I was bringing half the bodyguard only because I'd taken what Eukairios had told me in Corstopitum seriously and involved myself in a lot of exasperating precautions against murder. I'd told the men of my dragon that we must be on guard against intruders into our camp, who might be relatives of the Pictish dead, seeking vengeance: this was a perfectly sensible move in its own right, and it meant that no Britons crossed the palisade unquestioned.

I was very careful of what I ate and drank—which had meant finding excuses not to share the food of my Roman colleagues. (I trusted them, on the whole, though with unhappy doubts about Comittus—but I didn't know or trust all their servants.) I'd also made a will. And finally, I'd forced myself to accept that I must not go anywhere alone, certainly not when others knew where I was going. In spite of all this, I had hoped that I'd be able to talk with Pervica quietly and in some reasonable degree of privacy. I had been wondering whether what I thought I'd seen in her wasn't a product of my own mind, confused from the touch of death, stunned and overjoyed to find itself still alive. Whether I loved her or not, though, I was certainly indebted to her for my life and bound to do what I could to repay her. I'd chosen a gift for her, and I hoped to be able to discuss the plan for the stud farm sensibly and thoroughly. In none of these things was it likely that Longus would help.

"Why do you want to come?" I asked him bluntly.

He gave one of his doleful grins. "Pure curiosity. But I think you ought to have a Roman officer with you. Have you thought of the effect on the inhabitants of a medium-sized British farm of the sight of sixteen armed Sarmatian horsemen galloping into their chicken run?"

I hadn't. "The chicken run is at the back of the house," I said. "We would have no cause to gallop into it. But come if you wish."

In the end, there were twenty of us who set out: myself, with Leimanos and fifteen of the bodyguard; Eukairios, whom I wanted along to take notes; Longus; and Flavius Facilis—who, however, was not going to River End, but to Corstopitum about some supplies for the festival, and who only joined us for the ride. We were all armed. I would have preferred to leave the armor behind, but (exasperating precaution) thought I'd do better to wear it. Comittus stayed behind to mind the fort.

It was a chill, overcast day, but not actually raining or snowing, and we rode along companionably, discussing the preparations for the festival until we were close enough to Corstopitum to begin looking for the farm. I was glad of Longus, in the end, since I had never actually ridden to River End Farm and hadn't been paying proper attention when I rode from it: we needed to ask directions, and none of the people we found to ask spoke Latin. Facilis abandoned us to our search and turned toward Corstopitum, saying that he would meet us on our way back if he could.

We found the farm shortly before midday: my heart rose when we saw the colonnaded wings of the courtyard before us, enclosed in a valley that the melting of the snow had left a deep green. I hadn't noticed before, but you could see the river shining in the distance as you rode down the mud track to the farm gate. Sheep dotted the hills to our left, and I wondered if Cluim was with them.

There was a shout as we reached the gate, and when we rode up to the courtyard, the redheaded servant Elen held the front door open for a man I hadn't seen before. He was a tall, solid man with iron gray hair, well dressed for a Briton, having a gold collar as well as a checked cloak with a fine pin. He stood in the middle of the porch with his legs apart and his arms crossed, glaring at us.

"Greetings," I said, stopping Farna in front of him. "Is the Lady Pervica at home?"

"Are you that Sarmatian she saved?" he demanded.

"I am. Are you one of her servants?"

His face reddened and he glared harder. "I am Quintilius son of Celatus, owner of Two Oaks Farm, and a friend and associate of Pervica. I was here doing some business with her and advising her."

I looked at him a moment. It was to be expected that an attractive young widow with a good farm had "friends and associates." I would have to discover how friendly and how close the association was. "Greetings, Quintilius," I said, politely. "May I ask that you tell the lady that Ariantes son of Arifarnes, commander of the Sixth Numerus of Sarmatian Horse, is here to speak with her about the stallion, as he promised?"

At this moment Pervica herself came to the door. She stopped, framed in it, and stood still, staring at me around the side of her "friend and associate." The moment I saw her I knew that what I had felt before was not mere fancy. I smiled at her and she smiled back. I dismounted and pulled off my helmet, holding it carefully so that the long red crest wouldn't sweep the mud, and bowed my head to her. "Many greetings, Lady Pervica," I said.

"Many greetings, Lord Ariantes," she replied, stepping around Quintilius and coming forward. "Did I hear you say you'd come about the horse?"

"Yes, Lady—and about another matter to do with horses, if you have time to discuss it."

"Of course. But I rather doubt that all of you will fit into my house."

I glanced back at my men, sitting on their steaming horses in their armor and grinning. "No," I agreed. "But if you will permit them to build a fire in back, they will make themselves comfortable while we are talking."

"I'll see if we can find them some beer and bread," she said. "Elen!"

"Pervica, no!" protested Quintilius. "I've told you, you should have nothing more to do with any of these barbarians! The gods know what the savages might take it into their heads to do—you've heard the stories about them! How can you—"

Longus burst out laughing. "Oh, tell me the stories about them, please!" he said, jumping off his horse and elbowing his way to the front. "I'm sure you don't know half of it, but tell me anyway." He bowed sweepingly to Pervica. "The name's Longus, by the way, most esteemed lady, Gaius Flavinus Longus, senior decurion of the Second Asturian Horse of Cilurnum. I'm sure my friend Ariantes would have introduced me in another minute. I hope there's room for me indoors. Unlike the Sarmatians, I prefer to rest indoors when it's cold."

The presence of a Roman officer silenced Quintilius, though he still looked deeply dissatisfied. Pervica smiled warmly at Longus, then turned to Elen and began giving orders about bread and beer. I turned back to my men and told them to go into the back and make themselves comfortable near the barn, but first to unload the present for Pervica from the packhorse and bring it into the house. Longus held the door for Pervica and followed her in; Quintilius, scowling, shoved in front of me. Leimanos followed me with the present, and after him came Eukairios with his tablets.

I clinked my way to the dining room, where I found a charcoal brazier lit for warmth and the rosewood tabletop covered with papers and a strong-box. Pervica stared when Leimanos appeared with the present. I'd rolled it in a carpet to keep it safe. "What's this?" she asked.

"A gift, Lady," I answered. "A small thing in token of my gratitude to you."

"It's beautiful!" she exclaimed, staring at the carpet, which Leimanos set down on the floor.

It was a good one, red wool patterned with galloping black horses and, in the center, a golden sun. I'd intended for her to keep it. But I smiled and knelt to unfold it. "This is the covering," I told her, undoing the knots that secured the carpet. I lifted the top fold away. "This is the present. You said you disliked the painting in this room; I thought you might prefer this one."

The painting was of a battle between the Greeks and the Amazons. I'd seen it in a villa I'd looted in Pannonia, and taken it home because one of the Amazons looked a bit like Tirgatao. She'd pretended not to like it for exactly that reason, so it hadn't been in the wagons when they were looted. I'd brought it with me thinking it might be useful to bribe a Roman with, but hadn't wanted to part with it, until now.

"Jupiter Optimus Maximus!" exclaimed Longus, staring at the painting, which was on a plank of wood about four feet long by two feet high. An Amazon astride a leaping white horse dominated its center, leaning down to slash at the fallen Greek below her, who'd caught her wrist and was pulling her off. Behind them horses danced, armor gleamed, cloaks flapped brightly, and beautiful men and women struggled with each other. The struggle did not seem terribly serious, and the battle was more of a festival frolic than a warlike contest. The whole painting bubbled with color and exuberance. The Amazon who looked like Tirgatao was in the upper left-hand corner, drawing a bow threateningly on a Greek in a gold helmet. You could see from the look on her face that she meant to hit him, but she'd probably kiss him afterward.

"This is really superb!" Longus observed, picking up the painting and setting it on the table, braced upright against the strongbox. "Where did you get it?"

"I had it in my wagon," I answered misleadingly. "I have been told it was painted by Timomachos of Byzantium and is quite valuable."

Eukairios made a strangled noise and dropped his tablets. "It's not genuine!" he said.

"Of course it is genuine," said Leimanos, offended for me. "The man we took it from wept, and said it was worth more than forty thousand denarii."

So much for my restraint.

"You stole it?" asked Quintilius, as though this confirmed his worst suspicions.

"My lord took it on a raid," Leimanos corrected proudly. "His planning and our strength had carried us almost to Segedunum, and we found the house of a former governor of Asia, a palace fit for a king. Ten *alae* of cavalry they had searching for us, and half a legion: we looted the house, drove off the cattle, ate, drank, and set out again. We met one *ala* and destroyed it, and went home safe to our own wagons."

"Leimanos," I said in Sarmatian, "these are Roman subjects. Telling them how we looted Roman subjects will not impress them."

"If it's that valuable, I don't think I should keep it," said Pervica quickly.

"It is less precious to me than my life," I said. "If it pleases you, it would please me if you kept it, Lady."

She shook her head. "I've told you already, you owe me nothing. I could hardly have let you die. No, it's a lovely painting, a beautiful painting, and thank you—but I'd never feel comfortable with something worth forty thousand denarii hanging in my dining room." She didn't add that she didn't want stolen property, either, but that was plainly the case.

I sighed. "If that is what you wish, Lady." I gave Leimanos an angry glance, and he looked away, embarrassed and ashamed. He'd boasted to impress them with my importance, forgetting that Romans boast of different things.

"Anyway," Pervica went on, trying to soften her refusal, "you've already done me a great kindness, Lord Ariantes. Thanks to you, my husband's debts are all paid off."

I looked at her in surprise, and she smiled. "I suppose I hadn't told you directly. My husband had left me with debts totaling some eighteen hundred denarii—mostly to Cinhil here." (I noticed that she cal! `d him by a British version of his name, and suspected that he only used "Quintilius" when he was trying to impress someone.) "I'd resigned myself to paying it off little by little for years to come. But with all the things your men gave Cluim, we paid everything. Cluim refused to touch any of it until we'd paid the debt. I was just collecting the note of the final discharge from Cinhil when you arrived. And Cluim still has nearly nine hundred denarii to spare!" There was such gladness in her voice that it shocked me: I realized how much the debt, which I had not been aware of, must have burdened her before.

"I am pleased, Lady," I returned. "But that was the debt my bodyguard paid to Cluim. I have given you nothing."

"Except thanks?" she asked, with the gentle ironic smile I remembered.

"Except those," I agreed. "Leimanos." I switched back to Sarmatian. "Take the picture out and see that it's wrapped in straw to keep it safe on the way back; let her keep the carpet, anyway. And don't come back in unless you can remember who you're talking to."

"I'm sorry, my lord," he said miserably, picking up the picture. "I thought . . ."

"I know, I know. You've learned Latin faster than you've learned Roman customs. Well, she might have refused it anyway, and it seems you and the bodyguard have already given her a thing she really wanted."

Leimanos went out, carrying the painting under his arm. The dark servant girl, Cluim's sister, bustled in from the back of the house, carrying a pitcher of hot spiced beer and a dish of nuts. While the girl poured the drinks, Pervica asked us to sit down. The couch only had places for three, and Quintilius plonked himself firmly in the center of it. Longus sat down beside him, but I preferred the carpet, and sat down on it with my bad leg bent and my good one crossed under it; I set my helmet down beside me. Pervica did not recline on the couch, but found herself a stool at the end of the table. In the end Eukairios took the other place on the couch.

"I also wished to speak with you," I told Pervica, as the girl handed me my drink, "about a different plan for your horse that might interest you." And I told her about the plan for the stud farms.

She listened intently, and her first question was, "What would the set price for the foals be?"

"That would have to be settled," I replied. "My scribe here, Eukairios, is very good with money. I have brought him to help you determine how much you should charge if you do decide that you are interested."

"You're not considering this plan?" asked Quintilius in a stern, masterful tone.

"Of course I am!" replied Pervica. "If the price was good, it would . . . it would make this farm everything poor Saenus always dreamed it would be! You know it would!"

"It's nonsense!" snapped Quintilius. "There probably isn't any serious plan to breed horses. This barbarian just wants some excuse to come here so he can try your virtue!"

The room went very quiet. Longus lost all his irony and looked alarmed. I was glad that Leimanos had gone. "You are unwise to say that," I said, looking at Quintilius levelly, "if you mean by it that I would ever do anything to harm a lady to whom I owe my life."

"What's unwise in suspecting an acknowledged thief of dishonesty?" Quintilius replied. "It'd be a fool who'd trust you!"

"Oh, Hercules!" groaned Longus.

I looked at Pervica. "Lady, is this man your friend?"

"He is an old friend of my husband's," she said earnestly, "and he's been very worried ever since he heard about you. I told you that there have been various stories about your people which have frightened many people. Please excuse him."

"I excuse him, then, for your sake," I said. "But, Quintilius, I would ask you to remember that we are both guests of this lady. You should not insult her guests in her house, out of respect for her, if you have none for them or yourself."

"If I'd had any say in it, she'd never have allowed you into the house in the first place." The masterful tone had become a bellow.

"But you had no say in it, and I am here. It seems to me that the lady is quite capable of managing her own affairs."

Longus leaned back, shaking his head in amazement. Pervica gave me a look I couldn't interpret, and began discussing the set price with Eukairios— hurriedly, before Quintilius could begin again. It didn't take them long to work one out.

"So," I said, when they'd finished, "I may tell the legate that you agree to the scheme, provided you get at least this much?"

"Yes," she said firmly.

"No," said Eukairios. "You'll have to tell him she wants at least ten denarii more. He'll expect to beat her down, my lord."

Pervica and I looked at each other. I spread open my hands. "Trust Eukairios."

"I believe I would," she told me, smiling. "Now, how many horses do you think the farm could take? You'll have to tell him that as well, and I've no experience in horse-rearing."

"Pervica, you must not accept this scheme!" exclaimed Quintilius. "As your husband's oldest associate and your closest adviser, I forbid it!"

Pervica got to her feet. "Cinhil," she said evenly, "I've been grateful for your help, over the years, and for your patience about the money. I've heard your advice and I respect it. But I'm quite certain that we have nothing to fear from Ariantes—and for that matter, he's proposing a scheme that would be administered by the office of the legate of the Sixth Legion, not himself. I can see absolutely no reason to reject it untried."

Quintilius was on his feet as well, towering over her. "Pervica," he began, "out of respect for Saenus . . ."—then stopped. For a moment he looked not so much angry as confused and betrayed. It was clear from the lady's calm resolution that she wouldn't obey his order, and he couldn't enforce it. Then the anger came back, hotter and wilder, and he turned to me. "No!" he exclaimed angrily. "You've fooled the lady into thinking you're harmless, but she's not without friends. *I* forbid you to come here. Take your men and get out!"

I stayed where I was. "Lady," I said, to Pervica, "does he speak with your authority?"

"No," she answered, but she'd gone pale and looked distressed. "No. Cinhil, please . . ."

I got to my feet. I was taller than Quintilius, which was satisfying. "Do you wish to fight me, then?" I asked him.

At that he went pale as well, but he was resolute. "Yes," he declared, "if it's man to man, and you'll take those gilded fish scales off."

I took off my coat and began undoing the buckles on my armor.

"Please!" said Pervica. "Please don't! Ariantes, he isn't a soldier, you mustn't fight him!"

"Ariantes," said Longus, "look, I know he wants to—we can all swear to that—but if you kill him, they'll still have to at least formally charge you with murder, and I don't like to think what your men would do if we tried to arrest you. In the name of all the gods, leave him be!"

"Do not be anxious," I told them. "I will try not to harm him." I unfastened my baldric, set the sword on the table, and pulled off the scale armor cuirass. The woollen shirt and trousers I wore underneath the armor were only light ones; it would be a cold fight. "Do you have your arms with you?" I asked Quintilius.

He licked his lips. "N-no."

"You may borrow my sword, then." I unfastened the belt of the armored trousers and began taking them off as well.

Quintilius picked up the sword, which was very like a Roman *spatha*, the long slashing sword of the cavalryman. The hilt was gold, with a dragon's head set with rubies forming a ring-clip on the end. He put his hand around it tentatively and drew it from the sheath; the blade gleamed with the serpent pattern of fine steel. He looked at it as though it might bite him.

"Is it too long?" I asked, setting the armored trousers beside the cuirass.

"I . . . I said I'd fight you. It will do."

"I am sorry if you prefer the short sword. I have none. Do you prefer to fight on horseback or on foot?"

"On foot," he whispered.

"Please!" repeated Pervica. "Please, this is pointless! Pointless! Cinhil, in the name of all the gods, apologize!"

"I'm going to fight the bastard here and now!" shouted Quintilius, abruptly going red again.

"I won't have men killing each other on my property!"

Quintilius simply ignored that. He pushed his way out, through the door that led into the kitchen and the back of the house.

"Would you prefer it if we went up to the road?" I asked Pervica.

"No! I'd prefer it if you didn't fight at all!"

"We must fight now. There is a code in such matters, and I at least could not back out without disgrace."

"And what about the disgrace to me?"

"Lady, I swear on fire there will be no disgrace to you. I have been insulted and I will defend my honor, but the responsibility for that is not yours, but his. I must go before he says something stupid to my men as well."

I hurried out, through the kitchen and into the backyard. My men had made themselves a shelter against the wind with some straw moved from the barn, built a fire in a sandy corner, and the cups and bowls of beer testified that they'd been relaxing comfortably. But they were all on their feet now and glaring at Quintilius, who was standing in front of the door clutching my sword nervously in both hands.

"Wait one minute," I told him. "I will make them swear not to harm you if you should win."

I pushed past him, went over to my men, and explained the situation to them. They were pleased—he had offended their sense of my dignity—and they grinned at each other and offered me their swords. I made them stretch their hands over the fire and swear that they would not harm my opponent or do any damage to his cattle, family, or property, in the event of my losing the contest. This done, I went back to the door. Quintilius had been joined by the others. Longus just looked resigned now, but Pervica and Eukairios were distressed.

"If you wish, we will go off your land and fight alone," I offered Pervica.

"Not knowing what was happening would be even worse," she answered wretchedly. "Please . . ."

Quintilius slashed the air with my sword, still holding it two-handed. The hilt was really too short for this, and he had to overlap his hands to manage it, but I supposed he was used to holding some weapon like that. "You haven't borrowed another sword," he said, harshly.

"No," I answered. "Do you require any other arms?"

"Come on! Let's get it over with! Go borrow a sword!"

I went back to my men and asked for a dagger. Their faces lit up, and they ran to fetch a coil of rope as well.

"Just a dagger," I said, and the glee ebbed away. There was a moment of horrified silence as they realized I meant it.

"Take a coil of rope as well, my lord, please!" said Leimanos. "That at least!"

"He isn't a warrior," I told them. "A lasso and a dagger against a sword is almost even odds, and where would the glory be in that? Give me the dagger, and remember what you swore."

"My lord," said Leimanos. "Please . . . your leg might fail you . . ."

"Leimanos, I don't correct you in matters that concern your own honor. Don't correct me in matters that concern mine."

They handed over a dagger reluctantly, and I walked back to Quintilius. He stared.

"What do you think you're doing?" he demanded.

"You are unaccustomed to my sword," I said, "and, if you will forgive my mention of it, you are somewhat older than I. Please allow me to even the balance." I felt suddenly and overwhelmingly happy, light-headed with the old wild thrill: my life in my hands, death before me, and glory either way. It was an intoxication I hadn't expected to feel ever again.

Quintilius almost refused the advantage—but couldn't bring himself to, and the fact that he couldn't enraged him. He gave a sudden howl of fury and leapt forward, swinging the sword into the air.

I could have stabbed him as he jumped, but I didn't want to kill him and I was wary of his unorthodox method of fighting. I leapt sideways—to my right, so as to land on my good leg—and stepped back quickly. The sword came down, then heaved up again, and he ran after me, waving it wildly above his head. I jumped to the right again, then, since he was almost on top of me, hurled myself forward. He spun about; again I might have slipped under the sword, which he was holding insanely high, but I didn't want to strike to cause serious harm. I jumped right, nearly crashed into the house wall, and jumped forward and to the left. I had to land on my bad leg this time, and it gave for a moment; I pushed myself up desperately—and saw that Quintilius had brought my sword down on the ground where I'd been, and buried it edgewise in the earth. I was astonished, and somewhat concerned for the blade. He heaved it out, bellowed, and ran at me, swinging it sideways this time. I dropped flat on the ground, and it whistled over my head; Quintilius tripped over me and fell. I rolled and got to my knees; he managed to sit up and swung the sword back at me, one-handed now. I caught it on the dagger and pushed. The knife slid up the sword-blade, over the guard, and sliced the backs of his fingers. He yelled and dropped the sword, then, to my amazement, balled his bleeding hand into a fist and slammed it into my face.

The world went red and black for a moment, and I heard behind me the angry roar of my men. Disbelievingly, I put my hand to my nose. Quintilius staggered to his feet. I covered my head just in time to keep the next barefisted blow out of my eyes. My left arm went numb. I struck upward with the dagger, blindly, and at the same time shoved toward him. Both the dagger and my shoulder hit something. He grunted; I dropped my arm, saw that the dagger had only sliced his sleeve but that the shoulder had caught him in the stomach.

This was no sword-fight. I grabbed the arm nearest to me in a wrestling hold and rose, throwing him over and onto his back with a thud, then turned, dropped to my knees on his chest, and put the dagger against his throat.

For a moment I thought he was going to try to rise anyway, but he didn't. He lay still, gasping, and looked at me without expression. I wiped my nose with the back of my numb hand, and saw that it was streaming with blood. "What sort of fighting was that?" I asked.

"Shut up and get it over with!" he returned.

I took the dagger away from his throat and got up. "You did not even know how to hold a sword!" I said, still hardly able to credit it. I looked around for my sword, limped over to it, and picked it up. It was covered with dirt.

Quintilius sat up slowly, clutching his stomach, still gasping for breath.

"Look what you have done to my sword!" I told him, wiping my nose again.

Longus started to laugh. I felt a fool.

"Don't you laugh at me!" Quintilius shouted—and gasped again. "Damn you!" He rubbed his stomach.

Longus offered him a hand to help him up. "I wasn't laughing at you. You're a brave man indeed, to fight Ariantes when you don't even know how to hold a sword. He's killed more men than you've got teeth in your head— ask his followers about it sometime. *I* wouldn't fight him, and I'm a decurion. But I hope now you'll admit that the lady has the right to say who is and who isn't allowed in her own house. If you make him fight you again, he'll probably insist on doing it blindfolded." He pulled Quintilius to his feet and looked around for something to bandage the cut hand with.

Leimanos came over and took the sword away from me. He rubbed some of the dirt off and began examining it carefully for chips in the blade. Another of the bodyguard collected a handful of wool to mop up the nosebleed. Then Pervica came over with a woollen rag instead. "You had better come into the house," she said quietly. "It's too cold to stand about in your shirt, and you should lie down with your head back." I nodded and, pressing the rag to my nose and feeling a complete idiot, went back into the house.

A few minutes later I was lying on the carpet I'd brought, with my head back, and Quintilius was recovering on the couch while the rest of them stood about the dining table. Leimanos had found another use for the handful of wool, and was cleaning my sword. "People who cannot hold a sword have no right to expect a scepter-holder to fight them," he said. He did not direct his comment to Quintilius, but he was careful to speak in Latin. "Herdsmen who cannot fight should keep silent before noblemen."

"He is not a herdsman," I said, through the rag. "He is a farmer. He owns land. Probably he has herdsmen working for him."

"He fights with his hands, like an animal. I do not believe he even owns a sword."

I shrugged, as well as I could lying down. "He owns a house, and probably he spends any surplus on it, instead of on swords. He owns a farm, and he spends his time working on it, and has no time to learn war, and expects other people to do any fighting that is needed. He is a Roman, Leimanos.

" *'Beyond the stars will stretch his lands*
Beyond the paths of the sun and years
Where heaven-bearing Atlas stands
Turning the earth between his hands
On its axis of stars that burn so clear.'

"Or so say the Romans."

There was a moment of silence. "Where the hell did you learn to quote Vergil?" asked Longus.

I didn't answer. I felt foolish and depressed. My grand heroic gesture had ended in a fistfight, and I was realizing yet again the terrible gulf between the world we had inhabited before and the world we lived in now.

Pervica came and knelt beside my head. "Thank you," she said. "You could have killed Cinhil and you took terrible risks to make sure you wouldn't."

"I would have been very ashamed to have killed a man who cannot even hold a sword," I replied.

Quintilius made an inarticulate noise of anger and resentment.

"I . . . I have something that we found on the riverbank, that we thought was probably yours," Pervica said, after a moment. "I think the water's spoiled it, but I was meaning to give it to you. I'll go fetch it."

She left, and Longus took her place. "Can I just make sure that the nose isn't broken?" he asked.

I lifted the rag and he inspected it. "No lasting damage," he announced cheerfully. "You ought to wash your face: your beard's full of blood."

The bleeding seemed to have stopped, so I sat up and looked for something to wash my face with. Leimanos brought the bowl of water he'd been using to wipe the mud off my sword.

Pervica came back into the room carrying my bow case. "Is it yours?" she asked, holding it out to me.

I took it; as my hands touched it, I remembered Aurelia Bodica saying, *I've given you the bow because they'll think you were hunting*—and her giggle as she pushed me toward the water. I sat still, staring at the water-stained red leather.

"What's the matter?" asked Pervica.

"I remember drowning now," I answered. I unlatched the case, opened it, and took the bow out to examine it.

"I'm afraid the water has spoiled it," Pervica repeated.

"No. The case has an oilskin lining, see? It is quite dry inside. It must have floated downstream and washed ashore."

"But the bow's bent backward."

I looked up and smiled. I'd forgotten that the Britons were unfamiliar with the recurved bow, with its layers of horn and sinew. There were no other units of eastern archers on this end of the Wall, and the native bows were weak and made entirely of wood. "They are always like that when they're unstrung," I explained. I slipped a string into the bottom nock, twisted the bow backward against my leg, and strung it. The string gave its sharp, buzzing hum as the bow pulled into its living shape.

"I thought you were hunting," said Longus, puzzled.

"And?"

"So why was your bow in its case, unstrung?"

I looked up at him, then looked down at the bow. I bent it and unstrung it again, without answering. I put it back in its case. "Thank you," I told Pervica. "They do not know how to make these here. My men can make them, but I think probably we could not get the best kind of glue here."

"I'm glad it's not broken," Pervica said, smiling. Then she sat back on her heels and rubbed the top of the bow case with her thumb. "About the horse," she said, watching her nail against the leather.

"Ah. I thought perhaps you might wish, after all, to keep him. He would be a valuable asset to the stud."

"No," she said, looking up and smiling at me again, "no, I can't manage him. I'd like to give him to you."

"If you kept him, you would have help with him. If you do not want to keep him, I must pay for him. I am far too deeply indebted to you to accept a gift."

"You're not in debt to me. That's why I want to give him to you."

"That is a woman's reasoning. I do not understand it."

"That's a man's arrogance. It's perfectly clear. I'm out of debt, thanks to you, and I have a chance at real and honest prosperity. I won't take anything more from you because of some imaginary blood debt. You gave me gifts today; I want to give one back."

"You refused the gift I gave you."

"You gave me the respect due a householder, Cinhil's life—and a carpet. I didn't refuse any of those."

I smiled at her. "I am glad of anything I have done that pleases you."

"Then take the horse."

I wanted to laugh. "I will take the horse and train it for you, but you must keep it and the stud fees when the time comes to breed it."

She did laugh. "Take it now, and we'll talk about that when the time comes!"

WHEN WE LEFT an hour later, it was with the stallion Wildfire tied beside the packhorse. To my delight, we also had Pervica's agreement to visit Cilurnum for the forthcoming festival. Longus, to my great surprise, came up with a widowed mother and married sister in the fort village, and offered Pervica hospitality on their behalf. It seemed that the sister was planning to drive to Corstopitum to shop two days before the feast, and could meet Pervica there, escort her back to Cilurnum, and host her in complete respectability over the holy days. This guaranteed, Pervica was delighted to come. Quintilius protested, but feebly. I was enormously contented, and took pains to tell Longus that I was grateful for his help, and glad after all that he had come.

We were just leaving the farm track and turning back in to the main road when Facilis hailed us, and we saw him trotting toward us. We stopped and waited for him to join us.

"What happened to your face?" he asked me, as we started together down the road.

"He got into a fight with one of the lady's friends," Longus answered for me. "Oh gods and goddesses, it was beautiful!"

"What happened to the friend?" asked Facilis, in alarm.

"Cut hand. Ariantes was never going to kill him. I, and more importantly, the lady, didn't want him to."

Facilis grunted. "Stupid to fight at all, then."

"It was the other man's idea. Oh gods! I'm glad I came! Marcus, it was beautiful. This friend was a big solid landowner, Quintilius son of Celatus by name, and it turned out he'd loaned a lot of money to the lady's husband and she'd been sweating blood to repay it. Reading between the lines, he hoped he could marry her and collect a tidy little property as well as the pretty widow. She thanked him for his patience about the money, but he wasn't the sort that lets go easily; he'd taken advantage of the debt to bully her and badger her just as much as he could. When she saved the life of our noble friend here, though, his grateful bodyguard showered her with gifts enough that she paid off the whole debt, with half as much again left over. It was the last thing the landowner wanted. He was there when we arrived, taking the final discharge of the debt, warning her about the lusts and treachery of barbarians, and promising her his matrimonial protection yet again."

"You do not know this," I said, taken aback.

"It's true, though, isn't it?" asked Longus. "Leimanos, don't you think it's true?"

"I had not thought of it," said Leimanos, frowning. "But yes, it is true."

"You are inventing it," I insisted.

"I'm not inventing a word!" exclaimed Longus. And he went on to tell Facilis about the painting and the conversation and the quarrel. "Quintilius was so beside himself with fury and frustration," he concluded, "that he said yes, he certainly did want to fight—provided our friend shed his armor. Well, he was out of the armor quick as boiling asparagus, out in the yard, swore all the bodyguard to keep hands off the landowner, and loaned the man his sword. It was a nasty moment for me, I can tell you. And it got worse: instead of borrowing another sword for himself, he borrowed a little dagger. A dagger against a long sword! I started imagining five hundred enraged Sarmatians at Cilurnum swearing vengeance, and I was scared sick. But, Marcus—this is the best part—Quintilius had never held a sword in his life! He waved it about in the air like a pruning hook, and when he'd had his hand cut, he abandoned it altogether and punched Ariantes in the nose."

Longus began laughing again. "You never saw anything like it. None of the Sarmatians could believe it. Leimanos here was purple with indignation and the rest of them were howling. It was an unnatural act. After all, the gods gave us hands to hold swords with, not to hit each other! Well, Ariantes ended it after that: he threw Quintilius down, sat on him, and put the dagger at his throat, just to make it absolutely clear that he could kill the fellow any time he liked—though that had never been in doubt. Then he got up again and picked up the sword, which the poor sod had used to hack the earth, and said, 'Look what you have done to my sword!' " Longus had a wicked knack at imitating, and I imagine his impersonation of me, bewildered, indignantly wiping a nosebleed, was devastatingly accurate.

Facilis started laughing, and Longus joined him. "You were funny!" Longus told me. "Gods, you were!"

Leimanos tried to look offended—prince-commanders of a dragon, especially your own, aren't supposed to be funny. But after a moment, he began laughing too. Another of the bodyguard rode up and asked him why, and he sobered quickly and said, "Flavinus Longus was saying how that herdsman fought, waving our lord's sword like a pruning hook."

At that, the bodyguard laughed too.

"So what did this Quintilius do?" asked Facilis.

"Not much he could do. Leimanos was announcing that commoners who didn't know how to hold a sword shouldn't expect the privilege of being chopped up by noblemen. And to tell the truth, I think that Quintilius had realized what a lunatic thing he was doing as soon as he had a look at the sword, and would have backed out then, if he could have: he certainly wasn't eager for a rematch, particularly when I told him of our friend's bloody reputation. No, Quintilius just sat and moped the rest of the time we were there."

"And the lady?"

Longus grinned. "The lady Pervica is exactly what you might expect," he declared, with great satisfaction. "Top quality from head to toe, a young widow of twenty-five, graceful, soft-spoken, and sharp enough to run a legion. She also, unless I'm much mistaken, has a will of iron. She doesn't like being bullied and she wouldn't have married Quintilius if he were governor of Britain. But she's already made up her mind on a certain subject, and her only hesitation is whether the subject means it, or whether he's just grateful. She's had enough of other people relying on her gratitude, and has no intention of playing that game herself. I won't say more, because the lady's coming to Cilurnum for the festival; she'll be staying with my sister, and I'm sure you'll meet her. I think she may be about for some time to come." He turned the grin on me. "Has it crossed your mind, Ariantes, that she won't want to leave a good stone house to come live in a wagon?"

"We can settle that when the time comes," I said contentedly. I thought privately that I'd sleep well even in a house, if I were sleeping beside Pervica.

XI

MY MEN RECEIVED their first pay packet the day Pervica arrived at Cilurnum, two days before the festival. All the other troops on the Wall had been paid already: our pay was late because of all the negotiations. The amount we were finally given was the standard auxiliary pay—two hundred denarii a year—plus an allowance for one and three quarter horses, with another extra amount for the upkeep of our armor. It was less than I'd wanted, but, it must be said, a considerable advance on the first offers and more than the Asturians were getting. The usual half had been deducted to pay for rations, and another variable amount for horse fodder and replacement of equipment. But I was pleasantly surprised to find that the total had been backdated to the time we left Aquincum: it was a substantial amount. Moreover, the captains were given seventeen times the basic rate of pay, an even more substantial amount, and one that could help smooth over any short-term troubles with debt. Since arriving in Cilurnum, we'd bought anything that needed buying with whatever money or valuables we'd taken with us, and I'd been watching the first stirrings of trouble with shopkeepers and moneylenders. Now we were in the clear again. With the pay we were also given a notice from the legate, relaxing one of the restrictions on us: the men could now apply to me for permission to leave the fort, in groups not smaller than three nor larger than sixteen, and could stay away up to three nights if that permission were granted. This meant that they could go hunting or ride into Corstopitum to spend their money, and otherwise behave more like free men than prisoners.

I drew the dragon up and made a severe speech warning the men against moneylenders and the dangers of getting into debt, then brought them all into the chapel of the standards in the fort headquarters, where the clinking bags were handed out beneath the impassive gaze of the statue of the man we'd sworn our oaths to at Aquincum. The men went off in a proper holiday mood to prepare for the Sada feast.

I found their excitement depressing. Six months before we had scarcely known what money was: now, even the slowest man in the dragon had been able to understand instantly that he earned more than the Asturians did. I was tired and irritable when I limped back to the chapel of the standards to check over the final accounts with Eukairios and the Asturians' treasurer, who had the key to the strong room. It was late in the afternoon by then. Halfway through the accounting, I noticed another pay box under the table, and I heaved it up and shoved it across at Eukairios. "What is this for?" I asked him. He answered, with a smile, "The commander's pay, my lord."

"Oh," I said. Eukairios went on copying pay chits into two registers. I sat beside him, ready to countersign the pages with the scrawled dragon mark I'd been using since Bononia. "How much is it?" I asked, after a minute.

Eukairios set down his pen and laughed. He shook his head, picked up the pen again. "I'll have to tell that one to Longus," he said.

"You'll have to tell me what?" said Longus himself, striding into the chapel.

Eukairios put down the pen again. "Lord Flavinus, I have written, at my master's dictation, some sixty or seventy letters about the dragon's pay and allowances. He's given presents to officials in the legate's office, the governor's office, the grain commissary, and the treasury. He has, as you know, come up with complicated schemes to pay for the horses. We've worried over the price of glue to mend bows and the cost of a blacksmith's furnace. Would you have thought there was any detail of this troop's finances he didn't know about?"

"No," said Longus—expectantly.

Eukairios pointed at the box. "The commander's pay."

"Isn't it thirty thousand a year?"

Eukairios started laughing again. I looked at him in exasperation. I was not in a mood for jokes. "You should not laugh at me," I told him.

He sobered quickly. "It is thirty thousand a year, my lord, as Lord Flavinus Longus said. Fifteen thousand now. Item: fifteen thousand denarii for the commander's pay, here." He flipped a page in his ledger. "You countersign there."

I countersigned and picked up the box containing fifteen thousand denarii. It was very heavy. Quite suddenly I loathed it, and hated the tomb-like, stone-walled chapel, the standards along the wall, and particularly the statue of the emperor with his preoccupied, philosophical face. I had been a prince, and owned herds and flocks; I had led raids, and traded with the East; I had held a scepter and judged the disputes of my dependants. Now I was a hireling. I wanted to hurl the box at that smug statue—but that would be sacrilege and treason. I put down my wages again.

"Put it back in the strong room for now," I ordered Eukairios.

"Yes, my lord." He put down his pen again and got up to obey, and I noticed that he looked even wearier than usual. He had, of course, done most of the work for the payday, checking over the accounts, keeping the books, writing out the five hundred pay chits that now had to be copied over in duplicate. "Wait," I ordered, and he stopped. I unlocked the box, picked up a stack of the coins, and counted out a hundred of them, the same amount as my men had been allotted for their first six months' basic salary. "A financial detail you also were unaware of," I said, pushing the money toward him. "The commander's scribe's pay."

I was unprepared for his reaction. He went white, then red, and stared at me as though I'd insulted him. He didn't touch the money. "You can't do that," he said at last.

"Why not?"

"You don't pay slaves!"

I didn't know how to answer that, so I shrugged. "I have chosen to pay you. If you do not wish to keep the money, dispose of it as you wish."

He picked up the coins with shaking hands. "All my life," he whispered, "all my life . . ." He looked up, blinking at tears, and seemed suddenly to register the amount. "No, you mustn't give me this much, my lord. It would offend the men of the dragon if I got as much as they do. Here . . ." He pushed three little piles of ten coins back toward me, then fumbled them into the box himself, closed it, and locked it. He looked at the seven piles remaining on the table and nodded. He wiped his eyes. "All my life," he said again, "I've been on the supplies ledger, not the pay ledger. Item one scribe, item rations for same."

"Does it make much difference?" asked Longus impatiently.

"Yes," said Eukairios, still staring at the money. "Yes, it does. It's almost like being free." He looked back at me and smiled shakily. He was beginning to recover himself. "Thank you," he said quietly. "I thought—I hoped—since you're generous, you might give me a denarius for the Saturnalia. I never expected this at all. I've never been paid before."

"Nor have I," I said. "I am glad you enjoy it."

"Oh, so that's it," said Longus. "It offends your princely dignity to get wages. I wish someone would offend me with the same amount. Look, I came to tell you that my sister has just arrived back from Corstopitum with a guest of yours, and if you're going to be a courteous host, you'd better come and greet her."

"I'll countersign the rest of the accounts later," I told Eukairios, and went out with Longus to welcome Pervica to Cilurnum.

THE FESTIVAL, WHICH we celebrated over three days, was a huge success. We lit the bonfires of the Sada, and the Romans chose the king of the Saturnalia, and we sacrificed to Marha and to Saturn side by side. I'd managed to locate some hemp seeds for my troops, and they were able to toast them in the traditional steam bath before the feast, from which they departed half-drunk on the smoke and howling with pleasure. Mare's milk, to make koumiss, the usual drink, had proved harder to find, and we had to make do with wine and beer. Still, there were plenty of those, and plenty of roast meat, and milk, and honeyed almonds; the Romans exchanged the little pottery dolls they give on the occasion, and we gave a few of them as well and wished each other a joyful festival. Roman troops always prepare entertainments for the Saturnalia, setting aside money for it from their pay packets over the whole year, and buying wild animals from hunting syndicates for spectacles, as well as laying up food and drink. There were bearbaitings, then, and wild beast fights with boars, dogs, and bulls. My men had never seen these before, and enjoyed them even more than the Asturians did, watching with whoops of excitement and going off full of praise for the courage of the dogs. We, for our part, had arranged horse races and tilting matches, which the Romans also enjoyed. Then there were songs in Sarmatian, in Latin, in British; there was music on the harp and the kithara, the flute and the drums; there was dancing and acrobatics.

Pervica enjoyed herself, though she didn't like the spectacles—she was sorry for the animals. Longus' sister Flavina proved to be a pleasant woman,

tall, dark, and mournful-looking like her brother, and with the same irre-
pressible sense of humor; she was married to another of the Asturian decurions, who, in the usual peculiar fashion of men on active service, was
expected to sleep in barracks in the fort, rather than with his wife in the village. Pervica got on well with her and with the widowed mother, who also
shared the house. (Longus told me afterward that he'd had some concern
about that side of things, as his mother had never forgiven me for tipping her
son off his horse.) But Pervica got on well with everyone. I introduced her to
my officers, and she greeted them as respectfully as they greeted her, and
they approved of her. She laughed at Longus' stories, particularly when they
were about me, and she listened attentively to Comittus and understood his
good sense. I noticed her at one point having a long conversation with Facilis,
and he was smiling at her. She slipped into the same effortless partnership
with Eukairios that I had myself. Everything was perfect; everything was almost too perfect. The days were of white sun and midwinter calm: perhaps
we could all feel the storms ahead, and decided to grab at our happiness
while it was there before us.

I felt pressed by that urgency from the first evening I saw her in Flavina's
house, smiling at me from beside the fire, as warm and shining as the light itself. Why, I asked myself, should I delay loving her? I had confidence in her,
her grace and dignity, her strength to deal with anything that might come, her
kindness—and every time I saw her, my confidence grew. Apart from anything else, so I told myself, delays would only damage her reputation. Everyone knew she was my guest, and had come because of me. Her name was
joined to mine: why not her body as well? I knew what I wanted and I was
fairly certain that she would not refuse. Why shouldn't I be reckless, and ask?

On the evening of the third and final day of the Sada celebrations, I had
my chance. Everyone was in the Sarmatian camp—my men, the Asturians,
nearly all the villagers, the inhabitants of both the brothels. There was music,
and a few strong fellows still had the energy to dance. All the officers, with
their various womenfolk, were by the main fire in front of my wagon, under
the awnings. The stars were white in the winter sky and the sparks leapt upward from the fire like a stream of molten gold. We were roasting chestnuts
and drinking a little hot spiced wine.

"This is lovely," said Pervica, dreamily. She was reclining against a bale of straw, and the firelight gilded her face and made deep shadows against the softness of her throat. "If you're used to this, Ariantes, I'm not surprised you don't like living in a house."

"I still think a wagon must be pretty damn drafty to sleep in," said Longus.

"It is very comfortable," I said. "In our own country there are often deep snows in winter, even before the solstice. But we are always warm."

Pervica twisted about to look at the wagon behind her. "Doesn't the wind come up through the floor?" she asked.

"It has felt on the bottom," I said, "and rugs. I will show you." I got to my feet and held out my hand to her. She hesitated only a moment before taking it.

It was dark in the wagon, and I left the door open as much for the firelight as to keep things respectable. She couldn't see the rugs, and tripped over the edge of the bunk. I caught her and steadied her, and she laughed. I did not. The desire I had felt for her ever since I saw her coming into the stables flared up when I touched her, like a dry pine branch on a fire, and I felt as though my heart had stopped.

"I've been wanting to see what they look like inside," she said, standing there with my arms around her, "and now I'm inside, I still don't know."

"You are free to come inside this one whenever you choose," I told her. I was saying more than I'd meant to, but I couldn't regret it. "If you want it, it is yours. I offer it to you now."

She laughed again. "You must have had too much to drink. I've told you, you shouldn't give me any more gifts. Certainly not your own wagon. Where would you live?"

"Here. With you."

I could feel the laughter go out of her, the muscles tensing under my hands. "I'm not sure what you mean," she said uncertainly.

I let go of her. I should have realized I would have to be more formal. She did not know our customs on such matters, and I was unfamiliar with hers. "I am sorry," I said. "I meant it honorably."

"What?" she said. "I still don't understand."

"I was suggesting marriage, Lady Pervica. That is the usual custom of my people when a man and a woman share a wagon." Repeating the offer in

Roman terms only made me more sure of myself. I wanted her, not just now, but to come home to over years; I wanted her in my wagon, loving and beloved, filling the chasm Tirgatao had left. She had called me back to life, and I wanted her to remain, life in the place of death.

"Oh! Oh . . ." She stood very still, staring at me through the darkness. I could hear the others talking outside, and farther away, a man singing a ballad at another fire, an old slow tale of the deaths of heroes. "You don't need to do this from gratitude," Pervica said at last, slowly and with great firmness. "I would much rather stay single than have a man marry me from some misplaced notion of gratitude."

I put both arms around her, pulled her against me, and kissed her. It was so desperately and impossibly sweet that I was shaken by it; I felt naked and helpless, as though it were the first time, the first clumsy passionate kiss of a young boy and girl. Pervica stroked my face, then held me hard. "You're not doing it from gratitude?" she asked again, still, still, unconvinced.

"No," I said, thickly.

She pressed her face against my shoulder. "Oh, my white heart, my dearest darling, yes. Yes. Yes."

I kissed her again, touching her body, which was smooth, and strong, and answered mine.

"You shouldn't have asked me, really," she said, breathlessly, when I let her go again. "It's just the way we met that's done this. If we'd met one another on the road or at the market, you wouldn't have noticed me, and I wouldn't have spoken to you."

"Perhaps," I said. "But why should you say that what we saw in that extreme is false, and how we appear at a market, true? The gods gave with both hands when they spared me from dying in the water. For my part, I mean to take their gifts and bless them."

"So I notice," she said, and I could sense the ironic smile, invisible in the dark.

I kissed it. "You are laughing at me," I told her. "People have been laughing at me a great deal recently. It is very bad for my reputation. I am supposed to be a bloodthirsty savage."

She giggled. "And staying in here with you much longer will be very bad for mine. I'm supposed to be a modest young widow. You're going to have to let me go back and reassure them all that I am a respectable woman, really."

Whatever reputation she got in the fort now, she would have to live with over many years. I helped her down from the wagon, and we walked back to the fire.

Longus' sister Flavina lifted her mournful dark face to Pervica and said, "So do you think it looks comfortable?"

Pervica sat down and hugged her knees, her face radiant. "Yes."

Flavina laughed. "And when are you going to move in?"

"That will have to be decided," I intervened. "But the lady has consented to marry me. Wish us joy."

They all jumped up exclaiming, and wished us joy.

By the end of the evening we had fixed a date for the wedding—early February, which I hoped would give us enough time to sort out all the details of houses and lands and legal arrangements. I was not eager to sort out anything just then, in that perfect hour. I stood at my wagon watching when Pervica at last walked back to the village with Flavina, past the fires, under the thick winter stars. Already the line of her back, the way she held her head and draped her cloak, the soft shadow of her hair, were familiar to me. In a little while, I thought, I would recognize even the sound of her voice calling in the distance, or her body in the darkness; she would become more familiar to me than my own face, a pillar of my world. For all my desire, I felt in that instant neither anticipation nor dread of anything that fate could hold, but I was wholly content, at peace in that one shining moment of time.

I turned to go back into the wagon—and saw Facilis, still sitting beside the fire that the others had now left. When he saw me notice him, he got up.

"I need to talk to you, Ariantes," he said harshly.

I sighed. "Tomorrow."

"No. Now."

I looked at him a moment in silence.

"There are some things I need to know," he told me. "And I suspect there are some things you should have heard before you asked that lovely young woman to marry you."

"If that is so, it is already too late."

"I know, I know, I should have talked to you before, but I didn't want to ruin the festival, and I didn't realize you were going to make up your mind so fast. Still, the sooner you hear it, the better."

"Very well," I said, reluctantly. "We can talk."

"Not here. It's too public. Come to my house in the fort."

I hesitated, and he added, very quietly, "I can vouch for your safety going there and back, and I won't ask you to eat or drink anything."

I should have realized that he would notice my precautions. I sighed again, and nodded.

He had one of the empty Asturian barrack blocks to himself, and lived in the decurion's quarters at the headquarters end. He'd bought one slave in Eburacum to look after it for him, a thin, ugly boy who was snoring by the hearth in the main room when we came in, flushed with festival drink and happily gorged with feasting. Facilis grunted, put a blanket over the boy, and left him asleep. He ushered me into the bedroom instead and lit the lamp. It cast a yellow light over the cold stone walls. The floor was packed clay, without even bracken to warm it, and the bed had been shoved into the corner to make room for a desk. It was so cold that our breaths steamed in the lamplight. If ever a room looked like a tomb, it was that one.

"Now," said Facilis, "First the things I need to know. What happened to you on the road back to Condercum?"

"That is common knowledge."

"The hell it is! You didn't go hunting. Longus told me: your bow was still unstrung in its case. The woman hadn't unstrung it, because she commented on the shape of it, and thought the water must have spoiled it. And it's a pretty odd hunter who wades into the river to collect a quarry he's killed with an unstrung bow."

"A bow can be unstrung after use, and put back, to keep it dry."

"It can be—but it wouldn't be, with a quarry about to be washed downstream. And I talked to your young woman. When you were found, you were lying on your back in the shallows—but your face was covered with mud. The lady's no fool: she understood what that meant, though she was trying to pretend to me that she didn't even when she told me about it. She can see for herself that you're not admitting to anything and she's going along with it, but she's worried, and was letting me know as much as she could. Come on! I *know* there's something going on. You've stopped eating in the fort, and you wear armor and take your bodyguard with you even to exercise your horses—you, the slip-in-and-out sick-of-war shirtsleeves one. Someone tried to murder you, and you think someone's going to try again. And I can guess why. Someone made you an offer, and you turned it down, didn't you? Who? What did they want? Has Arshak accepted it?"

"Facilis," I said slowly, "I am sorry."

"Please!" His voice cracked. "I'm not your enemy. I was an idiot on the way from Aquincum, I can see that now. But I was sick with grief, I thought then it was my one chance to get a little of my own back, and I never expected to want to make alliances later. Look, what we used to be died at the ocean, and we know each other better now. You're a brave man, and an honorable one, and a damned fine officer who'll do anything to look after his lads, but you can't handle this alone. I want to help. Trust me, please! This is my fort now, and your people are my lads, too, and we're in the thick of somebody's plot to make them die in a mutiny like Gatalas and take a few thousand Roman lives as they do it."

"Facilis . . ." I began again, then stopped. "You are right, we know each other better. You are also a brave man, and an honorable one, and, I would guess, by nature a kind and decent man as well. I do trust you. But if what we were died at the ocean, it has left ghosts to haunt us, and one of those ghosts is a bullying centurion who tormented us from Aquincum to Bononia and tried to make things difficult for us even in Britain. My people have a saying: 'Some horses cannot be driven in pairs.' To Arshak's people, and to many of Siyavak's, and perhaps even to some of mine, I am damned as a Romanizer already. Arshak at least holds it against me that you, you specifically, vouched for me to the legate. Siyavak is my ally now, but he hates the Romans, and I dare not do anything that would lose him. I cannot make an alliance with you."

"You've lost Siyavak already. I saw him in Corstopitum, while you were recovering from drowning, cozily chatting with Arshak and . . . a certain lady."

I shook my head. "I have not lost him yet. But if Arshak and the lady you mention knew that, he would die. You see, I do trust you."

"May I perish! So Siyavak is spying on them? Things have gone further than I thought." He was silent for a minute, then said, "And do you understand why? And who? Because I still don't."

This I could answer. I told him, quietly and quickly, what Eukairios had told me about the druids, though I said nothing about the man he had mentioned, Cunedda. I did not trust Facilis not to investigate him further, and that investigation could put Eukairios' life at risk.

"May I perish!" he said again, when I'd finished. "That fits." After a moment, he asked, "Who told you all this?"

"Another ally."

"Roman? Sarmatian? British?"

"What are the things that I should have heard before I asked Pervica to marry me?"

He shook his head in frustration, then drew a deep breath. He sat down at the desk and took out a strongbox from beneath it. "The day you went to your young woman's farm, I went to Corstopitum." He set the box on the desk. "It's true, what I told you: I did have some shopping to do for the festival. But I'd also had a letter from Titus Ulpius, the prefect of the Thracians there, telling me that there was something I ought to see. I'd made a point of getting friendly with him and with a couple of the town magistrates, so they could keep an eye on things for me. It's an important place, Corstopitum: all the messages and messengers to Condercum and Cilurnum go through it, and all the traffic north as well. I went into the military compound, and Titus gave me this." Facilis unlocked the box and took out a roll of something dull and gray. He handed it to me.

It was a scroll of lead sheeting. I unrolled it carefully. There were two lines of writing on it, the letters made by points pricked out on the soft metal by the point of a knife. The first line was the writing Eukairios had called druidical; the second looked like Latin. The hollows of the knife-pricks were stained with what looked like blood. There was something evil about the thing, and it made my hair stand up to touch it. "What does it say?" I asked.

"It says, 'Ariantes son of Arifarnes,' " replied Facilis. "It was stuck in the mouth of a body found hanging from an oak tree in a sacred grove."

"Marha!" I set the thing down, and stretched my hands toward the lamp flame to invoke the god's protection. The heat from the lamp trailed a spot of warmth across my fingers, holding back the cold. I had been cursed before, but never like this, never with another man's life taken to fix death on me. My people believe that besides Marha and the heavenly gods, there is a dark power under the earth. We call it "the Lie" and do not worship it, but sometimes we curse by it. We say that it claims all oath-breakers and those who murder treacherously. I told myself that I had never sworn falsely or killed except in a fair fight, and I prayed to all the good gods to defend me from it.

"He'd been stripped and painted blue before he was strung up, and stabbed afterward," Facilis went on, harshly. "It was done the night of the midwinter solstice, the longest of the year. When Titus told me I didn't know what you told me about the druids, but it sounded like a ritual murder to me even then. And Titus didn't want to talk about it, and the magistrates didn't want to talk about it, and it's perfectly clear that nobody's even going to look for the people who murdered that poor bastard. Because they're afraid— and probably that means that the people who did it are numerous and powerful. But you can be sure that soon the whole countryside will know about it, and know that these druids hate you and have cursed you in the name of their gods, consigning you to perdition by another man's death. And you should have known that before you proposed marriage to that sweet young woman and decided to leave her, engaged to you, sitting out on an isolated farm in a region where your enemies have friends."

I couldn't breathe. I went to the window, which was closed and shuttered, and leaned my head against the sill where the winter air seeped through. After a moment, I slammed my hand against the frame. I had taken the gifts of the gods and blessed them, and because of it Pervica's life was in danger.

"What happened on the way back from Condercum?" asked Facilis.

"What you think," I said, without turning round.

"Was it the lady Aurelia?"

"Yes. She said that Gatalas' death had been a mistake, that it had been intended for all his dragon to mutiny. She said that what she wanted was a kingdom of the Brigantes, and that there was a good chance of getting it, since the Romans had already abandoned the Picts as too troublesome to govern, and might be persuaded to do the same with the Brigantes. She said that the natural allies of the Sarmatians are the Britons, not the Romans. Arshak believes it all. I think he is in love with her, and expects to reign as her consort when she is queen."

"What? She's an adulteress as well?"

He was shocked, which seemed ridiculous to me. After all, she was betraying her husband whether she was sleeping with Arshak or not. But Romans take adultery much more seriously than Sarmatians do. Even the husband can be prosecuted if he's thought to have tolerated it—though he can sleep with any unmarried woman he pleases, and commit no offense. My own people consider it a woman's business who she sleeps with. "I do not know," I told Facilis. "It would be risky for them, would it not? And difficult to find privacy, in Eburacum. But does it matter?"

He snorted: yes, it did, but he wasn't going to argue about it. "And what did she offer you?" he asked instead.

"We did not get that far. I told her I would as soon lead my men on horseback into the sea as trust them to her good faith."

"And what happened then?" He asked it in a whisper. "That was the bit that made no sense, that you ended up in the water with no sign of a fight. Did she . . . You said they're supposed to know magic, these druids . . ."

"They may, but she did not rely on spells. When she met us, she brought out wine, saying that by this she put the whole conversation under the sacred bond of hospitality. My cup was drugged. Even before I refused her, she had drugged it." It was unexpectedly humiliating to admit it, and remember my helplessness. "Arshak was angry at first; he wanted to fight," I continued, after a moment. "But she told him he would be accused of murder if he did and sent him off with the hunting story. She did not want him there when she drowned me—I think because she did not want him to see how much she enjoyed it." I turned away from the closed window and went back to the desk, where the lead roll with my name on it lay cold and lethal in the lamplight. "But I think I owe my life to that drug. I was weak with it, and chilled, when she put me in the water: I could not struggle. She said she had never drowned a man before, only animals, and animals would have fought. She must have turned me over and decided that I was dead before she left me, and so I was still alive when I was brought to Pervica. Marcus Flavius, what am I to do? I thought it was only my own life that was threatened. But they would kill her from sheer malice."

"You could go to the legate, or write your friend the procurator of the fleet, or even the governor."

"I? There is another ghost that haunts us—a prince of Iazyges who led raids across the Danube and drank from a Roman skull. I am on trial already. You yourself were commanded to put me under arrest earlier this very month. Who in authority would believe what I said about the wife of a legate?"

"I'd vouch for you."

"You could not vouch for what you did not see. Anything you said would offend Siyavak more than it helped me. I would be arrested for slander, and my men would mutiny, and probably I would be murdered in the prison, unable to defend myself. And what of the others here? Would Comittus vouch for me? Or would he say what his kinswoman asked him to?"

"Gods! I don't know. I like Lucius—but I don't know. What we really need are some allies in the British camp. Well, what about this other friend of yours, the one who isn't Roman, Sarmatian, or British? Couldn't he testify for you?"

"No. If he or his friends went before a magistrate, they would be sentenced to death."

"What are they? Smugglers? Christians? Never mind. So you're sitting and waiting, and hoping that they, or Siyavak, turn up something that you can use as evidence?"

I nodded. "I was a fool even to think of getting married," I said bitterly. "No, there is only one course. I must tell Pervica everything. She must either stay here with me and send her people safely away from her farm—or she must declare that, on reflection, she does not want me, and leave as though she were my enemy." I picked up the lead sheet. "May I show her this?"

He nodded. "I'm sorry, Ariantes."

I shook my head. "No—I am grateful to you. If she had gone home and died because of me, I would . . ."

I didn't know what I would do, and my mind suddenly threw up before me the image of Tirgatao, vivid as a thing seen through a window—torn open, a horse-head thrust in her womb, burning on the corpses of our children. I nearly dropped the lead sheet, and I had to set my teeth together hard to stop myself from screaming.

"Are you hurt?" asked Facilis. He tried to take the cursing tablet away, as though afraid it might have poisoned me.

I rolled the lead sheet slowly into its scroll and shook my head. It wasn't true, of course. I was hurt. I had been hurt badly early that summer, and the wound had just been kicked open. "I am sorry we cannot be allies, Marcus Flavius."

"What do you mean?" he asked. "We *are* allies. But I'll keep quiet about it."

THE NEXT MORNING I rode down to the fort village early, knocked at the door of Flavina's house, and asked to speak to Pervica. She herself came running at the sound of my voice, and greeted me with a smile so joyful I felt sick with fear and grief.

"I must speak with you privately," I told her.

"If you like," she agreed, her eyes dancing. "But not too private: spare my reputation before the wedding, please!"

"Come up to the camp with me, then," I said, "and we will find somewhere suitable."

We walked back up to the camp, leading my horse, because she was reluctant to ride through village, fort, and camp perched before me on the saddle. My leg ached by the time we arrived back at my wagon, I was tired from a night spent sleepless, and I was in a very black mood, which the cheerful greetings and congratulations of everyone around us only made worse. I pulled some rugs over from in front of the ashes of the fire and set them by the door of the wagon, right at the back of the awning. "Is this suitable?" I asked. "We can be seen here, but will not be overheard."

She laughed. "Very scrupulous! I wish we couldn't be seen either—but reputations are like eggs: there's no mending them once they've cracked." She sat down on the edge of the wagon, inside the open door, and stared curiously backward into it. "You know, it *is* pretty in there. It's like . . . like the inside of a jewel box. All those rugs and swords and things. What's the hairy thing over on this side?" She reached under the bunk, by the door, and pulled out the pile of the scalps I had removed from my horses' bridles when I first arrived in Britain.

I pushed them hastily back, and she looked at me in surprise. I drew my finger across my forehead and around the side of my head.

She didn't understand for a moment—and then she did. She looked at the scalps again, this time in revulsion.

"I am sorry," I said. "It is a custom of our people."

"There are a lot of them," she said quietly.

"Twenty-eight. All men I have killed with my own hands. There were others, too, whose scalps I had no opportunity to collect. I have stopped collecting them now, because the custom horrifies the Romans, but most of my men took some from the Picts we defeated, and I have said nothing to them about it. They take great pride in their strength and skill, and so they should."

"I suppose I will have to get used to it," she said slowly. "But I'd like it if you'd bury these."

I sat down on the rug at her feet and leaned my head against my bad knee. Her calm resolution to adjust to everything made it harder for me. "Pervica," I began helplessly—and stopped.

She stroked my hair away from my face and rested the long, firm hand on my shoulder. "I'm sorry," she said humbly. "I know you're not Roman. I don't expect you to become Roman either, really, but it's just hard for me to . . . to grasp it all at once."

"That is not it! Pervica, I was wrong to ask you to marry me."

All the joy went out of her in an instant: she stared at me with a face like a woman glimpsed by lightning, white and terrified. I turned and caught both her hands in mine. "Listen to me," I said. "I have enemies. I knew my life had been threatened, but I was confident they could not reach me here, in the middle of my own camp among my own men. I thought that no one would trouble the innocent, that no one would know or care about you, secure in the countryside, but I see now that I was wrong, and I have put you in danger. Look." I pulled out the lead scroll, which I'd shoved into my belt. "Facilis showed me this last night. It was found in the mouth of a man who'd been murdered in a sacred grove."

She took it slowly and unrolled it, then stared blindly.

"It is my name," I told her.

"I can read," she replied, sharply. "If you don't want to marry me, say so plainly. Don't make excuses."

"Do not be a fool. I wanted to badly enough that I forgot to think, to take any precautions. I was stupid and made a serious mistake: we must do what we can to retrieve it now. You must not go back to your farm as my betrothed. Either we must marry at once or you must pretend to quarrel with me, say that the engagement is off, and go home as though you were angry."

"And which would you prefer?" Some color had come back to her face, and there was a hint of anger in her voice.

"I would prefer it if you married me, of course. I would give you an armed escort back to River End, and you could send your people to safety, then return here."

She stared at my face searchingly, then slowly relaxed. She dropped the lead sheet onto the carpet beside me and stared at it, as though only now was she able to take in all that it meant. "Who did this?" she demanded in a whisper. "You know, don't you?"

I hesitated, then took her hands again. "I will tell you," I said, looking into her face, "but you must tell no one else."

I told her everything I'd heard or guessed about Aurelia Bodica from the time I arrived in Britain up to that moment. I told her hurriedly and angrily, and she sat and listened in silence. At the end she covered her face with her hands.

"I am sorry!" I said, wretchedly. "I should not have involved you, and I regret it."

She leaned over and grabbed my shoulders, looking angrily into my eyes. "Don't regret," she commanded. "I love you. How can you regret loving me?"

"I do not," I answered. "But I regret very much that I have put you in danger."

"If you don't regret loving me, then I will *not* pretend to quarrel with you and go home angry."

"Then we must marry at once. I will try to find out what the legal situation is today. I am not a citizen, and it may need some special—"

"I won't do that either! I'm not going to be chased about by these people, or send Cluim and the others away from their own home. I know a druid.

He blesses our orchard every year, and we give him a basket of apples and a jug of mead made with our own honey. I will talk to him about this Aurelia Bodica and her vile cruelty, and see what he has to say for himself! Give me this!" She snatched up the cursing tablet. "I'll take it to the temple of the Mothers. I've worshipped them all my life, and they've always been kind. This . . . this is wicked. Calling on the gods to commit murder is a crime against gods and men both."

"No!" I said, now very alarmed.

"You know nothing about the old religion. This"—she hit the leaden scroll—"this is a twisted parody of it, a gall, a deformity. They have no business murdering anyone, and most of them know it. And I am not someone they could murder. Everyone knows me, Saenus' widow Pervica. Everyone knows I honor the gods. They couldn't string me up just because they hate you."

"If they want this kingdom of the Brigantes, they would accuse you of treachery for opposing them."

"*They* may want one, but 'want' must be their master. There are men, no doubt, who long for revenge on an enemy, or an escape from their debts; there are ambitious nobles who dream of holding power in their own hands instead of bowing to legates and prefects; there are druids who long for an end to persecution. There are probably enough of them in all that when they talk among themselves they think everyone supports them. But there won't be any more general uprisings of the Brigantes, certainly not here near the Wall. We depend on the army here for our livelihoods: without the troops to buy our grain and our meat, the whole region would wither away. And an alliance with the Picts which involved giving them our farms to plunder—no, no, no! It's as ludicrous as the idea of a princess of the Coritani calling herself queen of Brigantia. No. You're not British or a farmer, or you'd realize at once that these people have no power in the countryside."

"They had power enough to murder at least one man and go unpunished through fear."

"Some townsman who'd done something to offend them! No. My darling, I'm far from saying that these people aren't dangerous. I know about them, I know they are—but not to me. To you, yes, because you're a foreigner and without a place here, and no one would risk offending them for your sake. But I can help you. I can talk to the people I know, the true followers of the old religion, not these visitors from the South. I think they'll help. They don't want the Selgovae and Votadini descending any more than the rest of us. All it needs is someone like me to ask them."

"Pervica!" I said, horrified, "You must not!"

"You forbid it, do you?" she asked, her mouth setting.

"I have no right to forbid. But you must not. Even if you were right to be confident of your own safety from the druids, still you would not be safe. Arshak is a powerful and arrogant man, and totally lacking in caution. He is to go to Condercum after the festival, with the second dragon, his followers, and if he learned that you were stirring up trouble against his lady, he would kill you first and think of explanations for the authorities afterward."

"He isn't British. Does he speak British? Then he won't know anything that's going on in the countryside. And the people I mean to speak to won't give my name away. Even if they don't help, they won't want me killed, and if they do help, they'll take the credit for their actions themselves."

"You cannot go back to your farm and . . . and spy for me. You cannot. You will be killed."

"I can, I will, and I won't be. I'm not going to abandon my property and my dependants, and you can't expect me to. Would you, in my place? And I'm not going to sit in your wagon like a piece of baggage while you run stupid risks and make terrible mistakes through not knowing things I could easily discover. I'm British: I have more rights in the matter than you do!"

I got up and walked off a few steps and slammed r y hand against the wagon. "And what if you are killed?" I asked her.

"What if you're killed? That's even more likely. I'm only incidental: you're the one they want."

"I have five hundred men at my command, and thirty in particular whose chief task is to preserve my life and honor. And even if they fail, I can face my own death."

She closed her eyes for a moment, then opened them again. "Don't you understand?" she asked. "Perhaps you could face your own death—but I couldn't. I never loved my husband. I liked him, I obeyed him willingly, because he was kind, because he loved me, but I could never give him either respect or love. When he died I thought I would spend the rest of my life in independence. I was content enough—until I went into my stable and saw you standing there, with Wildfire eating from your hand. Then I knew that I had never been alive at all. I don't care if I die now, but I'm not going to live without you."

I went back and knelt before her. "Pervica, please!" I said. "You have seen what I have done with your horse, how he is beginning to trust me, how he comes to me for protection from the cold, and expects me to feed him? If he came, and I beat him till he staggered, who would he trust then? Do not die, Pervica. It would destroy me."

She put her arms around my neck. "I will not die," she told me solemnly. "But I won't do what you ask."

XII

*P*ERVICA WENT HOME that afternoon in exactly the situation I liked least—formally engaged to marry me, planning to continue on her own till the date set for the wedding, and totally determined to carry out her inquiries among her druidical friends. I loaned her a wagon to drive herself back, and I and the bodyguard escorted her all the way to River End, but my continued protests only made her angry. As Longus had remarked, she had a will of iron and she hated to be bullied. I was miserably aware that I had made my explanations to her very badly, driven as I was by my own memories.

When I'd seen her home I rode back to Cilurnum like a thundercloud. I found Kasagos and told him about the cursing tablet—the news was bound to reach the camp within a few days, and I wanted the protection of our own gods; the thing had unsettled me. He was predictably outraged. We sacrificed to Marha, and he lit a ring of fire about my wagon to invoke the god's protection and keep back the power of the Lie. Then he counted out the divining rods, but their message was ambiguous and uncomforting. I snarled at the bewildered bodyguard, ignored the puzzled questions of my Roman and Sarmatian friends, and went off to work with my horses.

The only other person I spoke to about the tablet was Eukairios. I was afraid that the murdered man was his friend, killed for his inquiries on my behalf, and I sent him into Corstopitum to check.

He returned the following afternoon to report that his friend was safe and well: the sacrificial victim had been a carpenter once accused of using wood from a sacred grove. He said besides that a lead scroll that was supposed to be the famous cursing tablet had been found that morning lying on the altar of the Mothers in Corstopitum. One of the local druids was said to have erased the name on it and to have denounced the ritual murder that produced it as blasphemous. The local people were delighted about this—the victim had been a townsman, and it was widely believed that the murderers were Pictish druids enraged by the failure of the raid on Corstopitum. The marketplace was rustling with whispers, and many of the citizens were going to the temple of the Mothers to see the scroll and leave an offering to the goddesses. This was comforting in that it did not sound as though the countryside was eager to harm Pervica, but unsettling in that if the cursing tablet *was* lying on an altar in Corstopitum, it must be because Pervica had put it there, and made public her opposition to everything it represented.

The news of the ritual murder and the cursing tablet seeped into the rest of the camp the same day, brought by the first people to visit Corstopitum after the festival. As Facilis had predicted, everyone knew what had been written on the tablet. The general conclusion was the same as in the town: that it had been the work of Picts angry at their defeat. I could see, however, that Comittus in particular was extremely unhappy about it. He lost all his bounciness and looked upset whenever he saw me. Several times he tried to speak to me, but I was still in a very black mood and ignored his tentative questions entirely. I think he and Longus both realized then that I hadn't shared their food or drink since the near-drowning. They were neither of them stupid, and the mutiny and the raid, the drowning and the curse, were obviously and suspiciously connected. Longus tried to talk, too—but I wouldn't discuss it with him, either.

A FEW DAYS later, on the second of January, I set out for Eburacum, as the legate had asked. I brought my bodyguard with me under Banadaspos, and Kasagos' squadron as well, but left Leimanos in charge of the rest of the dragon. We took our wagons to sleep in. I brought Eukairios, both to have his help with the arrangements for the stud farms and also because he wished to consult his fellow cultists in Eburacum and hear their verdict on an alliance. Facilis came as well, muttering some excuse about legion business—though it was clear to me that he came because he wanted to pursue his own inquiries about Aurelia Bodica.

I also took along the stallion Wildfire. I'd had considerable success training the animal already, partly because he wasn't used to being outside in cold weather and forgot his distrust of humans in his desire to come under the awnings and be warm. I'd just begun breaking him to the saddle and I judged it would be bad for him to interrupt the training for the time needed for the journey.

On the second day of the journey we met Arshak and his dragon, riding up the north road from Eburacum to their posting at Condercum. It was a cold gray day of intermittent snow, but the sun came out just before we met them and we saw the glitter of their arms in the light while they themselves were only a shadow on the road ahead. They'd spread out across the verges of the road, as we had ourselves, trying to spare the unshod hooves of the horses. Arshak was riding in the vanguard beneath the golden dragon of his standard. As we rode on toward him, he slowed, and when we were almost level, he stopped, and all his men halted behind him. I stopped as well, only a few paces from him, and we stared at each other for a long time in silence. I noticed that he was wearing his coat of scalps. His liaison officer, Severus, looked puzzled.

"Greetings," he said at last. "I didn't see you when you were last in Corstopitum. I wanted to tell you how pleased I am that you're still alive." He smiled.

I knew that smile: he'd given it to Facilis often enough. I thought of asking him if he had a cup of hospitality he wished to share with me—but there was no point baiting him. "Greetings," I said, instead. "I'll be pleased to meet you any time, now that we are to be neighbors."

He smiled again and ran a hand caressingly down his spear. "You're a true nobleman, in most ways," he commented. "You're bound to Eburacum, you and your"—his eyes raked Facilis—"your good friends?"

I nodded and gathered up Farna's reins. "And you're bound to Condercum. I won't keep you—unless you have business with me now?"

His eyes lit, but he shook his head. "I wish I did. But not now. Still, I'm glad you didn't drown. A prince of the Iazyges should die by the spear."

"I will die as the god wills it, and by the hand he appoints," I replied, "as you will yourself, Arshak." He flinched slightly, as though the connection between gods and killing made him uneasy. "A pleasant journey to you," I told him, and started my horse forward.

He moved his white Parthian aside to let me pass, and turned in the saddle to watch me as I rode on. When Facilis passed him, he smiled again and fingered the neck of his coat—then gestured for his drummer to give the signal, and continued on.

"Have you quarreled with Lord Arshak, my lord?" Banadaspos asked me unhappily, when our party was through the long coils of the dragon and on the clear road behind it.

I looked at him. "You should not ask such questions, Banadaspos," I said. "I don't want dueling between his men and ours. Whatever is between him and myself is our own business."

He was not satisfied with this reply. "It is our business to guard our prince," he said sullenly. Then he added, in a whisper, "That story Arshak told of chasing a boar never made sense. But I don't see how . . ." He stopped. He didn't see how a quarrel with Arshak could end in a drowning and a lie.

"This affects my honor, not yours," I said; and at this he fell reluctantly silent.

The rest of the journey to Eburacum was uneventful. We arrived in the middle of the afternoon of the fourth day after leaving Corstopitum.

Eburacum, which we had last visited early in the autumn, lies in green, fertile valley land upon a river, and just south of the Highlands of Brigantia. Besides being the home for the Sixth Legion, the city is the base for the civilian administration of the whole of the northern half of the province—which is run by the legionary legate, though he is officially subordinate to the provincial governor in Londinium. Being in a position of such importance, Eburacum has naturally prospered. The stone-based half-timbered buildings crowd unpleasantly close together, overshadowing the street, and the main market square seems in contrast very bright, surrounded by the white facades of the grand public buildings. The shops sell everything from hunting dogs to imported glassware.

The legionary fortress lies the other side of the river from the market square, a severe castle frowning upon its ostentatious neighbor. All forts are much alike. All have the same shape, rectangular with rounded corners; all have the same two main streets, the Via Principalis and the Via Principia, running from the four gates past the neat barrack blocks, and where those two streets meet, the headquarters building and the commanding officer's house invariably face one another. I had always found the uniformity repellant before, and this time was unsettled to discover that it merely seemed convenient.

We were met at the fort gates and escorted first to the stable yard, where we were instructed to leave our horses and the wagons, and then to the places where we were supposed to sleep—a guesthouse for Facilis, the tribune's house recently vacated by Arshak for myself, and barracks for the rest of the men. I did not argue, but I told my men, in Sarmatian, that they could stay in their wagons if they wanted to. We were hardly going to be pushed into the barracks by force, and the wagons could be parked as comfortably in the stable yard as anywhere else, so why quarrel over what can be ignored? I left the others to settle in, and, though it was late in the afternoon, took Eukairios and went at once to see the legate.

I was admitted immediately. Priscus seemed pleased to see me, and was happy to get down to business. He had chosen a number of farms for the horses, but he was perfectly happy to add River End to the list. Eukairios and I had a tentative list of mares to breed in the next season, and stallions to cover them, and the arrangements as to which farm would take how many horses were soon made. Priscus then turned to the "other business" he'd mentioned, and my apprehensions about it turned out to have been entirely misplaced. Another eight dragons of Sarmatian cavalry were expected to arrive in Britain between April and July, and the legate wanted my advice on how to accommodate them. I was surprised and delighted, particularly when it turned out that one of the companies was the fifth dragon, commanded by my elder sister Aryazate's husband, Cotys, a friend as close as any I'd had in my life. These troops were wintering in various locations between the Danube and the ocean but would cross the Channel as soon as the weather permitted. I gave Priscus a great deal of advice on the spot, mostly to do with choosing sites that had enough grazing and allowing the troops the use of cattle to produce all the milk they'd need. Even when the legate had had enough for one day and dismissed me, I kept thinking of other things to tell him, and ordering Eukairios to write them down. Eukairios was impatient to stop work and go see his fellow Christians, and eventually said so.

"You'll simply have to learn to write," he told me, while I chewed on my lip in frustration. His eyes were glinting with amusement.

"But I have heard that writing is difficult, and one must learn very young, or not at all."

He smiled, putting away his pen. "Now, if I were to assure you that writing's easy, I might find myself in the same position as your men did when they promised me that riding a horse is the easiest thing in the world, and that human beings just naturally stay on—and then were unable to account for it when I fell off. I certainly don't find writing difficult. But I did indeed learn it very young, if not quite as young as you Sarmatians learn riding, since you seem to sit on the saddle behind your mothers before you can even walk. All I can say is I think you'd be able to learn it and you'd undoubtedly find it useful if you did. But I must go speak to my friends as soon as possible, so that we can make arrangements for . . . if they agree."

"Very well, very well!" I said, thinking of something else that I would now simply have to try to remember. "Meet me in the morning, and we will finish this then. I will sleep in my wagon tonight, but you may use the tribune's house they allotted us, if you prefer—or stay with your friends."

Between thinking of arrangements for the other eight dragons and worrying about Pervica, I had trouble getting to sleep that night. I tossed and turned in my wagon, and at last got up, pulled on my coat, and stepped outside. The night was clear and very cold and the moon was waning. It was about midnight and everything lay still, the stone of paving and walls white in the moonlight, the shadows very black. I limped slowly toward the stables to check on my horses. I was about halfway there when I heard the shouts, faint with distance, and smelled smoke. Then the trumpets sounded from the gates, and there was a sound of feet running. I ran back to the wagon, grabbed my sword and my bow case, and ran in the same direction as the feet, thinking wildly that the city was under attack.

But the alarm had been raised for a house on fire. I arrived at the row of tribunes' houses on the Via Principalis to find flames pouring from the windows of one of them and half the Sixth Legion, in various states of undress, lining up with buckets to fetch water from the aqueduct. A centurion was shouting at some men to hurry up with an oak beam. I registered all this before I realized that the house was the one I myself had been allotted, and that Eukairios might be inside. I pushed past the legionaries and hurried toward it.

The stone walls of the house radiated heat like an open oven, and the slates of the roof were cracking like chestnuts in a fire and falling into the flames below. The buckets of water hurled by the legionaries hissed deafeningly on the flames, and clouds of smoke and steam billowed out to choke anyone who went near. The centurion bellowed at his men, striking them with his vine staff and pointing at the door; they raised the oak beam and struck with it, trying to batter down the door.

"Is anyone in there?" I shouted.

"That Sarmatian commander!" the centurion shouted back. "The one that arrived today! If he's yours, help!"

I caught the end of the beam as they swung it back. "I have a slave . . ." I began—but didn't finish, since the legionaries swung the beam. I leaned with them into the stroke: the door held. We struck again, and it gave. A wave of heat so great that it seared the lungs struck our faces; I saw the inside of the house incandescent, the walls dressed with fire, and the remains of something black across the door. The man nearest the door screamed soundlessly and flung himself backward, and his friends caught him and drew him away coughing and choking, his hands burned and his hair singed.

"If anyone's still in there, he's dead," the centurion declared, as we retreated. He looked at me again. "What were you saying? Is that your commander's house?"

"It was meant to be mine," I said, staring back at it, "but I did not use it." I looked at the centurion. "Someone had blocked the door. There was something across the inside."

"Someone did the whole damned thing!" he returned. "I've never seen a good stone house go up like that, and the first lad to get here said the smoke reeked of lamp oil. And the windows were bolted on the outside. Did you say *you* were meant to be in there?"

I nodded, staring at the house. The roof was collapsing now, but the legionaries still hurled their buckets of water. "My slave may be in there." Burned alive. Murdered by fire, and burned.

"But no Sarmatian commanders? And no one else? Just a slave?"

I shook my head.

"Well, thank the gods for that!"

There was a stir in the now thick crowd that had gathered in the street, and I noticed Julius Priscus pushing his way into the mob, his crimson cloak askew and his sandals unlaced; he was staring at the flames. I started toward him. The centurion of the Sixth began by following me, but confronted with a wall of backs, pushed in front and cleared a path with his vine staff.

Priscus heard him coming and turned, his face grim—then he saw me, and his eyes flew open in amazement.

"Ariantes!" he exclaimed, and reached over to grasp my hands. "Thank the gods! However did you get out of that . . . that Phlegethon?"

I was not sure who or what Phlegethon was, but his meaning was clear enough. "I was never in it, my lord. I prefer my wagon. But my slave may be in there."

"Well, for once I'm pleased with your savagery!" exclaimed Priscus, ignoring my reference to a slave. "Publius Verinus"—to the centurion of the Sixth—"what happened here?"

"Clear case of arson, sir," the centurion replied smartly. "One of my lads was coming back from a night out, and he smelled smoke as he passed it— and said it reeked of oil. He saw fire through the cracks in the shutters, and tried to open the door, but it was locked. By the time he'd raised the alarm, the whole place was ablaze. When we battered the door down, we found that someone had put something right across it. The shutters were bolted, too, on the outside." He gave me a level look. "Somebody wanted to kill the commander here pretty badly."

A wall of the house collapsed, its stones cracking explosively. The fire, though, seemed to be dying now under the constant stream of water from the buckets. It must have burned everything in the house that could burn. I prayed silently that that did not include Eukairios.

Priscus gave me the same level look. "Who wants to kill you?"

I was silent for a moment, struggling with myself. The name of his wife was in my throat, choking me. I had a friend who had, perhaps, just died horribly, and whose life was considered a thing too inconsequential even to discuss. I wanted badly to revenge him. But I could not say Bodica's name: I still had no proof. Besides, I didn't know for certain that Eukairios was dead. He'd preferred staying in his friends' houses in the past, and might well be comfortably asleep in the town outside the fortress gates. "There was . . . an object found near Corstopitum," I said at last. Someone was bound to tell Priscus this if I didn't. "A lead scroll, pushed into the mouth of a murdered man found hanging from a tree in a sacred grove. It had my name written on it. The general conclusion was that it was the work of some Picts, resentful of their defeat."

Priscus drew in his breath with a hiss and blinked at me several times.

"There are no Picts in the middle of a legionary fortress at night," declared the centurion of the Sixth. "They might, just, slip into the town, though even that's pretty unlikely this far south—but they'd never get over the walls of the fort."

"No," I said, giving him the level look back. "So it must have been a Roman. And why the Romans would wish to kill me, I do not know—though my men, and the men of the fourth dragon, will doubtless think of a reason. With your permission, Lord Legate, I think I must go back to my men now, or they will be alarmed."

Priscus caught my arm. "There's nobody under my command who wants to kill you," he said harshly. "May the gods destroy me if it's false! You're the one we can work with, and worth all the other Sarmatian officers put together."

"Sir, I do not doubt your goodwill. But it would be better if you did not use such terms, as it would offend the other officers. May I go reassure my followers?"

He let go of me, and I bowed and walked off.

I was halfway back to the wagons when I heard a shout behind me, and I turned to see Eukairios running toward me through the moonlight, waving both hands wildly. I gave a cry of relief and ran toward him.

"Thank God!" he said, and, "I thank the gods!" I exclaimed, at almost the same instant. I caught him by the shoulders and shook him, to make sure he was really there and not ashes in the burned house. I was smiling so hard my face hurt.

"The house is burned down," I told him. "I was afraid you were inside it."

He shook his head. "No, I was staying at a friend's in the town. But I heard the alarm, and came to see what was happening. I didn't *think* you were in the house, but I wasn't completely sure. Was it . . . was it arson?"

I nodded.

"Everyone thought you were there. Everyone except your own men."

"Yes. I do not know what to say to the legate. It is clear now that it must have been a Roman who arranged it: only army people are allowed in the fortress at night. They will think of the message that was sent to Gatalas. They will start guessing. But we still have no evidence, and how can I speak without it? It would be easy for them to kill me, if I were arrested here. Something in the prison food while I awaited trial for slander, another fire—nothing would be easier. Marha! I do not know what to say."

I started back toward the wagons, and Eukairios fell in beside me. "You're very upset about it," he remarked. He sounded surprised.

"I am very glad you are alive," I told him, beginning to recover myself. "I thought you were dead and your body burned."

He stopped a moment. "Oh," he said. "Oh, yes—of course." He hurried to catch up with me again, and we walked on together, as though we were members of one household. We arrived back at the wagons, where my men were gathered in an anxious knot that broke in shouts and exclamations of relief when I appeared.

THE FOLLOWING MORNING Eukairios was eager to go back into the town: he hadn't finished arranging matters with the Christians when the fire started. "I spoke to the . . . the *presbyteroi* of the *ekklesia* yesterday," he said. "The elders of the assembly, that is. They've prayed about the alliance. They are mostly Brigantians, and they don't want to see a rebellion or an invasion of the northern tribes—but they're not quite sure. They want to meet you."

"Meet me? Why?"

"My lord . . . we can be injured very easily. One has only to go to a magistrate and say, 'He's a Christian,' and that in itself is a sentence of death. And we don't want to start a struggle with the druids: we'd be crushed. If we're to commit ourselves to the risks of an earthly alliance, we have to be sure of our allies. They—one of them in particular—isn't sure about you at all. I've vouched for you—but I'm your slave."

I shrugged. "But what do they expect to gain by meeting me? They must know that I am not of your faith, that I am . . . how did you put it once? . . . a man who decorates his horses' bridles with scalps and drinks from a Roman skull."

"You don't, anymore. They just want to know if you're the sort of man they can trust not to betray us. Please, sir, I don't think they'll help if they haven't met you."

I was not eager to meet Eukairios' friends. I preferred not to know the sordid details. But I did want their help in keeping contact with Siyavak and whatever knowledge their contacts with that other illegal cult had to offer me. "Very well, very well!" I said irritably. "You may tell them that I will meet them at midday, in a place of their chosing. But be back as soon as you can. I wish to have a list of proposals ready for the legate when we meet him this afternoon."

He saddled my red bay carriage horse and galloped off almost as briskly as a Sarmatian.

Without Eukairios to help me with my list, I had the morning free. I considered trying to arrange some meeting with Siyavak—but decided that however I did it, I might endanger him, and it was safer to allow him to choose his time to meet me. I worked with the stallion Wildfire instead.

I'd accustomed the horse to the feel of a saddle while we were still in Cilurnum, and I'd ridden him for short distances beside Farna while we were on the road. It was probably fortunate that he'd been trained only as a carriage horse before. The saddle held no particular terrors for him—unlike the bridle, the very sound of which made him roll his eyes and lay his ears back. His mouth was so badly scarred, anyway, that he was unable to feel anything short of a wrestling hold on the reins, so I left him with his head in a halter and trained him only to the signals I gave him with my feet. He already knew the Latin carriage calls for "stop" and "go," so it was easy to teach him that, and he learned to turn quickly. I rode him round and round the stable yard that morning—turn to the right, good lad, turn to the left, good, my brave one, stop! good, very good, here is some grain for you; turn to the left, trot, to the left, yes, good—and he was working well, still nervous of strangers or any sudden sound, but enjoying himself, wanting to please and be praised. When he'd walked and trotted for about an hour, I stopped him in the middle of the yard and began to show him that riders can do odd things in the saddle but that these are nothing to worry about. I stood up in the stirrups, moved over to one side, moved over to the other, leaned down, talking to him quietly all the while. He stood still, flicking his ears backward and forward, and only occasionally trying to move off. I praised him, then drew my legs up and knelt in the saddle. My left knee was stiff, but did not threaten to give under me. I stood up, carefully—and felt ridiculously proud of a feat of balance I'd once taken for granted.

All of a sudden we heard voices at the end of the stable yard, and Wildfire laid his ears back and shied violently. I managed to drop back into the saddle, though he had moved so that I landed hanging sideways by one leg; he leapt across the yard stiff-legged, prancing and snorting, with me hanging off on one side and dragging myself up by his mane. He nearly crashed into the wagons, shied again, twisted about, and neighed loudly, kicking. I had my hands full trying to stay on, and my men began running to help. Wildfire backed among the wagons, kicking and rolling his eyes. I slipped off and caught his head, put my arm about his neck and crooned into his ear. He stood still, shivering. Banadaspos ran over and caught the other side of the stallion's halter, while I stroked the damp neck and whispered to the animal. I heard the rattle of a carriage crossing the yard, but was far too busy to pay any attention to it—until I heard Bodica's voice, very close, saying, "Having trouble with your horse, Lord Ariantes?"

Wildfire neighed again and tried to rear. I put my coat over his head, but he still shifted, trembling and snorting.

"I think perhaps he remembers you," I told Bodica, not looking up. "If you will please move away, Lady Aurelia, I can put him back in the stables."

I led the horse past her without looking at her, only vaguely aware that she was sitting in her chariot and watching me. Wildfire calmed a little as I brought him into the stable. I put a blanket over him, and asked Banadaspos to walk him up and down and give him a drink of water when he was cool. Then I went back into the yard.

Bodica was still there, standing and leaning on the chariot rail now, letting the flower-bordered edge of a new white cloak drape elegantly over the painted side. "I think you're right," she told me, smiling. "I believe I did own that horse once. But he turned vicious and I sold him. I didn't know you were interested in secondhand animals."

I had wondered before if the stallion had ever been hers. While there are plenty of people to mistreat animals, few could afford to abuse such a fine one, and she obviously liked driving large and powerful stallions. "Most creatures turn vicious if they are punished unreasonably," I told her. "Did you wish to speak to me, Lady Aurelia?"

"My husband and I wanted to invite you to dinner tonight, Lord Ariantes," she said, smiling sweetly. "I hope you can come. We would be most offended if you couldn't."

I set my teeth. I'd been afraid of this, and had tried to think of a good excuse not to share a meal with my commanding officer. I'd been unable to. I would simply have to hope that she would not poison me at her own table, where her husband might discover it. "I am honored," I told her, bowing my head. "I will come."

"Good!" she said, and sat down again, "We'll expect you about five o'-clock then." Her driver shook the reins, and the chariot moved off. I watched the white stallion trot smartly out of the yard, and wondered how long it would be before he "turned vicious," too.

EUKAIRIOS RETURNED ABOUT the middle of the morning and said that the Christians had agreed to a meeting, though they wanted it to be discreet. I was still angry and anxious when I set off with Eukairios for this. Eukairios wanted to go as inconspicuously as possible, and he asked that I not wear my armor. I very much disliked the feeling of setting out with my back unprotected. (Eukairios also considered it conspicuous to go on horseback, but I told him that Sarmatian princes do not walk, and I would be even more conspicuous if I did—though I took my courser instead of Farna.) I did not bring any of the bodyguard, of course. They were very unhappy at this, since they understood that someone had not only tried to murder me the night before, but chosen a particularly horrifying method for it, and they guessed now that the cursing tablet had not been the work of any Pict. They were deeply offended that I should leave them behind at such a time, and they protested angrily and swore to their loyalty. In the end I had to issue a flat order that they stay behind and keep quiet, and they watched me ride off very resentfully.

We trotted through the east gate of the fortress, then down the road and into the marketplace—like Corstopitum, Eburacum had grown from a mere army base into a proper city. Despite the cold weather, the market was busy, and the people there all looked at us twice. Eukairios glanced at me nervously and shook his head. "Couldn't you have worn some other coat?" he whispered. "That red one is very conspicuous . . ."

"I have no plain coats," I replied. "Your friends were the ones who wanted this meeting."

Eukairios sighed. "Yes, my lord," he said, very tense and unhappy now the time had come. "Well, we'll have to go round the back, and then I'll have to go on ahead, and make sure it's clear, and get someone to hide the horses somewhere . . ."

We had to do as he said—out of the market, down a street, through an empty alleyway, into an even narrower back alley that smelled of boiled cabbages. Then I had to wait with the horses by a rubbish heap while Eukairios vanished into one of the houses ahead, and came back a little while later with a frightened girl, who whispered that we could put the horses in the shed with her goats. I looked at her remotely and said nothing. If the Christians decided not to help, after all this ridiculous performance, I was going to be seriously angry. But I tied up my courser in a shed in a back garden beside two nanny goats, and followed Eukairios through the back door of a private house. We emerged in a kitchen, very low and smoky, and were ushered through it into a middle-class dining room. The room was warm and bright, heated by a brazier, and the winter sun shining through the glass windows made watery patterns upon the red and white tiles of the floor. There were three men there, all in their forties. Two wore the gray-brown tunics and trousers and checked cloaks one could find on any man in the marketplace, and the third, who was clean-shaven, wore Roman dress. All three came over to me when I entered and shook hands, with me and with Eukairios.

"Lord Ariantes," said the one in Roman dress. "Thank you for coming. I'm sorry we can't give you our own names: it's probably better that you don't know them." He sat on the middle couch of the three dining places, and gestured to the couch on his right. "Please, sit down."

If an army officer had said that, I would have taken off my sword and made some effort to sit or recline in the usual Roman fashion. But I wasn't going to make myself uncomfortable for a pack of cultists. I sat down on the floor in front of the couch he'd indicated, with my good leg crossed under me and my bad one pulled up before me, adjusting my sword so that it didn't pull on the baldric. The two other Christians gave me an odd look, then sat down on the central couch beside their spokesman, watching me with wary curiosity. Eukairios, after a moment's uncomfortable hesitation, sat down behind me.

"Our brother Eukairios," said the Romanized Christian, "has explained to us that there may be a plot to make this region, Brigantia, our home, rebel against the provincial government. He's said that someone is trying to involve Sarmatian troops like the one you command in mutinies, and has actually called in the Selgovae and the other Pictish tribes as invaders to occupy the army so the rebellion can succeed. He says further that the person at the center of this plot is . . . a lady reputed to be a follower of an extreme druidical sect, who wants to make Brigantia a druidical kingdom, with herself as queen. He says that while you know of this plot, you have no other witnesses or material evidence for it, and that your word alone would not be sufficient to convince the authorities. Is that a fair summary?"

I was relieved to have it all set out so clearly and unemotionally, though the open discussion of the details made me feel even more exposed than riding through the marketplace without armor had. "Yes," I agreed.

"And he says further that you want our help for two purposes: first, to keep in contact with a friend of yours in Eburacum who is trying to discover the details of the plot; and secondly, to make use of our knowledge of, and contacts with, the druids."

"That is so."

There was a moment's silence. Then one of the other Christians asked bluntly, "Why should we help you?"

"Because," I answered, "you are British, and Roman, and, I think, Brigantian, and the kingdom that this plot would produce would be unwelcome to you on several counts."

"The present government does not love us," the other replied. He was a serious, dark-eyed man. "We are persecuted in every corner of this empire, and treated like sheep to be slaughtered. Our kingdom is not of this world, and we have no business interfering in the counsels of princes and legates."

"And if the Selgovae and Votadini came up to this city and began to sack it?" I asked. "Would you interfere with them?"

"We would not shed their blood," said Dark Eyes solemnly. "We would oppose them, and die in the name of Christ our Lord."

"That wouldn't do our neighbors any good!" replied the other British Christian, before I could say anything. "Nor our brothers and sisters, nor our wives and children! We are Brigantian, as he said: why shouldn't we defend our home? And the man is asking us to carry letters, not to shed blood."

The Romanizer held his hand up. "Not in front of our guest!" he said. "Lord Ariantes, our brother Eukairios has vouched for you in the strongest terms, and said that you are kind, generous, and a peacemaker. He says that by helping you, we might prevent a cruel and bloody rebellion. We know . . . something . . . of the people involved in this affair, and we're inclined to believe him. But your people also have a very evil reputation, and it's hard for us to . . . How shall I put it?"

"Make an alliance with a Sarmatian."

He grinned at me quickly, and suddenly I liked him. "Well, yes," he said. "I wouldn't have thought a dragon was the natural ally of a flock of doves."

I spread my hands before me. "Granted. But I already have as an ally a Roman who before was a bitter enemy. If I can make an alliance with the eagles, I can make one with a flock of doves."

"Eagles have more in common with dragons than doves do," said Dark Eyes. "They are both killers."

"Eukairios said he was a peacemaker," said the Brigantian champion.

"He doesn't look it," said Dark Eyes. "Sitting there on the floor with his sword on his back and his hand on his dagger! And the stories I've heard say he's killed dozens of men with his own hands."

I took my hand off my dagger and looked at Dark Eyes thoughtfully, rubbing my knee. I wondered who and what he was, and who'd told him about me. "I have killed above thirty men," I answered. "I have stopped counting. It is true, we are not a peace-loving nation—and we were sent to Britain as soldiers, and could not choose peace now even if we wished to. But I do not want there to be a war."

"What do you want?" asked the Romanizer softly.

I gave him the honest, shameful truth. "I would like my dragon to rest quietly in Cilurnum, with nothing more to do than patrol the Wall, put down occasional raids, and breed horses. But I confess to you honestly that my own men might ask the gods instead for glory and victory in war."

"That's what I've heard," said Dark Eyes. "There is nothing, I was told, that gives a Sarmatian more pleasure than killing any man whatsoever."

I looked away, down at my hands now resting crossed on my torn knee. "In ten years' time," I said quietly, admitting another shameful truth that I'd known now for some time, "there will be no real Sarmatians in Britain. I am not what I was, nor is Arshak, nor are any of us. If you live in one place under an alien code of discipline, collect your wages four times a year, and spend your time drilling and patrolling, you are not the same as a nomad who lived by his herds and made war for pleasure. The only question has been, what do we become instead? I have answered it, 'Roman soldiers.' Arshak says, 'British warriors.' And perhaps there is no great difference in it. We are killers, in your terms, whatever we do—though you would do well to remember that as soldiers, we would defend you, while as warriors, we would become your oppressors. But I do not like the company we would keep as warriors, and I think even if we succeeded, we would succeed only to the destruction of all that is best in us. We used, in the past, to love truth, respecting our friends and keeping our oaths; we used to fight fairly, and spare the helpless. Those are the customs I wish us to keep, whatever else we may lose. I swear it on fire"— I raised my right hand and stretched it toward the brazier—"that I have asked for your help in a good cause which I believe ought by rights to be your cause, and that I will deal with you justly and without treachery."

"It is our cause," said the Brigantian.

"It is not!" said Dark Eyes.

"Christ is our cause," said the Romanizer. "Him and him alone—but to serve him may mean serving goodness and justice wherever we may find it, as it is written: 'and they said to him, Lord, when did we see you hungry and feed you, or thirsty and give you drink? and he replied, Amen I tell you, whenever you gave it to the least of these my brothers, you gave it to me.' "

"He is not a brother!" exclaimed Dark Eyes angrily. "Least or greatest!"

"He is a neighbor, then," snapped the Brigantian, "and engaged in a struggle with *our* enemies, who, by all accounts, have called on the aid of demons to curse him and have tried to murder him in this very city. Should we pass by on the other side, in the vain hope that the brigands won't actually threaten *us?*"

"We put our trust in God, come what may," replied Dark Eyes. "Not in princes."

"We've prayed over this already, and argued it," said the Romanizer. "I had a strong conviction of our Lord's guidance in this before, and meeting the man has only reassured me. I'm sorry, brother, that it hasn't helped you."

Dark Eyes scowled. "He could have been worse," he said, after a pause. "So you're determined to go through with it?"

"For Christ's sake!" exclaimed the Brigantian. "It's our own city and our own homes at risk!"

"We have a clear choice between helping a man who is working for peace," said the Romanizer, "or standing aside and letting the forces of destruction and violence take their course. I am for peace." He stood and walked over to me, holding out his hand. "You have your alliance."

XIII

*T*HE CHRISTIANS WERE helpful as soon as their decision was made, even Dark Eyes, though it was plain he was reluctantly going along with the majority. They provided the name of someone who could write letters for Siyavak, a password and means to contact this person, and promised that any letter he wrote would be passed swiftly and secretly to me. Then the Romanizer produced a set of wax tablets. "We drew this up last night," he said. "It is a list of people we know to be druids, together with their hiding places, and officials known to be sympathetic or bribable. But before I give it to you, you must swear not to show it to the authorities. Most of these people are innocent of any crime, and many of them abominate the practices of the extreme sects—but any of them would suffer cruelly if their sympathies were known."

I put my hand over the fire and swore that I would not betray the information to the authorities, but only use it to defend myself and to collect evidence against the plotters, and I was given the tablets. I thanked the Romanizer with some warmth.

"No, we must thank you," he returned. "You're the one running the greatest risks in this contest. We will pray for your safety."

I was contented when I rescued my horse from the goat shed and rode back along the cabbage-scented alleyway. My allies seemed both efficient and reliable. Eukairios was very silent. When we were riding back through the gates of the fortress, however, he gave one of his sudden dry chuckles, and I gave him a questioning look.

"Nothing," he said, shaking his head. But his eyes were dancing.

"I did something you think is funny?" I asked resignedly.

He chuckled again. "The way you sat there on the floor, my lord, the perfect picture of a noble savage, telling Senicianus that you'd lost count of the number of men you'd killed! He was so shocked I thought he'd fall off his seat. I thought you'd lost them all, I really did. But it worked: they could see that you were being completely honest with them, and they realized that they could trust you."

I snorted. "I was not trying to be amusing. And you must not go about telling people that I am a peacemaker. It is a disgraceful thing to report of the commander of a dragon."

He chuckled again. "Not to Christians. But I will keep my mouth shut in future on that shocking truth."

I looked at him with affection. There he sat, a small dark man in his forties, perched clumsily astride my red bay carriage horse and grinning at me. Riding, the cost of horse fodder and size of stud farms, the Sarmatian language: he had struggled valiantly to master them all. By rights he ought to hate me. He had been given to me very much against his own wishes, snatched away from home and friends and forced to adapt himself to a world nearly as alien to him as it was to me. "What would you do if I freed you?" I asked him.

The grin vanished. We were crossing the bridge from the city to the fortress now, and for a long minute we rode in a silence stirred only by the soft clopping of the hooves of our horses. "Would you do that?" Eukairios asked, in a strained voice.

I stopped my courser. "If you would agree to stay in my service, as a paid secretary, yes. But if you would go back to Bononia, no. I am sorry, but I cannot afford to lose you."

He clenched his hands together on the reins and stared at me in consternation. "I hated Bononia!" he exclaimed. "I found that out within ten days of leaving it. All the stupid petty rules, and the short rations and the beatings if I complained or made a mistake; the way my supervisor loaded me with other people's work and took the credit for mine. I loved my friends there, who supported me and cared for me when times were bad, but I was utterly wretched. But I didn't even realize that until it ended; if you've staggered a long way under a burden, you don't really know how heavy it is until you put it down. I've been very happy working for you. Hadn't you realized that?"

I thought he had not been unhappy, but this astonished me. I shook my head.

"I would be very glad to go on working for you, my lord, very glad, in any circumstances."

"If you want your freedom, then, you may have it," I told him. "You know my people do not keep slaves. You can . . . How does one go about freeing a slave?"

He laughed out loud, a laugh that ended in something very like a sob. " 'She may sing, but we are dumb,' " he said, quoting verses in a voice suddenly harsh with both triumph and extraordinary pain.

> " *'Oh, when will my spring come?*
> *When will I be like the swallow, and renew my tongue?*
> *By silence my song has perished, and Phoebus looks aside.*
> *Thus Amyklai raised no alarm, and by its silence, died.*
> *Whoever's never loved, love tomorrow;*
> *love tomorrow, whoever's loved before.'*

"I can draw up a document for you."

I had a sudden conviction that he had quoted those lines before, in the days when he had talked back to his superiors and been beaten for it. He had watched love passing him by then, and cried out for the spring of freedom that came now, too late. It was as though the solid rock of my own identity shivered, and I reached at the unimaginably foreign state of what I might have been if I had been born a slave.

What Eukairios cried in that moment was for himself, and I had no business intruding into it. "Then do so this afternoon," I ordered. "But now we must hurry or we will be late for our appointment with the legate."

We left the horses in the stable yard, which reassured my men, who were fretful as heifers that have lost their calves. We were not late arriving for the meeting with Priscus, which was just as well, since we were very late leaving. To my relief, the legate made no reference to the events of the night before and began at once to discuss the arrangements for the other dragons instead. We'd talked for a couple of hours and written a few letters when the legate's secretary stuck his head round the door and announced that Siyavak and Victor had come, as ordered. Priscus told the secretary to admit them—in just a minute.

"I want to extend the plan for the horses to their *numerus*," he explained. "But I don't want any talk about the other Sarmatian troops in front of Siyavak. It will be some time before the Fourth Sarmatians live down their previous commander's mutiny, and it would be better if they didn't know how many other Sarmatians there are in Britain or where they're posted. Do you understand me?"

I nodded, though I was taken aback. I had, of course, noticed that I was being trusted with knowledge, but I'd assumed that the information was no longer considered sensitive. It was obviously not as sensitive as it had been, but still too delicate for Siyavak's attention. I was being rewarded for my Romanizing. Priscus gestured to his secretary to let the others in.

Siyavak looked tired and strained. I thought he was pleased to see me, but he would not look at me for long and sat at the opposite end of the room. I wished that I could talk to him: I had no idea whether he was still my ally, after all this time spent with Bodica. We discussed how many horses the fourth dragon could spare as brood mares and afterward some other business that affected both our companies, until the secretary stuck his head around the door again and said that it was time for the dinner party. It seemed we were all expected to be there—except, of course, Eukairios.

"Hercules!" exclaimed the legate. "Is it five o'clock already? Well, we'd better go then. Not polite to keep a lady waiting!" He stamped out the door. Victor hurried after him, trying to discuss some bit of legion business that had been pushed aside before, and Siyavak slipped out behind them. I paused to say good night to Eukairios and arrange to meet him in the morning, and started after the others. When I stepped into the corridor, I found Siyavak waiting.

"I thank the gods!" he whispered hoarsely. "I was beginning to think I'd get no chance to speak to you at all."

"Are you safe?" I asked him.

"For the time being. She thinks I'm drunk with admiration for her, like the rest. Have you thought of a way for us to communicate? I don't dare speak long now: if we come in to this dinner together, she'll notice."

I took a deep breath, prayed to Marha, and gave him the name and password that the Christians had given me that afternoon. "That is a man who can write letters for you," I said, "and send them secretly. He's a kind of ally—but I beg you, make no mention of him to anyone. He's a member of an illegal cult, though a different one from the druids, and he'd die for his faith as much as they would for theirs if his allegiances were known. But do you want to arrange a meeting with me now?"

"I want to, oh gods!—but it's not wise, Prince. She has spies everywhere in this city, and I've seen what she does to people who betray her. I must go *now*, or she'll become suspicious." He pressed my hand and hurried ahead, and I followed, slowly, dreading it.

There were seven of us at the dinner: Siyavak and Victor; Priscus and Bodica; myself and Facilis—and the centurion I'd met the night before, Publius Verinus Secundus, who turned out to be fort prefect for Eburacum. We were seated in the three places in those pairs, with Secundus sharing a couch with me and Facilis, on our host's right. (I took my sword off and hung it on the arm of my couch when I arrived.) Bodica looked more beautiful than ever, dressed in a gown shot with the silk we'd given her husband, her hair arranged very simply with a few gold hair combs. But, to my surprise, she was in an obvious and appalling temper. The reason soon emerged: her hairdresser had gone missing.

"The silly little slut's still gone!" she was telling her husband while the slaves were showing me to my place. "She's been missing since this morning now, and you said it was nothing to worry about! I told the duty officer to keep an eye out for her on the gates—I'm sure the little bitch is hiding somewhere, and means to run away for good. She knows I was angry with her and she's trying to get out of being punished. When I catch her, she'll—"

"Now, now," said the legate soothingly, "you know she had that baby recently. It disturbs the minds of even freeborn ladies, losing a baby, and she's just a feebleminded girl. She's probably just panicked and run off to cry over it."

"But look at my hair!" protested Bodica. "I don't dare let that idiot Vera curl it, she never gets it straight, and now we've got all the officers here and it's twenty years out of fashion!"

"My dear, you look lovely as ever," Priscus said gallantly, taking her hand and escorting her to the couch, "and I'm sure the officers agree with me. Gentlemen don't notice fashion nearly as much as you ladies seem to think we do, and who cares for curls when the hair and face are so charming without them?"

We all agreed, and Bodica, though still seething, settled down to her part as hostess. I remembered how Facilis had been enraged by Bodica's treatment of this slave girl before, and glanced at him. He reclined stolidly on the other end of the couch, looking expressionlessly at nothing in particular. The slaves handed us our cups of wine.

We talked harmlessly about the wine and the food and what we'd done during the Saturnalia through the first courses. I deliberately spilled my first cup, managed to wipe my plate off before eating from it, served myself the appetizers from the opposite ends of the serving dishes, and then ate as little as I decently could. Facilis noticed, of course, but said nothing. Bodica noticed as well, and gave me a sweet smile and a dangerous glare. I assumed that the wine was safe: it was served, as always, from a common mixing bowl, and the slave had no opportunity to slip anything into my cup alone. I was aware, halfway through the main course, that I was probably drinking too much of it. But I was hungry—the meeting with the Christians had caused me to miss my lunch—and very tense, and the slaves kept refilling my cup as fast as I emptied it.

When the main meal was finally over, Priscus swung his legs off the couch, sat up straight, and gave all of us a benevolent smile. "Now," he said, "to what I really wanted to discuss this evening. Ariantes, who is trying to kill you?"

I stared at him, shocked by the suddenness of the bolt after the earlier lulling silence. I wished I'd left the wine alone.

"Don't try to pretend you don't know what I mean," Priscus said, when I'd sat stupidly for so long that it became awkward. "You have an enemy: who is it?"

"My lord legate," I said at last, "I have told you I trust your goodwill. Why should you believe that I know?"

He snorted. "This whole affair reeks of conspiracy so badly they can smell it in Londinium. The commander of the fourth *numerus* was sent a message purportedly from this very fortress, a piece of Sarmatian paraphernalia with British writing which made him mutiny. At just that time the Selgovae and Votadini staged a major raid, and prisoners interrogated afterward revealed that they'd been forewarned of the mutiny—by an unknown person whom they believed to be a senior officer of this legion. You, who stopped the raid, went to look at the treacherous message and reconcile the rest of the men to Roman service, and you very nearly never came back. Your good friend and brother prince, Arsacus, who was with you, says it was a hunting accident; you claim to remember nothing about it. But you had no business going in the water with a bow case if you were after a boar, as Arsacus says, and if you were after wildfowl, why was your bow found unstrung in its case?" I glanced quickly at Facilis, who looked away; Priscus noticed. "Yes, of course I've talked to him about it!" he snapped. "Him and others. A man is then murdered near Corstopitum, and a cursing tablet with your name on it is shoved in his mouth. You come here, and the house in which you're thought to be sleeping is set on fire as soon as you arrive—the house that *was* the house of your friend and brother Arsacus, which he could easily have prepared for you. Come *on*! I've been patient, man, I think highly of you, I think I understand your motives for silence—but I'm not a damned imbecile! You know something, somebody else knows you know, and you'd better spit it out before the somebody's efforts succeed!"

He was not a damned imbecile: he'd pieced more together than I'd realized. I even wondered for a moment if he was right that Arshak had prepared the house for me. He had wanted to set fire to it—but that was impossible: when I'd met him on the road there'd been no suggestion that he was contemplating such a cruel and alien method of murder. It was much more likely that Bodica's friends had done it. If they'd told him they wanted to burn it after he'd left, he would have been pleased and asked no further questions. And I was still afraid to accuse the legate's wife, particularly here in this fortress where she had spies "everywhere"—though a glance showed me she'd gone still and was watching me in terror.

"No Sarmatian would murder by arson," I told Priscus. "My brother Arshak favors the spear, but even if he would dishonor himself with murder, he would not use fire. It is sacrilege to pollute Marha's image with death. That is a Roman custom. And the man killed at Corstopitum was not killed in any manner familiar to my own people."

Priscus was silent a minute, blinking, as he had when I first informed him of the cursing tablet.

"I can't believe you're right to be suspicious of Arshak, Tiberius," Aurelia Bodica put in, rushing the words, her eyes dark. "He's not the conspiring sort; you must have seen that. He revels in killing, yes, but he's not a planner."

Priscus grunted and stood up. "Very well," he said, picking up a lamp from the stand in the corner. "It's pretty clear that there are Britons involved. Very well, maybe Arsacus wasn't guilty of that particular effort; maybe he's not guilty at all, though if he isn't, I don't see why you're keeping your mouth shut, Ariantes. It makes a lot of sense that you'd try to settle Sarmatian quarrels in Sarmatian ways: you're vulnerable to accusations of Romanizing even without informing on a fellow commander. But maybe I'm wrong." He set the lamp down on the table in front of me. "Put your hand over this and swear your people's oath on fire that you believe Arsacus is innocent and you don't know who's trying to kill you or why."

I stared at him, appalled. "Sir," I said at last, "if I have suspicions, I have no evidence. And I have no wish to be accused of slandering eminent Romans without evidence. When I do get evidence, you may be sure I will tell you of it."

He glared at me. "Eminent Romans, is it?" he asked. "Eminent Romans and Arsacus, or eminent Romans alone?"

I put my hand over the flame of the lamp; it made a spot of gold warmth on my palm. "I swear that when I told you I did not remember what happened on the way back from Condercum, I was telling the truth," I said. "I swear that I believe Arshak to be innocent of the arson, and of the murder in Corstopitum." The spot of warmth was becoming uncomfortably hot. I struggled to remember what else I could truthfully swear to, couldn't think of anything, and took my hand away.

"That's a long way short of what I asked you to swear," observed Priscus.

There was one other thing I could swear to. I put my hand over the flame again. "I have not lied to you, my lord, nor broken the oath I swore at Aquincum in any way; on fire I swear that now." I put my hand down and held on to the arm of the couch; my fingers were starting to shake. "If you like," I added, "I will have my scribe write an account of what I believe to be the truth of these matters, and should my enemies' efforts succeed, you may have it."

"That's not good enough! What are you afraid of?" demanded Priscus. "Do you think I'd let you be murdered while the business was investigated?"

"I have told you, sir, I have no evidence and no witnesses to call, and without them, I cannot speak." I climbed to my feet, unsteadily—I felt as though I'd been riding hard all day. "May I go and rest, Lord Legate? I did not sleep well last night, and I am tired."

Priscus swore, glaring at me. Facilis got up and straightened his cloak. "I'll walk him back to his friends, sir, with your permission."

"You won't get anything out of him," growled Priscus. "Ariantes, you are disobeying a direct order from your commander in chief. That is rank insubordination and punishable. Are you going to tell me the truth—or do I have to send you to prison?"

I said nothing. I stood there with the wine ringing in my head, looking at him. I was horribly aware of my sword, hanging from the arm of the couch, its hilt a few inches from my fingers. It would solve nothing. Prison for insubordination or prison for slander, death and disgrace either way. And what would my men do then?

Verinus Secundus, who had sat stony-faced through all of this, stirred and spoke for the first time. "But supposing he's right, sir?" he asked. "The kind of murder there was at Corstopitum—there's a lot of that, even in the legion. I've heard the lads whispering. We can trust his own men not to kill him, but if we put him in prison, who's to guard his guards?"

Priscus grunted. After a moment, he nodded, and gave me a gesture of dismissal. I picked up my sword, slung it over my shoulder, and limped out, followed by Facilis.

When we were in the street outside the commandant's house, and alone in the cloudy moonlight, I stopped and turned on Facilis angrily. "Why did you tell him?" I demanded. "Do you know what would be done to me in a prison? Do you know what my men would do if I were put in one?"

"He's not putting you in one," Facilis replied. "And what was I supposed to say when he asked me? He may be a cuckold, but he's no idiot. He doesn't suspect her yet, but he will, and why should we suppress evidence to slow him down? But I didn't come along with you to talk about this. Ariantes, I need your help."

"My help! Marha!" I turned on my heel and began to stalk off. Now that I'd escaped, I was furious, with the legate, with his wicked murderous wife, with the Romans in general and myself for Romanizing, and particularly with Marcus Flavius Facilis, for making himself my ally and then going some way to betraying me. And I had no idea what would happen next, whether I'd be allowed to leave Eburacum without confessing what I knew, whether I'd live another day.

"Your help!" agreed Facilis, running after me. "Look, that girl . . ."

"What girl?"

"Vilbia. Bodica's little slave. I've got her in my house."

"What!" I stopped again, and Facilis stopped, facing me, panting a little.

"I'd said a few kind words to her on the way from Dubris," he said, "and she turned up at my door last night, the poor little bitch, clutching her baby, and she cried, and she begged me to save the brat and to protect her from her mistress. May the gods destroy me in the worst way if I don't. I've got to get her out of the fortress somehow, and that wagon of yours is the best way I can think of. Nobody's going to look for her in that."

"With a baby?" I asked incredulously. "I thought Priscus said she had lost one."

"She bore a healthy son eight days ago, but her mistress had no use for a baby and tossed it out. The little bastard was the only thing the poor girl had to love in all the world, and she slipped out of her slave's cell, all bloody from childbirth, and crawled through the streets at night, and found the baby on the dung-heap before it froze, and wrapped it up warmly, and hid it. She's been running to it every night, to feed it and care for it, but she's had to leave it in the day to look after that witch's hair. The little bastard didn't thrive on the treatment, of course, particularly in this cold weather; in a few days it was clear he'd die without better care, and the girl couldn't stand it. She ran to me because of a few kind words. May the gods destroy me in the worst way if I give her back!"

"Bodica threw a baby, a healthy, living child, on a dung-heap to die?" I asked in horror.

"Oh gods, Ariantes! They all do that. What else do you do with a slave brat if you don't want it?"

"Marha! Romans!"

"The baby won't make much noise," he said. "It's a feeble little thing now, and even when it cries you can barely hear it—but she doesn't let it cry. You don't need to worry that it would give her away."

"I will take her out in my wagon," I said, and began to walk on. "If I am not allowed out, I will see that she escapes somehow. I have allies who might help."

"You're allowed out. You're allowed out tomorrow. Did you really think he was going to imprison you? Hercules! Don't be an idiot. With a conspiracy boiling away in his half of the province, stirrings across the border, and suspicions attached to all his British senior officers, the last thing he wants is more trouble with your people. And he's seen a lot more of Sarmatians than he had last September: he knows that if he tried to imprison the prince-commander of a dragon, any dragon, he'd have to imprison his bodyguard as well, and half the men at least, and that would mean a major military operation. He can't afford that. Besides, you're the loyal, responsible one: who's going to help him manage the next four thousand Sarmatians if anything happens to you?"

I stopped again and stared at him. "I do not understand you Romans at all," I complained. "Why did he threaten to imprison me if he had no intention of doing so?"

"To let you know that he was seriously annoyed with you, of course. You bastards hate lying so much, you don't understand how we use it. When he asked you to swear that oath, it never even occurred to you to lie, did it?"

"I have never sworn falsely in my life! And with a curse hanging over my head, how could I afford to?"

"That's what I mean. You've Romanized full tilt since you got to Britain, but you've been pretty damned careful *how* you Romanize. So I can put the girl in your wagon?"

"Yes. If I can leave tomorrow, I will do so. You should bring her tonight."

He beamed at me and clasped my hand. "Thank you. I knew I could rely on you. I'll bring her at the second watch, when it's quiet. You're going to have to tell your men to expect us. With things as they are, anybody they find creeping up to their precious commander's wagon in the dead of night is likely to be chopped to pieces. Will they accept it? You don't need to say *who* I'm stealing the girl from."

I nodded, then shook my head in bewilderment and began walking again. Just before we reached the stable yard, I thought to ask, "Who is the father of this baby?"

"How would I know?" asked Facilis. "Some guard or groom or slave who said something nice to her once, and dumped her when she got into trouble. She's not interested in him at all, just the brat."

When we reached the wagons I told my men that Facilis would come back in the middle of the night, bringing a stolen slave girl and her baby, and explained to them that Romans kill unwanted slave children. They were as horrified by this as I was, and stunned to think that Facilis, whom they still disliked, had the courage and piety to defy his own people's laws and save them—particularly when they counted off the months and saw that the baby couldn't possibly be his. For their part, they would have been willing to help even if their commander hadn't been there to require it, and they grinned at Facilis and slapped him on the back, which disconcerted him.

I SLEPT SOUNDLY that night, and woke quickly when the cautious knock sounded on the side of my wagon. I got up, picking up my sword just in case, and found Facilis and Banadaspos standing outside the door, with a shape huddled in a cloak between them. The wagon's awning was stiff with frost, and rang when my hand brushed it. The moon had set, and it was dark and bitterly cold.

"This is Lord Ariantes," Facilis whispered to the faceless girl. "He'll take you out of the city in his wagon tomorrow morning."

"But . . . but," the girl whispered back, soft-voiced and stammering, "but this is the man my lady wishes to kill! She's tried twice to kill him, and cursed him with death!"

Even in the dark, I saw how Banadaspos stiffened, and I groaned. His Latin had become fairly fluent, and he'd had no trouble understanding. "Banadaspos!" I ordered him quickly, speaking in Sarmatian. "You must not repeat to the others what she just said."

"My lord," he shot back, "whose slave was she?"

"If I'd wanted you to know, I'd have told you. I want no trouble between you and the Romans."

I should have known it was useless to try to avoid the confrontation. "You're treating us shamefully!" Banadaspos exclaimed furiously, so loudly that there was an answering stir in the wagons around us, as my men woke up and started listening. "You've quarreled with Arshak, and the Romans have tried to murder you, and you treat us, your bodyguard, as though we had no right to know anything about it! You go slipping off into the city with Eukairios instead, and plot there with strangers. I am your man, and have been since I took my first scalp. How well I have served you, no one knows better than you yourself. I've always been proud of my commander, and prouder to think that I was entrusted with your life. I've never been guilty of any disloyalty. I swear it on fire, none of us have! You've got no right to treat us like this!"

"Banadaspos!" I exclaimed, jumping down from the wagon and catching his shoulder. "Yes, I have a Roman enemy who's tried to murder me. And I know you and all the bodyguard are proud and courageous, and would be ashamed to cower before Roman authority when your prince's life was at stake. That's the reason I've told you nothing. I've been afraid where your pride and your courage might lead you—and your loyalty, which I know and trust absolutely."

"Who is this enemy?" Banadaspos demanded—and then answered himself. "A woman, the girl said. A Roman inside the fortress walls. And a friend of Arshak, whom you've quarreled with. The legate's lady." He glared through the night at my face. "When she came today, I thought she seemed to hate you, but I put it down to her anger at seeing you manage a horse she'd ruined. Twice, the girl said; twice she's tried to kill you. Once by water and once by fire. My lord, you should have told us."

Those responsible for keeping you alive have rights in your life. I could not answer Banadaspos at all, and I stood there helplessly, ashamed, exasperated, and exhausted. At that minute there was a feeble snuffling cry from the shapeless cloak around the girl, and she jumped and clutched something under it.

"Oh, please!" she said, turning to Facilis. "He's hungry, and it's cold.

Please, find me somewhere else to go! I'm afraid to stay here, with a man my lady's cursed with death."

"Your lady's curses haven't hurt Ariantes," Facilis told her soothingly. "He's a good man, and has invoked the protection of his own gods. And I don't know how else to get you out of the city, darling, if you don't go in his wagon. They're watching for you at the gates, and your lady was in a very ugly mood when I saw her this evening." She was silent, cradling the now feebly wailing bundle under her cloak. "That baby will die if you don't get out of the city with him," Facilis told her, his voice so gentle I wouldn't have recognized it.

"Oh! Oh yes." She was tearful now. "I'm sorry, Marcus Flavius, I don't mean to cause trouble. I'm sorry, Lord Ariantes. I do thank you for helping me."

I sighed, offered her my hand to help her into the wagon, and followed her into it. I'd already cleared a place for her on the opposite bunk. "You may sleep there," I told her, taking her hand and letting her feel the bed in the deep darkness inside the wagon. "Do you have what you need for the child?"

"Yes, sir." I could hear her moving in the dark, sitting down, unpinning her tunic to give the baby her breast. The weak snuffling cry stopped abruptly and was replaced by the sound of sucking.

"Stay there quietly, then. It would be better if you do not leave the wagon once it's light, though my men all know you are here and can be trusted. You can lie on the floor of the wagon, under the bunk, and pull a carpet over you if you are afraid of discovery."

"Yes, sir. What if I need to . . . uh, use the latrine?"

"You will have to get out of the wagon for that, and find somewhere in the stable yard. Try not to do it after dawn, and I will try to see that we leave promptly. I will be back in a few minutes: I must speak to my men."

"I'm so sorry. I've upset your friend, haven't I? I shouldn't have said anything; she told me never to say anything about you to anyone. But I've finally got away from her, and I was so surprised when Marcus Flavius said who you were, and I'm so tired. She cursed you . . ." The girl trailed off. "I'm sorry," she finished miserably.

"It is for the best," I told her. "Rest quietly. We will allow no one to harm you or the little one." I climbed down from the wagon.

Banadaspos was still there, and others of the bodyguard were joining him. Kasagos and his squadron were up as well: they were all whispering together, explaining to each other what had happened. "... the legate's lady ..." I caught, "... a witch, a follower of the Lie ... fire ... her slave ... Arshak ... no accident ..." Facilis was slumped wearily against the side of the wagon. I ached to go back to bed, but I could only stand still and wait for what my men had to say to me. At least, I told myself, it's Banadaspos, and not Leimanos. The claim the commander of my guard had on me was just that much greater than his deputy's, and my failure to tell him anything just that much more shocking.

The murmured explanations stopped. "My prince," said Banadaspos, stepping forward and speaking for them all, "who are your enemies?"

I told them what Bodica was and what she wanted. They listened in silence, though I could tell that they were all very angry, and when I'd finished, they remained silent.

"I do not want a battle with the Romans now," I said flatly. "My fellow *azatani,* I relied on you even though I kept secrets from you. You know how I've taken you with me even to exercise my horses. Perhaps you thought I was taking precautions against the Picts: now you know better. I trusted you with my life no less than I ever did before—but I didn't trust you to stay patiently quiet when I was threatened, and that is what is needed. You must show me now that I was wrong to doubt your restraint."

"What can we do?" asked Banadaspos, now anxious as well as angry.

"What you were doing before," I replied. "Keep my enemies' knives out of my back, defend me from the Lie by your prayers and your honesty, and wait. I have hopes now that we'll get evidence against our enemies, evidence that will ruin and disgrace them. I've made alliances and I hope they'll bear fruit. But if we strike now, we're the ones who'll be disgraced, dying at the Romans' hands with the world reproaching us as oath-breakers and slanderers. I know you're angry with me, but I both beg and command you: be patient, and keep this quiet!"

"My prince, you can't blame us for being angry," said Banadaspos. "Without you, we might as well drag our standard in the mud for all the honor we'd get from anyone. If it hadn't been for you, we'd have arrived in Cilurnum disarmed and scarcely better than prisoners, and we'd have stayed there when Gatalas mutinied instead of winning the glory of a victory. We'd have lost our wagons, like the other dragons, and we'd have to eat grain and beans like the Romans. We'd be paid shabbily and grub about in debt, and everyone would treat us with contempt. Even the Asturians would boast in front of us! We've gloried in how much the legate esteems you, sending for you to advise him on the other dragons; we've reveled in the knowledge that even when the other dragons do get the same wages and advantages as us, they owe them to our prince, not their own. And now we learn from a slave that your enemies have nearly murdered you without our even knowing— twice! It disgraces us, my lord, it disgraces us immeasurably. Give us another chance to prove our worth. Please, my prince, though we've failed you, trust us now!"

I was astonished. I looked around the group, and when I could see no hint of disapproval for what Banadaspos had said, I was stunned. I had Romanized full tilt, as Facilis had said, but always with a glance backward, painfully aware how far I'd come, anxious that I was leaving my people behind. I should have realized that my men had, as always, followed me every step of the way. In August, for their commander to be summoned by a Roman legate as his esteemed adviser would have been something to be ashamed of; now, not six months later, it was something they gloried in, something they would boast about in front of the other dragons. And probably even in the other dragons, the boast would be treated as real and not an empty sham. They had all seen clearly where honor lay among the Romans, and like true Sarmatians, they'd run after it. I felt ashamed of myself for my stupidity in underestimating them—and I felt acutely and utterly ridiculous.

"My dear friends and kinsmen," I said, "in all the time you've followed me, you've never failed me once, let alone twice. You are my glory and my pride, and my chief concern all along has been for your honor and safety, compared to which my own life is a small matter. As I said before, I have no doubt whatever of your loyalty, your courage, or your strength, and I've relied on you to preserve my life from the moment I knew it was in danger. All I ask of you now is that you wait with me quietly for evidence that will satisfy the Roman authorities as to my enemy's guilt. I want no violence, and I want no rumors spread. If we move without proof, the contest is lost. This very night I refused to answer the legate himself when he asked me my enemy's name: don't give away what I kept secret. Swear to me now, all of you, that you'll stay quiet about this until I give you leave to speak."

"May I speak to Leimanos?" asked Banadaspos, after a moment's hesitation.

"To him, and to the rest of the bodyguard," I conceded, "but to no one else."

They swore it, all of them, stretching out their hands over the embers of the evening fire. Kasagos and his squadron looked smug, and I could only hope they really would stay quiet when we were back in Cilurnum, and not hint to the rest of the dragon that they shared a secret from which the other squadrons were excluded. But at least there'd be no crisis in Eburacum tonight, and I could go back to bed—though not, I found, to my own bed.

"My lord, you must not share a wagon with your enemy's slave," Banadaspos declared firmly, as soon as he'd sworn the oath. "Even if she was honestly asking for help when she went to Facilis, it might occur to her that if she murdered you, her mistress would forgive her anything. I will sleep in your wagon tonight, and you take my place in mine. It will be safer, anyway, for you to rest where we can guard you."

I thought it quite absurd to suggest that Bodica's poor frightened little slave would put down her baby and knife me, but I owed the bodyguard some respect, and I yielded meekly. When I went over to my wagon with Banadaspos to explain to the girl, Facilis, whom I'd almost forgotten, picked himself up.

"Settled 'em?" he asked me.

I nodded.

He gave a snort of amusement and rapped on the side of the wagon. "Are you still awake, Vilbia?" he asked.

"Yes, Marcus Flavius," came the sleepy reply.

"Ariantes won't be in the wagon tonight. His men want him in another wagon where they can keep an eye on him and be sure he's safe. The one who'll be sharing this wagon with you is called Banadaspos—so you don't even have to be afraid of curses. Is that all right?"

"Oh! Oh yes, thank you."

"Good night, then. I'll see you tomorrow, on the road." Facilis turned to us and added, in an undertone and to Banadaspos, "The poor little bitch has suffered enough. I hope I can trust you not to take advantage of her."

"Do not insult me," Banadaspos whispered back, stiffening.

"Sorry," said Facilis. "Just my slave-owning suspicious Roman nature." He turned to go.

"Marcus Flavius," I said, and he turned back and gave a questioning grunt.

"Perhaps I do not understand how you Romans use lying," I told him, "but I have just understood that, as liars go, you are a consummate one."

"To what do I owe that tribute?" he asked.

"We said nothing in Latin about Banadaspos sleeping in the wagon. And you have assured us all the way from Aquincum that you speak no Sarmatian."

He was silent a moment, then gave a bark of laughter. "The trouble with you, Prince," he said, in the most villainously accented Sarmatian I'd ever heard in my life, "is that you do not allow a poor lying centurion to make a mistake once, even in the small hours of a cold night. Sleep well."

XIV

*W*HEN I WENT into my wagon early next morning to collect my armor, I found the slave girl and her baby still asleep, though Banadaspos was up by then. Vilbia lay on her side, huddled under the blankets, a pitifully thin girl with a white exhausted face. Of the baby I could see only the top of a head with a few curling wisps of black hair, cradled on her arm. The rug had slipped loose from on top of them, and I pulled it up; as I did so, I saw the marks on the girl's bare shoulder. Scar on top of scar, and some of the slashes were new. I remembered that Facilis had said she had given birth only eight days before: she should not have been up at all, let alone beaten for slowness. I straightened the rug and went out, feeling angrier with Bodica than I had since I met her. To try to drown a strong opponent because he might prevent you getting a kingdom where you can practice your religion freely is understandable; to torture a miserable girl who only wants her baby back is unforgivable.

Eukairios arrived a little later to find us harnessing the horses, and was shocked. Although we'd concluded most of the business we'd had in Eburacum, he'd expected us to stay another day at least, to tie up any loose ends and to rest the horses. He'd bought some good parchment and drawn up a manumission document in triplicate, all ready to be signed and witnessed. But he wanted seven witnesses to make things absolutely beyond legal question, preferably mostly Roman citizens, and preferably mostly literate since I was unlettered: it was clear that now he'd have to wait until we were back in Cilurnum. However, he swallowed his disappointment quickly when I explained what had happened at the dinner party, and wrote two letters for me, one to the legate, apologizing for my insubordination and excusing myself, and the other to Siyavak with reassurances and promises of help. I sent one of the bodyguard to the commandant's house with the first letter, and Eukairios to the Christians with the second, and the rest of us set out at once. I was apprehensive when we rode up to the gates, but we were allowed through

without question. When the fortress was safely behind us, I sighed with relief and touched my horse to a canter. Eukairios and the other messenger had
to gallop hard to catch up with us.

Facilis didn't catch up with us until the middle of the morning, when we
stopped for a meal at a roadside farm where we could buy some milk.

"You were in a tearing hurry to get away," he observed, dismounting
beside me. "Were you still worried that the legate wasn't going to let you go?"

I had been worried about precisely that, of course, and he saw it and gave
a bark of laughter. The slave girl Vilbia, who'd been hiding in the wagon,
heard and recognized that laugh at once, and stuck her head out. "Is that you,
Marcus Flavius?" she called.

"It is indeed," he said genially. "And have you seen where we are, girl?"

She hadn't—we'd woken her when we harnessed the horses, but she'd
crawled under the bunk with the rug over her—and she jumped down from
the wagon beaming delightedly. "We've escaped!" she exclaimed. She flung
her arms about Facilis and kissed him on the cheek. "You got me out! They
never even thought of looking for me in that wagon! Oh, Marcus Flavius,
thank you; may the gods bless you!"

Facilis grinned and patted her on the back.

Eukairios was staring in shock: he hadn't known that Vilbia was there.
"Isn't that . . ." he began.

Someone explained to him what she was doing there, and he shook his
head in amazement. After a moment, he started smiling. Someone else
brought Vilbia a bowl of warm milk from the farm for her breakfast, with a
piece of our bread ration from Eburacum, and she went back into the wagon
to be with the baby while she ate.

"You've left the fortress as stirred up as if you'd looted it," Facilis told me,
grabbing a piece of bread for himself and sitting down on the drystone wall
of the field where we'd halted. "I was up to headquarters first thing this morning, and everyone was suspecting everyone else and cursing you. When I left,
Priscus had just got your letter excusing yourself: I think if you hadn't sent
it, he'd have been annoyed enough to have you summoned back."

"I had no wish to offend him," I said.

"So you said in your letter. It made him slightly less offended than he
would have been otherwise. Publius Verinus has been told to investigate the

arson attack on you, though I don't think he'll get anywhere. I've been detailed to find out about the ritual murder in Corstopitum, and I have letters authorizing me to pursue inquiries. I just hope nobody finds out I've stolen my commanding officer's wife's slave. *Me miserum!*" He took a big bite of the bread.

I nodded, taking my own piece of bread and sitting down beside him. "What will you do with her now?"

"One step at a time!" he replied. He frowned. "I don't dare keep her in Cilurnum. It's a small place, I'm known, people may recognize her. Comittus certainly knows her. Corstopitum's probably a better place for her, though still a bit risky. It's bigger, and she should be all right if I can find a safe house for her to stay inside. I'd ask your young woman to take her on that farm, but . . ." He stopped himself.

But he was as unsure of Pervica's own safety as I was.

"I have a friend in Corstopitum," said Eukairios, coming over. "He could find somewhere for her to stay."

"Thank you!" Facilis exclaimed, surprised and pleased. "This is the 'correspondent' who sent you that letter about the mutiny, is it? Does he have a house of his own?"

"No, sir. But he'll know who might be able to arrange things. Would you be prepared to"—he rubbed his fingers together significantly—"if it's necessary?"

"If it gets the poor little bitch a safe refuge, yes."

"My friend won't want any money himself," Eukairios explained, with some embarrassment. "Not when I tell him there's a child's life at stake. But hiding runaway slaves . . . well, you know how it is."

"Hercules, Eukairios!" exclaimed Facilis, greatly amused. "Anyone would think *you* know how it is!"

"Eukairios," I said, "do you have the tablets we were given yesterday?"

He nodded, becoming all at once very tense and unhappy. "Yes, my lord. I . . . looked at them last night. They . . . they contain at least one very unpleasant surprise."

"Fetch them now," I ordered.

He went off. Facilis looked at me suspiciously. "This is the result of the 'plotting with strangers' your men were so worked up about last night?"

"Yes. You have authority, you say, to pursue inquiries. I have information that might help. I cannot give it to you directly, though. I swore on fire that I would not show these tablets to the authorities, as most of the people whose names are written on them are innocent of any wrongdoing but would still suffer if their sympathies were known."

"Whose are the names, then?"

"I have not had time to read them. It is a list of known druids, together with those who have helped them and the places they have hidden."

"Jupiter Optimus Maximus! How on earth . . ." He stared at me in disbelief. "Is it from Siyavak?"

I shook my head. "When I hear from him, I hope to end the contest. This merely begins it."

Banadaspos' eyes lit up.

"Then how in the name of all the gods . . ."

Eukairios came back with the tablets. He stood holding them under one arm, looking at Facilis apprehensively. If Facilis used the list openly, the druids would probably realize where it came from, and then Eukairios and the Christians would suffer in turn.

"Very well," Facilis said, swallowing his astonishment. "I won't ask how you got them. I won't ask to see them. I won't charge anybody just because they're on that list. I'll simply go and visit them privately, with you, if you like, and use my authority to search for evidence. There's no point me swearing it on fire, because I'm no Sarmatian, but I promise you solemnly not to abuse your sources, and may the gods destroy me in the worst way if I do. Does that satisfy you?"

I nodded. I didn't trust him not to break his oath, but I did trust him to honor mine and to avoid cruelty.

"What's the nasty surprise, then?" Facilis growled, turning to Eukairios. "Who's on the list?"

The scribe opened the tablets and looked down them, and set his finger against one entry. When he spoke, it was in a low voice that even the rest of our party, eating their bread and drinking their milk a few feet away, could not hear. "There is the name of a man believed to be from the city of Lindum, who came to Eburacum about a year ago, and has been active among the druids there on occasions since. The name, as reported here, is Comittus son of Tasciovanus. He is described as a young man, and believed to be an army officer."

"Hercules!" whispered Facilis; "Marha!" exclaimed Banadaspos.

"The only thing I'm not sure of is the patronymic," said Eukairios. " 'Javolenus' is, of course, a Roman family name, and would not be used for . . . religious purposes. Lindum as origin is, I believe, correct, and the time matches."

"It makes sense," whispered Facilis. "He's had one foot in the British camp all along, his cousin got him his place, and he admires her. He always swears by the divine Mothers and Maponus and the other old gods of the Britons. It fits horribly well."

"Do the tablets say if he follows the extreme sect?" I asked.

"No," replied Eukairios, closing them. "That detail's been included when it's known—but usually our . . . informants . . . wouldn't know that."

Lucius Javolenus Comittus. *You can call me Comittus, because you're not a Roman either.* I remembered him smiling as he praised Bodica, and weeping over the Picts. I also remembered him lending me his horse, and making room for me on his couch in Dubris, and vouching for me to the legate—and arriving at River End Farm with Leimanos, overjoyed to see me still alive. And I remembered, with sudden uncomfortable vividness, his misery when the news of the cursing tablet reached Cilurnum, and his hesitant attempts, repeated attempts, to talk to me about it—attempts I, in my distress over Pervica, brushed impatiently aside.

"He is not a follower of the extreme sect," I said. "He did not know what Bodica had done until news of it reached the whole camp, and he was distressed when he learned it."

"I think you may be right," said Facilis grimly, "but I think he's got a few explanations to make to us, nonetheless."

"I pray to all the gods that he is innocent," said Banadaspos. He spoke softly and with passionate sincerity. But his hand was on the hilt of his dagger, and it was perfectly clear what would happen to Comittus if he were guilty.

I looked at him levelly and said, "You swore to me that you would stay quiet and do no violence until I gave you leave to strike."

Banadaspos looked back, then let his breath out unhappily through his nose and took his hand off his dagger. He nodded.

"I think that he is innocent," I consoled him.

WE MADE THE journey back as quickly as we could—though this was no great improvement on our time for the journey down, given the short days and the appalling weather. Eukairios and I went over the list of names and passed on to Facilis a few whom the Christians of Eburacum had considered ringleaders. He did not press us for more; he in fact seemed very relaxed, and more cheerful than he had been since I'd known him. He rode beside the wagon and talked to Vilbia, he played with the baby—whose thin cry grew stronger and louder by the day—and in the evenings he chatted with my men, making no further attempt to disguise his knowledge of our language. It emerged that he'd learned it much as I'd learned Latin, from a settled farmer on our side of the Danube whom he'd paid to teach him when he was still a private soldier, hoping to make himself useful enough to his superiors to win promotion. He genuinely was what he had told Valerius Natalis and Julius Priscus, a legionary expert on Sarmatians, and he had been advising his superior officers on us for years.

"Well, what did you expect?" he asked me, when I expressed my surprise at this. "You knew that the emperor had appointed me himself. Your three dragons were the first to be sent west, and two of them were considered particularly likely to be difficult. Naturally the emperor looked for an officer with some experience to put in charge of you. He made a mistake, and I botched the job—but he chose sensibly on credentials."

"Why was Lord Gatalas considered likely to be difficult?" asked Banadaspos, who was with us during this discussion.

Facilis gave him a snort and a bob of the eyebrows. "Gatalas wasn't. *He* never looted the villa of a governor of Asia, or drank from a centurion's skull. Even when I decided to follow you lot to Britain, I was more worried about your own commander than either of the other two. It's why I asked for Cilurnum."

We arrived at Corstopitum around noon on the fourth day of the journey. When we reached the bridge, I arranged that Facilis and Eukairios would go into the city to see if they could arrange a place for Vilbia. Kasagos and his squadron would stay with the wagons and, when somewhere had been found for the girl, take them on to Cilurnum. I and my bodyguard would ride at once to River End Farm. I was very anxious to see Pervica.

I found the farm this time without difficulty. I reined in my horse at the top of the hill and sat looking for a moment. There had been snow during the night, and the fields were white and smooth; the river beyond flashed icily silver in the fitful sunlight. The farm buildings nestled in their hollow, whitened thatch above gray walls, kitchen smoke rising in a thin blue column from the back. It was a scene of such peace that my eyes stung to look at it. I'd been afraid that when I crested that hill I'd see only blackened ruins.

I dismounted, unsaddled Farna—leaving the armor on her—and saddled and mounted Wildfire instead. I thought Pervica might enjoy seeing her horse ridden, and the stallion was now well trained enough to manage about a farm, though I wouldn't have taken him into a city, let alone a battle. I started him down the hill at a slow trot, with my bodyguard jingling after me.

We were about halfway to the farm when I heard a shout of terror to my left, and I glanced over to see a sheepskin-cloaked figure—surely Cluim—running frantically toward the farm. He jumped the wall, hurtled across the yard, and plunged into the house, still shouting. Then Pervica walked out onto the porch—even at a distance I recognized her grace, and the way she held her head. She stood there, directly before the front door, her arms crossed; as I drew nearer, I saw that her face was set in anger and a kind of proud desperation. I slowed Wildfire to a walk, then stopped him altogether at the yard gate, and sat still, looking back at Pervica in confusion.

The anger flickered, then suddenly vanished. Her face opened into a flood of an equally desperate joy. "Ariantes!" she shouted, and ran toward me.

I bent down in the saddle, unlatched the gate, and pushed it open; Pervica ran through, her arms stretched up, and I caught her, pulled her onto the saddle in front of me, and kissed her. Wildfire snorted in alarm and put his ears back, rearing, and I patted him hastily with my free hand. "It is only Pervica," I told him. "You know her."

"Ariantes," she said again, holding me tight.

"Pervica," I answered. "You are well? You are safe?"

"I'm fine," she replied. "You're riding Wildfire!"

"*We* are riding Wildfire," I corrected. The horse knew where he was, of course, and was eager to go back to his nice warm stall in Pervica's barn: he danced impatiently beneath us. I clicked my tongue to him and made him trot about the yard in a circle to keep him steady, then, to show off, made him turn and circle the other way. Pervica laughed. She started to put her head against my shoulder, then pulled away again hastily.

"I can't hug you," she told me, smiling into my face. "You're too scaly!"

There was an anxious shout from the doorway, and I saw Cluim again, standing in the doorway with a boar spear in one hand and my dagger in the other. Pervica waved to him. "It's Ariantes!" she told him, and he slumped in relief and sheathed the dagger.

I suddenly understood, and stopped Wildfire. "Arshak has been here," I said. "You thought I was him."

Her smile vanished. She let go of me and slid to the ground, then stood there with one hand on the saddle, looking up. Her expression was unmistakably one of grief. "You both have the same kind of armor," she admitted quietly.

I dismounted and faced her. "When did he come? Has he threatened you?"

She sighed and swept both hands over her face upward, pushing her hair back. "We can talk about it in a minute, inside," she said. "Do your men want to stop in the back again? I'll tell Elen and Sulina to get them something warm to drink."

I put Wildfire in his stall, and left most of the men to build their fire; Cluim came to join them rather nervously, breaking into a grin when they made him welcome. But I asked Banadaspos to come into the house with me: I felt already that this would be something my bodyguard would have to know about.

Pervica led us into the dining room. The carpet I had given her now adorned the floor; she sat down heavily on the couch. I sat down on the floor next to her, leaning against the couch, sideways to allow space for my sword, with my arm on the cushion beside her.

"When did Arshak come?" I asked again.

"Two days ago," she told me, very calmly.

"Was he alone, or did he bring his men with him? Did he threaten you?"

"I . . . no. He didn't hurt me, and he made no threats. He came with about thirty men—his bodyguard, I suppose. He said he'd heard that I'd saved the life of his brother prince, and that you were going to marry me, and so, he said, he'd come to greet me. I think . . . I think he just wanted to know where I was." Her face had closed up again.

"Then why were you so afraid, you and Cluim?"

"Nothing. Just what you said about him before. And I hadn't realized. You'd said he was arrogant and dangerous, but I just hadn't realized. He's like some beautiful predatory animal, a golden eagle or a wildcat, which kills by nature. The way he smiled frightened me."

And that was plainly true, but her face was still closed. There was something he had said or done that she did not want to tell me. "But what did he say to you?" I asked, putting my hand against her knee. The muscles tightened under my touch with a little shiver.

"Nothing." The bolts were being shot home behind her eyes. "Nothing that bears repeating."

I was silent a minute. "He insulted you?" I asked at last.

She gave a weak smile. "He was not polite."

"What did he say?"

"Never mind. It's my affair, not yours."

"It is my affair," I said. "If he insults you, he insults me. Please, tell me what he said to you."

"It was only *words*! It was a ridiculous thing to do, to ride over from Condercum just to say a few insulting words to a woman he'd never met. People round here will only laugh at him for doing it. People don't take it seriously."

"My people and Arshak's do."

"No! Look, please! I don't want to tell you because I don't want you to fight him! He's not like Cinhil; even I could tell that! In any fight with him, someone would die—and if it wasn't you, you might still be charged with murder afterward. He did this to provoke you: don't you see that?"

"Pervica," I said, "this concerns my honor."

"Oh, that's the ultimate reason, is it? The one to which all other considerations must bow down!"

"Yes. If you do not tell me, I must go to him in Condercum and ask him what he said. His bodyguard will doubtless boast of it."

"Oh, no! No!"

"He expects nothing less."

"So you'll oblige him? Just like that?"

"Yes. We are enemies now; that is beyond retrieval: we have chosen different paths, and he watched while I was drugged and taken off to die shamefully. I would prefer to settle the matter between us like Sarmatian noblemen, and I think he would prefer to do the same, rather than allow his allies to kill me by sorcery or treachery, which is why he is trying to provoke me. I met him on the road to Eburacum and I let him understand then that I would fight him whenever he wished. But whatever happens, one or the other of us will be dead before this is over. You must understand why he came here. I am his enemy, and he wished to triumph over me in you, to dishonor me. In our own country he would have burned your wagons and driven off your flocks. But here he would have to account for his actions to the authorities—so instead he insults you, which is a thing the authorities will take no notice of, but which I cannot ignore. Without honor, I am nothing at all. My men are disgraced in me, and I am powerless to command them."

She looked down at her hands, twisting together in her lap. "Maybe we shouldn't get married, after all," she whispered; then, "I know we shouldn't get married, after all."

I took my hand off her knee. "You cannot mean that. You know that I want you, and I thought you wanted me."

Now her face twisted as well, fighting the tears, but she still would not look at me. "It's not what I want that matters. I thought of this earlier; I didn't want to say it, but I must. I see it now. We shouldn't get married."

"Even if you refused me now," I said, after another moment of silence, "I would still have to fight Arshak."

"Oh, no!" She pressed her hands to her face.

"Tell me exactly what he said, please. I would rather learn it from you than from him."

She sat still with her hands over her face. "When I saw him coming," she said, slowly, "I ran out to meet him. I thought he was you, and by the time I realized my mistake, his men had surrounded me. Nobody threatened me, but they sat there on their horses like so many steel statues and stared at me. He . . . greeted me. He was very polite at first, and said what I told you, that he'd heard you were going to marry me, and he'd come to pay his respects. Then he smiled and said that it was an odd thing for a king's nephew to be paying respects to a common herdswoman. He said that in your own country, you'd married the daughter of a scepter-holder, a lady descended from princes and great warriors, famous for her spirit; while here, he said, you Romanized, and courted a soldier's bastard out of gratitude for the tatters of your life." Banadaspos caught his breath, and she dropped her hands and looked up at him quickly. "Please!" she said to him. "I don't want him to fight Arshak. There's no point. I am a soldier's bastard, and it was gratit—"

"It was not," I said quickly. "I told you that before. It is not."

She looked unhappily into my face. Her hands made a quick, abortive gesture, as though she had been about to reach toward me, and stopped herself.

"And was that all?" I asked.

She took a deep breath. "You want the part his men will repeat, don't you? He said, 'It was different in our own country. Ariantes was famed as a warrior there and men admired him. But he was injured in the war, and it broke his spirit. Now one leg and his courage are crippled, and he contents himself with a thing like you after loving a golden princess.' I told him to get off my land. He didn't go, of course, so I turned and tried to go back to the house. His men wouldn't let me; they closed in all around me. I tried to duck under the horses, but one of them caught my arm, and his friend caught my other arm, and they both held me, facing their master. He picked up his spear, and I thought for a moment he was going to kill me. Then I realized that he wouldn't, he wanted me alive to tell you this. I understood—of course I understood—that he only wanted to humiliate me to provoke you. He rode toward me, smiling that horrible smile, and caught my cloak pin with the tip of his spear, and then he turned aside, and his men let him through the ring and fell in behind him; the men who'd held me threw me down in the mud and followed as well. He'd pulled my cloak off my shoulders, just like that, without scratching me: he shook it off his spear as he rode off, and the horses of his followers trampled it. The pin was broken. That is what happened, and that is everything that happened."

"You ordered him to leave your land, even though you were alone and surrounded by his men?" asked Banadaspos. "And when he threatened you with his spear, you faced him in silence?"

Pervica glanced at him impatiently and nodded. Banadaspos smiled fiercely. He would report it to the rest of the men, I knew, and they would all be pleased that Pervica had the kind of courage they expected of their commander's lady.

I sat in silence for a minute. There were two sides to this. One was what Arshak had meant by the visit. That was perfectly clear, and would be settled between us. The other was what Pervica had thought and felt because of it, and of that I was deeply uncertain.

"Banadaspos," I said—in Latin, as a courtesy to Pervica—"go and explain to the bodyguard what happened; tell them that the dishonor will be revenged."

He stood. He was stiff with excitement and apprehension. "Do we ride for Condercum now?" he asked.

"Gods, no! The horses are tired. His whole dragon is there, and I could not guarantee the security of the rest of you once the duel is over. Besides, do you think the Romans will allow us to fight? We will go back to Cilurnum tonight, send messengers, and make the arrangements."

He nodded, bowed, and jingled out. I turned to Pervica. "Why do you say we should not marry?" I asked her. "Because you think that if we are not going to marry, there is no cause for me to revenge the insult to you? Or for some other reason?"

She bit her lip. "There are other reasons."

"We are of different nations, whose customs and ways of life are very far apart. My life is threatened, and by that, yours is as well. I am the slave of my honor, which must always be the chief consideration, to which all others bow down. Those reasons?"

"No!" She looked intently into my face again. "No, I think I guessed all that before. I won't say I understood it, but I think I could see it was there. No, it's because so much of what Arshak said was true. You were born a prince in Sarmatia—not just one of the provincial nobility, a member of the equestrian order, but one of the really great families, the senatorial aristocracy of your own people, the consulars. I hadn't understood it before. I'd been thinking of you as though you were just the prefect of a wing of cavalry, which was a rank above me but not out of reach. But I realized it when I met Arshak. There's no equality between us, and a marriage without equality is dangerous—particularly to the lesser partner."

"It is a very long ride from here to the Danube, and further to cross it," I answered sharply. "Here I am only a cavalry commander. And anyway, it is not the same among us as among the Romans—we have no 'provincial nobility' and no 'consulars,' only scepter-holders, nobles, and commoners. You own flocks and have dependants, so by our own reckoning you are noble. For a scepter-holder to marry a member of the lesser nobility is no disgrace to anyone. Arshak said what he did to insult you, nothing more. And here near Corstopitum, some people must take another view of the whole matter. Here they must think, 'Pervica is a landowner, a beautiful young widow with a prosperous farm and a position in the region. She can choose to marry anyone she pleases. What does she want with an illiterate barbarian who's happier in a barn than in a house, and expects her to sleep in a wagon?' "

She flushed. People—probably Quintilius—had obviously not just thought it, they'd said it, and to her. "There is another reason!" she said, breathlessly, and I saw that the other had made her uncomfortable but that this was the real heart of it. "I don't want you to remember your first wife, and then look at me and feel ashamed."

"I would not."

She shook her head. "I know you loved her. I knew that even before I knew your name or who you were. And I'm sure she was all that Arshak said she was. I thought I wouldn't mind coming second to her, but I see now that it's a mistake, *you* would mind, and I could not bear that. I will not be a rag tied to your tail, a disgrace—not even for you. The gap's too big. In time you'd grow to hate me."

"No."

"I think you would."

"Pervica." I reached up and caught both her hands, forcing her to look at me. "I would not."

Her eyes were full of tears, but her mouth was set in determination. The hands in mine did not twist, but they did not hold.

"I would not," I told her again. "Listen, I have lived in two worlds, the one across the Danube and the one here; I was once a prince of the Iazyges, and I am now the commander of a unit of cavalry for the Romans. But there is a part of me that is neither of those things. I know, because I have balanced on it, shifting from one to the other. It has neither rank nor wealth nor title nor honors. All those things are gifts of either world, and have changed; it has not, and so it could choose a path in a land where all was unknown. That is the part of me that loves you. And because it owes nothing to either world, it cannot compare one with the other, or cheapen your great worth falsely beside the value of Tirgatao—whom, it is true, I loved dearly. Love is not like water in a bucket, which is full or poured out; it is like a river, which will flow where it can find a channel, and if it is blocked in one place, strives to find another pathway for itself, a new person to love. I will have no less love for you because I loved her first. I would not hate you, Pervica. I could not."

Her mouth crumpled, and the hands clenched suddenly on mine. Then she flung her arms around me, dropping onto her knees beside me, and cried against my shoulder, scales and all.

She stopped crying soon and let me kiss her and hold her for a little while—and then she wiped her eyes, and sniffed, and sat back on her heels. "I'm sorry," she said.

"So, we will be married, after all," I replied, wanting it to be perfectly clear and agreed.

"Yes," she sniffed, smiling ruefully.

"Good." I smiled back.

"Yes," she repeated, then added, "if you are still alive on the wedding day."

I wanted to encourage her, so I told her most of what had happened in Eburacum, leaving out only a few details about the Christians. As I spoke I felt my own hopes rising. The balance was shifting. Before, my enemies had struck at me from under a cloak of secrecy, like the invisible warriors of the tales, and I had been helpless to strike back. But now I had a list of names and an ally with authority to investigate them—and I had great hopes of getting more from Siyavak. Stripped of their invisibility, it was they who would be helpless.

"Opposition to the conspiracy has been growing here, too," Pervica told me eagerly. "I spoke to Matugenus, the druid I told you about. He was afraid to do anything at first—he thought that all the supporters of the old religion would damn him as a Romanizer and a heretic—but in the end he decided that trying to use the gods to commit murder was blasphemous, and that he would oppose it even if he died for it. He erased your name from the tablet and we left it on the altar of the Mothers. Ever since then, people from all around have been finding excuses to call. It's partly curiosity, but also partly to show their sympathy for me. They even have some sympathy for you. Nobody liked that carpenter who was killed, but people have been outraged that he was murdered to put a curse on the man who saved us from the Picts. Matugenus has called for a convocation of druids such as there hasn't been in the North for years, and he's beginning to think that he can count on substantial support. Apparently many of the more moderate druids have been unhappy with the position of the extreme sect for some time, but they'd all been too unsure of themselves to say so until now. At times I've thought I could feel our strength spreading out through the countryside like fire spreading in tinder." She smiled shakily, and added, "It helps that you're still alive. Cunedda had cursed you; Matugenus revoked the curse. The gods obviously listened to Matugenus, not Cunedda. Ariantes, how good a fighter is Arshak?"

I shrugged. "Very good. Particularly with the spear. You have seen that. I would say that my horse is better trained, though: he has not the patience to put an animal through a maneuver again and again. It will be an equal contest, and the outcome is in the hands of God. Marha has favored me up till now. I will try to arrange the meeting with him for ten or twelve days from now, which I hope will give me time to resolve some of the other aspects of this. But you must not stay here if there is such a long delay. He is an impatient man, and will be ashamed that he restrained himself out of fear of the authorities: he might very well come back here, determined to injure you this time. You should stay in Cilurnum, you and Elen and Cluim and his sister. I could rent you a house."

"What about my sheep? And the farm?"

"Is there so much that needs doing at this time of year that a neighbor could not do it for you? You said you had two other tenant families living elsewhere on the estate in their own houses. Could they not see to the sheep for ten days or so?"

She leaned wearily against me. "Very well, then. Yes, I'll come."

It took her a little while to arrange for others to tend the sheep and cattle, and for her and the three servants to collect their things and pack them in the farm cart. It was dusk when we set out for Cilurnum. Pervica stopped the cart on top of the hill and looked back at the farm, dark now in its hollow under the scudding clouds. I knew she was wondering if she would ever see it again. But she said nothing, and looked back at me with a rueful smile before shaking the reins and starting on.

XV

I DREAMED I was riding across a wide meadow in the sunshine, riding a strange horse, a beautiful white stallion that stepped as lightly as snow falling. It was early summer and the grass was purple with vetch, red with poppies, and scented with meadowsweet. I rode over a hill and saw my own wagons below me beside a stream, and my own horses grazing beyond them. Tirgatao was sitting beside the campfire, with Artanisca beside her and a baby on her lap. I gave a shout of joy and galloped down to them. She stood as I approached, but when I dismounted, she waved me back with her hand, laughing. Artanisca jumped up and down, shouting, "Daddy! Daddy!"—but he did not clutch my leg.

"Look!" said Tirgatao, and she held up the baby. It was fair-haired and blue-eyed, and smiled into my face. I smiled back, reaching out my finger for it to grab—and then I remembered that it had died before it was born, and I drew back.

"It's all right," said Tirgatao, understanding. "I wanted you to see her."

"You were burned," I said, in a whisper. "My dearest light, they burned you."

"That doesn't matter anymore," she replied, smiling at me as though I'd made a joke.

"I was going to marry again, if I lived," I told her, awkward and ashamed.

At that she laughed out loud. "I know. Oh, my darling, don't look at me like that! The dead don't marry, and it would be a waste for you to stay alone, when you can love so well and there are so many living who can only hate. I met Marha in the fire, and I asked him for your life. Tell Pervica that now I give it to her."

I looked at her in astonishment, and she laughed again. "I love your face when you're surprised," she said tenderly. "All that serious princely dignity looking silly: you were made to be teased. Tell Pervica she must tease you. Yes, my golden hero, I met Marha, I myself, and he didn't harm me. Eukairios was right: it's what we are alive that counts, not what happens to us when we're dead. Fire can only purify the good, not destroy them."

"How do you know Eukairios?" I asked.

"I don't," she replied, still smiling. "You do. Look, your mount wants attention."

I looked, and saw that the white stallion had become a dragon, golden, fire-eyed, bright-winged; it spread its wings and roared, its long tail cracking like a whip. It was still harnessed with my own saddle and bridle. I accepted it unquestioningly, as one does in dreams, and caught the bridle. The dragon tugged impatiently at the reins, just as a horse does when it wants to go home. I turned back to Tirgatao—but she was gone, and the children and the wagons with her; the stream bank was empty. I cried out and vaulted onto the dragon's back. Its wings cracked as it galloped into the air. The meadow swung away beneath me, empty, all empty, and everything had gone still and pale, and the only sound was the muffled rush of the wind in my ears. Then we were flying higher still, and around us the stars were singing while the wind stung my face. I was cold. From a great height I looked down, and I saw for a moment clearly, as though it were a still spot in a rushing stream, a clearing in a wood, a charcoal burner's hut with an ash heap beside it, and a gilded, red-crested helmet on a stake thrust into the ground. Then my eyes burned with the cold and I closed them.

I groaned and woke up. I was lying on my bunk in my own wagon, still cold; I'd thrown off the blankets in my sleep. I sat up and rubbed my hands through my hair, drugged with the dream, trying to make sense of it. After a moment, I went to the door.

The morning fires were burning under a bright winter sun, and it was late to be just rising. Facilis, Eukairios, and Flavinus Longus were sitting in front of the wagon under the awning, together with Banadaspos and Leimanos; they were all drinking something and talking to each other. I looked at them for a moment, and suddenly everything seemed to fall into place, and I was happy. Tirgatao, dead, suffered no more; I stood living in the sunlight, watching my friends eat breakfast peacefully together. One moment, ordered, ordinary, and without hatred: my life was worthwhile.

I sat down to put my boots on, the wagon creaked, and they all looked round and greeted me. In another minute I had my coat over my shoulders, a cup of milk in my hands, and was sitting beside them. It was a relief not to have to put the armor on, for a change.

"My sister tells me you've installed the lady Pervica with her again—with three servants this time," Longus remarked. "She said to tell you that she likes having Pervica, but that the posting inn is actually down the road, next to the fort. She thought maybe you didn't know that."

"Thank your sister for me again," I replied. "It was late when we arrived last night, and there was no time to arrange other accommodation. I will try to rent a house today."

"Oh, don't! Flavina would be most offended if you did," said Longus. "The posting inn was a joke; she does like Pervica. So do we all. I'm glad you persuaded her to come to the fort: I didn't like to think of her out there alone, after that tablet they found at Corstopitum."

Facilis grunted agreement. I almost asked him what kind of accommodation he'd found for Vilbia—the girl was not in my wagon, and Kasagos had told me that she'd been found a refuge somewhere—but I remembered that Longus knew nothing about her and probably shouldn't be told. So I simply nodded instead. For my part I had no intention of telling the Romans about Arshak, knowing they would certainly try to prevent the duel if I did. Even Eukairios would, I thought, struggle with his conscience and then tell Facilis: he understood a little what honor meant to me, but he would not believe an insult worth dying for. I'd warned Banadaspos and the rest not to discuss the matter in front of any Roman and made Pervica promise to keep quiet about it as well.

"I've been telling Gaius what happened in Eburacum," Facilis growled, shattering the peace of the morning.

Longus snorted. "Gods and goddesses! I should have realized, Ariantes—but you should have said something. Why won't you tell the legate who's trying to kill you, if you know?"

I glanced at Facilis quickly; he shook his head: no, he had not told Longus more than I had told Priscus.

"Without evidence, it would only cause trouble," I answered, making a quick decision. "But I can tell you a little more than I told him. Banadaspos, Leimanos—"

They both looked up, then stood, looking suspicious. "You don't mean to send us off?" asked Banadaspos.

"My dear brothers, there are some things I must say which concern the honor of a colleague. I believe he's innocent of wrongdoing, but he will have to be questioned. I would not subject you to such questioning before your men, and you should not witness this, though the Romans must."

I could see that Banadaspos had told Leimanos about Comittus: they both understood instantly who I meant. They looked still more suspicious. Longus watched blankly, not understanding the conversation, which was held in Sarmatian.

"It does not concern my safety—unless he's guilty," I told my men. "And I will tell you the outcome."

They sighed, bowed, and walked resignedly off. It would console them, I thought, when I sent one of them with a message to Arshak to arrange the meeting and it was the Romans' turn to be excluded from a secret.

"Shall I go as well?" asked Eukairios. He did understand Sarmatian, enough to follow most of what had been said.

I nodded. "But fetch that document you drew up in Eburacum, and bring it to headquarters later. We should have some witnesses for it there."

That cheered him up: he walked off almost jauntily. I turned back to Longus and told him what I knew of the druids and the plot to establish a Brigantian kingdom by the help of the Picts and my own people. He was horrified and profoundly shaken. But when I finished by telling him of the list, and the fact that it contained Comittus' name, I was amazed to find that it didn't surprise him in the least.

"Oh, Lucius isn't one of your extreme sect! He's very much of the main school of druidism, and pretty junior in that," he exclaimed, as though this were the most ordinary thing in the world to say. "And he's been in an absolute stew over the whole business ever since that tablet was found. He told me all about it after the Saturnalia—though he was a bit surprised to find out I knew it already."

"You knew he was a druid?" asked Facilis in bewilderment.

Longus shrugged. "People *are*, you know. Some of my squadron always slip off from the Saturnalian celebrations at night to go to the temple of

Mithras over at Brocolitia, which is legal—and some slip off to celebrate the midwinter solstice at the sacred grove down by Blackwater Stream, which isn't. I don't ask for details about either, but I know about it. When I saw Lucius riding back into camp with a few others in the middle of the morning of the solstice, with the edge of a white robe sticking out from the corner of his saddlebags and a sprig of mistletoe in his cloak pin, it didn't take much guessing. There's a lot of druidism about—it is the old religion, after all, and people who're allowed to worship the gods unhindered don't see any point to banning the priests. Nor do I, for that matter. In my view, they ought to legalize it and set up a proper druidical priesthood like they have in Gaul. Then all this murder-in-the-dark business would shrivel away."

"Why didn't you say anything before?" Facilis shouted, going red in the face.

"I didn't know it was significant!" Longus snapped back. "Not until that tablet was found, and you and Ariantes nipped off to Eburacum pretty shortly after that. I tried to talk to Ariantes about it, but all I got was the I-didn't-hear-you look and a change of subject. Lucius tried as well and got the same treatment."

"I am sorry," I said. "I was concerned for Pervica." I was suddenly amused. Pervica had been right: foreigners like Facilis and myself obviously understood nothing about druidism. Even Eukairios, a Gaul, hadn't understood its commonplace nature in its own country. He'd seen only its dark, secret and illegal side.

Longus snorted. "Well, as I said, I'm pleased you persuaded her to come back to Cilurnum. The murder-in-the-dark business isn't something it's safe to be the wrong side of. I suppose you told me this, and sent the others off, because you wanted me to be a witness when you talk to poor Lucius."

I nodded, finished my cup of milk, set it down, and got to my feet. "I thought we might discuss it with him now."

"I think I should do the talking," growled Facilis. "I was appointed to investigate, after all."

"Poor Lucius," Longus repeated, now very unhappy. "Gods!"

Comittus was in the dining room of his house, reading. I noticed again at the door how pleasant the room was—its mosaic paving of birds and animals, the good glass windows that made it light but not cold, its decorated plaster walls. The floor was deliciously warm underfoot, heated by the hypocaust without smoke. For the first time I wondered if I might live in such a house—one day in the future, still distant but no longer out of sight.

Comittus noticed us standing silently in the door, and stopped reading in midsentence. He smiled widely and jumped up, rolling up his book.

"Welcome back!" he exclaimed, putting the book down, and he came over to shake hands.

Facilis ignored the outstretched hand, and Comittus took a step back, the smile fading from his face. He looked at Longus in alarm: Longus shook his head sadly.

"I have some questions to ask you, Lucius Javolenus," said Facilis. "I think we'd better sit down."

When Facilis charged him with being a druid, Comittus admitted it, and wept. He turned to me and sobbed, "I'm sorry, Ariantes!" But it soon emerged that he had not actually done anything he needed to be sorry for. He was a druid because he wanted to worship his people's gods in the way they had always been worshipped, and he was, as Longus had said, still very junior, studying the sacred teachings of his religion at a very basic level and assisting another priest. He'd known nothing about the killing in the grove near Corstopitum until the news had reached the whole fort after the Saturnalia— and then, again as Longus had said, he'd got into "a stew" about the whole business. The killing, and the fact that it had been done to injure me, his colleague and a man he knew had never committed any sin against druidism, had shaken his faith in everything he'd been taught. And he had instantly associated it with the Pictish invasion and seen that his friends were guilty of rebellion against Rome. Roman and British, a legionary tribune and a student of druidism, a nobleman of the Coritani and a member of the equestrian order—all his life he had stood with one foot on each side of a gaping crevice. Now it had torn apart beneath him and left him plunged in confusion, racked by contradictory loyalties. He almost welcomed Facilis' accusations, though he assumed that he was about to be arrested and carted off to disgrace, ruin, and possible death. Facilis bullied him cruelly, trying to find out more about how many druids there were in the region, how they were organized, and who was behind the murder. But Comittus knew little more than the Christians in Eburacum had, and was reluctant—honorably, in my opinion—to name any names. He did not mention Aurelia Bodica. He admitted that "some friends" had asked him about me, and that he'd answered them freely, but only until the raid. Then he'd become suspicious. After the curse, he'd refused to see those friends at all, though one of them had sent him a message asking for a meeting. He said passionately that druids weren't *all* like that, that some druids were opposing the extreme sect, that there was going to be a convocation to consider whether the human sacrifice had been blasphemous . . .

"Consider?" demanded Facilis. "Your gods are the sort, then, who leave such matters open to question?"

Comittus shook his head, lower lip trembling like a child's. "We've been persecuted for a long time, Marcus," he protested wretchedly. "When people have hurt you, it's natural to hate them. I haven't suffered myself, so I can't condemn . . . that is, I don't say it's right, but . . . but can't you understand?"

I was sure Facilis understood perfectly, but he showed no sign of it. He cursed Comittus for a traitor and a hypocrite. Then he whipped out the writing leaf with the list of suspected ringleaders. The evidence of how much we knew shook Comittus so badly I thought for a moment he would faint, but still he did not want to speak, though he eventually confirmed two of the names in a voice thick with distress. One name was Cunedda's.

Facilis pounced. "The archdruid," he said contemptuously. "The Brigantian poisoner who dreams of dragons fighting, the man the person at the head of all this chose as chief adviser. Yes, of course we know who the leader of this conspiracy is! We know where that person is; where is this Cunedda?"

Comittus began to cry again.

"You know," said Facilis mercilessly. "He's one of the friends who asked you questions about Ariantes, isn't he? And he's the one who sent you a message after the curse, trying to arrange a meeting, isn't he?"

Comittus nodded.

"You know what he wanted then, don't you? His curse wasn't working, so he wanted you to help him murder the prince. Just think of that! If you'd gone along with that, you could have painted this fort with blood. Gods and goddesses! He's a murderer, Lucius, and by your own reckoning he's a blasphemer as well. Why are you protecting him? You say you think he's wrong. Who's going to believe that when you try so hard to shield him? You're in trouble anyway: why should you make your own sufferings worse to protect him? Come on! If he proposed a meeting, he must have told you where you could reach him. Where was it?"

Choking, almost unintelligible with grief, Comittus named a place, then covered his face and doubled over sobbing.

It was enough, and I finally put a stop to his misery. "Comittus," I said, "the authorities do not know your name and we will not betray it to them."

Comittus uncovered his face and stared, first at me, then at Facilis.

Facilis gave me a look of intense annoyance, then sighed and nodded. "I've been given the responsibility for investigating that sacrificial murder," he said, "and the only people I want punished for it are the guilty ones. You and these convocation-calling friends of yours weren't there and I'm not going to bother you."

At this Comittus wept again and thanked us, clutching all our hands. We left him in his house to calm down and went across to headquarters to discuss what to do next.

Eukairios was waiting in the commander's office, his three sheets of parchment sitting on the desk, rolled neatly and tied with a cord. "The mysterious document!" observed Longus, but the usual facetious words were spoken in a voice uncharacteristically tired and unhappy. "I hope it's not another nasty surprise, Ariantes."

I shook my head. "It's Eukairios' manumission. How many witnesses do we have here at headquarters?"

Facilis gave a bark of laughter. "I should have guessed it. Eukairios could have invested in a red hat months ago."

"A red hat?" I asked, puzzled.

"A freedman's hat," explained Longus. "He puts it on and everyone knows to congratulate him. A red hat with a peak. Like yours, but a little floppier and without the earflaps."

"Like mine?" I demanded, horrified: had I been wearing a hat that marked me as a freed slave?

Longus and Facilis both began laughing. "Oh gods, Ariantes, didn't you know?" said Longus, forgetting his unhappiness. "No, I suppose not! Nobody dared say anything."

I took my hat off. They both laughed again.

"Ariantes, nobody in their right mind ever mistook you for a freedman," Longus told me. "Nobody. The thought of you as a slave—it's like that play where the god Apollo gets made the slave of some Thracian as a penance, and his master runs around fetching things for him. And that hat isn't really the right shape—it's just that it's red."

I shook my head. I would have to buy a hat of some other color. "Do you need a red hat?" I asked Eukairios.

He began laughing as well, but stopped himself. "Yes, my lord. I hadn't bought one, in case it brought me bad luck."

I handed him mine. "Let us sign the document, and then you can put it on."

He unrolled the document and read it out, and I signed it, in triplicate ("You make your mark *there*, my lord, and I write 'Unlettered' *here*"), and after me Facilis, Longus, four Asturians who were working in the headquarters as clerical staff, and Leimanos, who'd come down to see if I'd finished with Comittus. Then Eukairios put on the hat, looking pink as a girl who's just been kissed, and everyone shook his hand and congratulated him. When it was my turn to shake his hand, he clutched my hand in both of his—then dropped it, flung his arms around me, and hugged me like a long-lost brother. "Thank you," he shouted, "Patron!" He was shaking with joy.

I had no heart then to discuss druids with Facilis, or mislead Longus about what I knew. I told Eukairios to go buy himself a drink, then told the others that I was going to visit Pervica. I wanted to tell her my dream. Leimanos left headquarters with me.

When we had collected our horses and were riding down the Via Decumana to the south gate, I remembered the other piece of important business I had to conduct that day. "Leimanos," I said, "has Banadaspos told you everything that happened in Eburacum, *and* at River End Farm?"

He stiffened, and his horse laid back its ears. "Yes, my lord," he answered quietly. "I'm sorry we didn't defend you better."

"I have no complaint against you in anything. I spoke because I want to send a messenger to Condercum."

He looked into my face and smiled, but I could see his knuckles whitening on the reins. An insult to his commander, even given through the commander's betrothed, was an insult to him. He'd had enough of Romanizing and restraint, of secrets and conspiracies: he wanted battle, and his honor avenged. But he knew that Arshak was a dangerous opponent, and he was afraid for me. "My prince," he said, very softly and humbly, "may I ask you to send me?"

He was taking a position of danger himself, offering to ride into Condercum and speak defiance to Arshak. Arshak's men might resent what he said even if their commander didn't. But it was also the position of honor, and I'd known that he would ask for it. I reached out and touched his hand. "Who else would I send, kinsman?" I asked him, and he smiled again.

I settled to the details. "Take the first ten of the bodyguard with you, and make sure you get guarantees of safe conduct before you enter the fort. I don't think Arshak would injure you, but I don't know now, he's not what he was before. Don't tell the Romans anything. None of the Roman officers in Condercum even realize we've quarreled, and it's better to keep it that way: speak in front of them as though you were bringing Arshak a friendly invitation to go hunting."

He nodded. "And to Arshak I should say?"

"Say to him, 'Son of Sauromates, when I met you on the road, I told you I would meet you whenever you wished. You had no cause to ride to Corstopitum to hurl a few cheap and ridiculous words at a noble lady you had never met, as though I would be timid unless I were provoked. Stop behaving like a herdsman, leave off your attempts to murder me through the hands of your lying and treacherous allies, and come meet me like a prince.' "

Leimanos' eyes glowed, and he tapped out the signal for the charge on his saddle. "That's the way to speak, my lord!" He repeated the message twice to make sure he had it, elaborating it slightly each time, and grinned.

"Though when we come to the arrangements," I confessed, "he cannot possibly meet me like a prince. The Romans would arrest us both if they knew we meant to fight. Make it clear to him that it's going to take ten days or so to set things up, and that if we're indiscreet, we'll lose our chance. I'm not in too great a hurry. I expect to be able to move against his allies soon, and it will be much the best if I fight him with their ruin hanging over him, whatever the outcome of our meeting. Then even his triumph would be clouded and short-lived."

Leimanos grinned even wider. "It's good to see you like this, my lord. Almost like the old days. You remember the message you sent Rhusciporis when we got back from Segedunum?"

I had flaunted a successful raid to a rival at home. But this was something more serious, though I used the same kind of bold language. I nodded and made no comment. "Look out for a good place to meet on your way to and from Condercum. We need somewhere off the road, somewhere we won't be seen by casual passersby, but it will have to have enough space for the horses. Suggest to Arshak that we each bring our bodyguard to the meeting, but leave the rest of our men behind—too many onlookers and the Romans will come searching for us. All the squadron leaders should be informed beforehand, though, and be made to swear that the contest will end with the death of one or both contenders. There must be no attempts at revenge and nothing that will cause trouble with the Romans."

Leimanos nodded, but he was frowning now. We had come out the south gate by then, and had reached Flavina's house; I reined in by the front door.

"What will the Romans do afterward?" he asked, in a low voice.

I shrugged and spread my hands. "I don't know. If Arshak has been exposed as a traitor already, they may not punish me. They will probably arrest me, though. And Leimanos, I will want you, and the bodyguard, and all who follow me, to bear that quietly. I'll require oaths from you on that, too."

He was silent.

"Even Gatalas required that from his men," I said.

"But not from his bodyguard."

"He meant to die in battle against the Romans. I don't."

He sighed. "I can swear to bear it quietly if they arrest you for killing Arshak, my lord. I cannot swear to stand by and do nothing if they decide to execute you for it."

"Leimanos, you are my heir. You know what I want."

He shook his head, and suddenly pressed both hands to his ears, covering them to show that he would not listen. "You want the honor and safety of the dragon. But I'm not you, my lord. You were a scepter-holder, and you had no son or brother to inherit the scepter. If you'd petitioned the king, he would have granted you the right to stay in our own country, granted it freely, and I would have been left to take the dragon to Aquincum in your place. You chose to give the scepter to your sister's son, instead, and come yourself, because you were our prince and we relied on you. We all know that, and we've been glad of it a hundred times over. I will not swear to stand by and watch the Romans execute you."

I was silent a minute. I had underestimated them all again. No one had ever said to me, "You could have stayed at home," and I'd thought that that realization had been mine alone. But my motives for coming had not been as pure as Leimanos seemed to think. I reached over and pulled one of his hands away from his ear. "That you relied on me was only one of the reasons," I told him quietly. "I had others."

He nodded. "And I know those, too, my lord—no wagon to ride home to, and imagined guilt because our raids helped to start the war. But the fact remains that you might be a prince and scepter-holder still, wealthy and powerful and able to choose a wife from among a kingdom of widows— and instead, you're here. If you die in combat, I must accept that as the will of God. But I will not accept it otherwise. I swear it on fire."

I let go and sat staring at him for a moment; he stared angrily back. I sighed and ran my hand through my hair. "Well," I said. "Well, chances are that either I will die in combat, or that the Romans will agree that Arshak was guilty of treason and do nothing to punish me. So long as you don't start shooting if they arrest me, I'll have to be content. And I've had a good omen, Leimanos. I met Tirgatao in a dream last night, and she said that she met Marha when she was in the fire, and that she begged my life from him. She said she gave it now to Pervica. I believe it was a true dream and that I will live to marry again."

His eyes opened, very wide and blue. Then he raised his right hand toward the sun. "I pray it was true, my lord! She'd come whole out of the fire, then, by Marha's kindness?"

"I met her in a meadow full of flowers, and the children were with her. The baby as well. And there was another thing in it that will please you: she gave me a dragon to carry me back to this earth, and it was our dragon, our standard."

Leimanos grinned. "I accept the omen!" he cried, raising his hand again.

"It pleased me too," I said. "I'm going to tell it to Pervica. If I had a kingdom of widows to choose from, Leimanos, I don't think I could choose better than I've chosen here."

"She is a brave and noble lady," he agreed, much happier now. "Give her my regards. I must go now and collect the men. We'll have to set out soon if I'm to reach Condercum today. I can tell Banadaspos what you've said?"

"Yes. Go with good fortune then, kinsman."

He grinned, made his horse dance as he turned it, and galloped back up the road.

When I had tethered my horse by the house, I found that Pervica and Flavina both had been watching us through the shutters.

"Wasn't that your captain Leimanos you were talking to?" asked Flavina, ushering me into the house. "Where's he off to in such a hurry?"

"I had an errand for him," I replied. "He sends his regards." I had no intention of discussing Arshak in front of her, either: she'd be sure to tell her brother.

Pervica remained in the doorway a minute, looking anxiously northward after Leimanos. "You were talking very seriously."

"Yes," I said. "I had a dream last night which I have taken as an omen. It was of great concern to you, so I have come to tell it to you." At this she looked so worried that I smiled and added, "It was a good dream."

Like me, and like Leimanos, she liked the dream and was cheered by it. Flavina, who remained with us the whole time I was there, to guard Pervica's reputation, was also impressed by it, particularly Tirgatao's instructions to Pervica to tease me. "But that's exactly the sort of thing someone might really say!" she exclaimed. "Did she tease you?"

"Yes," I replied. "Always. We first met when she beat me in a horse race, and she always said that I married her to get the horse." I realized as I spoke that it was the first time since she died that I'd been able to think of Tirgatao without being tormented by the image of her burning, to remember her as she was, laughing and alive.

Flavina giggled. Pervica put her hand over her mouth. "What happened to the horse? Did you bring it with you?"

It was an unfortunate question. "Ask the Second Pannonian Cavalry," I replied bitterly.

"The Sec . . . What do they have to do with it?"

"It was Tirgatao's favorite horse, and she had it at our own wagon when she was killed. The Second Pannonians drove it off with the rest of the cattle."

"Oh!" said Pervica, going white. "Oh, I'm sorry. I didn't . . . I didn't even know . . . I thought she'd died naturally. You hadn't said."

I hadn't said, to her, and stared a moment in amazement, realizing suddenly how little we knew of each other. I would have to tell her one day how Tirgatao had died. But there was enough death about without darkening the day with that now.

It was Flavina who broke the uncomfortable silence. "It's hard to remember that you used to be . . ." she began, then stopped herself. "I was going to say, 'on the other side of the Wall.' But it was the other side of the Danube, wasn't it? Gaius says your men are always boasting of what they did on raids. It just seems very odd to think of you doing that."

"It seemed the natural thing at the time," I replied.

"Why?" asked Pervica. She, too, must have realized how little we knew of each other, because she leaned forward a little on the couch, watching me intently. "I can't imagine raiding seeming natural to you."

"Things are different on the other side of that river," I told her. "My reasons for raiding seemed good to me at the time. I needed goods, and there they were across the Danube. Everyone always praised the daring and skill of any commander bold enough to go and take them, and I needed a reputation in war even more than I needed goods."

"Why did you need goods and a military reputation?" asked Pervica.

"Oh, that is complicated!"

"Go on!" She was smiling now. "Tell me!"

I hesitated, then yielded and spread my hands. "My father, Arifarnes, had an enemy called Rhusciporis, with whom we had a dispute over grazing rights in the summer pastures. The king, of course, does not like his scepter-holders to have disputes with one another, as it weakens the nation, but he does not like to offend any of them that are powerful. He would not adjudicate the matter, and it dragged on and on. Then one day Rhusciporis attacked my father when he was out inspecting the herds of a dependant, and they fought. Rhusciporis triumphed and took my father's head for a trophy. My father had no brothers to inherit from him and no sons but me—and I was out of the country. With no one to hold the scepter, my family had to agree to accept a blood price for my father's life, and made a compact of peace with his murderer. They could not even demand the head back: Rhusciporis kept it, and made the skull into a drinking cup, which is a custom of ours with enemies who matter to us. When my mother and sisters had sworn the peace, Rhusciporis took the matter of the grazing rights back to the king, and the king decided in his favor—I was still out of the country, and anyway, I was barely eighteen at the time, so he had no concern about offending me."

"Where were you?" asked Pervica.

"I was beyond the Caspian Sea when my family's messenger found me and called me back. I'd been planning to ride with my companions as far as the Jade Gate of the Silk Country."

"Why?" she asked, dizzy with the distance. "Why so far?"

I laughed. "This story grows longer with every question. For glory! I was mad for glory when I was young. I wanted to fight a griffin in the mountains of the North and steal its gold; I wanted to ride the horses of the sun, and rescue a princess from a tower of iron. I wanted to do anything great, daring, and splendid. I was impatient with the world, and wanted more than it offered me. And at any rate, I wanted to see more of the world than my own country. We had traveled slowly, taking time to see everything, and my family's messenger caught up with us without difficulty, but still, it took months to come home."

"I've never been further from Corstopitum than once to Eburacum," Pervica said, in a low voice.

"It is easier for my people to travel than it is for yours," I said. "When we set out for the Jade Gate, we brought our wagons, and flocks to support ourselves, and asked grazing rights from the people we journeyed among. It was not very different than moving from spring to summer grazing grounds. And we were among Sarmatian tribes as far as the Caspian Sea, and after that among the Massagetae and Dahae, who understand our language."

She nodded, then suddenly gave me a radiant smile. "You'll have to tell me. I want to hear everything about it. The Jade Gate of the Silk Country! It sounds like a song."

"I never reached it," I said—and remembered the morning when I turned back, how I stood in the dry scrubland beyond the Caspian and strained my eyes to catch the shadow of the distant mountains of the East, and saw only the sun rising bloodred over an endless plain. I had dreamed of those mountains, and I'd known then that I would never see them. I wept as much for that as for my father's death—though I'd loved him.

I bowed my head at the memory and went on. "When I returned and received the scepter, I found that the fortunes of my family were staggering. We had lost dependants along with the grazing rights, and many of our people were trickling away to other lords, thinking that the luck of our inheritance had failed. It was clear to me that I needed to obtain honor and a reputation as a leader in war, and that I needed wealth in goods and in flocks, both to encourage the waverers to return to us and to reward those who were still loyal. I could obtain everything I needed if I crossed the Danube. Everyone relied upon me to go. So I did. I wanted glory, anyway." I was silent, thinking of where I, and other daring raiders like me, had brought us all.

"What happened to Rhusciporis?" asked Flavina, after a minute.

"When I was successful, I got the grazing rights back, or most of them. I made presents to the king from the spoils of my raids, and asked him to adjudicate again, and he decided in my favor, and made Rhusciporis return my father's skull as well. I taunted Rhusciporis with my successes, and my followers swaggered before his just as they now swagger before the Asturians. But we never fought. We had sworn peace. He died in the war."

I hesitated. I knew that Pervica was deeply unhappy about the planned duel with Arshak, and I wanted to explain to her why it was necessary. A Sarmatian woman might have been eager for me to revenge the insult to her dignity, but even if she hadn't been, she would never have questioned the need to do it. But to Pervica the whole duel was unnecessary and senseless, and it hurt me to think how she would feel if I died in it. "You see," I went on, slowly, "honor is everything to us. It was the fact that we had glory, not the gifts, that made the king decide for us. Here if a man is appointed to command a troop of cavalry because he bribed the legate, and if he is corrupt and cowardly, still he will be obeyed, because the soldiers respect their discipline. You have an altar to discipline in the chapel of the standards and you worship it as though it were a god. But our people know nothing of that. They expect their commander to bring them honor. If he is weak, they will still try to take pride in him, because their honor is bound to his and they wish to be proud—but if he brings them disgrace, they will begin to desert him, though they will grieve very bitterly over it and reproach themselves as disloyal and reproach him for making them so. Our honor is dearer to us than our blood, and to lose it kills us."

Pervica looked at me and smiled sadly. "I understand," she said.

I could see that she did. It was a hard thing to ask of a woman who loved me, that she should allow me to die for a cause she considered senseless—but she understood that I had to uphold my honor or be ruined, and she would not oppose me. I smiled at her and touched her hand. I was content.

XVI

THE FOLLOWING DAY I received three messages.

The first, which arrived at about midday, was a very short letter from Facilis, who had gone druid-hunting in Corstopitum.

"Marcus Flavius Facilis to Lord Ariantes and to his freedman Eukairios sends greetings," it said. "I found Cunedda. He was killed trying to escape. Farewell."

My first reaction was one of relief: now the druid could inform on no one. My second was of shame: that had almost certainly been Facilis' intention. The centurion had undoubtedly known how to do it: the few words in the ears of the Asturians he brought along to guard the prisoner ("Look, lads, you know what this fellow is. He'll talk about some of your comrades if the law gets him")—and then the offered opportunity, the guards apparently asleep or inattentive, the waiting horse, the struggle and the sprint and the spear in the back. Killed trying to escape. A minor disgrace to Facilis ("I caught him, sir, but there was no chance to question him"). For Bodica in Eburacum, anger and relief: she lost her chief adviser, but she was spared exposure. Release to Comittus and perhaps to some other moderate druids in the region—and to Eukairios, salvation. I wondered if the centurion had guessed what Eukairios was, and if that was the reason the letter had been addressed to both of us. It seemed very likely.

My scribe was certainly very shaken by the letter, understanding it as I had. I gave him the rest of the day off.

The second message, which Leimanos delivered to me about the middle of the afternoon, was from Arshak.

"He made no problems about the safe conduct," my captain reported, "and he treated me honorably. He was pleased with your message, and said to tell you this: 'Son of Arifarnes, I am glad to see that you haven't Romanized away your courage. My blood is royal, and I will meet you as what I am. Meet me as what you were, and I will drink to my victory from your skull.' "

Leimanos gave a snort of anger and contempt, then continued, "The Romans in Condercum, I'm certain, suspect nothing—though they're unhappy with him, because his men quarrel with theirs and he does nothing to stop them. Half the dragon was confined to barracks when I arrived, and a man had been executed for dueling. When Arshak went to River End he'd slipped out without permission, and now they have the Dalmatian troops from Vindovala guarding all the gates. It was hard to breathe in that fort, my lord, the air was so thick with anger: I thanked the immortal gods for Cilurnum. The Romans were pleased to think that Arshak would go hunting with you. They'd heard that we manage things better here, and they hope you'll convince him to behave less arrogantly. Arshak is perfectly happy to take precautions against his liaison officer discovering anything and has no argument with a delay to arrange things. He suggests twelve days, in fact, rather than ten, and we tentatively scheduled the meeting for the twenty-third of the month."

I frowned at this. This patient caution was not like the Arshak I knew. I wondered if his allies had another scheme under way. Aurelia Bodica must feel threatened by the proposed druidical convocation and the investigations now being carried out in Eburacum and Corstopitum. She would certainly try to move quickly if she could.

"I would prefer ten days to twelve," I told Leimanos. "Shall we say, eleven? I will send to suggest it to him—let Banadaspos take the message this time. Did you find a place for the meeting?"

"Not yet. We've agreed to look between Hunnum and Vindovala, about ten miles away from both of us, and to send a messenger when we've found somewhere suitable."

"I hope he understands to send his messenger *carefully*. The Romans here are less ignorant than the ones in Condercum. Facilis in particular is hard to fool. If he discovers that I've had any dealings with Arshak at all, he'll suspect."

"Arshak does know we have to be cautious, my lord. And he is very eager to fight you." Leimanos looked me over anxiously, appraising my strength for the meeting. He was unhappy with what he saw. "I hope that your leg . . ." he began.

"If I have to use my leg, I am a dead man. I will rely on Farna's."

He didn't like it, and I could see him remembering what I'd been like on our raids, comparing it with my crippled present. He sighed. "Yes, my lord."

The third message arrived at night. I had just gone to bed when Eukairios came and knocked on the side of my wagon, and I got up to find him standing outside in the frost. It was the dark of the moon, and the campfire had died to embers: I recognized Eukairios only by his voice. With him was another man whom he introduced as Protus, his friend from Corstopitum, a scribe in the office of the municipal archivist.

I jumped down from the wagon, pulling on my coat. "I believe I am much indebted to you," I told Protus, shaking his hand. "You sent Eukairios a letter, did you not, when Gatalas mutinied?"

"You're not indebted to me for that," he told me. "I've never been so glad of anything I've done in my life as I was of sending that letter. God must have helped me write it. If you and your men hadn't arrived so quickly, the barbarians would've sacked Corstopitum. I've brought you another letter tonight, Lord Ariantes. I borrowed a horse and rode over with it when I'd finished my work, because the person who gave it to me said it was urgent. It came from Eburacum." He set it in my hands. The wax seals were stamped with a curving pattern my fingers recognized as a dragon cloak pin. Siyavak.

I thanked Protus and asked him if he needed food (he did, and I had one of the bodyguard search out some bread and leftover stew for him) and a place to sleep (he said he must ride back to Corstopitum that same night, as he was expected at work in the morning). While he was eating the stew by the rebuilt fire, I lit an oil lamp and took Eukairios into my wagon to read me the letter.

It was everything I could have asked for. Arshak and Bodica had accepted Siyavak as theirs, and he knew names and places and points of assembly enough to damn them both. He set it out in a few lines, short, sharp, and deadly. The letter concluded,

Recent events have alarmed her. There is opposition to her plans among the druids, and talk of a convocation which she fears may condemn her. She has decided to risk moving at once, before it can meet. Arshak has been asked to mutiny on the twenty-fourth of January, and there is to be an invasion of the Selgovae and Votadini at the same time. She wants my dragon to mutiny on the same day; she has allies within the legion [and he gave names] *who will mutiny with us, and let us out of the fortress if things go badly. There are also to be uprisings in* [and he gave more names and places]. *I have sent this in haste. If you act quickly, Prince, they are in your hands, but if you delay, we are ruined. I will not mutiny, but if I speak defiance to her openly, my life is ended. For the love of honor, act at once! She is a witch and a servant of the Lie and I am afraid of her. I was glad, the god knows it, of the letter you left with me, and the man who writes this letter has spoken comfort to me, but the night is dark. I await your answer.*

He had dated the letter the sixth of January, which was the day I'd left Eburacum; it was now the eleventh. The triumph was like a blaze of lightning. We could strike in force.

I dictated a reply on the spot:

Ariantes to Siyavak lord of the fourth dragon sends greetings. Lord, by your courage and loyalty, Gatalas is avenged. Have no fear of me or my love for honor. I will act at once, and our enemies will be destroyed. For your part, continue your pretense and allow yourself to be arrested with the conspirators, for thus you will be safe from their vengeance. As soon as they are secure, you will be released and honored for your loyalty in revenging your lord's death. This I swear on fire.

I signed the letter, sealed it, and brought it out of the wagon. I was so stiff with excitement and joy that I wanted to shout. Protus was just finishing his stew. (The firelight revealed him as a round-faced man a bit younger than Eukairios, plainly dressed and with identically ink-stained hands.) Leimanos and Banadaspos had both appeared, tousled and sleepy, from their own wagons, which were, of course, nearby. They were convinced that something was up and determined not to miss it, and they sat watching Protus sullenly: another of their lord's foreign allies, involved in plans from which they had been excluded.

"I am indebted to you," I told Protus. "You said you had borrowed a horse: may I give you one?"

He gaped. "I . . . I couldn't keep a *horse*, Lord Ariantes! I don't have the money or the place to put it. And I can barely ride."

I went back into the wagon and fetched my last gold drinking cup—the others had all gone in bribes—and went to the supply of silver I'd put under the bed to keep handy. I filled the cup with silver and brought it out to Protus. "Take that, then, in token of my gratitude to you for riding over tonight," I told him. "Another man might have left it until the morning. When do you ride back?"

"I have to go as soon as I've finished eating, sir," Protus stammered, looking from me to the cup and back again. "I don't dare be away from work in the morning. I'd be beaten for it. I . . . These are denarii! Lord Ariantes, you can't mean—"

"I said it was a token of my gratitude. Do you think my gratitude is cheap? Here is an answer to the letter you brought; I ask you to see that it is sent with the same haste as the one you delivered to me. If you are leaving now, we will have your company on the road." I turned to my captains and switched to Sarmatian. "Leimanos, Banadaspos, our enemies are in our hands, and they will be ruined before the month is out! Tell the bodyguard to arm: we ride tonight."

They both jumped to their feet, sullenness vanished in triumphant delight.

"Tonight?" Eukairios echoed, in Latin, behind me.

"Tonight, and you as well," I told him, switching back to that language. "If you can sleep now, I admire your coolness. Facilis is still in Corstopitum, and we will need his help. We might as well ride now as in the morning. Leimanos, I'm leaving you in charge of the dragon."

"My lord . . ." began Leimanos, ready to protest.

"There won't be any fighting," I promised him, back in Sarmatian again, grinning. "They will die by ink and a few leaves of beechwood. I only want the bodyguard to protect my back. Eukairios, be sure you bring writing supplies. Leimanos, I'll tell Longus where I'm going as I leave. Don't bother Comittus about anything to do with this."

"You said he was innocent!" objected Leimanos.

"And so he is—but he has friends who aren't, and is it honorable to ask him to assist in their destruction? Do you know if Longus is in his house?"

"He said he was going to Fortunatus' place."

"Good. Someone point it out to me, and I'll say good-bye to him there."
I clapped my hands. "To arms!"

A few minutes later we were galloping out from the camp, thirty-one armed Sarmatians and two rather stunned scribes. It was just over an hour later when we rode into Corstopitum.

We dropped a shaken Protus off by the municipal buildings, and rode up to the gates of the military compound shortly before midnight. The guards were initially alarmed to see us, but relaxed when I asked for Flavius Facilis: they knew he was investigating the druidic murder, and midnight alarms were to be expected in such a case. They admitted us, sent a message to the commandant's house where Facilis was staying, and allowed us to stable our horses in the military stables. When we arrived at the commandant's house, it was to find the lamps lit and Facilis and the prefect of the Thracians, Titus Ulpius Silvanus, sitting in the dining room looking anxious and sleepy, waiting for us.

"What the hell are you doing galloping into Corstopitum at this time of night?" was Facilis' greeting to me.

"I have had some important news," I told him. "But there is no need for all of us to stay awake for it. Lord Prefect, is there anywhere for my men to rest?"

I managed to send him off to sort out the barracks, and as soon as he was gone, I handed Facilis Siyavak's letter.

The centurion read it with a look of growing disbelief, and when he'd finished, sat staring at it numbly. "Jupiter Optimus Maximus!" he exclaimed, and looked back up at me.

I ran my forefinger across my forehead and around the side of my head.

"Gods!" he agreed. "This will finish them! The other names you got were good: that Cunedda had kept a ring that belonged to that poor bastard of a carpenter he sacrificed, which pins the murder on him, and now that he's dead, there've been people coming forward to inform. The countryside and most of the druids in the region have turned against his sect. I thought now we could start to put up a fight. But this! This is the Venus toss on the dice, and the other players are out of the game shirtless."

"There is not much time," I said. "We should move at once."

Facilis nodded. "We need to write some letters."

When Titus Ulpius came back in, yawning, we had the writing leaves out and were sharpening the pens. "What's happened, then?" he asked.

Facilis looked at him reflectively a moment—then he handed the letter to him. The prefect began to read it in a mumble. He stopped yawning after the first line; after the fourth, he stopped mumbling and read silently. He looked up at Facilis, wide-awake and terrified. "Is this true?" he demanded.

"Yes," replied Facilis steadily. "But you don't need to take our word for it. When those bastards are arrested, they'll find proof of the lot, I'm sure of that. We need to get them all at the same time, so that they can't warn each other and hide the evidence. Best if it's done just a day or so before the uprising's scheduled to begin. You're prefect of a cohort, Titus, you can help. I don't have the authority to order what I need to, and nor does Ariantes."

"But the legate . . ."

"We tell the legate."

I made a gesture of caution, and the centurion turned on me. "You said you'd tell him when you had evidence, and by all the gods and goddesses, you've got it now. Nobody's going to arrest you here, with your own men at hand, and once he's arrested this lot, it will confirm everything. We tell the legate: you can dictate the letter yourself. But we tell the others, as well—the officers of all the forts involved—just in case he doesn't, or can't. And we write the governor down in Londinium." He turned back to Titus Ulpius. "Do you have a license to use the post? Then we send a fast courier off first thing in the morning, to Eburacum first, and then to Londinium. We give him strict instructions that the letter to the legate is on no account to be given to him if his wife is present. Come on! Let's get started!"

Letters. "Ariantes, commander of the Sixth Numerus of Sarmatian Horse, Titus Ulpius Silvanus, prefect of the First Thracian Cohort, and Marcus Flavius Facilis, centurion of the first order, *hastatus* of the Thirteenth Gemina, to Quintus Antistius Adventus, *legatus Augusti pro praetore*, governor of Britain . . ." "Ariantes . . . to Julius Priscus, legate of the Sixth Victrix, many greetings. My lord, when we spoke in Eburacum I swore that when I had evidence, I would give it to you. I have been informed that . . ." And letters as well to the prefects of half a dozen forts scattered around Brigantia, to the grain commissary, which was responsible for all intelligence operations, and to Marcus Vibullus Severus, Arshak's "liaison officer" at Condercum. Eukairios and Facilis wrote; I dictated; Ulpius, subdued and frightened, signed.

At four o'clock in the morning the letters lay in neat stacks on the prefect's desk, carefully sealed, the names of their addressees written neatly across the back. I looked at them, and thought how strange it was to fight a battle that way, boxing an absent enemy into a death cell by words scarcely whispered aloud. And even as I thought it, I realized that my part in the battle was over already. The letters would be sent. They would reach their destinations. All over northern Britain, men would be put under surveillance and houses would be searched, and a few days later, an uprising would be strangled the day before it could begin. The elation I had felt vanished suddenly and absolutely in a tide of grief. I was glad I was fighting Arshak, and would never see him arrested. I wished I'd agreed to fight him at once.

"Arshak won't be imprisoned," Facilis told me. He had written that letter. After a moment, he added, very gently, "I think that most likely he'll die resisting arrest." I looked up and saw him looking at me with almost as much tenderness in his heavy face as he'd had when he looked at Vilbia and her baby. "You were grieved for him," he said.

"Yes," I replied. "I am grieved."

"Go to bed," he told me. "Nothing's going to happen for days, and there's nothing more for you to do when it does."

But when I returned to Cilurnum the following afternoon, I found that Arshak had sent a messenger to arrange the location for the duel.

THE NEXT NINE days seemed unreal. The real war that I had launched had flown like an arrow from the string, and I saw nothing more of it. Arshak agreed to my suggestion of eleven days from the time I sent Leimanos, and the meeting was set for noon on the twenty-second of January. The business of the camp continued as peacefully as sleep. I drilled myself with the spear and the sword until my arms ached, and worked Farna until she'd obey a breath. Leimanos rode out to inspect the meeting place, and returned to say that it was acceptable. I waited in silence for something to happen, but nothing did.

On the evening of the twenty-first I summoned all the captains and told them what I was going to do. They had heard, from the bodyguard, what Arshak had done, and they would have been horrified and ashamed if I hadn't agreed to fight: they approved my announcement with a shout. They were less happy when I made them promise to say nothing about the duel until it was over, forswear revenge, and promise obedience to the Roman authorities, but they did as I required. I rose early next morning and sacrificed to Marha as the sun rose, praying for his protection. The fields were white with frost, and glittered pink in the early light; the bare branches of the trees burst with transient flowers of ice. It was good weather for fighting, clear and dry, and I judged that the frost would vanish as the sun rose. I armed myself and saddled Farna with her blanket of armor, but didn't mount her: there was no point in tiring her on the journey to the meeting place. I wanted her to be fresh for the combat, and I mounted Wildfire instead. I rode through the fort with my bodyguard behind me, as though we were going out for a gallop to exercise our horses. But I turned aside into the village and stopped at Flavina's house.

Pervica came to the door; she must have heard us jingling down the street, and rushed from dressing, because her hair was still loose over her shoulders, and she was in her stockinged feet. I dismounted, came over to her, and kissed her.

"It's today, is it," she said, in a flat voice.

I nodded. I took one of her hands and kissed that as well.

She closed her eyes. "I pray to all the gods you come back!"

"So do I," I said. "The omens are good."

She opened her eyes again, and linked both hands behind my head. Her face was so lovely it made me want to weep. "I haven't told anyone," she said. "And oh gods! I've wanted to."

I kissed her again. "I trusted you would not."

"I'm never going to be able to tease you, you know," she said, as though this were the thing that mattered.

I smiled. "Not everyone is the sort that does. Besides, everyone else laughs at me here: better not to receive it from my wife as well. Good fortune, Pervica."

"The only good fortune I want is for you to come back! Come home!"

I kissed her hand again, touched it to my forehead, and got back on my horse. I did not dare look back as we rode out of the village.

It was a white, shining morning of clean bright air and radiant skies, and as we rode along the military way I was light-headed with joy at the beauty of it. The golden stone of the Wall running up and down the crags, the green of the grass, the sheep grazing, the blue hills falling away to our right, a small brown bird pecking at a delicate sheaf of orange berries—everything seemed full, bursting with a splendor that took it out of itself and filled it with glory. I repeated to myself, tempting my own delight, all the things I would never do if I died before the evening. I would never ride Wildfire into a city or greet my brother Cotys when he arrived in Britain. I would never learn to write, never own a house, never see my schemes to breed horses come to fruition in a field of healthy foals. I would never marry Pervica, never sleep with her, never see our children. I would never reach the Jade Gate.

I laughed. Leimanos edged his horse beside Wildfire and looked at me questioningly.

"We never saw any griffins," I told him. He had come along on that journey.

He looked puzzled.

"When we rode east," I explained.

"Oh! No, my lord." He was still puzzled. After a moment, he added, "We saw plenty of other strange things, though. Do you remember the tiger?"

"Yes," I agreed, contentedly. "It's a lucky man who leaves his life complete."

"My prince," he said firmly, "I trust Marha that you will not leave your life today."

"It's in the hands of God," I replied. "I'm not afraid."

We rode through the infantry fort of Hunnum just past the middle of the morning, and it was still before midday when we turned off the road. Leimanos, who had inspected the location, led us across two fields, over a stream, and into a patch of woodland. In the middle of the wood was a large clearing, with a charcoal burner's hut surrounded by ash heaps; it, and the woodland, were empty. I realized that I'd seen it before, in a dream. It was another good omen, but I could not tell Leimanos, though I knew it would reassure him. What I felt that morning was a joy so private that I could not speak of it at all.

I had dismounted to inspect the ground, and my men were building a fire to warm themselves, when Arshak and his party arrived. He left his followers beside mine, by the hut, and rode over to greet me. His armor gleamed golden as he rode out of the shadows of the trees into the sunlight at the center of the clearing, and I stood holding Wildfire's bridle and smiling as he approached.

"Greetings," he said, stopping in front of me. "Is the ground acceptable?"

"Greetings," I replied. "I have no quarrel with it." I remounted Wildfire and gathered up the reins. "Shall we take the oaths from our men? Or do you wish to rest your horse first?"

"It was a short ride," he said, smiling back at me. "We'll take the oaths now."

We rode back to the hut, where my men had started the fire, and first one party, then the other, stretched out their hands above the freshly smouldering heap of charcoal, and swore that the contest would end with the death of one or both contestants, and that no revenge would be taken.

"What shall we do about the body?" asked Arshak, when that was finished.

"I believe you had a plan for a drinking cup, if the gods favor you," I replied.

He smiled. "True—but your friends the Romans might disapprove."

"You don't care about that, do you?" I asked. I could have added, "You are assuming that you only need to hide the body for two days anyway"—but I didn't. The exaltation I felt would only be cheapened by triumphing over him, and I might endanger the lives of his colleagues at Condercum if I spoiled their preparations. "The corpse can be buried here," I said instead. "But the Romans are likely to find out and arrest the survivor anyway. You're not afraid of them, are you?"

He smiled again, then suddenly extended his hand to me. "I'm glad it ends like this, Ariantes," he said. "For what my allies tried to do, I am sorry."

I shook his hand. "Spoken like a prince, Arshak. I'm glad to settle with you."

We turned back, each to our own party, and made the final preparations. I tightened the girths on Farna's saddle, checked the buckles of the armor, and unfastened my bow case, handing it to Banadaspos. I took off my coat and passed it to Leimanos, and mounted. My men spread out down one side of the clearing from the fire; Arshak's down the other. I looked at Arshak, now sitting high in the saddle of his white Parthian mare. "You are a king's nephew," I told him. "I yield the honor of first choice of position to you."

He bowed his head and, without another word, rode into the center of the clearing; he made the mare rear up, gleaming, and turned her, lifting his spear. I nodded. He understood as well as I did that my hope was in the training of my horse, and he would make me come to him. I turned Farna and cantered her round to the west end of the clearing. The sun was high and would not get in his eyes much, but it might yet help. I raised my hand in salute to it, and saw Arshak answer with the same gesture. I was perfectly content when I lowered my spear and touched Farna into a gallop toward him.

He did not move from his place, only braced himself in the saddle, holding his spear ready. I watched his face as I approached rather than that bright edge: I knew he could move it quicker than I could see. When his eyes flickered, I dropped from the saddle sideways and touched Farna to make her veer off; the tip of the lance whispered through the air above my head, and I heard a shout from the onlookers. I stabbed toward him with my own spear as I passed, but he had already kicked his mare and made her bolt out of the way. I slithered back upright, spun Farna about on her hindquarters, and started her back. His horse was a shade slower than mine and was still turning; he had twisted and was looking at me over his shoulder, grinning with excitement. My chance. I braced myself for the impact, aiming the tip of my lance at his chest.

He kicked his feet out of the stirrups, spun in the saddle, and swept his lance across sideways. It caught me on the left side; my spear was swept out of line, and I almost fell. I pressed my face against Farna's armored side, trying not to clutch at the saddle in case I dropped my spear. I was slow to pull myself back up; my left knee ached, and would not obey my command to lift me, and I'd almost lost my right stirrup. Over the shouts I could hear the hoofbeats of Arshak's mount following me.

"Go, sweet one," I told Farna, nudging her with my elbow since my feet and hands were busy. She flicked her ears and lengthened her stride, staying ahead of the other. I managed to get my right foot back fully in the stirrup and push myself upright. Arshak slowed his mount, straightening his spear. I galloped round the ring once, the onlookers merely a blur of metal, collecting myself again. Arshak followed on the inside, then turned his mount and rode in the opposite direction, speeding up again. Again I watched his face as he galloped toward me.

There was no flicker of the eyes this time: they were fixed and merciless, impossibly blue. I veered Farna sharply left, turned her almost on top of the onlookers, and galloped in the opposite direction, with Arshak galloping after me and his men jeering. "Run, darling," I whispered to her, and she heard and galloped with all her brave heart, gaining lengths. When I had space, I turned her again, into the center this time, and tried to cut in beside my opponent. But he dragged his mount to a halt and waited for me with his spear braced. I veered off again and circled round once more. Arshak again galloped in the opposite direction, bearing down to meet me. I veered left, right, left again; the spear point followed me unerringly. I brought Farna rearing to a halt, spear level, bracing myself for the impact.

He ducked as his mare took the last few steps, dropping so quickly that my spear hissed through the air above his shoulder, and his own spear twisted down so fast I had no idea where he'd aimed it, until I felt the pain white-hot in my bad leg. Through the shouts and the burning I could hear, small and distinct, the snap as the weak bone broke. Gasping, I whipped my spear about sideways, but he brought his free hand up, and the shaft slapped into his palm. His fingers locked on it, and I was too dizzy with pain to hold on. Somehow I drove my left heel against Farna's side—and the twist of the bone as I did nearly made me scream—and she leapt sideways. The spear lifted my leg, tugging as it came out, and I could feel the blood gushing warmly down my shin. Farna galloped in the direction I'd sent her. I glanced back, and saw Arshak wave my spear triumphantly before flinging it to the ground.

It would have to end quickly, or I'd faint from the bleeding. I drew my sword, and fumbled with stiff fingers at the buckle of the baldric. It came loose, and I tore off the sword's sheath and coiled the long leather strap about my hand. Arshak was waiting for me, watching, grinning triumphantly. The edge of his spear was dark now.

I turned Farna round to the right—it had to be to the right, my left leg wasn't working—and cantered back toward my opponent. "Good girl," I whispered, leaning forward onto her neck. Sweet, steady, patient Farna: I'd been right to choose her from among the thousands of horses I'd once owned, and take her with me. Holding the sword low against the armored blanket, looking up to watch Arshak's face, we galloped up for the last time. My only hope was that he thought he'd won already, and might be careless.

He was not actually careless, but he didn't mind if I veered left or right, and made no attempt to force me left, and that was enough. I saw the flicker in his eyes—he had to aim carefully this time, with me so low on the horse— and veered right. The crest of my helmet slapped against his spear shaft; I pulled Farna left sharply with the reins, and she crashed against his mount, making both horses stagger. I was up in my saddle, slashing down with the sword. But Arshak already had his spear back in line, and my blade chopped into the shaft. I dropped it and flung myself out of the saddle against him, knocking him out and over, reaching for my dagger as we fell. With another part of me, I heard screams and shouting and the clatter of arms; I saw the grass etched in a thousand tiny blades, shining with melted frost—and Arshak landed with a grunt, and I twisted my broken leg as I fell on top of him, and screamed, and found my dagger. Arshak rolled desperately away even as I struck, and the blade slid uselessly across the golden scales of his armor. I pulled myself up onto one knee, bracing myself with the other. My left leg was twisted so that the foot stuck out limply, sideways and almost upside down, and the blood was still streaming. A few more moments, I thought, and I'll faint. Arshak leapt to his feet and drew his sword.

The long strap of the baldric uncoiled as I lashed out with it. The end caught about his leg, and he fell as I jerked it back again. I half kicked, half dragged myself toward him; he rolled, got to his knees, and swung his sword at me. I caught it in the leather strap and flung it out of his hand, and then I was on top of him, knocking him flat. He had his hand on his own dagger. Lying on top of him, I struck downward at his throat with all my strength; the knife glanced off his jaw and skidded across his armor. He screamed, a scream full of blood, pulling his own knife from its sheath, but too late. I struck again, and this time the knife went home. The blood spurted hot over my hand and into my face, blinding me. I let go of the knife and lay still. I felt his heart pounding beneath my cheek; I felt the instant when it stopped, and I was sick with grief. Around me, the world went gray.

The next thing I remember is someone pulling at my shoulders: my leg twisted and I lurched back into consciousness with a cry of pain. There was a pause, and then I was lifted again and turned over, and someone said, in Latin, "We've got to stop the bleeding." I looked up and saw Facilis standing over me.

"You bastard!" he said vehemently. He was very red in the face. "You slippery bastard!"

I looked away. I knew vaguely that he wasn't supposed to be there, but I didn't want to think about it. I felt very faint and sick, and the pain in my leg was terrible.

"Do not stand there!" Facilis shouted, in his villainous Sarmatian. "Your lord is bleeding to death. We must get his armor off and stop it." I realized he hadn't been addressing me this time.

I fainted when they took my armored trousers off, and probably screamed as well; I don't remember. They pulled my leg straight, stitched the big vein in the leg, which had been torn but fortunately not severed, put a compress on the wound to stop the bleeding, splinted the whole, and tied it up: I woke up again during the last part of this, and saw that it was Comittus who was tying the knots. I remembered he had said he knew some field surgery, but I was still too faint to wonder how he'd come there. I was relieved, though, when Leimanos brought a stretcher up: I'd known that he was there.

They moved me next to the fire, covered me with horse blankets, and gave me a drink of wine from a flask. I lay still for a while, listening without understanding to the voices, Latin and Sarmatian, speaking around me. After a time, Facilis appeared overhead again. He knelt down beside me.

"We've rigged a horse litter," he told me, "and we're going to take you to Corstopitum. Incidentally, you're under arrest."

I nodded weakly. "What are you doing here?" I asked him. My voice came out very faint and far away.

He snorted. "I could ask the same question of you, and with much more justification. You bastard! There was no reason for you to fight him. The whole thing was going to be over with tomorrow anyway."

"Honor," I said, and smiled.

"*Vae me miserum!*" he exclaimed in disgust. "Sarmatians!"

"If you are taking me to Corstopitum," I said, "could someone ride to Cilurnum and tell Pervica and the others that I am still alive?"

"You don't deserve to be!" he told me. "Lucius!" Comittus appeared again. "He wants someone to ride to Cilurnum to tell the lady Pervica that he's alive, and the rest of his precious savages as well. You go, and take Leimanos with you to make sure the others know it's true and behave themselves. Keep the bastards confined to camp."

Leimanos himself appeared, with Banadaspos, both looking distressed. "Is he going to live?" they asked anxiously.

"Unless the wound takes the rot," replied Facilis impatiently. "Though if we hadn't come along, you lot would probably have stood about lamenting his injury and praising his courage while he bled to death. Sarmatians!"

"I will not leave my lord to be imprisoned by you," Leimanos declared angrily.

"You think he's going to be imprisoned, in the state he's in?" asked Facilis. "He'll be shoved straight into the fort hospital. They've got a proper doctor there, not just a couple of orderlies like at Cilurnum. He'll be fine."

"I will not leave him," Leimanos insisted, glaring at Facilis as though he suspected the centurion of plotting to clap me in irons and rack me on the hospital bed.

"You will go back and reassure the men," I ordered him. "You have sworn me an oath on fire, and you will keep it." He looked at me in distress, and I added softly, "We will reach the Jade Gate yet."

He caught my hand, kissed it, and went off. Banadaspos looked at Facilis silently.

"You can come," the centurion told him. "You and ten of the bodyguard can keep him safe. The rest go back to Cilurnum with Leimanos."

"What are you doing here?" I asked Comittus.

"Marcus thought you might try to do something like this," he replied. "He asked Severus at Condercum to tell him if you'd sent any messages to Arshak, and we found out the time of the meeting. We were planning to stop you on the way. But Severus got the day wrong: he thought it was tomorrow, and nobody realized until this morning after you'd left the fort. We came pelting after you with all five squadrons of Asturians, but we missed you on the road, and only arrived in time to see the end. Severus still isn't here."

"The day was changed," I said.

"You slippery bastard," Facilis grunted. He picked up one end of the stretcher; Leimanos took the other. They carried me over to the horse litter they had rigged, put me down on it, very gently, and strapped me in so that the movement wouldn't jar my leg. I looked back and saw my helmet sitting on a stake, as it had been in my dream. I guessed that the pack below it contained my armor. I turned my head and saw Arshak's body lying at the other side of the clearing, still in its golden armor. His face was covered with blood, and his men sat in a circle about him, disarmed, watched by some of the Asturians. Leimanos followed my gaze.

"Do you want me to collect his scalp?" he asked.

"No," I answered. "The customs are different here."

XVII

I was in the hospital in Corstopitum for fourteen days. I didn't need to stay there so long, but I was technically under arrest for the whole of that time, and no one wanted to put me in the prison. Pervica came down from Cilurnum with Eukairios, and they found a place to stay in the town and came to keep me company. Eukairios started to teach me to write, and read me letters about what was happening elsewhere.

The mutiny was strangled on the twenty-third of January, the day before it was scheduled to take place. The legate Julius Priscus ordered the arrest of a number of his officers, then resigned and allowed the spies of the grain commissary to arrest his wife. Bodica wrote a letter to Arshak, not knowing that he was already dead, and poisoned herself in the prison. A lot of people afterward who hadn't seen the letter claimed they had, and cited it as scandalous and salacious, but it wasn't; Facilis showed it to Eukairios, who repeated it to me. "Aurelia Bodica, to Arsacus, prince-commander of the second dragon, greetings," it said. "My white heart, we have been betrayed. I would have made you a king, as you deserve, but the gods have decreed otherwise. The purposes of the Hooded Ones are hard to understand. They did not effect my curse and my prayers have gone unheard. Yet I beg them again to hear me, and to receive my spirit, and yours. Farewell."

I still don't know if she had, as Facilis thought, committed adultery, and it still doesn't seem very important. She had undoubtedly betrayed her husband, but at least she genuinely loved the man she had chosen in his place. I did not forgive her for her pleasure in drowning me, let alone for Vilbia, but it was some relief to learn that she was, after all, a human being, and not the demon she had appeared.

Siyavak, who had indeed been arrested with his pretended allies, was released on Bodica's death and publicly proclaimed the discoverer of the conspiracy, a hero of the Roman state—which cannot have pleased him—and the revenger of Gatalas, which I know did. He was given the kind of decorations Romans always give to award conspicuous courage—a silver spear, a golden crown, and an assortment of armbands, torques, and medals. He was also confirmed as commander of the Fourth Sarmatians, and his liaison officer, Victor, was recalled to the headquarters of the Sixth Legion. Siyavak sent me a letter announcing his satisfaction at revenging Gatalas' death and at receiving honors from the Romans, which, he said, had greatly pleased his men. He also congratulated me for killing Arshak. "I've heard that the Romans revile you for fighting him when he would have been arrested anyway," he wrote, "and the man who writes this letter deplores it. But it was honorably done, Prince, and I was glad to hear of it, for I would have been ashamed to see him, the descendant of kings, imprisoned and executed by the Romans. I look forward to seeing you again, and hearing of the combat, which I've been told was terrifying both for its skill and for its ferocity."

Pervica had one very surprising piece of news from her druid acquaintance. It seemed that the druids of the North had held their convocation and that, with Cunedda dead and the rest of the extreme sect in fear, the whole meeting had swung over to her friend Matugenus. Instead of being branded a heretic lover of Rome, he was a hero of the true religion. The meeting had denounced "those who betray their own people to foreign plunderers out of hatred of their enemies," and voted that human sacrifice of an unwilling victim was blasphemous. The followers of the old religion all over the North were delighted with Matugenus, and Matugenus was enormously pleased with himself. Through Pervica he sent me a message saying that he would pray for my swift recovery, and offering me the friendship of his order.

That was immediately after the rebellion was crushed. A few days later we heard that the grain commissary, less careful than Facilis, was arresting any druids they could find and torturing them until they confessed to having some part in the conspiracy. Unlike Facilis, the commissary struck blindly. They had no list of druids, only the reports of their own informers. They didn't take many men, but they did grab everyone whose name was reported to them. Matugenus' name was on everyone's lips—and he was among those taken.

Pervica went to Facilis and told him that Matugenus was innocent, that he'd led the opposition to Cunedda. Facilis told me that he knew that from others and had said as much to the intelligence officers, but that the only interest they took in it was to ask him who his informants were: for him to intervene again would be no help to Matugenus, and could put more lives at risk. There was nothing we could do.

The governor of Britain, Quintus Antistius Adventus, arrived in Eburacum to decide what to do about the mess of the northern army on the eighth of February. The summons for me to go there had come some time before, on the third. I was carried down in a horse litter, much to my disgust. I told everyone that I had ridden seven hundred miles from Aquincum with my leg in a splint, so I could perfectly well ride a mere seventy-five or eighty to Eburacum, but everyone disregarded me completely. The doctor in Corstopitum said I must not put any strain on the bone, that my riding with it in a splint had done it considerable damage before, and that the only good thing about it breaking again was that now it could at least set straight. Even my bodyguard sided with the doctor, and Facilis gleefully pointed out that I was under arrest and had no choice about which way I traveled. So I went to Eburacum lying on my back in a litter, like a Roman senator's wife.

Facilis rode along beside me, with Longus, a squadron of Asturians, and a cavalry cohort from the First Thracians under Titus Ulpius Silvanus. Eukairios and Pervica came as well, Pervica driving her farm cart and Eukairios riding my red bay, but all of my own men were left at home. Facilis promised them that the arrest was only a formality, but said that even so, a man charged with murder really could not go to trial with a bodyguard and several squadrons of armored horsemen at his back. They protested angrily at this. I had to have all the captains summoned to the hospital, so that I could command them to obey their oaths. The Romans promised them that no one was likely to execute me, reminding them that the arrest was just a formality. Eventually they yielded, though sullenly. I charged Leimanos and Banadaspos with making sure they behaved with grace during my absence. Comittus also stayed behind, partly because the fort required at least one senior officer, but also, I think, because he didn't want his own connections inspected at Eburacum.

When I arrived in Eburacum, I was put in the fort hospital—again to keep me out of the prison—while my friends found lodgings in the town or squeezed into fort buildings already crowded with the governor's staff. The next morning a party of soldiers in old-fashioned strip armor and cap helmets marched into my room carrying a sedan chair and asked if I were Ariantes, commander of the Sixth Numerus of Sarmatian Horse. I agreed that I was.

"Then we'll take you to see the governor," said their spokesman. "We're with the Second Numerus of the Consular Guard. He's sitting in judgment now, and your case is next."

I looked down and rubbed my knee, trying to collect myself. I felt very nervous and unsure of myself, now that it had come to the point. I did not believe that the authorities particularly wanted to punish me for killing Arshak, now that he had been exposed as an oath-breaker. On the other hand, duels between commanders were not something that the Roman state would want to encourage. They might punish me with demotion to make an example of me to the next eight dragons. They could even conceivably execute me. I was glad that my bodyguard had been left behind in Cilurnum, but I wished I had a friend with me now.

"Do you want to change?" suggested the leading consular guardsman, misunderstanding my hesitation. "If you have Roman dress, we'll give you time to put it on."

I had my own clothes, and my friends had seen to it that they were clean. I put on my best shirt to see the governor, and pinned my coat loose across my shoulders. I had a new hat—black, with gold embroidery—but for weapons I had not so much as a dagger, and I felt exposed and ashamed. It was worse when the guardsmen brought up the sedan chair for me. "I will walk," I told them.

"We were told you couldn't," said their spokesman. "Just sit down in it, sir. I don't want to get in trouble with the doctors. The governor must have finished the last case by now, and they'll all be waiting for you."

I sat down in the sedan chair. I felt utterly ridiculous.

The governor was seated at the tribunal in the great hall of the headquarters of the Sixth Legion. The courtyard outside was full of his personal guard, and the hall itself was so full—with his staff, with officers of the legion, with prefects of all the auxiliary forces of the North—that it was hard to see any known face among all the faces. I noticed Julius Priscus, though, standing behind the tribunal. He looked shrunken and aged since our last meeting, and he stood with his shoulders slumped. His eyes met mine as I was carried in, and his mouth twisted. He looked away. Everyone else in the room seemed to be staring at me.

The guardsmen who were carrying the sedan chair set it down, and I stood up, balancing on my good leg. The governor sat with his hands on his knees, looking down at me. He was a middle-aged Numidian, grizzled brown and dark-eyed, and in honor of the military occasion he was wearing gilded armor under his gold-fringed crimson cloak. The emperor's statue watched with a preoccupied frown from the chapel of the standards at the side of the hall.

I saluted the governor. "Greetings, my lord Antistius Adventus!" I said. "Greetings to you all."

The governor clear his throat. "You are Ariantes, son of Arifarnes, commander of the Sixth Numerus of Sarmatian Horse?"

I bowed my head in agreement.

"You have been accused of murdering the commander of the Second Numerus, Arsacus son of Sauromates."

"I killed him, my lord, in fair combat," I corrected him.

One of the governor's staff coughed. "Were you aware that he was plotting a mutiny?"

"I was."

"Was the fight perhaps connected in some way with that mutiny?" the same staff member prompted.

"We had chosen different sides, sir," I said carefully. "He wished to fight, and took steps to provoke me."

"You might have taken steps to inform your Roman liaison officer, or your camp prefect," put in a different man, this one an army commander in the red cloak and sash of a prefect.

I had no intention of discussing Comittus and his druidical connections. "I had informed both of them," I said instead, politely, "of the conspiracy against Roman power in this region. I had informed them, and the legate, and you, my lord governor, and all who were concerned, of Lord Arshak's involvement in that conspiracy, as you all know. But I was provoked, as I said, to fight him. And I thought also that for him to die at the hands of the Roman state would be crushing to his people, to mine, and to those of our nation who have yet to arrive in this province. He was the nephew of our king.

Moreover, it seemed to me very likely that many lives would be lost over-coming him, for he was a powerful man and a brave one, and would have fought his arrest. I therefore fought him privately, and the gods granted me victory."

"You are a loyal servant of the emperor?" asked the first prompter.

"I am faithful to my oaths," I replied.

My prompter turned back to the governor. "You notice that he was aware of everything that the centurion told us?" he asked. "That this man Arsacus would have been an immense embarrassment to us if he had been arrested and executed, and that many Roman lives would have been at risk in any attempt to arrest him? Isn't it far better that this loyal commander killed him in a duel?"

"Yes, I did notice it, Quintus Petronius," answered the governor, testily. "But I'm still not going to give him a gold crown for it. I agree that it was a mercy of the gods that this fellow Arsacus was taken out quietly and in a way that his followers don't too much object to, but dueling remains a practice I do not wish to encourage in the British army. Ariantes son of Arifarnes, it's plain that the man you killed was a rebel and traitor and that you killed him largely because of it, and I therefore have no hesitation in proclaiming you innocent of murder. But I cannot give you the reward you may have expected, because of the *manner* in which you killed him. In future, you must respect Roman discipline."

I bowed my head to hide my surprise. I heard someone laugh over to one side, and I glanced round to see Longus and Pervica, squeezed in the door that led from the courtyard, watching me, in Longus' case, with delight.

"However"—and the governor smirked, and began to speak in a peculiar booming voice which I later realized was the way they're taught to talk in rhetorical schools— "it is clear that the province of Britain owes you a debt for the prompt way in which you reported this treason to the authorities, for your tenacity of purpose and loyalty when faced with threats against your life, and for the encouragement you gave to Siau . . ."—he had trouble with the name— "Siauacus, the commander of the Fourth Sarmatians, in his brave and loyal service in uncovering the conspiracy. Moreover, I have taken note of the high regard in which all your junior officers hold you, and the tributes paid to your administrative ability by the procurator of the fleet and the former legate of the Sixth Victrix. In respect of the services you have rendered us—but *not* the killing—I have decided to award you the silver spear, the medals, and the armbands normally given to honor valor. In appreciation of your proven loyalty and abilities, I have decided to do away with the need for a Roman liaison officer in your case and to allow you the supreme command of all the troops at Cilurnum, including the five squadrons of the Second Asturian Horse. As a temporary measure, I would also like you to take charge of the Second Sarmatian Horse."

My head was swimming, and I was afraid my leg would give way. "My lord," I said, spreading my hands helplessly, "that I cannot do. They are Arshak's men, and I am their lord's killer. They will not revenge it, because it was fair combat and they had sworn to abide by its result—but they would not obey me. I suggest that you allow Siyavak to choose one of the squadron captains as commander of the dragon, and appoint him jointly with a Roman."

The governor frowned, looking offended—then shrugged. "Very well," he said. "We'll resolve that matter later. In the meantime, Ariantes, I wish to offer you, in the emperor's name, a reward greater than any of those I have mentioned so far: the citizenship of Rome."

I bowed my head again, to conceal my feelings. The citizenship of Rome. I, become a Roman. Become a countryman of Tirgatao's murderers. I did not want it.

But the governor had taken my gesture as one of awed consent, and he smirked as he instructed one of his staff to draw up the papers. Another staff member was already sorting out a memorandum about the next case, and the audience whispered to each other about it and about the business they had just seen finished. I asked if I were free to go. I was told I could, impatiently, by the officer who'd been annoyed with me about dueling, and I began to limp heavily out of the hall. Longus and Pervica pushed their way in through the door and forced me back into the sedan chair. After a moment, the consular guardsmen picked it up and carried me out.

I made them stop before they took me back to my hospital room, and they put me down outside in the hospital courtyard, where there was a garden. Pervica and Longus hurried up behind them. Longus was laughing. I climbed out of the chair and steadied myself against a potted shrub. "Should we take the chair back then?" asked the leading guardsman. "Or will you need it later, sir?"

"I do not want it!" I said, with some force, and he grinned.

"Very good!" he said cheerfully, and gestured for the others to take it away. "Sorry they didn't give you the crown, sir. You deserved it. But that's the senior command: they always come down hard on a breach of discipline. Good luck!" And he and the rest marched off.

Longus laughed again. "Hercules!" he said. "You looked so stupid when the governor said you couldn't have a golden crown."

"I thought I would be punished," I told him.

He laughed again. "That's what Marcus Flavius said. You have a very low opinion of Romans, don't you? We'd be a pretty ungrateful bunch to punish you after you saved the province—or the north quarter of it, anyway. And you standing there, wobbling on one leg, the other injured in your struggle against the enemies of Rome—Hercules! Half the governor's staff think he's treated you very unfairly as it is. Of course, you gave them presents when you were trying to increase the pay offer, didn't you? They had a high opinion of you anyway."

I shook my head in bewilderment. I told myself how pleased my men would be when they learned that the Romans had honored me—but I realized even as I thought it that they would find out that I might have been given a gold crown, and they would instantly forget their relief and resent the lack of it. Siyavak, they would tell each other, had been given a gold crown, and he wasn't even a scepter-holder. And the next time they met up with the men of the fourth dragon, they'd quarrel with them. As Facilis said, Sarmatians!

"So," said Longus happily, "now you're officially prefect of the *ala* of the Second Asturians—my prefect, my lord"—he swept me a mocking bow— "as well as commander of the Sixth Sarmatians. And Comittus goes back to being a staff officer of the Sixth Legion. You'll have to move into that house after all, you know. You're a Roman citizen! What are you going to call yourself?"

I shrugged. Pervica came over and put my arm over her shoulders, helping me to balance. "You don't want to be a Roman citizen, do you?" she asked gently.

"No," I agreed.

"You can't refuse!" exclaimed Longus, losing his mockery.

"It would insult the governor if I did, would it not?" I said evenly, "And it would give me . . . advantages, I suppose, which would be useful. No, I cannot refuse." I looked sourly at the hospital. "If I am not technically under arrest, I do not need to stay here, do I? But my wagon is in Cilurnum."

"I'm sure they'll find you a house," said Pervica.

I put my arm around her waist and looked at her. I could feel her hipbone against my wrist, and the smoothness of her stomach under my hand. I suddenly wanted her very badly. I knew that she was staying in an inn in town, and I didn't want to leave her there. "If I am a citizen," I said, "it will make it easier to marry legally. I suppose I could tolerate a house, if you shared it."

Her fingers tightened on my shoulder. "It will probably take longer than one afternoon, though, to sort it out," she said quietly.

"Let us try!" I said, urgently now. "We can have a wedding feast back in Cilurnum: see if we cannot sort out some kind of contract today!"

She flushed bright red and kissed me. "Yes!" she cried, suddenly enthusiastic. "Yes, right now! Gaius and I will go and see what we can do. I'll find Eukairios, and he can find Marcus Flavius: they'll know how we can do it."

I stayed in the hospital garden while they searched, sitting down beside the fountain. It was a warm day, for February: the sun was shining, and the early crocuses had shoved their blunt snouts above the ground. Hellebore was flowering, white and sweet-scented, and the water was dark and clear. After a while, Facilis trotted into the courtyard. He seemed unusually pleased with himself.

"Congratulations," he said. "Honors all round. Gaius tells me you want to get married today."

I nodded. I had another thing to say to him first. "I understand you spoke to the governor on my behalf, urging him to give me honors for killing Arshak."

Facilis grunted. "I pointed out to them that you solved a very sticky problem for us."

"You slippery bastard," I said, with feeling.

He barked, and sat down on the fountain beside me, grinning. "We'll

have you speaking Latin properly yet!" he exclaimed. "About the marriage—
I can help arrange it for you, if you like. I'm going to the public archives myself this afternoon anyway."

I eyed him suspiciously. "Why?"

He grinned at me. "A manumission and an adoption."

"What?"

He gave a pleased grunt. "I told Julius Priscus last night that I'd . . . um,
found Vilbia, with her baby, in Corstopitum, and that I'd, um, *apprehended*
them. But I said I'd taken a liking to the girl and wanted to buy her. He had
no objection. He doesn't want anything that ever had anything to do with his
wife, poor bastard; he's sick with the whole business, ruined and disgraced.
His administrative career is finished, though I can't see anything he did that
was worthy of blame. Anyway, he gave me Vilbia on the spot, I drew up the
manumission papers, and I'm going to get them witnessed this afternoon and
legally adopt the girl."

"As your daughter?" I repeated, bewildered.

He barked with laughter. "You want a wife, but that doesn't mean everyone does. I had one once, and that was enough for me. But I also had a
daughter once. She died when she was seven. I've always had it in the back of
my mind, 'What would have happened if she'd lived? What would she be like
now?' Probably not a bit like Vilbia. But the girl has suffered, and she needs
someone to care for her. She's a sweet, kind girl, and brave, to defy her mistress over the baby—you know she believed in Bodica's magic absolutely, and
was terrified of her. I want a daughter; she wants a father. These things sort
themselves out. One little piece of parchment and instantly I'm a father again,
and a grandfather as well. Flavia Vilbia and Marcus Flavius Secundus, citizens
of Rome. How about that, eh?"

"Congratulations," I said, smiling at him. "I wish you all much joy."

"We're going to move to Eburacum," he went on. "I'm being promoted,
to *primus pilus* of the Sixth Victrix! Think of that! All those years I sweated
in the Thirteenth Gemina, and I thought *hastatus* of the first rank was as high
as I could get, and now I'm *primus pilus* for a year, over the heads of two others, and afterward something senior. No more muddling about with a lot of
barbarians who always smell of horses."

First the news that Comittus would be recalled to the Sixth; and now Facilis as well. "I will miss you," I said, and it was perfectly true.

He slapped my shoulder. "You don't intend to forget me completely, then? You remember that?"

I nodded.

"I'll miss you, as well." He added it very quietly, as though it embarrassed him to say it, and hurried on, "But it's been pretty damn clear ever since we reached Cilurnum that you never needed me to keep an eye on you. And I imagine you'll be in and out of Eburacum fairly frequently, as well as down to Londinium, advising people on how to treat Sarmatians: we'll see each other from time to time. Anyway, there is a quick way of getting married, without going through all the ceremonies. You have Eukairios draw up a legal contract expressing your intent to marry a Brigantian citizen, one Pervica, and arranging your various properties however you wish. Then you sign it, she signs it, three witnesses sign it, and that is sufficient evidence of *affectio maritalis* to satisfy any court in the land. I'll file it for you when I go down to the archives, and the job's done. You'll need your citizenship papers, though. I can collect them for you from the governor's staff. What names do you want on them?"

I shrugged. Roman names.

"Well—to whom do you owe your citizenship?"

"First to the governor, then to the emperor."

"Quintus Antistius Ariantes? Marcus Aurelius Ariantes?"

I flinched. "Marha!"

He grinned at me. "A bitter mouthful, is it? You'll get used to it. Which one shall it be?"

"Marcus Aurelius."

"The safest choice. The governor would be flattered if you used his names, but his term of office ends in a year or so, and he can't be offended at you choosing to honor the emperor. I won't call you Marcus, don't worry." He got to his feet. "I'll go arrange it for you. Good health!"

Eukairios arrived a few minutes after he'd gone. "Pervica said you wanted to see me, Patron," he said.

"I wanted to marry her today," I said. "Marcus Flavius says that you can draw up a marriage contract concerning our property, and that we need three witnesses for it. He says he will collect my citizenship papers from the governor's staff, take them down to the public archives, and file the contract for us. Is that all it needs?"

"That should be— What citizenship papers?"

I looked at him sourly. "I am rewarded with Roman citizenship."

"Oh." He sat down beside me and stared into the fountain. I noticed quite suddenly that his eyes were red.

"What is the matter?" I asked.

He looked away from the water reluctantly and rubbed his eyes. "I . . . was visiting the brothers here, and they had a letter for me from the *ekklesia* in Bononia, the one I used to belong to. Three of my friends have been arrested, and were sent to Augusta Treverorum to die in the arena."

"I am very sorry," I said, after a moment's silence.

He shook his head. "We say it's a glorious death, to die praising Christ in the arena." His voice had thickened. "We say that it's the sure road to the Heavenly City, and that God will wipe away every tear from their eyes."

"But you wept, nonetheless."

"They were always so *kind*!" he exclaimed passionately, beginning to weep again. "Especially Lucilla. There was never a stray cat that went hungry from her door, and if she saw a child crying in the street, she comforted it. She used to send me honeyed wine when I'd had my rations stopped, and charcoal to warm my cell in the winter. Oh God, God, I loved her! They are going to throw her to the wild beasts." He looked up at the dull sky, his face contorted and streaming. "I want to take the soldiers who arrested her, the magistrates who ordered it, the jailers who keep her prisoner—I want to take the whole howling mob of people who are going to watch it—I want to take them all, and cast them into the lake of Hell, and watch them burn!"

"I am sorry," I said again.

"Vengeance is evil. I should forgive my enemies." He was back in control of himself. "Otherwise the wounded strike the wounded, and so the world is chained in suffering. I should be glad for my sister and my brothers: they are leaping from a moment's pain into eternal glory. I am confident that Christ will give them strength and bring them home."

There was another minute of silence. I thought about the kind Lucilla, doomed to die in the arena; about the Pictish prisoners we had taken; about the druids imprisoned in this very city. I thought about Tirgatao's death.

"So," said Eukairios, after another minute of silence, "they've given you the Roman citizenship."

I nodded. "Tell me, Eukairios, should I refuse it?"

"No!" he said, in astonished disbelief. "Of course not!"

"I do not want it. The gods know, I do not love Rome."

"But you've risked so much to defend Roman power!"

"I had a choice between that and joining its enemies, who seemed to me much worse. I was not offered the choice my heart would make; one never is."

"What choice would that be?"

I was silent for a long time. I did not want to be a Roman, but I already knew that I was no true Sarmatian anymore—and I still had no clear idea of what the Britons were like. What world would I chose, if I had my freedom?

"A world without hatred," I said at last.

Eukairios looked away, into the fountain. He reached over and stirred the stagnant water with his hand. "You're right," he whispered. "That's not a choice we're ever offered."

I touched his shoulder.

Pervica came into the garden and hurried over to me. I stood up, balancing on one foot, and let her take my left arm. "Facilis says he can arrange for us to be married today," I told her. "Eukairios can draw up the contract, and Marcus will take it to the archives this afternoon."

"I went to see Publius Verinus, the camp prefect here," she replied, "and he says we can have a guest room in the commandant's house, despite it being so crowded. He was very pleasant when I told him we wanted to get married, and wished us joy."

Her face, turned up to mine, was flushed and radiant. I smiled into it. In that part of me that was neither Roman nor Sarmatian, I kicked shut the doors of all the worlds that offered, and chose the one that no one would give me, the way to the Jade Gate, where I could never go.

Historical Epilogue

*T*HE SARMATIANS WERE a real people. Nomadic speakers of an Iranian language like their cousins the Scythians, their different tribes—Iazyges and Roxalani, Alans, Aorsi, and Siraces—at one point extended from the plains of eastern Hungary as far as the Caspian Sea. They appear in the art of the Greek cities of the Black Sea and on Trajan's column; at one point in the late third century, the Romans appear to have regarded them as the greatest of all the barbarian threats.

The historical peg on which this book has been suspended—the presence of some 5,500 Sarmatians in the Roman army in Britain—is also genuine. The fragmentary remains of book 72 of Dio Cassius' *Roman History* preserve this detail of the peace settlement that in 175 ended the Danube campaigns of the emperor Marcus Aurelius. That the Sarmatians arrived in Britain and remained for some time is attested by a tombstone from Chester, an inscription relating to a settlement of Sarmatian veterans at Ribchester, and some probably Sarmatian fragments of armor and definitely Sarmatian beads at a few sites—including the fort of Chesters (Cilurnum) on Hadrian's Wall. Of such bits and pieces is history constructed. My own construction is, of course, full of details, but it's only fair to warn the reader that many of these are invented or borrowed. For example, it isn't clear that the cavalry surrendered to Marcus in the settlement of A.D. 175 were all armored: the British bits and pieces suggest armored units, and it makes sense that Marcus would demand this if he could, but the Iazyges did use unarmored mounted archers and could have sent principally these. Another bit of historical cheating is my use of the "Thundering Victory." This actually took place in a *different* Danube campaign of Marcus Aurelius. But the only battle Dio describes with the Sarmatians—a dramatic encounter on the frozen Danube—is pretty clearly a minor skirmish, only recounted because the old Greek liked melodrama: it wouldn't do for the end of a war. Better a real battle misplaced than an invented one, I thought.

For descriptions of Sarmatian customs my principal sources are Ammianus Marcellinus (on the Halani or Alans, a Sarmatian tribe, XXXI.2.16ff), Strabo, and, to a lesser extent, book IV of Herodotos (his "Sauromatai" are generally considered to be the ancestors of the later Sarmatians). Most of the archaeological work is in Russian or Hungarian, and hence inaccessible to me, but I've read what I could find in English. I must mention in particular T. Sulimirski's *The Sarmatians* (Thames and Hudson, 1970), a nice clear archaeology book with excellent illustrations, though a bit careless with references. A couple of other books that were generally very useful were Ann Hyland's *Equus: The Horse in the Roman World* (B.T. Batsford, London, 1990) and Anthony Birley's *The People of Roman Britain* (B.T. Batsford, London, 1979).

A couple of other points need to be mentioned. First, anachronism spotters will have noticed that my Sarmatians ride with stirrups. I am sorry to disappoint you (she lied, smirking), but this is *not* an anachronism: Sarmatians were using stirrups in the first century B.C., when grave goods in tombs near the Sea of Azov included saddles equipped with them (M. I. Rostovtzeff, *Iranians and Greeks in South Russia*; some discussion by W. W. Tarn, *Hellenistic Military and Naval Developments*; see also Sulimirski, *The Sarmatians*). I am fully aware that many scholars—principally medievalists—say that stirrups were invented by the Goths in the fourth century A.D. or the Franks in the seventh, or even the Normans in the ninth, and use them to account for everything from the fall of the Roman Empire to medieval feudalism. I read and believed those books myself. I was flabbergasted to discover that they were wrong. If any scholars are reading this, may I beg you to go check the evidence?

That is a scholarly error: I wish also to address a popular one. Readers may have noticed that Natalis' bireme is rowed by sailors who live in barracks, and wondered what happened to the galley slaves. There is, in fact, no evidence for galley slaves on Roman warships—or, for that matter, on any other naval vessel of the ancient world. (For a good summary of the evidence for oarsmen on ancient vessels, see L. Casson, *Ships and Seamanship in the Ancient World*, Princeton University Press 1971.) *Ben Hur* got it wrong.

The Roman Empire in 175 undoubtedly anticipated a long peace, particularly when Marcus Aurelius easily succeeded in suppressing the rebellion of Avidius Cassius in the East and returned in triumph to Rome. However, Marcus died in 180, and left his conceited and incompetent son Commodus to succeed him. Things soon began to fall apart—particularly in Britain. There was a major invasion across Hadrian's Wall in the mid 180s: Corstopitum (Corbridge) appears to have been sacked, and some important Roman commander (it's not clear who, but possibly a legionary legate) was killed in battle. Commodus seems to have ordered no action to rectify the situation, and the troubles went on for some years. The angry British army even made an attempt to make the legionary legate of York emperor before things settled down again, and discontented rumblings were heard from it for even longer. But that, as they say, is another story.